Grandmaster of Demonic Cultivate

MO DAO ZU SHI

5

墨香銅臭

Grandmaster of Demonic Cultivation

MO DAO ZU SHI

5

WRITTEN BY
Mo Xiang Tong Xiu

TRANSLATED BY
Suika & Lianyin
Pengie (EDITOR)

COVER ILLUSTRATION BY
Jin Fang

BONUS ILLUSTRATION BY
ZeldaCW

INTERIOR ILLUSTRATIONS BY
Marina Privalova

Seven Seas Entertainment

GRANDMASTER OF DEMONIC CULTIVATION: MO DAO ZU SHI VOL. 5

Published originally under the title of 《魔道祖师》
(Mo Dao Zu Shi)
Author ©墨香铜臭(Mo Xiang Tong Xiu)
English edition rights under license granted by 北京晋江原创网络科技有限公司
(Beijing Jinjiang Original Network Technology Co., Ltd.)
English edition copyright © 2023 Seven Seas Entertainment, Inc.
Arranged through JS Agency Co., Ltd
All rights reserved

《魔道祖师》(Mo Dao Zu Shi) Volume 5
All rights reserved
Illustrations granted under license granted by Istari Comics Publishing
Interior Illustrations by Marina Privalova
US English translation copyright © Seven Seas Entertainment, LLC

Cover Illustration by Jin Fang
Bonus Color Illustration by ZeldaCW
Special Thanks to Shiei

Seven Seas press and purchase enquiries can be sent to Marketing Manager Lianne Sentar
at press@gomanga.com. Information regarding the distribution and purchase of digital
editions is available from Digital Manager CK Russell at digital@gomanga.com.

Seven Seas and the Seven Seas logo are trademarks of
Seven Seas Entertainment. All rights reserved.
sevenseasentertainment.com

TRANSLATION: Suika, Lianyin
EDITOR: Pengie
INTERIOR DESIGN: Clay Gardner
PROOFREADER: Meg van Huygen, Jade Gardner
COPY EDITOR: Nino Cipri
IN-HOUSE EDITOR: Tamasha
BRAND MANAGER: Lissa Pattillo
PREPRESS TECHNICIAN: Melanie Ujimori, Jules Valera
EDITOR-IN-CHIEF: Julie Davis
ASSOCIATE PUBLISHER: Adam Arnold
PUBLISHER: Jason DeAngelis

ISBN Standard Edition: 978-1-63858-549-7
ISBN Barnes & Noble Exclusive: 978-1-68579-839-0
ISBN Special Edition: 978-1-68579-840-6
Printed in Canada
First Printing: May 2023
10 9 8 7 6 5 4 3 2 1

CONTENTS

Contents based on the Pinsin Publishing print edition originally released 2016

21
Hensheng: To Hate Life

— PART 1 —

WEI WUXIAN RAN DIRECTLY to the city's Guanyin Temple with Wen Ning in tow. He and Lan Wangji had scouted a path earlier in the day, intending to examine it more closely at night to crack the magic array. That would allow them to determine exactly what the array was keeping sealed away and whether it would help them face Jin Guangyao. But he'd just had to sleep all the way until xu time, and when he woke, *that* had happened.

Their plans were a bust, and Wei Wuxian was sorely agitated. What better time than the present to cause some trouble for that sneak, Jin Guangyao?

All was tranquil in the deep of the night. Every household had extinguished its lights, and the doors of the Guanyin Temple were shut. From his spot outside the tall walls of the enclosure, Wei Wuxian could see it was pitch-black inside the courtyard. He started to climb the wall, then halted abruptly.

Something's not right, he thought.

Wen Ning stopped in his tracks as well. "A barrier has been set," he murmured.

Wei Wuxian gestured, and the two dropped silently back to the ground. They left through the front gates and headed to a nook behind the Guanyin Temple. It was there that they cautiously scaled the enclosure wall. After they had hidden themselves behind a beast statue on one of the roof's ridges, they peered into the courtyard once more.

And were struck dumb by what they saw.

Lights shone bright inside the temple. The complex was filled with standing figures. Half the crowd were monks and the other half cultivators wearing the Sparks Amidst Snow uniform. The two groups were milling together, all wielding bows and swords. They seemed to be guarding something. They were clearly ready for battle and would occasionally exchange hushed words as they remained on standby.

A special concealment barrier had been set up around the temple. From the outside, it looked like all was still, dark, and silent. None of the lights or voices within could be seen or heard.

What shocked Wei Wuxian wasn't the barrier, though, and it wasn't the cultivators or fake monks. It was the white-clad man standing in the center of the courtyard.

It was Lan Xichen.

He was not bound or restrained in any way. Even his xiao Liebing and his sword were still fastened at his waist as he stood calmly among the crowd. The monks and cultivators also treated him with the utmost respect, some going as far as to respond to his statements with docile murmurs.

After observing them for a while, Wei Wuxian whispered to Wen Ning, "Hurry back to the inn and bring Hanguang-jun here as quickly as possible!"

Wen Ning nodded. The next second, he was gone.

Wei Wuxian hadn't spotted Jin Guangyao. He didn't know whether the man was here too, nor whether he had the Yin Tiger Tally in his clutches. After contemplating the situation briefly, he bit his finger, planning to entice a few minor minions into helping him summon some more powerfully sinister creatures.

But just as he was about to stick his bleeding finger into his spirit-trapping pouch, the sound of a dog barking came from the end of the long street outside the temple.

Wei Wuxian was promptly scared out of his wits. He nearly ruptured his internal organs trying to repress the urge to leap straight into the clouds. Instead, he latched on to the beast statue near the top of the wall, shuddering in terror as he listened to the barking come closer and closer.

Save me, Lan Zhan, save me! he chanted to himself unconsciously.

Chanting the name seemed to help him muster some courage. With one last shiver, he forced himself to calm down, praying desperately that the dog was a stray without a master and that it would quickly go the hell away.

Alas, the lord of heaven was in an uncooperative mood. A young man's bright, clear voice could be heard amidst the barking.

"Shut *up*, Fairy!" the young man scolded. "Are you trying to wake everyone on this street in the middle of the night?!"

It was Jin Ling!

Lan Xichen's expression stiffened. Most of the cultivators from the Jin Clan of Lanling recognized the voice of their little young master, and they exchanged looks before nocking arrows to their bows all the same.

It wasn't long before the boy and dog arrived at the front entrance of the Guanyin Temple.

"*Shh! Shh!* Keep barking and I'll turn you into stew!" Jin Ling quickly hissed. "...Where are you taking me?"

Wei Wuxian's heart was so full of a myriad of fears that he was scared it would hurtle out of his body.

Jin Ling, you unlucky little thing. Get outta here!

Of course, Jin Ling just had to stop outside the temple. Fairy kept howling. It sounded like it was circling around, pawing at the dirt and wall.

"Are you taking me here?" Jin Ling wondered.

After a brief silence, he actually knocked on the door.

"Is anyone there?"

Inside the courtyard, every Jin cultivator was holding their breath. Their attention and their arrows were both aimed at the front gates, though they did not fire. They seemed to be waiting for a command.

"Do not hurt him!" Lan Xichen hissed. The temple's barrier kept his voice from being heard outside it.

But the cultivators did not relax their guard, nor did they drop their bows. Jin Ling also seemed to have noticed something was off. Even if no one was patrolling the temple grounds at night, he had rapped on the door hard enough to shake the heavens. Anyone inside should've been jolted awake by the racket, making the complete lack of movement suspicious. Thus, he remained silent where he stood outside the door.

Before Wei Wuxian could exhale the breath he was holding, there was another round of crazed barking. Jin Ling was furious.

"Hey, why are you running back now?!"

Wei Wuxian was overjoyed. *Good Fairy!*

"Fairy! Come back! Fucking hell!" Jin Ling cursed.

Little ancestor,[1] *please just leave and take the dog with you! I'm begging you!* Wei Wuxian pleaded in his head.

Shortly after, he heard the barely perceptible sound of a piece

---

1   "Ancestor" is what one can call someone who is being difficult and demanding. It usually expresses exasperation, though it can also be used affectionately.

of rock being knocked loose. At first, he didn't know where it had come from. Then cold sweat drenched him as the realization hit.

Oh no, the brat's scaling the wall!

The moment Jin Ling reached the top of the wall, he saw the sea of arrows aimed at him. His pupils contracted.

One of the monks had probably never seen Jin Ling before, or was perhaps determined to eliminate any intruders. He let his arrow fly. It shrieked toward Jin Ling with a sharp, piercing whistle that told Wei Wuxian the archer was an expert. If the arrow hit its target, it would surely run Jin Ling's chest through.

Wei Wuxian only had one thing on him that could immediately block the shot. In a moment of desperation, he leapt onto the wall and flung it out.

"Run, Jin Ling!" he yelled.

He had thrown the bamboo flute that he'd kept on him ever since his rebirth. It knocked the menacing arrow off course, but the flute splintered into pieces on impact. Jin Ling had vanished from atop the wall—he'd probably run away, but in giving him that opportunity Wei Wuxian had revealed his own position. Hundreds of arrows came flying toward him, turning the stone beast into a porcupine.

That was close, Wei Wuxian thought. Every single one of those archers was a crack shot, and their cultivation was likely excellent as well. Whether Jin Ling would actually be able to escape remained to be seen.

He formed a hand seal as he jumped down from the wall, and was just about to whistle when a chuckle sounded behind him.

"I'd advise Wei-gongzi to refrain. Your flute shattering would be nothing in comparison to the misery of losing your fingers and tongue, no?"

Wei Wuxian immediately dropped his hand. "You're very right," he agreed.

The man beckoned him. "Would you kindly follow me?"

Wei Wuxian nodded. "Very kind of you indeed, Sect Leader Jin."

"My pleasure," Jin Guangyao said with a smile.

They strolled the grounds as if nothing had happened, and Wei Wuxian was speechless as they went. After several large, winding turns, they arrived at the entrance of the temple proper.

The front doors were open. As Wei Wuxian suspected, Jin Ling hadn't been able to escape: he was surrounded by several monks with swords pointed at him. After a moment of staring, he hesitantly decided to greet them.

"Xiao-shushu."

"Hello there, A-Ling," Jin Guangyao replied amiably.

Jin Ling then stole a glance at Wei Wuxian. Since there was no dog at the lad's side, Wei Wuxian was finally able to regain his scattered wits.

"Child... It's so late, what are you doing bringing a dog here all alone?" he asked, grimacing.

After Wei Wuxian left Lotus Pier by boat with Lan Wangji and Wen Ning, Jin Ling had secretly set off to find him. When he found no trace of him, he threw a fit at his uncle—who had apparently gone insane and was running around making everyone try to pull some crappy sword from its scabbard. Jin Ling had pointed an accusatory finger in Jiang Cheng's face and shouted at the top of his lungs that he was the reason Wei Wuxian had run off, and was subsequently smacked to the ground for the comment.

Refusing to rest until Wei Wuxian was found, Jin Ling had pursued him with Fairy in tow. Fairy had lived up to expectations by accurately tracking Wei Wuxian's scent all the way to the grounds of this Guanyin Temple. Sensing a surge of murderous intent within, it had abruptly changed tack when Jin Ling started knocking on the door, trying to warn its owner by biting his clothes and barking nonstop.

Unfortunately, there was clearly something odd about the temple. Jin Ling had felt that he should check it out, even if Wei Wuxian wasn't there. And so, he had still fallen into the enemy's hands.

Of course, he wasn't about to tell them all of that. So he only snorted at Wei Wuxian in response.

Jin Guangyao led the group inside the temple. As the front doors were about to close, he turned to ask a subordinate, "Where's the spirit dog?"

"That black spirit dog is unusually ferocious," one of the monks replied. "It bit whoever came close. Our efforts were in vain, and it escaped."

"Pursue and kill it," Jin Guangyao said. "The dog is quite intelligent. We don't want it going to fetch anyone."

"Yes, sir!"

The monk left, sword in hand, and the front doors closed after him. Jin Ling was left dumbstruck and horrified.

"You're really gonna kill Fairy?" he blurted. "You gave it to me!"

Jin Guangyao didn't answer him, but asked instead, "A-Ling, what are you doing here?"

Jin Ling stole a glance at Wei Wuxian, hesitating. Suddenly, Lan Xichen spoke up.

"Sect Leader Jin, Jin Ling is still a child."

Jin Guangyao turned to look at him. "I'm aware."

"And he is your nephew," Lan Xichen pressed further.

At a loss for words, Jin Guangyao laughed out loud instead. "Er-ge, what are you implying? Of course I know Jin Ling is a child, and that he's my nephew. What did you think I was going to do? Kill him to seal his lips?"

Lan Xichen did not reply, falling silent instead. Jin Guangyao shook his head and turned to Jin Ling.

"A-Ling, you hear that? If you try to run away or scream, it seems I might do something terrible to you. I'll let you decide."

Jin Ling had always had a good relationship with his little uncle, who doted on him. Jin Guangyao wore a genial expression even now, but it was very hard for Jin Ling to continue to see him the same way, given the circumstances. He walked over to Wei Wuxian and Lan Xichen in silence, apparently on his best behavior.

Jin Guangyao whirled around and questioned his subordinates, "Have you still not exhumed it? Tell them to hurry up in there!"

"Yes, sir!" one of the monks answered before charging into the temple's main hall with his sword at the ready.

Only then did Wei Wuxian notice an odd, repetitive noise from inside Guanyin Hall. It sounded like earth being moved, as though there were many people digging.

What's he digging for? Wei Wuxian wondered. *Making a tunnel? Excavating the Yin Tiger Tally? Unearthing the thing that's sealed in here?*

"Speaking of which," Jin Guangyao said, "I still haven't asked how Mister Wei knows of this place. Don't tell me you and Hanguang-jun chanced upon it during your wanderings?"

"Lianfang-zun hid an important-looking land deed inside Fragrance Palace's secret chamber. It was placed next to my manuscripts, remember?"

"Ah. That was indeed an oversight on my part. I should've stored them separately."

"Either way, we can't escape your clutches," Wei Wuxian said.

"Won't Lianfang-zun tell me what is sealed here, inside the temple? Just so my curiosity is satisfied."

"That information isn't cheap, Wei-gongzi," Jin Guangyao answered with a pleasant smile. "Are you sure you want to pay the price?"

"Oh. Never mind, then," Wei Wuxian acquiesced.

Lan Xichen walked over to him. It was then Wei Wuxian noticed that though the sword hung on his waist was unsheathed an inch, no spiritual light coursed through the blade.

"Zewu-jun, your...?"

"Much ashamed. I was deceived, falling for a trap that cost me all my spiritual power," Lan Xichen explained. "Even though I have both Shuoyue and Liebing with me, I am unable to help."

"There's no shame in that," Wei Wuxian said. "Lying is Lianfang-zun's forte, after all."

Considering the scene Wei Wuxian had witnessed during his session of Empathy with Nie Mingjue—the one in which Meng Yao had pretended to commit suicide to deceive him—and comparing it to the news of Lianfang-zun being "seriously injured," it wasn't hard to guess how Lan Xichen had lost his spiritual powers.

"Construct an array before Hanguang-jun gets here," Jin Guangyao ordered several monks. "Anything that can obstruct him will do."

"Why are you so sure Hanguang-jun is coming?" Wei Wuxian asked.

His mind was still racing, plotting whether to come up with a lie to get Jin Guangyao to drop his guard. But Jin Guangyao smiled briefly, seeming to see through him.

"Of course he is. Since Wei-gongzi regards this Guanyin Temple with such suspicion, it would be impossible for Hanguang-jun not to as well. Do you really think I will believe it if you claim he isn't with you?"

"Smart man," Wei Wuxian said.

Lan Xichen spoke up. "Wei-gongzi, if Wangji is nearby, why didn't he come with you?"

"We split up," Wei Wuxian said.

Lan Xichen blinked at his response. "I heard you were injured upon your return from the Burial Mounds. Why would he leave you at such a time?"

"Who'd you hear that from?" Wei Wuxian wondered.

"Me," Jin Guangyao replied.

Wei Wuxian shot him a look, then turned back to Lan Xichen. "It's like this. I couldn't sleep tonight, so I went out to take a stroll. It was pure chance that I happened to wander this way. Hanguang-jun was in another room, so he didn't know I left."

Jin Guangyao found this strange. "You two stayed in separate rooms?"

"Who said we were sharing?" Wei Wuxian retorted.

Jin Guangyao smiled at that, but didn't respond.

"Oh, I see." Realizing Lan Xichen must have been the one who told him, Wei Wuxian remarked, "You two really do tell each other everything."

Lan Xichen, however, was not joking around. "Wei-gongzi, did something happen between you two?"

The usual gentle smile on his face was gone, replaced by sternness. It made him look even more like Lan Wangji.

Wei Wuxian couldn't understand why he was getting such a severe reaction. Already feeling guilty, he answered, "Sect Leader Lan, what could possibly happen between us? Let's focus on dealing with this guy first, shall we?"

He gestured at Jin Guangyao with his eyes. It was only at this reminder that Lan Xichen relented and said, "I have been impatient. My apologies."

Jin Guangyao laughed, however. "It seems something really *did* happen. Something big, at that."

Wei Wuxian sneered. "The entire cultivation world is poised to embark on a crusade against you, Lianfang-zun. You seem so carefree. Do you still have time to worry about other people, or get chatty with them?"

"Please, I am simply marveling. Hanguang-jun endured the wait for so many years, but even now, his efforts have come to naught. Not only does Sect Leader Lan have reason to be impatient—it is also difficult for those of us watching from the sidelines to bear."

Wei Wuxian abruptly shifted his gaze to him. "Waiting for what? What efforts?"

His questions surprised both Jin Guangyao and Lan Xichen. The two of them looked Wei Wuxian over seriously, critically, as if trying to discern whether he was just pretending to be this obtuse. Wei Wuxian's heart suddenly started pounding, like the thing that had been dead for half the night was gradually being revived.

"What do you mean?" he asked with forced calm.

"What do I mean?" Jin Guangyao echoed his question, then asked in amazement, "Wei-gongzi, do you *really* not understand? Or are you *pretending* to not understand? Whether you mean it or not, Hanguang-jun would be rather hurt if he heard you."

"I really don't understand. Just tell it to me straight!" Wei Wuxian exclaimed.

Lan Xichen was dismayed. "Wei-gongzi. Do not tell me you know nothing of Wangji's feelings, despite having been with him for so long?"

Wei Wuxian grabbed him. He was nearly on his knees, begging him to just tell him everything clearly and all at once. "Sect Leader Lan, Sect Leader Lan, you...you said Lan Zhan's feelings. What feelings?! Does he, does he..."

Lan Xichen yanked his hand out of Wei Wuxian's grip. "It would seem you truly do not know," he said in disbelief. "Have you so easily forgotten how he received the discipline whip scars? Have you not seen the brand on his chest?"

"The discipline whip scars?!" Wei Wuxian exclaimed as he grabbed Lan Xichen again. "Sect Leader Lan, I really don't know anything. Please tell me. Where did those scars come from? Could they have something to do with me?!"

Irritation appeared on Lan Xichen's face. "If not because of you, would he have done that to himself for no reason?"

Zewu-jun had always been faultlessly decorous, but he was moved by genuine anger now that the matter concerned Lan Wangji. However, his rage dimmed a bit upon scrutinizing Wei Wuxian's expression. He ventured a tentative guess. "Your...memory is damaged?"

"My memory?" Wei Wuxian asked, then immediately tried to think back on whether he'd forgotten anything. "I don't remember when my memory might've been... Wait, yes, it is!"

There was indeed a period of time when his memory was particularly hazy—

The Nightless City Massacre!

That night, he had thought the Wen siblings were reduced to ashes. He had heard the major clans' impassioned speeches as they began their crusade against him. He had even witnessed Jiang Yanli die in front of him. Madness had finally overtaken him, and he'd joined the two pieces of the Yin Tiger Tally and gone on a killing spree.

The tiger tally controlled the bodies of the dead. The people the dead slew turned into fierce corpses in turn, creating an infinite army of murderous puppets. The scene had quickly become a blood-soaked vision of hell.

Although Wei Wuxian was still able to stand afterward, he felt himself leave the ruined city-turned-slaughterhouse in a trance. He remained senseless and oblivious for a long time. By the time he could think clearly again, he had already been sitting at the foot of Yiling's Burial Mounds for a long, long while.

"Is it coming back to you now?" Lan Xichen asked.

"Was it that time at Nightless City?" Wei Wuxian mumbled. "I...I'd always been under the impression that I wandered back by myself in a daze. Could it be..."

Lan Xichen was exasperated enough to laugh. "Wei-gongzi! How many cultivators waged war against you that night at Nightless City? Three thousand! No matter how much of a genius you might be, how could you possibly have withdrawn unharmed?!" he rebuked.

"Lan Zhan... What did Lan Zhan do?" Wei Wuxian asked.

"If you do not remember what Wangji has done for you, I worry he will never tell you himself. Nor will you ask him to," Lan Xichen said. "Very well. Allow me to tell you.

"Wei-gongzi, you took the two halves of the Yin Tiger Tally and combined them into one. After killing to your heart's content, you were completely spent. Wangji was hardly in a better state, having been wounded during your bout of madness. He was barely hanging on, only able to stand with Bichen's support. But even so, he followed you immediately when he saw you swaying on your feet as you left.

"Not many were still conscious at that point. I, myself, was almost immobile. I could only watch helplessly as Wangji hobbled after you, even though he was obviously almost completely drained of his spiritual powers. He lifted you, mounted Bichen, and flew away at once on the sword.

"It took four hours for my spiritual powers to recover. I hurried back to the Lan Clan of Gusu to request reinforcements, worried that Wangji would be considered an accomplice if the other clans caught up to the two of you first. The best-case scenario would see his reputation tarnished, blemished for life. The worst-case scenario would see him killed without mercy. Uncle and I selected thirty-three seniors who had always thought highly of Wangji, and we launched a secret search. After two days, we finally found signs of your passage within the boundaries of Yiling. Wangji had hidden you inside a cave. By the time we arrived, you were sitting on a rock, staring into nothingness. Wangji held your hand in his own, speaking quietly and ceaselessly to you as he transferred you his spiritual power.

"But the entire time, you only repeated the same two words to him: '*Get lost!*'"

Wei Wuxian's throat was dry, his eyes were rimmed with red. He couldn't say a single word. Lan Xichen continued his explanation.

"My uncle stood before him and rebuked him harshly, demanding he provide us an explanation. It seemed he had already expected we would find him. He told us there was nothing to explain. That that was all there was to it. He'd never once talked back to Uncle or me, ever since he was young. But for you—not only did he talk back, he raised his blade against his fellow members of the Lan Clan. In the resulting fight, he seriously injured the thirty-three seniors we'd asked to come along..."

Wei Wuxian dug his fingers into his hair. "...I...I didn't know... I really..."

He didn't have much else to say, other than repeating those words.

Lan Xichen could restrain himself no longer. "*Thirty-three* lashes from the discipline whip!" he exclaimed. "All in one sitting. One per senior. You must know how painful the lashes are, and how long one must lie in bed to recover! After he stubbornly escorted you back to the Burial Mounds, he returned morosely on his own to receive his punishment. Do you know how long he knelt before the Wall of Discipline?! When I went to check on him, I told him this: *Wei-gongzi has already committed a grave crime. Why must you add to them?* Yet he told me...that while he could not say whether your actions were right or wrong, he was willing to carry the burden with you, regardless.

"It has been said that he spent those years facing the wall in reflection. In truth, he was too injured to do any such thing. And even so, when he learned of your death, he had to go to the Burial Mounds to see for himself, forcibly dragging his body there in such a state...

"When he whisked you away and hid you inside that cave, the way he spoke to you, the way he looked at you...even if you were blind or deaf, it would have been impossible not to understand his feelings. That is why Uncle was beyond outraged. Wangji has been the Lan disciples' role model ever since he was young, and later, a distinguished cultivator in the cultivation world. He has been proper and righteous his whole life, untouched by the corruption of the secular world. The only mistake he has ever made in his life is *you*! Yet you say...you say you didn't know. Wei-gongzi, in how many ways did you profess your feelings and pester him after your return via sacrifice? Every night... Every night you were determined to... And yet you say you didn't know. If you did not know, why did you act that way?!"

Wei Wuxian really wanted to go back in time to those very moments and kill his past selves. It was precisely because he *hadn't* known that he had dared to act that way!

He was suddenly seized with terror. If Lan Wangji hadn't known that he essentially remembered nothing of the days after the Nightless City Massacre...if Lan Wangji thought he'd always known about his feelings...then what the hell had he been doing to him since his return?!

Wei Wuxian's initial, exaggerated buffoonery had been intended to repulse Lan Wangji and goad him into throwing him out of the Cloud Recesses as soon as possible. They would then go their separate ways, never to meet again. It was impossible that Lan Wangji hadn't seen through him and known his intentions. Even then, he had still...stubbornly kept Wei Wuxian by his side and protected him. He hadn't given Jiang Cheng a chance to draw near or make things difficult for Wei Wuxian. He had answered Wei Wuxian's every question, heeded his every whim; ridiculously indulgent, absurdly tolerant. Not to mention that, even in the face of Wei Wuxian's multitude of tricks, the awful teasing and flirting, he had still managed to maintain decorum without ever overstepping boundaries.

When he suddenly shoved Wei Wuxian away at the inn earlier that night, could it have been because...because he thought it was just another of Wei Wuxian's wanton whims?

Wei Wuxian really couldn't bear to follow that line of thought any further. He abruptly bolted toward the door, but several cultivators immediately blocked his way.

Jin Guangyao began to speak. "Wei-gongzi, I can understand your excitement..."

Wei Wuxian only wanted to rush back to the inn—rush back to Lan Wangji's side—and babble all his feelings to him. With a strike of his hand, he knocked down two of the monks who were trying to restrain him.

"Like hell you do!" he growled.

Seven or eight others tackled him as soon as he struck, and Wei Wuxian's vision went dark.

Jin Guangyao was determined to finish his sentence. "...I just wanted to tell you there's no need to head out in such a rush. Your Hanguang-jun is already here."

An icy blue sword glare streaked down from the sky. Whistling sharply, it forced back the figures crowding around Wei Wuxian before returning to its owner's hand.

Lan Wangji landed silently in front of Guanyin Temple and cast a glance at Wei Wuxian. Though his expression was the same as always, Wei Wuxian was seized with nervousness. Everything he had wanted to say earlier suddenly crumpled into a ball and shrank back into his chest. His stomach twisted.

"Lan Zhan..." he mumbled.

Jin Ling, left completely stunned by Lan Xichen's story, was overjoyed to see Lan Wangji arrive. But his expression turned odd again when he saw the look Lan Wangji was exchanging with Wei Wuxian.

Jin Guangyao sighed in awe. "See, Wei-gongzi? As I said, as long as you're here, Hanguang-jun will surely come."

Lan Wangji flicked the wrist of the hand holding Bichen, about to make a move—but was interrupted by a chuckle from Jin Guangyao that suggested he should reconsider.

"Hanguang-jun, you had best take five steps back."

Wei Wuxian suddenly felt a subtle yet sharp pain around his neck.

"Careful," Lan Xichen hissed. "Do not move!"

Lan Wangji's gaze landed on Wei Wuxian's neck. His face paled slightly.

A light gold guqin string, so thin it was barely visible, was wrapped around Wei Wuxian's throat.

The string was incredibly fine, and painted a special color to boot, making it almost impossible for the human eye to catch. And Wei Wuxian had just been thrown for a loop, too distracted to pay attention to his surroundings. It was no wonder he'd ended up in such a perilous predicament.

"Lan Zhan, don't!" Wei Wuxian called. "Don't back away!"

But Lan Wangji retreated five steps without hesitation.

"Excellent," Jin Guangyao said. "Next, will you please put Bichen away?"

Lan Wangji immediately complied, sheathing Bichen with a *sching*. Wei Wuxian was furious.

"He gives you an inch and you take a mile!"

"This is 'taking a mile'?" Jin Guangyao asked. "If I tell Hanguang-jun to seal his own spiritual meridians next—what would you call that?"

Wei Wuxian sputtered angrily. "You—"

Before he could say another word, a sharp pain stung his neck. It felt as though his flesh had been cut, accompanied by something wet rolling down the line of his throat. Lan Wangji turned deathly pale.

"How can he disobey me, hmm? Think for a moment, Wei-gongzi. I have his life strung between my fingers."

"Do not touch him," Lan Wangji said, enunciating each word clearly.

"Then Hanguang-jun knows what he should do," Jin Guangyao replied.

After a moment, Lan Wangji said, "Very well."

Lan Xichen heaved a sigh. Lan Wangji raised his hand and heavily struck his acupoints twice, sealing his own spiritual meridians.

Jin Guangyao gave a light smile and murmured, "Honestly..."

Lan Wangji glared at him. "Let him go."

Suddenly, Wei Wuxian cut in. "Lan Zhan! I...I have something to say to you."

"Wait until later," Jin Guangyao said.

"No, it's urgent," Wei Wuxian insisted.

"Then you can say it as you are," Jin Guangyao said.

While that was only an offhand statement, realization dawned on Wei Wuxian.

"You're right," he said. Then he yelled, with all the breath he could pull into his lungs, "Lan Zhan! Lan Wangji! Hanguang-jun! I... I genuinely wanted to sleep with you earlier!"

"..."

"..."

"..."

Jin Guangyao's grip slackened, and the guqin string around his neck fell away. Wei Wuxian lunged at Lan Wangji the moment the stinging pain disappeared, unable to wait another moment.

His earth-shattering confession impacted Lan Wangji's body like a lightning bolt, striking him so hard he had yet to come around. His normally unflustered expression showed a trace of stunned bewilderment. While it wasn't the first time Wei Wuxian had seized him around the waist in a tenacious embrace, this time, Lan Wangji seemed to have turned into a block of wood. He was so stiff that he didn't know where to put his hands.

"Lan Zhan, did you hear everything I just said?!" Wei Wuxian asked urgently.

Lan Wangji moved his lips, but it was a while before he managed a response. "You..."

He had always spoken concisely and succinctly. Never before had his words been so broken, so unbelievably hesitant and tentative. He got a hold of himself and tried again.

"You said..."

He seemed to want to repeat what Wei Wuxian had said to confirm his ears didn't deceive him, but such words were much too difficult for Lan Wangji to speak aloud. Wei Wuxian, not missing a beat, was fully ready to repeat himself.

"I said, I genuinely wanted to..."

"*Ahem!*"

Next to him, Lan Xichen had folded his hand into a fist and placed it against his lips to give a polite cough. After a moment of deliberation, he sighed.

"...Wei-gongzi, you certainly know how to pick a time and place."

"So sorry, Sect Leader Lan," Wei Wuxian said, though the apology was not in the least bit sincere. "But I really couldn't wait any longer."

Jin Guangyao didn't seem like he could wait any longer either. He turned his head to ask, "Have you still not exhumed it?"

One of the monks answered him. "Sect Leader, you buried it so very deep..."

Various shades of blue and white flashed across Jin Guangyao's face. He seemed extremely upset. Despite that, he did not berate his subordinates, but only urged them, "Quicken the pace!"

He had only just spoken when a blinding flash of lightning splintered across the horizon. Moments later, thunder roared. Jin Guangyao glanced at the sky, gloom lightly clouding his expression.

It didn't take long before slanted threads of rain began to descend from the skies. Wei Wuxian held Lan Wangji tightly. He had initially planned to allow millions of words to burst through the dam of his chest, but the icy rain on his face cooled him down a little.

Jin Guangyao turned to Lan Xichen. "Zewu-jun, it's raining. Shall we go inside to take shelter?"

Despite having Lan Xichen at his mercy, Jin Guangyao still treated him as he always had: with politeness and respect. He was even perhaps a bit *more* polite than usual, as that made it harder to fly off the handle at him in a fit of temper—one does not slap the face of the smiling, as they say. Not that Lan Xichen had much of a temper to begin with.

Jin Guangyao was the first to cross the threshold of the main hall. The others followed after him.

During their daytime visit, Wei Wuxian and Lan Wangji had noted the grandiosity of the main hall, with its spacious interior and fresh, new red paint and gold lining on the walls. It was obvious this place was meticulously maintained. A group of cultivators and monks were digging behind the grand hall. They seemed to have been at it for some time, but had yet to unearth whatever Jin Guangyao had buried in the past.

Wei Wuxian glanced up and was taken aback.

Upon the divine altar, there stood a statue of Guanyin, the Goddess of Mercy. But in contrast to more common depictions of the idol, the statue's features and expression were crafted with less of a focus on compassion and benevolence, and more on delicate beauty. What really astonished him was that this particular Guanyin statue looked vaguely familiar. It resembled someone—specifically, Jin Guangyao himself.

The statue alone was fine, but the more one compared it to Jin Guangyao in the latter's presence, the clearer the similarities became. Indeed, it was too similar by half.

Is Jin Guangyao such a narcissist? Wei Wuxian wondered. *Was it not enough for him to preside over the cultivation world as the*

Cultivation Chief? Did he also feel the need to sculpt a divine statue in his own image for millions to prostrate themselves before and worship? Or is this some sort of wicked magic I don't know about?

"Sit," Lan Wangji's voice suddenly echoed next to his ear.

Wei Wuxian was immediately pulled back to the present. Lan Wangji had brought over four prayer cushions, giving one each to Lan Xichen and Jin Ling, and keeping two for Wei Wuxian and himself. For some reason, Lan Xichen and Jin Ling set their cushions down far, far away from them, both keeping their gazes trained on something in the distance that only they could see.

Jin Guangyao and his men had gone out back to check on the progress of the excavation. Wei Wuxian tugged Lan Wangji down to sit. Lan Wangji might still have been a little dazed, for he stumbled a bit at the tugging before steadying himself in his seat. As he tried to calm himself, Wei Wuxian stared at Lan Wangji's face.

Lan Wangji's downcast gaze made it difficult to tell what he was feeling. Wei Wuxian knew what he'd said earlier, by itself, was probably not enough to make Lan Wangji believe him. He'd been enduring lingchi for so long, with his incredibly clueless, disreputable tormentor smiling all the while—disbelief was the natural response.

As he reflected on this, Wei Wuxian's chest tightened with heartache until he was trembling all over. He didn't dare think any deeper on the subject. In that moment, the only thing he knew was that he had to treat Lan Wangji with some stronger medicine.

"Lan Zhan, l-look...look at me," he stammered. His voice was still a bit taut.

Lan Wangji complied. "Mn."

Wei Wuxian inhaled deeply, then began to quietly confess. "...My memory is really bad. There's a lot from the past I don't remember—

which includes that time at Nightless City. I don't remember a single thing that happened after that night."

Lan Wangji's eyes slowly widened.

Wei Wuxian seized Lan Wangji by the shoulders. "But! But from now on, I'll remember everything you've said to me, everything you've done. I won't forget a thing!"

"..."

"You're especially wonderful. I like you," Wei Wuxian said.

"..."

"Or, in other words—I fancy you, I love you, I want you, I can't leave you, I whatever you."

"..."

"I want to go on Night Hunts with you for the rest of my life."

"..."

Wei Wuxian pressed three fingers together in a solemn vow. He pointed to the heavens, then to the earth, then to his heart. "I also want to sleep with you every day. I swear this isn't a whim—I'm not messing with you, like I have in the past, and I'm also definitely not saying this because I feel like I owe you something. No more of that nonsense. I just really like you so much that I want to sleep with you. I don't want anyone else but you. It has to be you. You can do anything you want to me, have your way with me however you see fit—I'll like it, no matter what. As long as you're willing to be with me—"

Before he could finish, a sudden gust blew into the hall and extinguished the rows of candles inside the temple. The drizzle had grown into a storm while they weren't paying attention, and the long-extinguished lanterns hanging outside swayed and knocked against each other in the whirling wind and rain. Everything sank into darkness.

Wei Wuxian couldn't speak another word. In the blackness, Lan Wangji had seized him and pulled him into a tight embrace that sealed his mouth against his chest.

His breathing was frantic and uneven as he rasped next to Wei Wuxian's ear, "...fancy you..."

Wei Wuxian returned the tight hug and exclaimed, "Yes!"

"...I love you, I want you..."

"*Yes!*" Wei Wuxian cried loudly.

"I can't leave you... I don't want anyone else but you... It has to be you!"

Lan Wangji repeated what Wei Wuxian had said over and over, his voice and body shaking alike. Wei Wuxian thought he seemed on the verge of tears.

With every repeated phrase, he tightened his arms around Wei Wuxian's waist. Though the constriction hurt, Wei Wuxian's only response was to embrace Lan Wangji's shoulders even more firmly. He was practically suffocating himself, but he was a glutton for the pain, hating only that he couldn't squeeze him any harder.

He couldn't see a thing. But their chests were pressed so snugly together that there was no ignoring the beating of their hearts. Wei Wuxian could feel Lan Wangji's wildly pounding heartbeat perfectly, and the scalding heat that seemed ready to burst out of his chest. And, though it might have been his imagination, he thought he felt a quiet teardrop fall on the nape of his neck.

Rapid footfalls echoed in the hall. Jin Guangyao had returned from the temple's rear grounds with several cultivators. Two monks had to brace themselves against the force of the gale and expend all their strength to close the front doors and pull the heavy latch into place. Jin Guangyao took out a fire talisman and gently blew on it to ignite it, then used it to relight the red candles. The row of dim yellow flames was now the only light inside the lonely temple battered by the night rain.

Suddenly, there were two brisk blows on the outside of the door.

Someone was knocking. Everyone inside the temple reacted at once, their gazes drawn toward the entrance. The two monks who had just closed the doors tensed as though they were about to face a great enemy. They silently pointed their swords at the gates.

Jin Guangyao, sounding composed, inquired, "Who is it?"

"Sect Leader, it's me!" someone answered from the other side.

It was Su She's voice.

Jin Guangyao made a gesture, and the two monks pulled at the door latch. Su She entered, accompanied by a blast of fierce wind that nearly extinguished the rows of candles. The flames flickered, dimming and brightening in turn.

The two monks closed and locked the grand doors anew. Su She was drenched by the storm, grim-faced and frozen through to the point his lips were visibly purple. He had a sword gripped in one hand and dragged a person behind him with the other. Once inside, he was about to toss the man to the ground when he saw Wei Wuxian and Lan Wangji sitting on a pair of cushions in the corner, loath to draw apart from each other.

Su She had only just suffered a terrible loss at their hands. His face fell. He immediately brandished his sword and looked to Jin Guangyao, then calmed when he saw the man was at ease, like nothing was the matter. He knew this meant the two of them were under Jin Guangyao's control.

"What's going on?" Jin Guangyao questioned.

"I ran into him on the way," Su She explained. "I thought he might be useful, so I captured him."

Jin Guangyao approached and looked down. "Did you hurt him?"

"No. He fainted from terror," Su She stated as he threw their new captive to the floor.

"Don't be so rough, Minshan," Jin Guangyao chided. "He's easily frightened and can't withstand falls."

"Yes, sir." Su She immediately heeded his words, lifting the person he had just dropped so haphazardly and laying him carefully at Lan Xichen's side.

Lan Xichen's attention had been fixed on this person since the moment he arrived. When he brushed the man's wet, mussed hair off his face, it was exactly who he'd suspected—Nie Huaisang, who had fainted from fright. He'd likely been on his way back to Qinghe after recuperating in Lotus Pier when Su She had intercepted and apprehended him.

Lan Xichen looked up. "Why have you detained Huaisang?"

"Having another family head here will make others more wary," Jin Guangyao replied. "But please rest assured, er-ge. You know how I've always treated Huaisang in the past. When the time is right, I will free you both without harming a single hair on your heads."

"Should I believe you?" Lan Xichen asked, his tone lukewarm.

"It's your choice, I suppose," Jin Guangyao said. "Regardless of whether you believe me or don't, there's nothing you can do about it, er-ge."

Su She turned his gaze toward Wei Wuxian and Lan Wangji. He let out a snort. "Hanguang-jun, Yiling Patriarch, I never thought we'd see each other again so soon. The tables have turned completely too," he taunted. "How does it feel, huh?"

Lan Wangji did not respond. He never paid any mind to this sort of meaningless provocation. Wei Wuxian, on the other hand, thought, *How have they turned? You were the one who fled the Burial Mounds. Aren't you still fleeing, even now?*

But Su She had probably kept this bottled up far too long and needed no provocation to launch into a resentful screed. He looked Lan Wangji over with a calculating eye.

"You're still putting on airs. You think you come across *so* calm and collected," he jeered. "How long do you plan to keep that up?"

Lan Wangji still did not respond, but Lan Xichen spoke up instead. "Sect Leader Su, I do not believe we ever mistreated you when you studied with our Lan Clan of Gusu. Why target Wangji in this way?"

"As if I'd dare target Lan-er-gongzi, the boy prodigy! I just can't stand the way he acts like he's all that."

Although this wasn't the first time Wei Wuxian had learned someone's hatred could be born without reason, he couldn't help but feel perplexed.

"Has Hanguang-jun ever said he thought himself to be that amazing? If I remember correctly, the Lan Clan even has an 'arrogance is prohibited' rule in their family precepts."

"How do *you* know what's in the Lan Clan precepts?" Jin Ling demanded.

Wei Wuxian stroked his chin. "Copy them enough times and you'll remember."

"And why were you copying the Lan Clan precepts?! It's not like you're..." Jin Ling blurted before trailing off. He had intended to say, *"It's not like you're part of the family,"* but realized how wrong that sounded and stopped himself with a dark look on his face.

Wei Wuxian laughed. "Was Sect Leader Su making assumptions simply because Hanguang-jun has always worn that cold, stoic expression? If that's the case, then you've wronged Hanguang-jun terribly. His face is like that around everyone. You should be glad you didn't study at Yunmeng."

"And why's that?" Su She asked coldly.

"I would've made you drop dead with fury long ago. When I was little, I thought I was a genius extraordinaire, a fucking marvel. And not only did I feel that way—I went around telling everybody all about it."

Veins popped on Su She's forehead as he cried, *"Shut up!"*

He lifted his hand to strike, but Lan Wangji pulled Wei Wuxian into his embrace and shielded him in the security of his arms. Su She faltered, and was hesitating on whether to follow through with the attack when Wei Wuxian poked his head out.

"Better not try it, Sect Leader Su. Lianfang-zun is still treating Zewu-jun with such respect—do you think he'd be happy if you hurt Hanguang-jun?"

Su She was concerned about that very thing, which was why he was inclined to withdraw. But he was sorely vexed now that Wei Wuxian had commented, and his indignation drove him to further taunts.

"To think the legendary Yiling Patriarch—who struck fear into the hearts of the living and the dead alike—would be so scared to die!"

Wei Wuxian was not abashed in the least. "You flatter me. But it's not that I'm *scared* to die, it's that I don't *want* to die."

Su She sneered. "Playing word games—how laughable. Is there a difference between being scared to die and not wanting to die?"

Nestled in the crook of Lan Wangji's arms, Wei Wuxian replied, "Of course there is. For example, I don't *want* to tear myself away from Lan Zhan right now. How is that the same as being *scared* of tearing myself away from Lan Zhan?"

After a brief moment of thought, he added, "Sorry, I take that back. Maybe those two things *are* pretty much the same."

Su She's face was turning red with rage. Infuriating him was precisely what Wei Wuxian was trying to do.

Just then, there suddenly came a very soft laugh from above him. It was so soft that almost everyone present thought they'd misheard.

But when Wei Wuxian's head shot up, he confirmed what he'd heard was real. He spotted a tiny smile at the corners of Lan Wangji's lips, like a ray of sunlight reflecting off snow. It had yet to fade away.

Now it wasn't just Su She who was stunned, but Lan Xichen and Jin Ling as well. It was common knowledge that Hanguang-jun was eternally taciturn and cold as ice, as though he'd been born with a disinterested look etched on his face. Almost no one had ever witnessed him smile—not even the smallest upturn of his lips. No one had ever expected to see him smile under *these* circumstances.

Wei Wuxian's eyes bulged. It was a while before he managed to swallow hard, throat bobbing with the effort. "Lan Zhan, you..."

Just then, another round of knocking came from outside the Guanyin Temple.

Su She drew his sword and wielded it with a firm grip. "Who is it?!" he demanded, sounding alarmed.

No one answered. And then, the doors were blown to pieces!

The wind and rain burst inside to herald Zidian's oncoming strike. Coursing with spiritual light, it struck Su She squarely on the chest and sent him flying backward. He crashed heavily into a round, red wood pillar and spat out a mouthful of blood. The two monks guarding either side of the entrance were also hit by the aftershock and sprawled on the ground, unable to rise.

A figure clad in purple crossed the temple's threshold and entered the main hall with long, steady strides.

Outside, the wind was howling and the rain was coming down hard. But the man was perfectly dry, only the bottom hem of his robe dampened to a somewhat darker shade of purple. Raindrops pelted and splattered off the oil-paper umbrella he held in his left hand. In his right hand he held Zidian, its cold light sizzling and flashing wildly. The expression on his face was darker than the stormy night.

"Jiujiu!" Jin Ling called, sitting upright at once.

Jiang Cheng glared at him. "*Now* you know to call for me," he snapped coldly. "Why did you run away, then?!"

Whether consciously or otherwise, his gaze fell on Wei Wuxian and Lan Wangji. The eyes of the two parties had yet to meet when Su She pushed himself up with the help of his sword and lunged at Jiang Cheng. Before Jiang Cheng moved, there was a flurry of barking. Fairy soared into the temple like a flying fish, pouncing straight toward Su She.

The moment Wei Wuxian heard the dog, his hair immediately stood on end and he shrank into Lan Wangji's embrace. Scared completely out of his wits, he cried out.

"Lan Zhan!"

Lan Wangji already knew to hold him. "Mn!" he assured him. "I am here!"

"Hold me!" Wei Wuxian pleaded.

"I am!" Lan Wangji replied.

"Hold me tight!" Wei Wuxian then specified.

"I am!" Lan Wangji confirmed.

Jiang Cheng wasn't looking at them, but their voices alone set the muscles on his face and the corners of his lips twitching. He seemed to want to look their way at first, but then kept his head from turning at all. Coincidentally, several monks and cultivators

had now emerged from the back of the hall, charging with their swords brandished. Snorting, Jiang Cheng lashed a dazzling purple arc with a swing of his hand, sending everyone it hit flying through the air. The oil-paper umbrella remained perfectly steady in his left hand all the while. When the hall was filled with the fallen, still shuddering and convulsing like they had current coursing through their bodies, Jiang Cheng finally closed his umbrella.

Su She was yelling angrily at the black-haired spirit dog who attacked him relentlessly, while Jin Ling shouted encouragement at his hound.

"Fairy! Watch out! Bite him, Fairy! Bite his hand!"

Lan Xichen called out a sharp warning. "Sect Leader Jiang, be careful of the guqin's sound!"

He had just spoken when a couple of guqin notes rang from the back of the room. But Jiang Cheng was on high alert, having already fallen for that wicked song back at the Burial Mounds. The notes had only just sounded when he kicked a fallen cultivator's longsword into the air with the tip of his foot, chucked the umbrella aside, and caught the sword. His other hand drew Sandu from his waist. Wielding a sword in each hand, he crossed them above his head.

The two swords scraped against each other with a harsh, piercing noise that drowned out the sound of Jin Guangyao's guqin. It was a very effective way of breaking the spell. There was only one downside—that the sound was *awful*, a horrid screech fit to pierce one's eardrums. It was even harder for people from Gusu, like Lan Xichen and Lan Wangji, to endure. The two of them knitted their brows faintly. But Lan Wangji had his hands full dutifully holding Wei Wuxian, rendering him unable to cover his ears. And so, Wei Wuxian reached up and put his own hands over Lan Wangji's ears, listening to the dog barking and shaking all the while.

Stone-faced, Jiang Cheng charged toward the back of the room as he continued wielding his two swords to produce the mood-killing, ear-splitting demonic noise. Before he could fight his way there, however, Jin Guangyao emerged on his own.

"Sect Leader Jiang, in consideration of the power of your attack, I concede defeat," he said as he walked out with hands covering his ears.

Jiang Cheng lashed out with Zidian, and Jin Guangyao dodged.

"How did you find this place, Sect Leader Jiang?"

Jiang Cheng didn't bother mincing words. Jin Guangyao knew his spiritual powers were no match for Jiang Cheng's and didn't dare face him head-on, but had to stay constantly on his toes to dodge while instructing his subordinates to surround Jiang Cheng.

Still unruffled, he continued his queries. "Was it because A-Ling ran off, and you found this place while in pursuit of him? Fairy must've led the way." He sighed. "I'm the one who gave him that dog, but the creature won't even grant me a bit of face."

Wei Wuxian wasn't as scared of the barking while enveloped in Lan Wangji's firm embrace. He was even able to think. Watching Jin Guangyao fight, his eyes shifting slyly and a smile forever plastered on his face...it reminded him of someone.

"He and Xue Yang really are cut from the same cloth," he whispered.

But Lan Wangji did not say anything. When Wei Wuxian heard no response, he looked up and realized he was still covering Lan Wangji's ears—he hadn't heard his comment, and therefore hadn't answered. Wei Wuxian quickly dropped his hands.

Jin Guangyao chuckled and abruptly changed the subject. "Sect Leader Jiang, what's wrong? Your attention has been drifting ever since you came here; it seems you're afraid to look over that way. Is there something over there?"

"Cut the bullshit!" Jiang Cheng spat. "You're the Cultivation Chief, so fight if you're going to fight!"

"Still dodging the subject?" Jin Guangyao pushed. "There's nothing over there except your shixiong. Did you really find this place by following A-Ling?"

"How else?! Who else would I be searching for?!" Jiang Cheng barked.

"Do not answer him!" Lan Xichen exclaimed.

Jin Guangyao had a way with words. As soon as Jiang Cheng allowed himself to engage in conversation with him, his attention was diverted and his emotions subtly manipulated.

"All right," Jin Guangyao said. "Mister Wei, did you see that? Your shidi isn't here to look for you. He doesn't even want to look at you."

Wei Wuxian laughed. "What a weird comment. It's not the first time Sect Leader Jiang has acted like that toward me. There's no need for you to remind me."

Hearing this, the corners of Jiang Cheng's lips twitched slightly, and veins bulged on the back of the hand that gripped Zidian. Jin Guangyao turned back to him, sighing heavily.

"You see, Sect Leader Jiang? It's not easy being your shixiong."

Wei Wuxian grew alarmed, noticing how Jin Guangyao kept bringing the conversation back to him.

"Sect Leader Jin, is it not even harder being your sworn brother?" Jiang Cheng retorted.

Completely ignoring whether or not Jiang Cheng was listening, Jin Guangyao continued to speak. "Sect Leader Jiang, I heard you caused a huge ruckus at Lotus Pier yesterday, completely out of the blue. You were running around with the sword that used to belong to the Yiling Patriarch, demanding everyone you encountered try to draw it from its sheath."

Jiang Cheng's expression became instantly terrifying.

Wei Wuxian suddenly sat up from Lan Wangji's arms, his heart lurching. *My sword? Is he talking about Suibian? Didn't I toss Suibian over to Wen Ning? No, it's true that I didn't see him holding it yesterday... How did it end up in Jiang Cheng's hands?! Why was Jiang Cheng making other people draw it?! Has he drawn it himself?*

He was tense all over, only calming slightly when Lan Wangji stroked down his spine a few times. Seeing Jiang Cheng suddenly fall silent, Jin Guangyao's eyes glinted.

"I also heard that while no one could draw the sword, you were able to do so. How very curious, indeed. The sword was already sealed when it entered my collection thirteen years ago. Absolutely no one could draw it aside from the Yiling Patriarch himself..."

Jiang Cheng summoned forth both Zidian and Sandu. "You shut your mouth!" he shouted furiously.

Jin Guangyao continued regardless, smiling pleasantly. "And so, I was reminded of how wayward and frivolous Wei-gongzi was in the past—never bringing his sword along, no matter where he went. He had a different excuse each time, and I always thought it strange. What do *you* think?"

"What exactly are you trying to say?!" Jiang Cheng growled.

Jin Guangyao raised his voice. "How absolutely incredible you are, Sect Leader Jiang. The youngest family head, the one who reestablished the Jiang Clan of Yunmeng by his own power alone. I am in awe. But I seem to remember you were never able to beat Mister Wei in anything. Might I ask how you were able to make such a comeback after the Sunshot Campaign? Did you perhaps consume some sort of golden core restorative pill?!"

The words "golden core" were enunciated exceedingly clearly

and cuttingly. Jiang Cheng's face contorted, and Zidian emitted a dangerously blinding light.

In his state of turmoil, his movements presented an opening. Jin Guangyao, who had been waiting for this chance, whipped out the guqin string he had on hand. Jiang Cheng immediately snapped out of it and met the strike, Zidian and the guqin string tangling together. Jin Guangyao's palm went numb and he immediately let go. But he chuckled lightly soon after—and lashed out another string, aiming it directly at Wei Wuxian.

Jiang Cheng's pupils contracted into dots. Moving as fast as lightning, he changed Zidian's course to intercept the string.

"Jiujiu, watch out!" cried Jin Ling.

Jin Guangyao had taken this opportunity to draw the softsword that had been wrapped around his waist all this time—and he stabbed Jiang Cheng in the center of his chest!

Steely faced, Jiang Cheng pressed his hand to his chest as blood poured between his fingers and rapidly formed a purplish-black blotch on his robes. Having blocked the guqin string, Zidian instantly returned to its silver ring form and slotted itself back on his finger. When their masters lost too much blood or were severely injured, spiritual devices returned to the form that required the least amount of energy to maintain.

Pressing the advantage, Jin Guangyao rushed over and sealed Jiang Cheng's spiritual meridians with two quick strikes. He then pulled a handkerchief from his sleeve and wiped his softsword clean before wrapping it back around his waist.

Jin Ling had already rushed to Jiang Cheng's side to support him.

Lan Xichen sighed. "Do not allow him to move rashly. Help him sit down slowly."

Although Jiang Cheng had been stabbed in the chest, the injury wasn't grievous enough to be life-threatening. However, it did make it temporarily inadvisable for him to move or use his spiritual energy.

He disliked letting anyone help him, all the same, so he said to Jin Ling, "Get lost."

Jin Ling knew Jiang Cheng was still furious with him for running off on his own. Knowing he was in the wrong, he didn't dare to talk back. The black-haired spirit dog's wild barking sounded in the distance, followed by a sudden howl of distress. Jin Ling gave a start. Recalling what Jin Guangyao had said earlier, he shouted into the night.

"Run, Fairy! They're gonna kill you!"

Shortly after, Su She returned from braving the heavy rain in a towering rage.

"Why haven't you killed it yet?" Jin Guangyao asked.

"This subordinate failed to do so," Su She admitted, biting out the words hatefully. "I can't believe that dog is so spineless. It acts all tough when there's someone to back it up, but flees the second it sees the situation taking a turn for the worse. And it runs faster than anyone here!"

Jin Guangyao shook his head. "It might lead more people here. We have to make this quick."

"Those good-for-nothings!" Su She said. "I'll hurry them along."

Jin Ling breathed a sigh of relief. Seeing Jiang Cheng sitting on the floor with a steely expression, he asked Lan Wangji after a moment of hesitation, "Hanguang-jun, are there any more prayer cushions?"

Lan Wangji was the one who had found the prayer cushions they were sitting on, but he could only find a total of four in the hall. After a moment of silence, he stood up and pushed over the one he had been sitting on.

"Thank you! But never mind. I'll just give him mine..." Jin Ling hurriedly said.

"No need," Lan Wangji said.

He then sat back down beside Wei Wuxian. Surprisingly enough, they both fit on one prayer cushion without being too cramped. Seeing that a spot had been vacated for him, Jin Ling scratched his head and dragged Jiang Cheng over to take a seat.

Jiang Cheng pressed on an acupoint on his chest to stop the bleeding. He sat, glanced over at Wei Wuxian and Lan Wangji, and then quickly lowered his eyes again. His expression was grim as he lost himself in his thoughts.

An ecstatic shout rang out from the temple's rear grounds. "Sect Leader! We got it! We've unearthed a corner!"

Jin Guangyao visibly relaxed. He walked briskly to the back of the hall. "Keep going! Be very careful. Time is running out."

Seven or eight streaks of pale lightning twisted across the sky and were followed by delayed claps of thunder.

Lan Wangji and Wei Wuxian sat together in the temple hall, while Jiang Cheng sat to the side. Jin Ling dragged his own prayer cushion over to sit near him. A long, awkward silence descended amidst the sound of pelting rain. No one took the initiative to speak up first.

But for some reason, Jin Ling seemed as though he really wanted them to communicate. His eyes darted between them before he suddenly piped up. "Jiujiu, good thing you intercepted the guqin string earlier, or it would've been bad."

Jiang Cheng's face darkened as he snapped, "Shut up!"

If he hadn't been so emotionally unstable, thereby giving Jin Guangyao the chance to find an opening and surprise him, he would not have failed to subdue the man—nor would he have fallen into the enemy's hands himself. Moreover, Wei Wuxian and Lan Wangji could have dodged the guqin string on their own. Even if Lan Wangji had no spiritual power and Wei Wuxian's was meager, they were still physically skilled. Even if they couldn't attack, they could evade.

Jin Ling was clumsily trying to speak up for his uncle, but the attempt was so obviously deliberate that it only made the situation even more awkward. Having been rebuked, he shut his mouth in embarrassment. Jiang Cheng pursed his lips and did not speak again, and Wei Wuxian remained silent as well.

Had this happened in the past, he would probably have laughed at Jiang Cheng for being so easily provoked and allowing others to exploit it. But thinking back on everything Jin Guangyao had said, it was obvious why it had worked.

Jiang Cheng already knew the truth.

Lan Wangji stroked down his back a couple more times. Wei Wuxian looked up. When he saw that there was no shock on Lan Wangji's face, that his gaze could almost be described as gentle, it clicked for him.

He asked in a whisper, unable to stop himself, "...You knew?"

Lan Wangji slowly nodded his head.

Wei Wuxian let out a soft sigh. "...Wen Ning."

Suibian had been with Wen Ning for safekeeping, but it was now in Jiang Cheng's hands. To think Wen Ning had actually kept mum about this when they were leaving Lotus Pier...

"When did he reveal it?" Wei Wuxian asked.

"While you were unconscious," Lan Wangji answered.

"*That* was how we escaped Lotus Pier?!" Wei Wuxian exclaimed.

If Wen Ning had been there, Wei Wuxian would've been glaring at him right then.

"He felt very apologetic about it," Lan Wangji said.

Wei Wuxian's words were laced with a tinge of annoyance. "...I told him over and over again not to tell anyone!"

Without warning, Jiang Cheng spoke, "Tell anyone what?"

Wei Wuxian gave a start. Jiang Cheng and Lan Wangji both turned their gazes his way.

Jiang Cheng covered his wound with his hand as he bit out a sarcastic reply. "Wei Wuxian, you're so selfless. So noble. Despite all the humiliation you've suffered, you've done every good deed in the world and kept them secret from everyone. How touching! Should I be down on my knees, weeping and thanking you?"

Lan Wangji's expression frosted over at Jiang Cheng's blatantly rude and mocking tone. His hostile expression made Jin Ling hurry to stand in front of Jiang Cheng, fearing that Lan Wangji would strike him dead on the spot.

"Jiujiu!" he cried out anxiously.

Wei Wuxian's expression began to darken. He'd never had any hope that Jiang Cheng would bury the hatchet if he ever learned the truth, but he hadn't expected him to still speak so unpleasantly to him either.

After a moment of silence, Wei Wuxian grumbled, "I'm not asking you to thank me."

Jiang Cheng snorted a laugh. "Right. Asking nothing in return for doing a good deed—you're in a league of your own. Unlike me, of course. No wonder my father always used to say *you* were the one who really understood the Jiang Clan's motto, when he was alive. That *you* were the one who acted as a Jiang should."

Wei Wuxian interrupted him, unable to listen any longer. "That's enough."

"What's enough?" Jiang Cheng snapped. "It's enough just because you say so? Yeah, you know best! You're better than me in every way, whether it be talent or cultivation, intelligence or temperament! You people know it all. I can't compare. What *does* that make me, then?!"

He suddenly reached out, as if about to grab Wei Wuxian's collar. Lan Wangji gripped Wei Wuxian's shoulder and pulled him behind him to protect him, using his other hand to smack Jiang Cheng away. His eyes blazed with an indistinct fury. Although the blow was not infused with spiritual power, it was a powerful strike, and the force of it caused the wound on Jiang Cheng's chest to tear open and gush blood once more.

"Jiujiu, your wound!" Jin Ling cried out in shock. "Hanguang-jun, please have mercy!"

"Jiang Wanyin, mind your tongue!" Lan Wangji responded coldly.

Lan Xichen stripped off his outer robe and used it to cover Nie Huaisang, who was shivering from the cold.

"Sect Leader Jiang," he said, "please restrain yourself. Your injuries will only worsen if you become agitated and shout like that."

Jiang Cheng shoved away a flustered Jin Ling, who was still trying to support him. Though he was literally losing blood, enough still rushed to his head to drown out all rational thought. His face alternated between white and red.

"Why? Wei Wuxian, just fucking why?"

"Why what?" Wei Wuxian responded stiffly from behind Lan Wangji.

"How much has the Jiang family given you, *huh*?" Jiang Cheng said. "*I'm* the son; *I'm* the successor to the Jiang Clan of Yunmeng, but all these years, you've one-upped me in every way. You repaid the kindness my family showed in raising you by forcing them to give up their lives—the lives of my father, mother, elder sister, and Jin Zixuan! Because of you, the only one left is an orphaned Jin Ling!"

Jin Ling jolted. His shoulders drooped, and his expression wilted too.

Wei Wuxian moved his lips, but was ultimately unable to say a word. Lan Wangji turned and caught his hand in his own.

Meanwhile, Jiang Cheng was still relentlessly hurling abuse at Wei Wuxian. "Wei Wuxian, who was the one who broke his own promise and betrayed the Jiangs? You said it yourself—that you'd be my subordinate and support me for life when I became the head of the family. The Lan Clan of Gusu has their Twin Jades, and the Jiang Clan of Yunmeng had our Twin Heroes. You said you'd never betray me or the Jiangs. Who was the one who said all that?! I'm asking you, *who said it?!* Did it all amount to shit?!"

He only worked himself into more of a fury as he kept yelling. "And what happened in the end? You went and protected outsiders, ha ha! And they were Wens, no less! How much of their rice did you eat? You defected at the drop of a hat, with not a moment's hesitation! What did you take my family for?! You did every good deed known to man, but when it came to doing *bad* deeds, it was always out of your hands! You had no choice! You had some difficulties you just couldn't mention! Difficulties, my ass! You never tell me anything. You treat me like a fool!

"How much do you owe the Jiang Clan? Should I not hate you? *Can* I not hate you? Why does it now look like *I'm* the one who let you down?! Why do I have to feel like I've been a fucking clown all these years?! What am I? Does it serve me right to be blinded by your brilliance?! *Am I not supposed to hate you?!*"

Lan Wangji shot to his feet. Jin Ling leapt in front of Jiang Cheng in a panic. "Hanguang-jun! My uncle is injured..."

Jiang Cheng smacked him to the ground. "Let him come at me! You think I'm afraid, Lan-er?!"

Jin Ling froze after receiving that single slap. And it wasn't just him—Wei Wuxian, Lan Wangji, and Lan Xichen had all gone still.

Jiang Cheng...was crying.

As tears streamed down his face, he hissed through gritted teeth, "...Why...why didn't you tell me?!"

He clenched his fists, looking like he wanted to punch someone. Like he wanted to punch himself. In the end, he smashed his fist into the ground.

He should have been able to hate Wei Wuxian without qualms, but the golden core circulating spiritual energy in his body made it impossible for him to justify such hate.

Wei Wuxian was at a loss.

He had decided not to tell Jiang Cheng precisely because he hadn't wanted to see him like this. He'd vowed to Jiang Fengmian and Madam Yu that he would take care of Jiang Cheng, and that promise was rooted eternally in his heart. If someone as competitive as Jiang Cheng ever learned of the core transplant, he would be left in anguish and sorrow for the rest of his life, unable to face himself, unable to overcome the hurdle the knowledge posed. He would always be plagued by the thought that his achievements were only gained thanks to someone else's sacrifice. None of the cultivation, none of the accomplishments were his. He'd lost, even if he'd won. He had long since lost the right to be competitive.

Later, after Jin Zixuan and Jiang Yanli died because of him, Wei Wuxian had felt even greater shame at the prospect of letting anyone know. To tell Jiang Cheng the truth after that would have been like refusing to take responsibility—like he was all too anxious to make it clear that he was a man of merit, like he was telling Jiang Cheng, *"Don't hate me. You see, I've also sacrificed for the Jiang Clan of Yunmeng."*

Jiang Cheng's weeping was silent, but his face was streaked with tears. In the past, it would have been unthinkable for him to cry in such an unsightly manner before a crowd. But as long as this golden core remained in his body circulating spiritual energy, he'd never forget this feeling—every moment, every second, every day.

His voice was choked with sobs. "...You said that when I became the head of the family, you'd be my subordinate and support me for life. That you'd never, ever betray the Jiang Clan of Yunmeng... You said it yourself."

Wei Wuxian could not find the words to respond. It was a moment before he said, "I'm sorry. I broke my promise."

Jiang Cheng shook his head and buried his face in his hands. After a while, he suddenly snorted out a laugh. "Making you apologize even at a time like this," he said, voice muffled and tone derisive. "I must be *so* important."

Sect Leader Jiang always spoke with some degree of derision, but this time, he was not mocking anyone but himself.

"I'm sorry," he blurted all of a sudden.

Wei Wuxian was taken aback. "...There's no need for you to say sorry."

At this point, there was no way to measure who let down whom.

"Consider it a repayment of my debt to the Jiangs," Wei Wuxian added.

Jiang Cheng raised his head and looked at him with bloodshot eyes. "...To my father, my mother, my sister?" he asked in a hoarse voice.

Wei Wuxian rubbed his temple. "Forget it. It's all in the past. Let's not bring it up again."

This wasn't something he liked to keep reliving. He didn't want to be forced to remember the sensation of having his core cut out while he was still conscious, nor want to be forcefully reminded of what a sacrifice it had been and what it had cost.

Had this incident been exposed in his previous life, he would most likely have laughed it off. He would have consoled Jiang Cheng with, *"It's really no big deal. Look at me, haven't I managed for this long without a golden core? I still beat up whomever I want and kill whomever I please."* But he no longer had the strength to keep up a nonchalant act.

Truthfully, he wasn't unaffected. Could a person so easily resign themselves to such a loss?

Of course not. It was impossible.

Wei Wuxian's own pride when he was seventeen or eighteen had been, in fact, on par with Jiang Cheng's. He had also been someone with strong spiritual power and exceptional talent. Even when he'd fooled around all day catching fish and shooting birds, and climbing walls and playing pranks at night, he had still been leagues ahead of his fellow disciples who actually studied hard.

But whenever he found himself tossing and turning in the dead of night, unable to sleep and plagued by thoughts of how he'd never again follow the orthodox path to the mountain's peak, never again display the astounding swordplay that made people's jaws drop...he would turn his thoughts around with a simple fact. If it had not been for Jiang Fengmian bringing him to Lotus Pier, Wei Wuxian might never have crossed paths with the cultivation world. He would never have been conscious of such a mystical and magnificent realm. He'd merely have been the leader of some homeless street urchins who roamed the streets and fled at the sight of dogs—or perhaps herded cattle and stole vegetables in the countryside, playing his flute and living one day at a time. He'd have had no way of cultivating, let alone a chance to form a golden core.

And at that thought, he'd feel a lot better.

So he treated it as a repayment of his debt, or an atonement for his sins. Treated it as if he had never obtained that golden core to begin with.

After bringing himself around so many times this way, he was almost able to actually feel as wild and carefree as he acted on the surface. He could even half-jokingly praise himself for the state of acceptance he had reached, while he was at it.

But all that was in the past.

"Uh," he began. "Stop...thinking about it all the time. I know you'll never forget it, obviously, considering what you're like. But how should I put this..." He tightened his hold on Lan Wangji's hand. "I really do think it's...water under the bridge. It's been so long. There's no need to dwell on it."

Jiang Cheng rubbed his face hard and wiped away his tears, then took a deep breath and closed his eyes.

At that moment, Nie Huaisang slowly woke up. Still covered with Lan Xichen's outer robe, he groaned softly as he shifted upright with difficulty. Blearily, he asked, "Where am I?"

He could never have imagined he'd be greeted by the sight of Wei Wuxian and Lan Wangji sitting snugly together on a prayer cushion as soon as he woke. The Yiling Patriarch was almost in Hanguang-jun's lap. Nie Huaisang yelped and looked like he was about to faint again.

At the same time, a series of strange spurting sounds echoed from the back grounds of Guanyin Hall, like something was spewing forth. A moment later, screams rang out from the group of cultivators who had been digging.

Everyone's expressions changed as a subtle yet pungent smell wafted into the hall. Although Lan Xichen covered his mouth and nose with his sleeve, his face betrayed a hint of concern. Soon after, two figures stumbled into the hall.

— PART 2 —

S U SHE WAS SUPPORTING Jin Guangyao, both their com-
plexions pallid. The wailing from the temple's rear grounds
continued on.

"Sect Leader, how are you feeling?!" Su She asked.

A bead of cold sweat trickled down Jin Guangyao's forehead. "I'm
fine. Thanks for earlier."

His left hand hung limply; he seemed unable to lift it, and the
entire arm was trembling. Enduring the pain, he reached his right
hand into his robe to retrieve a bottle of medicine. Opening it with
one hand proved to be an inconvenience. Seeing him struggle, Su
She hurriedly took the bottle and tipped a pill into Jin Guangyao's
hand. Frowning, he lowered his head to swallow it. His brows
promptly relaxed.

Lan Xichen hesitated briefly before asking, "What happened to
you?"

Jin Guangyao looked slightly taken aback. Some color returned
to his face then, and he answered with a forced smile. "A momentary
carelessness."

He retrieved some medicinal powder and sprinkled it on his
hand. There was a patch of red on the back of his left hand that
stretched to his wrist. On closer inspection, the skin looked like
fried meat. The flesh was completely ruined.

With shaking fingers, Jin Guangyao tore a piece from his snow-
white lapel. "Minshan, wrap this around my wrist tightly."

"Is it poison?" Su She asked.

"The toxin is still flowing upward, against the flow of circulation,"
Jin Guangyao said. "It's not a problem. It can be purged with some
regulated breathing."

Once Su She had treated his wound, Jin Guangyao made to return to the temple's rear grounds to check on the situation.

Su She spoke up hurriedly. "Sect Leader, let me go!"

The pungent smell gradually dissipated. Wei Wuxian and Lan Wangji stood up as well and followed.

Behind the temple was a tall mound of earth piled beside a deep pit. An exquisitely fine coffin lay within. Its lid was crooked, and a pitch-black chest sat atop. The chest was also already open, and there were still thin wisps of white smoke slowly escaping from within. The pungent smell came from the smoke, which was undoubtedly some kind of deadly poison.

A jumble of corpses lay all over the ground beside the coffin. These were the cultivators who had been hard at work digging earlier, now dead and thoroughly cooked through. Even their Sparks Amidst Snow uniforms and monk robes had been corroded to the point that only scorched black shreds remained. It was clear just how toxic the white smoke was.

Jin Guangyao beat the others there and dispelled the residual corrosive smoke with his sword qi. The tip of his blade flicked the pitch-black metal chest, and it fell to the ground—completely empty inside.

Unable to wait a moment longer, Jin Guangyao stumbled to the edge of the coffin. In an instant, his face drained completely of color again. His expression alone was enough to tell the others that the coffin, too, was completely empty.

Lan Xichen came over, looking shocked at the horrid state of things. "What exactly did you bury here? How could this happen?"

Even a cursory glance at the scene made Nie Huaisang keel over from fright and start dry-heaving. Jin Guangyao's lips quivered, but he did not speak. A bolt of lightning flashed, illuminating the ghastly paleness of his face. His expression was so horrible that it seemed to send a shiver of terror down Nie Huaisang's spine. No longer daring to keep retching so loudly, he shrank back behind Lan Xichen, trembling from cold or fear.

Lan Xichen turned his head to say a few words of comfort, but Jin Guangyao no longer had the energy to keep up his gentle and amicable front.

"Zewu-jun," Wei Wuxian piped up. "You've wronged Sect Leader Jin on that front. He wasn't the one who buried *that* thing here. Even if he did originally, someone else must've swapped it out a long time ago."

Su She raised his sword to point at him and demanded in a cold voice, "Wei Wuxian! Was it you who messed with it?!"

"Not to brag, but your sect leader would probably be missing more than an arm if I was the one behind it," Wei Wuxian replied. "Sect Leader Jin, do you recall the letter Qin Su showed you at Golden Carp Tower?"

Jin Guangyao's gaze slowly shifted over to him.

"Madam Qin's former handmaid Bicao was the one who told Qin Su about all those wonderful things you did," Wei Wuxian continued. "As for why Bicao would decide to tell all so suddenly... Do you seriously think there was no one incentivizing her from the shadows? Then there's Miss Sisi, whom you had locked up. Who saved her, and who told her to go to the Jiang Clan of Yunmeng with Bicao to expose your secrets in front of everyone? Whoever it was, they were able to uncover your concealed past. How hard would it be for them to get here before you did and replace whatever you wanted to dig up with a surprise gift of toxic smoke, just for you?"

A monk spoke up then. "Sect Leader, the soil here shows signs of having been turned before. Someone dug their way in from the other side!"

Sure enough, someone had beaten him to it and gottten there first. Jin Guangyao whirled around and punched the top of the empty coffin. His face was hidden from them; all they could see were his slightly shaking shoulders.

"Sect Leader Jin, has it ever occurred to you that while you might be the mantis tonight, there's an oriole behind you?" Wei Wuxian continued with a laugh. "The person behind all this might be watching your every move from the darkness, even as we speak. Or perhaps they're not a person at all..."

Muffled thunder crashed and the torrential rain poured. A flash of what could almost be called fear streaked across Jin Guangyao's face at the suggestion of an inhuman pursuer.

Su She sneered. "Wei Wuxian, enough with the empty threats..."

Jin Guangyao raised a hand to stop him. The twinge of fear on his face ebbed in no time as he swiftly brought his various emotions under control. "Don't waste your breath on a pointless battle of words. Treat your injuries. Prepare the remaining men and be ready to set out immediately once I purge myself of the poison."

"Sect Leader, what about whatever was dug up and taken away?" Su She asked.

Jin Guangyao's lips blanched a little. "Since it's been taken, it is most certainly a lost cause at this point. We should not remain here."

"Yes, sir!" Su She responded.

Su She had gotten scratched in many places during his earlier fight with Fairy, and his robes were ripped along the arms and chest. Particularly the chest—the dog's claws had torn his flesh so deeply that the bone showed through. His white clothing was heavily stained with blood. If he did not treat his wounds promptly, he might not be in a position to deal with unexpected situations later.

Jin Guangyao took a packet of medicine from the folds of his robes at his chest and handed it to him.

Su She accepted it with both hands. "Yes, sir."

He turned around and undid his clothing to treat his own injuries, dropping any further engagement with Wei Wuxian.

Jin Guangyao's burned left hand still did not heed his commands, so he could only sit and focus on regulating his breathing to expel the poison. The cultivators who were still alive patrolled the Guanyin Temple's grounds with their swords at the ready. Nie Huaisang's eyes bulged when he saw the bright, gleaming blades. Without his bodyguards around, he didn't even dare breathe heavily, but cowered in a corner behind Lan Xichen and sneezed quite a number of times.

Su She is so condescending toward everyone, and especially resentful of Lan Zhan. But he treats Jin Guangyao with such respect, Wei Wuxian thought.

He unconsciously turned to look at Lan Wangji, catching an unexpected flash of frost in his eyes.

"Turn around," Lan Wangji coldly commanded Su She.

Su She was turned away from them, head lowered, busy applying ointment to the claw marks on his chest. Lan Wangji's sudden, authoritative tone made him unconsciously obey the command.

As he turned, Jiang Cheng and Jin Ling's eyes both widened. The smile on Wei Wuxian's face died instantly.

"...So it was you!" he blurted in disbelief.

It was then that Su She realized his mistake, immediately covering his chest with his clothes. But everyone present had already gotten a clear look at what he had exposed. The skin near his heart was densely pockmarked with dozens of hideous-looking black holes of varying sizes.

Marks from the Thousand Sores and Hundred Holes curse!

And these were clearly not the result of being the curse's *target*. Had that been the case, then judging by how far the holes had spread, Su She's internal organs and golden core would have been riddled too, leaving him unable to use his spiritual powers. But he could still use transportation talismans regularly, which consumed an enormous amount of spiritual energy each time. There was only one explanation for the marks—they had been left behind thanks to curse rebound after he had cast the spell on someone else!

It wasn't like Wei Wuxian hadn't tried to find the spell caster to clear his name, but it was like finding a needle in a haystack. And merely finding the culprit wouldn't have resolved everything that came after, so he had stopped holding out hope. Who could've imagined he would chance upon the culprit tonight? Truly, you can wear out iron shoes searching in vain, only to effortlessly stumble on what you seek by sheer luck.

Jin Ling didn't understand, and Nie Huaisang probably didn't either. But Lan Xichen was already looking at Jin Guangyao as he asked, "Sect Leader Jin, was this also part of the plan for the Qiongqi Path Ambush?

"Why would you think that?" Jin Guangyao answered with a question.

"Do you even need to ask?" Jiang Cheng said coldly. "If Jin Zixun hadn't been hit by that curse, nothing that transpired after would have happened! That one incident helped you dispose of both Jin Zixuan and Jin Zixun, who were juniors of the same generation as you. It removed every obstacle in your path to succeeding the leader of the Jin Clan of Lanling and taking up the position of Cultivation Chief. Su She cast the curse, and he's your trusted aide. Is there even a question of whose orders he acted on?!"

Jin Guangyao didn't comment, appearing to be concentrating on regulating his breathing.

Wei Wuxian was so furious he had to laugh. "Have I ever offended you?" he questioned Su She with a glare. "I bear you no grudge and have no feud with you. Heck, I barely even know you!"

"Wei-gongzi," Jin Guangyao said. "Shouldn't you understand this better than anyone? Does having no grudges or feuds mean you can live in peace? How is that possible? Everyone in this world starts out without grudges or feuds, but someone will always stab first."

"*Evil scum!*" Jiang Cheng spat hatefully.

Su She only sneered in response. "Stop thinking so highly of yourself. Who said I cursed Jin Zixun to frame you? I wasn't even under Sect Leader Jin's command at the time. I cast that curse because I wanted to!"

"Did you have a feud with Jin Zixun, then?" Wei Wuxian asked.

"Haughty people like him—I'll kill every single one I come across!" Su She said.

Wei Wuxian knew the "haughty" person he detested the most had to be Lan Wangji. He couldn't help but ask, "Exactly what dispute do you have with Hanguang-jun? How is he supercilious?"

"Am I wrong?" Su She said. "If Lan Wangji hadn't been born into a good family, what reason would he have to be so conceited? Who is he to say that I imitate him?! Everyone praises him for his noble character. Yeah, right. The renowned cultivator, Hanguang-jun, so noble he gets up to all sorts of sordid, scandalous acts with the Yiling Patriarch—who is wicked beyond redemption and condemned by all! What a joke!"

Wei Wuxian was about to speak when he suddenly realized Su She's gloomy, resentful expression was familiar. He'd seen it somewhere before.

Suddenly, it dawned on him. "It was you!"

The disciple whose sword had fallen into the Waterborne Abyss in Biling Lake at Caiyi Town, and the disciple who had shoved Mianmian forward in the cave of the Xuanwu of Slaughter—both had been Su She!

Wei Wuxian suddenly erupted in laughter. "I get it now."

"What is that?" Lan Wangji asked.

Wei Wuxian shook his head.

He knew the kind of person Jin Zixun was. Jin Zixun often turned up his nose at the people from clans affiliated with the Jin Clan, considering them no different from servants. He even found it beneath him to attend the same banquets as them. As a member of one such affiliate clan, Su She inevitably made frequent trips to Golden Carp Tower to attend these banquets and inevitably ran into Jin Zixun. One was narrow-minded and calculating, and the other was pompous and arrogant. If there had been any unpleasantness between them, Su She might very well have borne Jin Zixun a grudge.

If this really was the case, then the Thousand Sores and Hundred Holes curse on Jin Zixun had nothing to do with Wei Wuxian at all. But he was the one who'd ultimately been slapped with the blame.

The Qiongqi Path Ambush had been launched because Jin Zixun was cursed with the Thousand Sores and Hundred Holes spell. Without that, the Jin Clan of Lanling would have had no justification for their actions. Wen Ning would not have lost control and gone on a killing spree, and Wei Wuxian would not have had to shoulder a weight as heavy as Jin Zixuan's death. And everything that followed after would not have happened.

Now, he realized the murderer might not have sought to frame him by casting the curse. It hadn't had anything to do with him at all!

It was truly a bitter pill to swallow.

As he laughed, Wei Wuxian's eyes reddened. In a tone both sarcastic and self-deprecating, he said, "I can't believe it was because of someone like you...for such a senseless reason!"

But Jin Guangyao seemed to have seen through him. "Wei-gongzi, you can't think of it like that."

"Oh?" Wei Wuxian said. "You know what I'm thinking?"

"Of course," Jin Guangyao answered. "It's easy to guess. You're undoubtedly thinking how unjust this is—but it's actually not. Even if Su She hadn't cast that curse on Jin Zixun, Mister Wei would have found himself besieged for some reason, sooner or later.

"Because that's just how you are," he continued with a smile. "To put it nicely, you're chivalrous and free-spirited. To put it bluntly, you offend people wherever you go. So unless everyone you offended remained safe and sound for the rest of their lives, you were sure to be the prime suspect if anything untoward happened to them or anyone plotted against them. Revenge would soon follow. That is something you can't control."

To everyone's surprise, Wei Wuxian laughed. "Oh dear, what should I do? I actually think you make a lot of sense."

Jin Guangyao added, "And besides, even if you hadn't lost control that time at Qiongqi Path, could you guarantee you would never have lost control for the rest of your life? And so, people like you are destined to have a short life. Now then, doesn't thinking that way make you feel a lot better?"

Jiang Cheng raged. "*You're* the one with the fucking short life!"

Disregarding his critical injuries, he grabbed Sandu and attempted to charge over. Fresh blood immediately gushed from his wound, and Jin Ling held him back. Unable to move, Jiang Cheng was forced to stew in his hatred.

"Son of a whore!" he cursed. "You have no shame whatsoever. All in the name of rising to the top! Weren't you the one who put Su She up to it?! Who are you trying to fool?!"

Jin Guangyao's smile froze for a moment when he heard the words "son of a whore."

He looked at Jiang Cheng and thought for a moment before saying dispassionately, "Sect Leader Jiang, calm down. I understand how you feel right now. You're furious because you found out the truth about your golden core. Looking back on what you've done over the years, your proud heart feels a little guilty. You're anxious to find a villain culpable for what happened to Wei-gongzi in his former life, a fiend whom you can saddle with the blame. Then you'll lash out against him to avenge Wei-gongzi—and to relieve yourself a little of the burden.

"Perhaps you think that blaming me for everything from the Thousand Sores and Hundred Holes curse to the Qiongqi Path Ambush can alleviate your troubles. By all means, go ahead. It doesn't matter if you think that way. But you have to understand that you are *also* responsible for what happened to Wei-gongzi. In fact, you played a large role. Why did so many people dedicate themselves to crusading against the Yiling Patriarch? Why did everyone involved—and even those who had nothing to do with the matter at all—donate their voices to the cause? Why was there such an overwhelming number of people baying for his blood? Was it really their sense of justice at work? Of course not. Part of the reason...was you."

Jiang Cheng scoffed. Lan Xichen, knowing Jin Guangyao was trying to sow discord again, growled, "Sect Leader Jin!"

Jin Guangyao remained unmoved and continued with a candid smile. "...At the time, the Jin Clan of Lanling, the Nie Clan of

Qinghe, and the Lan Clan of Gusu contended with one another to divide the lion's share of the cultivation world among them. The other clans only had crumbs to nibble on. You had just rebuilt Lotus Pier, and you also had the immeasurably dangerous Yiling Patriarch in your corner. Do you think the other clans were happy to see such a young family head with such power? Fortunately, your relationship with your shixiong seemed strained. Everyone saw this was something they could exploit, so naturally, they tried their best to add fuel to the flames if it would make you two fall out with one another. They were making themselves more powerful by keeping the Jiang Clan of Yunmeng from growing stronger.

"Sect Leader Jiang, if only your attitude toward your shixiong had been just a little better in the past... It would've made your bond seem unbreakable, which would have made everyone aware the odds were stacked against them and abandon their attempts to sow discord. If you'd shown more tolerance after the incident, then things would not have ended up the way they did. Which reminds me, you also led one of the main forces in the Siege of the Burial Mounds..."

"Looks like 'son of a whore' really is Sect Leader Jin's sore spot," Wei Wuxian said. "No wonder you killed Chifeng-zun."

At the mention of Nie Mingjue, Lan Xichen's expression changed. Jin Guangyao's smile also froze for a moment. Then, he stood. Having regulated his circulation, he tried flexing the fingers of his left hand, which could finally move freely.

"Give the order to set off," he said immediately.

"Understood!" Su She heeded.

Two monks on the left and right kept Lan Xichen restrained between them. Just as the main door was about to be opened, Jin Guangyao suddenly said, "Right, I forgot."

He turned to Lan Xichen. "Judging by the time, the seal on Zewu-jun's meridians should be released soon."

Lan Xichen's cultivation was much higher than his. If Jin Guangyao wanted to seal his meridians, he had to redo it every two hours, or Lan Xichen would be able to break free on his own.

Jin Guangyao walked up to Lan Xichen and said, "Pardon me."

He was just about to reach out when something white plummeted through the air and landed heavily before him. Jin Guangyao, on the alert, sidestepped and looked closer.

It was a pale human body!

A naked woman was sprawled on the ground, twisting her body and limbs as if she wanted to crawl to Jin Guangyao. Su She thrust out his sword. The woman let out a shrill scream, and her entire body suddenly burst into flames. She stood and continued to stumble her way to Jin Guangyao, hands grasping. Her body and face had been scorched black by the flames, but the profound hatred in her eyes was clear for all to see.

With another slash of his sword, Su She cut her down, and she dissipated into smoke.

Jin Guangyao took several steps back and tripped over something. He looked back, only to see two entangled human bodies. One of them reached out and caught his ankle.

The sound of a whistle rang out behind him.

"Wei Wuxian!" Su She spat hatefully.

Without anyone noticing, someone had scrawled a number of spells in blood upon the Guanyin statue in Guanyin Hall.

The heart of Guanyin Temple's array was right in this hall. Wei Wuxian had broken it while the others were distracted, and the creatures that had been sealed within were now swarming out in a never-ending stream!

Jin Ling cried out in alarm. "What's happening?!"

Jiang Cheng kept slapping at his robe, the hem of which had spontaneously combusted. Jin Ling was one of the more fortunate ones. Several monks were already engulfed in flames, screaming as they writhed on the ground.

Su She and Jin Guangyao knew they had to wipe away the traces of blood Wei Wuxian had drawn on the Guanyin statue, but they were hindered by the cultivators on the floor and the incessant stream of evil, naked beings. The nude men and women obeyed Wei Wuxian's command and did not attack Jiang Cheng, Jin Ling, or the rest, but Jin Ling still stiffly held Suihua at the ready.

"What are these creatures? I've never seen such..."

Such naked and shameless evil beings!

Jin Guangyao's eyes blazed with fury as he struck out with his palm, blasting a path through the flames. He finally made it to the Guanyin statue, and was about to wipe away the spells that Wei Wuxian had painted on it when he suddenly felt a chill at the small of his back.

"Do not move," Lan Xichen ordered in a low voice.

Jin Guangyao was about to counterattack when Lan Xichen struck him on the back with his palm.

"Zewu-jun," Jin Guangyao said. "...Your spiritual powers are back."

Lan Xichen had yet to answer when Su She lunged at Wei Wuxian with Nanping. It hit another longsword, however—one with a sword glare that was similar, but coursing with brighter and clearer spiritual light.

It was Bichen!

Both swords collided—and to everyone's shock, Nanping snapped in two.

In that instant, the flesh between Su She's thumb and index finger split apart, and blood gushed forth. Even the joints in his arm cracked from the impact. Nanping's hilt hit the ground, and he covered his right arm with his left hand. His face was ashen.

Meanwhile, Lan Wangji held Bichen with one hand while the other caught Wei Wuxian around the waist to bring the latter behind him for protection. Wei Wuxian didn't actually need to be shielded, but he still leaned on him, playing along with relish.

This series of events took place in a flash. Only now did the cultivators from the Jin Clan of Lanling realize what had happened. By then, Su She's chest wound had split open as he clutched his bleeding right hand, and Bichen's tip was pressed against Jin Guangyao's throat.

With their master restrained, they did not dare to act rashly.

Lan Xichen was about to speak when the expressions of those in Guanyin Hall underwent a sudden change.

"Wei-gongzi, please... Please put those creatures away first," Lan Xichen said.

Not only were the evil specters naked and indecent, but they were also making extremely embarrassing moans. The sound was enough to tell one what they were doing.

No one present had ever seen such outrageously obscene, malicious spirits before. Lan Xichen turned his head to the side to avoid looking at them, Jiang Cheng looked absolutely livid, and Jin Ling alternated between blushing and blanching. Wei Wuxian looked at Lan Wangji beside him, worried that it was unbecoming to let someone who used to fly into an embarrassed rage at the sight of erotica glimpse something like this.

"I meant to release the evil he'd suppressed in the temple, to delay him for however long we could," he defended himself. "How could I have known I'd wind up letting these kinda things out...?"

Lan Wangji only took one glance at the vengeful spirits before averting his gaze as Lan Xichen had. As he looked in another direction, he stated, "Fire."

Wei Wuxian immediately nodded and agreed in a serious tone. "Yeah. These vengeful spirits were burned to death. Looks like a fire once broke out in this place, killing many people. Then Sect Leader Jin built a Guanyin Temple here in an attempt to pull the wool over everyone's eyes, as well as to suppress these spirits who turned malevolent after their fiery deaths."

"Sect Leader Jin," Lan Xichen asked, "did you have something to do with this fire?"

"Those vengeful spirits obviously hate him with every fiber of their being. It's impossible that he had nothing to do with it," Jiang Cheng said coldly.

"Sect Leader Jin... Might you explain?" Lan Xichen asked.

Jin Guangyao said nothing. His knuckles had gone faintly white.

"Looks like Sect Leader Jin isn't willing to talk," Wei Wuxian said. He raised his hand, and a naked female corpse instantly popped up under his palm. He placed his hand on her head of jet-black hair. "But even if you don't say a word, do you seriously think there's no way for me to find out?"

As soon as he started his session of Empathy—even before he opened his eyes—Wei Wuxian found himself surrounded by the strong fragrance of rouge and powder. A coquettish voice came out of his own mouth.

"...Her? Of course she wants to marry someone. She was already over twenty when she met that guy. She's not young anymore, and her popularity will no doubt plummet after a few more years. That's why she insisted on giving birth to a son, even at the risk of punishment—she just wants a chance to break free, no? But the man in the equation *has* to be willing to cooperate."

He opened his eyes and saw before him a magnificent, spacious main hall. There were dozens of large round tables, each seating multiple patrons and attractive women. Some of the women were bare-shouldered, some had let their silky hair loose. There were some sitting on customers' laps, while others fed liquor to the men around them. Every single one of them wore a saccharine, drunk expression.

Anyone could tell what kind of place this was with a single look.

So this spirit who burned to death in Guanyin Temple was actually a working girl, Wei Wuxian thought. *No wonder the vengeful spirits are all naked. They were probably all prostitutes and their customers.*

A patron who was drinking at the side laughed. "The son is still his, after all. Don't tell me the guy doesn't want him?"

"She said herself that the guy is a big shot from a cultivation clan," the woman answered, "which means he must have a lot of sons back home. Anything one has in abundance is no longer precious. Why would he care about this son outside? She waited and hoped, but nobody came to take her away, so she could only raise the child herself. It's now been fourteen years and counting."

Several of the customers said, "Big shot? Is that true?"

"Oh please, why would I lie to you about such things? Her son is currently doing odd jobs around here. There, that's the one." The woman twisted at the waist and beckoned to a young boy carrying a tray. "Xiao-Meng! C'mere!"

Sure enough, the boy walked over. "Anxin-jie, what can I do for you?"

In that instant, Wei Wuxian understood everything.

The men sized up Meng Yao with scrutinizing eyes.

"Is there something I can do for you?" Meng Yao asked again.

Anxin answered with a smile. "Xiao-Meng, are you still studying all that stuff on your own?"

Meng Yao blinked. "What stuff?"

"The stuff that your mom told you to learn," Anxin said. "Calligraphy, etiquette, swordplay, meditation... How are your studies?"

A few customers snorted with laughter before she could finish, as if they found the idea extremely hilarious. Anxin turned her head.

"Don't laugh, gosh. I'm telling the truth. His mom is raising him like a wealthy young master. She taught him how to read and write, bought him a whole stack of swordplay manuals, and even wanted to send him to school."

"Send him to school? Did I hear that right?" a customer exclaimed in surprise.

"Yup!" Anxin said. "Xiao-Meng, tell these young masters that you've been to school."

"Is he still attending?" a customer asked.

"No, he returned after a few days and refused to go there again," Anxin said. "Xiao-Meng, is it studying you dislike, or was it the place?"

Meng Yao said nothing, and Anxin giggled. She jabbed his forehead with a finger, the nail painted with bright red polish.

"Are you upset, little guy?"

Her forceful jab left a faint red mark at the center of Meng Yao's forehead, like the shadow of a cinnabar mark. He touched the spot as he replied, "No..."

Anxin waved her hand dismissively. "All right, that's it for now. You may go."

Meng Yao turned around and had barely taken a few steps when she picked something up from the table.

"Here you go," she coaxed him. "A fruit for you."

The moment Meng Yao turned around, the ripe fruit smashed into his chest and fell to the ground before rolling away.

"Why are you so slow-witted? You can't even catch a fruit?" Anxin rebuked him. "Pick it up now. Don't waste it."

Meng Yao tugged the corner of his lips into a smile. He should be fourteen years old by now, but he only looked to be twelve or thirteen due to his particularly scrawny stature. It was extremely disconcerting to see such a smile appear on his young face.

He slowly bent down to pick up the fruit, then wiped it on the front of his clothes. His smile deepened. "Thank you, Anxin-jiejie."

"You're welcome," Anxin answered. "Now get back to work."

"Call me again if you need me," Meng Yao said.

After he walked away, one of the patrons piped up. "If my son was living in a place like this, I'd take him home at all costs."

Another customer chimed in. "Is his father really a big shot in a cultivation clan? Shouldn't it be easy for him to buy a prostitute's freedom and give her a stipend to raise her son? It'd only take a single lift of a finger."

"How can you believe everything that woman says?" Anxin said. "Even believing half of her story is too much. She's the one who claims that he's a big shot. If you ask me, he's probably just some rich merchant that she exaggerated..."

A shrill scream suddenly rang out from the second floor, along with the sound of shattering cups and saucers. A jade guqin tumbled end over end through the air and landed in the middle of the hall with a thunderous crash, breaking into pieces. The people drinking and making merry at the tables nearby were so startled that they broke out into a chorus of swearing. Anxin almost fell out of her seat.

"What happened?!" she shrieked.

"Mom!" Meng Yao cried out.

Anxin looked up, only to see a large, burly man dragging a woman out of a room by her hair. Anxin grabbed the customer beside her and exclaimed in a tone that could have been excitement or anxiety, "She's at it again!"

Meng Yao rushed upstairs. The woman was clutching her scalp and desperately pulling her clothes over her shoulders. The moment she saw Meng Yao running over, she ordered him hurriedly, "I told you not to come up here! Go down! Go downstairs now!"

Meng Yao attempted to pry off the customer's hand, but was sent tumbling down the stairs by a kick to the stomach. Alarmed exclamations rang out around him.

This was the third time Wei Wuxian had seen him getting kicked down the stairs.

The woman screamed aloud and was promptly seized by the hair again. The customer dragged her all the way down the stairs, stripped her, and then tossed her onto the street. He spat a mouthful of saliva on her naked body and cursed.

"Ugly hags cause the most trouble. Old whore still thinks she's fresh meat!"

The woman was stricken with panic as she lay prone in the middle of the street, too scared to get up. She would bare herself completely for all to see if she moved. The street's pedestrians were both shocked and excited, and vacillated between staying and leaving as they pointed fingers at her with gleaming eyes. The brothel's entrance was also packed with the women inside. They giggled under their breath as they gloated and told the customers beside them about this old, wretched woman, the same way Anxin had.

Only one young woman squeezed her way outside. She took off her sheer and flimsy robe, revealing her extremely slender waist and half of her ample snow-white bosoms, which were wrapped in a bright red undergarment. She was so eye-catching that street gawkers all turned their gazes to her instead.

The young woman spat and cursed, "What the fuck are you looking at?! You people think you can ogle me for free? You gotta pay for each look. Pay up! Gimme the cash!"

As she berated them, she really did extend a hand to demand money from the onlookers. Some of the crowd dispersed, after which she tossed her sheer robe over the prone woman and wrapped her in it.

"I told you to change your ways a long time ago," she scolded the woman as they staggered back inside. "Who are you putting on airs for? And you're suffering for it now, aren't you? Get it through your head!"

That woman looks a tad familiar. Where have I seen her before? Wei Wuxian wondered.

"A-Yao, A-Yao..." the woman whispered.

Meng Yao had yet to recover from being kicked; he was sprawled on the ground, unable to get up. The young woman grabbed the mother and son, one in each hand, and pulled them up before leaving the main area.

A customer beside Anxin asked, "Who's that beauty?"

Anxin spat out two melon seed shells before she answered. "She's an infamous shrew. And awfully scary."

"So that's the talented courtesan from way back when, Meng Shi?" someone said in disappointment. "How did she end up like this?"

Anxin swapped to a smiling face. "That's it. Just like *that*. She insisted on giving birth—can a woman retain her good looks after bearing a child? There probably wouldn't be many willing to grace her with their business these days, if not for her so-called 'talented' reputation, which she counted on back then to ply her trade. If you ask me, those books she read were what ruined everything."

One customer agreed heartily. "Right. For some reason, anyone who's touched a book always has their nose in the air. They're always reluctant to give up their little dreams of being better than anyone else."

Anxin clicked her tongue. "If she could support herself with the books she reads, then I'd have nothing to say. But it's just a gimmick to attract customers. Not to be rude, but we're all whores. Does reading a few books make you better than the rest of us? What's the point of acting so high and mighty? It's not just the people outside who look down on her—do you think any of the sisters here like her? The customers who come to this sort of place occasionally consider it a novelty to have a delicate young girl in her teens put on such airs. How can she seriously expect people to pay to see an old hag? Her days of fame ended a long time ago. Everyone knows that. She's the only one who still can't see it..."

Someone tapped Anxin from behind. She turned around, only to see the young woman from before standing behind her. The young woman raised her hand and slapped her.

Anxin was stunned for a moment by the resounding slap before flying into a rage. *"Bitch!"*

"Slut!" the young woman shouted back. "Gossiping all day long. Your tongue got nothing better to do?!"

"What I say is none of your damn business!" Anxin shrieked.

The two young women scuffled with each other in the hall on the first floor, quite literally fighting tooth and nail as they yanked each other's hair and swore up a storm. They were screaming things like *"I'll cut up your face sooner or later,"* and *"nobody wants you even if you pay them,"* and the coarse language was vulgar to the ears.

Many of the prostitutes went to stop the fight. "Sisi! Stop it!"
Sisi?

Wei Wuxian finally realized why the young woman's face
was familiar. Add seven or eight blade scars, and wasn't that Sisi,
the woman who had come to Lotus Pier with secret intel?!

All of a sudden, a wave of searing heat assaulted his face. The main
hall was instantly engulfed in a sea of crimson-red fire. Wei Wuxian
hurriedly extracted himself from the session of Empathy and opened
his eyes.

"How was it?" Lan Wangji asked.

Lan Xichen, too, said, "Wei-gongzi, what did you see?"

Wei Wuxian sucked in a breath to compose himself a little. "My
guess is that this Guanyin Temple is where Sect Leader Jin grew
up."

Jin Guangyao remained unperturbed.

"Where he grew up? Didn't he..." Jiang Cheng trailed off. Before
he could state that he thought he grew up in a brothel, it suddenly
clicked with him as well. "This temple used to be a brothel. He
burned it down and built a Guanyin Temple in its place!"

"Were you really the one who set the fire?" Lan Xichen asked.

"Yes," Jin Guangyao answered.

Jiang Cheng sneered. "How candid of you to admit it."

"At this stage, will it really make a difference if I admit to one
more thing?" Jin Guangyao asked.

After a moment of silence, Lan Xichen said, "Did you do it to
hide your origins?"

Although many people knew that Lianfang-zun grew up in
a brothel, the passage of time had left most unsure exactly *which*
brothel it was. A strange thing, in retrospect. Everyone knew
Lianfang-zun must have deliberately manipulated things from

behind the scenes, but few would have expected him to actually raze to the ground the place where he was born and raised.

"Not entirely," Jin Guangyao said.

Lan Xichen sighed but did not continue the conversation.

"Aren't you going to ask me why?" Jin Guangyao asked.

Lan Xichen shook his head. He replied after a while, without answering the question. "It wasn't that I didn't know of the things you'd done. But I used to believe you had your reasons. However, you have gone too far. And I...do not know if I should believe you anymore."

His tone was one of profound weariness and disappointment.

The storm raged on outside the temple, accompanied by peals of thunder. Wind leaked through the cracks of the temple doors. Amidst the mournful howls, Jin Guangyao suddenly dropped to his knees.

Everyone was stunned. Wei Wuxian, who had just seized the sword from his waist, was shocked as well.

"Er-ge, I was in the wrong," Jin Guangyao said meekly.

Wei Wuxian was left speechless by this. Even he felt embarrassed on Jin Guangyao's behalf. He couldn't help but say, "Uh, about that... Let's skip the talking and fight it out. Can we just fight?"

This man changed face at the drop of a hat and kneeled on a whim. He had no dignity or air of authority to speak of. Lan Xichen also had an indescribable look on his face.

"Er-ge, you and I have known each other for years," Jin Guangyao continued. "No matter what anyone says, you are well aware of how I've treated you. I have no more designs on the position of Cultivation Chief, and I have already completely destroyed the Yin Tiger Tally. After tonight, I'll travel to Dongying and never return in this lifetime. Please spare my life for these reasons."

Plainly put, he planned to flee to Dongying. Disgraceful as it was, Jin Guangyao had always been known for his smoothness and flexibility. He preferred to bend than to break. If he could use a softer approach, he'd never meet force with force.

The Jin Clan of Lanling could crush one or two clans with their martial prowess, perhaps even three and four. But if every clan, both big and small, were to join forces in a crusade against him, it'd only be a matter of time before they met the same fate as the Wen Clan of Qishan. Rather than dragging things out until that time came, it was logical for him to withdraw and lie low to conserve his strength. He might even find a future opportunity to stage a comeback and rise to power once more.

"Sect Leader Jin," Wei Wuxian said, "you said that the Yin Tiger Tally has been completely destroyed. Can you show me the pieces?"

"Wei-gongzi," Jin Guangyao answered, "the restored parts are not the original, after all. There's a limit to how many times it can be used. It's already useless now. Besides, you know best just how heavy that thing is with malevolent energy. Do you think I'd carry around useless scraps that would only serve to invite calamity upon me?"

"I don't know about that," Wei Wuxian said. "What if you're able to find another Xue Yang?"

"Er-ge," Jin Guangyao pleaded, "everything I've said is the truth."

His words were earnest and sincere, and he had indeed treated Lan Xichen with courtesy and respect ever since he had taken him captive. Unable to bring himself to cut ties with him on the spot, Lan Xichen could only sigh.

"Sect Leader Jin, as I said when you obstinately insisted on creating the havoc at the Burial Mounds, there is no need for you to call me 'er-ge' again."

"The recent incident at the Burial Mounds was a grave error; I behaved like a man possessed," Jin Guangyao said. "But it is no longer possible for me to turn back."

"What do you mean by that?" Lan Xichen asked.

Lan Wangji frowned slightly and said in a frosty tone, "Xiongzhang, do not speak to him too much."

"Sect Leader Lan, do you still remember what you told Sect Leader Jiang?" Wei Wuxian reminded him as well. "Do not speak to him too much."

Lan Xichen knew how deadly Jin Guangyao's tongue could be, but given the possibility that there might be more to the story, he couldn't help but want to listen. And this was what Jin Guangyao latched on to.

He dropped his voice and said quietly, "I received a letter."

"What kind of letter?" Lan Xichen asked.

"A threatening letter," Jin Guangyao said. "It mentioned...*those* incidents, and that they would be made public in seven days. It stated that I must either take the initiative to confess and apologize for my crimes, or...wait for death to claim me."

The others understood now. Jin Guangyao naturally would not sit and wait for death to come. Rather than wait to fall from grace and end up mocked and overthrown by the other cultivation clans, he might as well gain the upper hand by making the first move. Even if the other party did expose the truth of his sordid past, everyone would be too weakened by the siege to raise a hand against him when the time came.

Unfortunately, this was an unlucky year for him. Wei Wuxian and Lan Wangji had ruined his plans.

"Even so," Lan Xichen said, "you cannot simply resign yourself to continuing the evil you started, seeking to murder people outright! If you act this way..."

It left Lan Xichen with no way to excuse him!

"What else could I do?" Jin Guangyao said. "Wait for everything to be exposed and the news to spread like wildfire? Until it's the talk of the town, until I'm reduced to being the laughingstock of the century among the cultivation clans? Wait until I'm forced to kneel before the world to apologize and beg for forgiveness, forced to present my face for their feet to trample? Er-ge! There is no third path—either they die or I die!"

A hint of indignation washed over Lan Xichen's expression. He took a step back. "Is this not because you...because you did all the things that were mentioned in the letter?! Had you not, there would be no opportunity for others to hold anything over your head!"

"Er-ge, listen to me," Jin Guangyao said. "I don't deny that I did those things—"

"How can you? There are witnesses and proof!" Lan Xichen exclaimed.

"That's why I said I'm *not* denying it!" Jin Guangyao retorted. "But why would I kill my father, my wife, my son, and my brothers if I had any other choice? Am I really such a maniac in your eyes?!"

Lan Xichen's expression calmed a little. "Very well. Let me ask you a few questions, and you can explain yourself one matter at a time."

"Xiongzhang!" Lan Wangji called out as he drew Bichen.

"Do not worry," Lan Xichen hurriedly told him, seeing he seemed ready to end Jin Guangyao right then and there. "He is injured and disarmed. He is already at a disadvantage, and cannot play any of his tricks with so many people around."

On the other side of the room, a kick from Wei Wuxian halted Su She's attempt to sneak forward.

"Go and deal with things over there. I will handle this side," Lan Xichen said.

Lan Wangji heard Su She's furious cry and walked over. Wei Wuxian knew Lan Xichen was still showing consideration for his sworn brother, still holding on to a small, inexplicable hope that compelled him to give the latter a chance to speak. Coincidentally, Wei Wuxian had his own reasons for wanting to hear Jin Guangyao's side of the story, and so he listened attentively.

"First of all," Lan Xichen began, "did your father, the previous Sect Leader Jin, really meet his end by your hand via such a method...?"

"I'd like to answer this question last," Jin Guangyao said carefully.

Lan Xichen shook his head. "Secondly, your...wife..." As if finding the word hard to say, he immediately corrected himself, "Your younger sister, Qin Su. Did you really go forward with the marriage despite knowing her relation to you?"

Jin Guangyao stared at him blankly. Tears suddenly streamed down his face. "...Yes," he replied in anguish.

Lan Xichen took a deep breath, his face turning ashen.

"But I really had no choice," Jin Guangyao finished in a whisper.

"No choice?!" Lan Xichen reproached him. "It was your marriage! All you had to do was to not marry her, no? Even if you broke Qin Su's heart because of it, it would have been better than destroying a woman who genuinely loved and respected you, a woman who had never looked down on you!"

"Did I not genuinely love her as well?!" Jin Guangyao exclaimed. "But I had no choice. There was nothing I could do about it! Yes, it was my marriage, but could I really decide not marry her just because I didn't want to?! Er-ge, there has to be a limit to your naivete. I suffered and struggled to get Qin Cangye to accept my marriage proposal. He and Jin Guangshan were finally satisfied as the wedding day approached. And you tell me I should've suddenly called off the wedding? What reason was I supposed to give? How was I supposed to explain it to those two?!

"Er-ge, do you know how I felt when Madam Qin suddenly came to me in secret to tell me the truth, just when I thought everything was perfect?! A thunderbolt descending from the heavens to strike me in the head would have been less terrible! Do you know why she didn't go to Jin Guangshan, but came under cover of night to plead with me instead? Because Jin Guangshan raped her! That *wonderful* father of mine wouldn't even spare the wife of a faithful longtime subordinate. He couldn't even remember when it resulted in a daughter! All these years, she never dared tell her husband of the matter. If I suddenly broke off the engagement, and they found out about it as a result, leading to Jin Guangshan and Qin Cangye falling out with one another, who do you think would be the one both sides would blame? Who do you think would suffer for it?!"

Although this wasn't the first time they'd heard of the despicable act Jin Guangshan had committed, everyone present was still beset by waves of disgust and horror which competed with each other for dominance.

"Then...then even if you had no choice but to marry Qin Su, you could still have neglected her," Lan Xichen said. "Why did you have to... And why go through the trouble of siring A-Song, only to kill your son with your own hands?!"

Jin Guangyao clutched his head in his hands and said in a bitter tone, "...After the wedding, I never touched A-Su again. A-Song... was conceived before we married. At the time, I was afraid that a delay would cause complications..."

So he and Qin Su had consummated their union in advance.

If not for that, he would never have ended up committing incest with his own younger sister. He didn't know whether he should hate his father, who was hardly a father at all, or his own paranoid, overthinking self!

Lan Xichen sighed. "Next—and do not attempt to prevaricate, but answer me. Did you intentionally plot Jin Zixuan's death?!"

Jin Ling was supporting Jiang Cheng, but his eyes instantly widened at the mention of his father's name.

Lan Wangji raised his voice a little. "Xiongzhang, will you believe his answer?"

Lan Xichen's expression was complicated. "I naturally do not believe it was by accident that Jin Zixuan happened upon the plot to stage an ambush at Qiongqi Path, but...let him speak first."

Jin Guangyao knew no one would believe him even if he denied it to the end, so he gritted his teeth. "...It was indeed no coincidence that I bumped into Jin Zixuan."

Jin Ling clenched his fists.

"But I did not plot all that happened after," Jin Guangyao continued. "Do not think I am *so* shrewd and calculating that I can devise such foolproof schemes. Many things are beyond my control. How was I to know that he would die by Wei Wuxian's hand, along with Jin Zixun? How could I have predicted with certainty that Wei Wuxian would lose control, and that the Ghost General would go on a killing spree?"

"You said you didn't bump into him by chance! You're contradicting yourself!" Wei Wuxian snapped at him.

"I don't deny that I deliberately told him about the Qiongqi Path Ambush," Jin Guangyao said. "The two of you had always been on bad terms, and I thought it would cause him some trouble to coincidentally run into you while his cousin was picking a fight.

Mister Wei, how could I have foreseen that you would simply kill everyone there?"

Wei Wuxian was so furious that he just had to laugh. "You're really..."

"*Why?!*" Jin Ling shouted all of a sudden.

He stood up from his spot at Jiang Cheng's side. The rims of his eyes were red as he charged over to Jin Guangyao, shouting, "Why did you have to do this?!"

Nie Huaisang hurriedly pulled back Jin Ling, who looked like he was about to fight it out with Jin Guangyao.

"*Why?*" Jin Guangyao echoed. He turned to Jin Ling. "A-Ling, can you tell *me* why? I always greet others with a smile, even though I might not receive one in kind, so why did everyone still flock around your insufferably arrogant father? Despite us being born of the same man, why was your father able to spend his leisure time at home with his beloved wife, playing with his child, while I didn't dare be alone with *my* own wife and my blood ran cold at the sight of my own son? I was even forced to carry out every wretched deed my father assigned me, as if it was only to be expected—such as ambushing and killing an extremely dangerous person who could go berserk at any moment and manipulate fierce corpses to massacre at will!

"Although we were both born on the very same day, why did Jin Guangshan host a grand birthday banquet for one son but allow his subordinate to kick the other down the stairs of Golden Carp Tower, watching him roll from the very top to the very bottom?!"

He'd finally revealed the source of his deeply concealed hatred— it wasn't Jin Zixuan or Wei Wuxian, but his own father.

"Stop finding excuses!" Wei Wuxian rebutted. "You can go ahead and kill whoever you hate, but why did you lay hands on Jin Zixuan?!"

"As you can clearly see, I did indeed kill them all," Jin Guangyao calmly answered.

"And in such a way," Lan Xichen commented.

With tears at the corners of his eyes, the still-kneeling Jin Guangyao straightened his back. "Yes. Such a death was quite well suited to that old, philandering stallion who constantly wandered around in rut, wasn't it?" he said with a smile.

"A-Yao!" Lan Xichen bellowed.

It was only after shouting that he remembered he had already severed his ties with Jin Guangyao and shouldn't address him as such. But Jin Guangyao didn't seem to notice, continuing to speak with an unperturbed expression.

"Er-ge, don't be misled by how I'm able to curse him with such harsh words. I once held out hope for that father of mine. I would carry out any order as long as it came from him, no matter how stupid it might be, or how abhorrent the act—whether it be betraying Sect Leader Wen, or protecting Xue Yang, or eradicating dissidents.

"But do you know what made me finally lose heart? I'll answer your first question now. It wasn't that a single strand of Jin Zixuan's hair or the few black holes on Jin Zixun would always be worth more than me in his heart. It wasn't that he took back Mo Xuanyu, or that he later tried to strip me of my power in every possible way. It was what he once confided to the woman drinking with him when he went out to make merry.

"Why was the head of a prominent clan, one who spent money like water, reluctant to make even the slightest effort to buy my mother's freedom? Simple—because it was *bothersome*. My mother waited for so many years. She fabricated so many excuses and situations that were beyond his control, invented so many predicaments that prevented him from coming for her. But as it turns out, the real reason was that it was *bothersome.*

"This was what he said: *'Women who have read a little always think they're a cut above other women. They have a lot of demands and the most unrealistic fantasies. It's most bothersome. If I bought her freedom and she found her way to Lanling, who knows if she'd continue to pester me? Let her remain where she is. With her qualifications, she'll probably be popular for a few more years. That should cover her expenses for the rest of her life.*

"*'Son? Hah, forget him.'*"

Jin Guangyao had an excellent memory. When he repeated Jin Guangshan's statement word for word, everyone could picture the drunken expression on the man's face when he had first said it.

Jin Guangyao laughed. "You see, er-ge, I'm only worth these words as my father's son: *'Hah, forget him.'* Ha ha ha ha…"

Lan Xichen looked pained. "Even if your father… But you also…" He couldn't think of an appropriate judgment to pass. He made as if to speak, but stopped instead and sighed. "What is the point of saying all this now?"

Jin Guangyao opened his hands and shrugged, smiling. "It can't be helped. Wanting others to pity me, even when I've committed every crime in the world—that's the kind of person I am."

At the word "person," he suddenly flipped his wrist and wound a red guqin string around Jin Ling's neck.

The corners of Jin Guangyao's eyes still had tears in them as he ordered in a dark voice, "Don't move!"

This time, they were truly caught off guard.

"Wei Wuxian!" Jiang Cheng bellowed. "Didn't you already disarm him?!"

In his moment of desperation, he'd actually shouted to Wei Wuxian in a tone that was exactly the same as the one he'd used as a boy.

"I definitely took away all his guqin strings!" Wei Wuxian shouted back. Jin Guangyao's cultivation couldn't possibly be high enough to conjure items out of thin air!

But Lan Wangji figured it out with a single glance. "He hid it inside his body."

At his prompting, the others looked closer. On one side of Jin Guangyao's abdomen, a patch of red was gradually spreading across his white garments. The guqin string was red because it was soaked in blood. Of course Wei Wuxian hadn't found it earlier—Jin Guangyao hadn't hidden it on him, but *inside* him. He had bided his time with conversation until the opportunity was ripe. When Lan Xichen was suitably worked up and everyone's attention was diverted, he provoked Jin Ling into charging him. Seizing the chance, he sliced his abdomen with his finger and dug the string from his body.

Who could have imagined Jin Guangyao would do such a thing to himself just to have one more trick up his sleeve? While the guqin string was extremely, extremely fine, it was still a metallic foreign object buried in his flesh, constantly shifting with his every movement. The sensation could hardly have been pleasant.

"A-Ling!" cried Jiang Cheng, aghast.

The shout made Wei Wuxian move unconsciously, but someone immediately grabbed him. When he looked back and saw it was Lan Wangji, he managed with some difficulty to compose himself and not lose his head.

Jin Guangyao rose to his feet, continuing to restrain Jin Ling. "Sect Leader Jiang, no need to get so worked up. I have also watched A-Ling grow up, after all. I'll say it again: let us each go our own separate ways. Naturally, A-Ling will return to you unharmed after some time."

"A-Ling, don't move!" Jiang Cheng cried. "Jin Guangyao, take me instead if you insist on a hostage. It's all the same!"

"It's very much not the same," Jin Guangyao replied frankly. "Sect Leader Jiang, you're injured and have difficulty moving; you'll only hold me back."

Wei Wuxian's palms began to sweat. "Sect Leader Jin, did you forget something? Your loyal subordinate is still here."

Jin Guangyao looked at Su She, who was being held hostage at sword point by Lan Wangji.

With some difficulty, Su She immediately shouted in a hoarse voice, "Sect Leader, no need to bother with me!"

"Thank you," Jin Guangyao answered with equal speed.

Slowly, Lan Xichen stated, "Sect Leader Jin, you have lied once again."

"Just this once," Jin Guangyao replied. "It will not happen again."

"That is what you said last time," Lan Xichen said. "I can no longer tell which of your words are genuine."

Jin Guangyao was about to speak when an unprecedentedly loud clap of thunder crashed through the air. Though far away, it sounded strangely close. He shuddered unconsciously and swallowed any further comments.

Three odd, loud sounds followed shortly after, coming from outside the temple door.

Thump!

Thump!

Thump!

The sound was less a knock on the door, and more a slam. It didn't sound like the pounding of a human fist so much as it did someone violently smashing a man's head against the wood, over and over again. Each bang was louder than the last, and the crack in the bolt holding the door closed grew increasingly larger. Jin Guangyao's expression was also growing more and more twisted by the second.

By the fourth slam, the bolt finally snapped. Heavy rain and a dark figure swirled in unison, crashing through the door.

Jin Guangyao jolted. He seemed to consider dodging, but very quickly suppressed the urge. The figure that flew in was not heading in his direction, but rather Wei Wuxian and Lan Wangji's. Moving with no particular hurry, both of them parted for a split second before coming back together in no time, standing shoulder to shoulder like it was the most natural thing in the world.

Wei Wuxian looked back. "Wen Ning?"

Wen Ning crashed into the temple's Guanyin statue. He hung there for a moment with his head down and feet up before falling to the ground with a thud. Only then did he greet Wei Wuxian.

"...Gongzi."

Jiang Cheng's and Jin Ling's expressions grew somewhat upset at the sight of him.

On the other hand, Nie Huaisang shouted, *"Da-ge!"*

Wen Ning's dynamic entrance aside...there was another figure standing at the temple doors. His silhouette was taller, sturdier, chiseled and solid, and his steely face had an ashen complexion. He stared at them with dull, lifeless eyes.

It was none other than Chifeng-zun—Nie Mingjue!

He stood before the Guanyin Temple in the torrential rain like an iron pagoda, obstructing everyone's path. His head sat squarely in place, and dense black stitches could be seen around his neck. Someone had sewn his head back onto his body with a single thread.

"...Da-ge," Lan Xichen called out.

"...Da-ge..." Jin Guangyao murmured as well.

There were three people in the temple who called out to Nie Mingjue's corpse with the address "da-ge," but each of their tones were poles apart. Jin Guangyao's face was awash with overwhelming fear, and his entire body started to shiver. In life or in death, his sworn brother was undoubtedly the one Jin Guangyao feared the most, thanks to his violent temper and unyielding character.

The moment his body began to shake, so did his hand. And with his hand, the bloody guqin string he clutched began to quiver as well.

Suddenly, Lan Wangji drew Bichen and slashed down. In the blink of an eye, he dashed over to Jin Ling and caught hold of something.

Jin Guangyao's arm felt oddly light. Slightly stunned, he looked down, only to realize that his right hand was gone—cleanly cut off at the forearm. What Lan Wangji had caught was the severed hand, still gripping the lethal guqin string.

Blood erupted everywhere in an instant. Jin Guangyao's face went ghastly pale with pain. He didn't even have the strength to scream, but only staggered back a few steps. Unable to remain steady on his feet, he fell to the ground.

In his stead, it was Su She who started to scream. There was a split second when Lan Xichen looked like he wanted to go over and support Jin Guangyao, but in the end, he didn't dare move.

Lan Wangji pried open the fingers of the severed fist, releasing the guqin string and finally freeing Jin Ling from danger. Jiang Cheng was just about to lunge over to see if he was injured, but Wei Wuxian beat him to it. He grabbed Jin Ling's shoulders and examined him carefully. Only when he confirmed that the skin on Jin Ling's neck was undamaged, without so much as a scratch, did he heave a sigh of relief.

Lan Wangji always left himself room to change tack whenever he struck with his sword, but this had been a dire situation. The guqin string was extremely sharp—in the hands of someone versed in the art of the Killing Chord, it could slice through flesh and bones like melons and vegetables. All it would take was for Jin Guangyao's hand to start trembling—for him to jerk one more time, or worse yet, forget he had someone in his clutches and make a run for it while still holding the guqin string...

If Lan Wangji had not acted with decisive speed and precision to sever the hand holding the string, Jin Ling may well have been decapitated by now, his blood spewing meters into the air!

The spray of blood from Jin Guangyao's severed arm hit Jin Ling dead on, staining most of his body and part of his face with blood. He was still in a daze, yet to grasp just what had happened.

Wei Wuxian gave him a fierce hug. "Stay far away from such dangerous characters next time. What were you thinking, standing so close earlier, brat?!" he scolded.

If Jiang Yanli and Jin Zixuan's only son perished before his eyes, he really wouldn't know what to do.

Jin Ling wasn't accustomed to being hugged like this. All at once, a blush blossomed on his pale face. He vigorously pushed at Wei Wuxian's chest, but was caught fast; Wei Wuxian hugged him a few more times, with greater ferocity, before patting him heavily on the shoulder and shoving him over to Jiang Cheng.

"Go! Stop running around and go over to your uncle!"

Jiang Cheng caught the still dizzy and disoriented Jin Ling and looked at Wei Wuxian and Lan Wangji as they stood together. After a moment of hesitation, he uttered a quiet *"thank you"* to Lan Wangji.

Although his voice was quiet, his words were not at all ambiguous.

"Thank you, Hanguang-jun, for saving my life," said Jin Ling as well.

Lan Wangji nodded and said nothing. Bichen was angled toward the ground, and the drops of blood slid swiftly off the bright, clear blade, leaving not a stain behind. He turned to aim the sword at Nie Mingjue, who was still standing at the entrance.

Wen Ning slowly climbed to his feet and popped his broken arm back into place. "Be careful... His resentful energy should not be underestimated."

Jin Guangyao gritted his teeth and tapped a few acupoints on his severed arm. He had lost too much blood and was feeling dizzy. All of a sudden, he saw Nie Mingjue take a step in his direction, eyes trained on him, and promptly lost his mind from terror.

Su She coughed up another mouthful of blood and bellowed at the top of his lungs, "Fools! What are you people standing around for?! Stop him! Stop that creature at the entrance!"

Only then did the dumbstruck Jin Clan cultivators move to surround him, their blades drawn. The two in the lead were instantly sent flying by a strike from Nie Mingjue's palm.

Using his left hand, Jin Guangyao sprinkled medicinal powder over his severed arm, but it was immediately flushed away by the flowing blood. He all but had tears in his eyes as he tore at the front flap of his robe, trying to find a way to bandage his arm and stop the bleeding. However, his left hand had been burned by the corrosive smoke inside the coffin and black chest earlier; it trembled as he attempted to rip a strip from his clothing, leaving him unable to exert any force. It was a futile effort and only added to his pain.

Scrambling to his feet, Su She lunged over and tore off his own white robe to bandage Jin Guangyao's arm for him. Su She patted himself down for any extra medicinal ointment or powder, but came up empty-handed. As it happened, Lan Xichen was shielding Nie Huaisang as he helped him retreat to a safe spot nearby, so Su She turned to him.

"Sect Leader Lan! Sect Leader Lan, do you have any remedies?" he pleaded. "Please help. Sect Leader Jin has always treated you with courtesy. Consider it a favor!"

Jin Guangyao was a wretched sight to behold, on the verge of passing out. Lan Xichen clearly didn't have the heart to see him in such a state—but just then, there was a series of blood-curdling screams. Nie Mingjue struck out hard with a heavy fist, and in one single strike, smashed three of the Jin cultivators into a bloody mass of flesh.

Wei Wuxian and Lan Wangji stood before Jiang Cheng and Jin Ling, shielding them.

"Wen Ning! How did you run into him?!" Wei Wuxian called out.

After popping his arm into place, Wen Ning did the same to his leg. "I'm sorry, gongzi..." he said. "You told me to look for Lan-gongzi. I couldn't find him at the inn, so I went searching for him outside. Before I could chance upon Lan-gongzi, I saw Chifeng-zun walking down the street. A group of beggars went to pester him when they saw him, not knowing how dangerous he was. Chifeng-zun has no conscious mind. He nearly tore them apart with his bare hands. All I could do was fight him the entire way here..."

There was no need for Wei Wuxian to ask why Wen Ning hadn't found Lan Wangji at the inn. He hadn't been able to fall asleep with Lan Wangji next door—how, likewise, could Lan Wangji have fallen asleep with *him* next door? He must have also stepped out to wander around and then run into Fairy, who had retreated with its tail between its legs to call for reinforcements.

The sudden thunderstorm must have started after Wen Ning and Nie Mingjue began fighting. Corpses naturally attracted the dark and the nefarious, and that effect would only be compounded with two extraordinary fierce corpses in one place.

Although the cultivators from the Jin Clan of Lanling were no match for Nie Mingjue, they kept bravely charging forward. But when their swords came down on Nie Mingjue's body, it was like they were trying to slice through the finest steel. They could not inflict even a single gash upon him.

Nie Huaisang peeked out from behind Lan Xichen. "D-d-da-ge, I...I'm..." he said, both terrified and hopeful.

Nie Mingjue's blank white eyes bulged with fury. He suddenly made a grab for Nie Huaisang, but Lan Xichen dipped his head, and Liebing let out a mournful moan. Nie Mingjue froze.

"Da-ge," Lan Xichen said, "this is Huaisang!"

"Da-ge doesn't even recognize me anymore..." Nie Huaisang lamented.

"It's not just you he doesn't recognize. He doesn't even know who *he* is now!" Wei Wuxian said.

Nie Mingjue was a walking corpse driven by overwhelming resentment. He was irascible and violent, and he attacked everyone, regardless of who they were.

Wen Ning took a moment to recover before stepping forward to get involved in the fight once more. But Wen Ning's resentful energy was not as intense as Nie Mingjue's, and his physique not as tall or strapping. In addition, Wei Wuxian's flute had been smashed. With him unable to provide any support, Wen Ning was at a slight disadvantage.

Jin Guangyao, who was lying on the ground, finally managed with some difficulty to staunch the bleeding from his arm. Su She climbed to his feet and lifted Jin Guangyao onto his back, seeking to escape during the mayhem…but the movement drew Nie Mingjue's attention to them again. He flung Wen Ning off of him and stormed over to Jin Guangyao with large strides.

"Xiaoshu! Run!" cried Jin Ling in spite of himself.

Seeing him actually warn the enemy, Jiang Cheng smacked him on the back of the head. "Shut up!" he barked angrily.

The smack brought Jin Ling back to his senses. Still, this was his little uncle, who had watched him grow up. Not once in the past decade had Jin Guangyao ever been unkind to him. When he'd seen his little uncle about to meet a horrible end at the hands of the fierce corpse, he hadn't been able to keep from blurting out a warning in haste.

When Nie Mingjue heard Jin Ling's shout, he turned his head with some measure of uncertainty.

Wei Wuxian's heart clenched. "Oh no," he muttered under his breath.

Now that Nie Mingjue had become a fierce corpse, most of his resentment was naturally reserved for his foe, Jin Guangyao. But fierce corpses did not distinguish between people using their eyes! Jin Guangyao and Jin Ling were closely related by blood. To a malevolent creature of the dead, these two living beings were similar in blood and vital breath; to a creature of the darkness in a state of chaotic confusion, it was even harder to tell them apart.

Blood was pouring from Jin Guangyao's severed arm. His breathing was weak, and he was practically half dead. Jin Ling, on the other hand, was still full of life and vigor. Nie Mingjue's dead, unthinking brain naturally gravitated more toward Jin Ling.

Lan Wangji unsheathed Bichen and struck Nie Mingjue squarely in the chest. As expected, the tip of the sword was halted as soon as it struck him. When Nie Mingjue looked down and saw the long, gleaming sword, he howled and reached for it. Lan Wangji immediately called Bichen back. It returned to its sheath with a *sching*, and Nie Mingjue caught only empty air.

Immediately after, Lan Wangji flipped his left hand to bring out his guqin, Wangji. Without wasting any time, he held it in his palm and strummed a few clear and far-reaching notes.

Lan Xichen also brought Liebing to his lips once more.

For his part, Wei Wuxian brandished over fifty talismans and flung them at Nie Mingjue. But before the talismans could get close to him, they were set ablaze by his resentful energy and burned to ash in midair.

Nie Mingjue let loose an enraged roar and made a grab for Jin Ling. Jiang Cheng and Jin Ling had already retreated to a corner of the room, with nowhere left to run. Jiang Cheng had to push Jin Ling behind him as he drew Sandu, which was temporarily unable to use spiritual energy, and braced himself to meet the attack head-on. Both guqin and xiao were already playing in unison, but it seemed they were not enough.

Nie Mingjue's strong fist punched through flesh.

But this flesh was not Jiang Cheng's, nor was it Jin Ling's.

Wen Ning stood in front of them, shielding them. He grabbed Nie Mingjue's steel-like arm with both hands and slowly pulled it out of his chest, leaving a massive hole behind that one could see straight through. Though he did not bleed, some black chunks of viscera fell out of him.

"Wen Ning!" Wei Wuxian cried out.

Jiang Cheng, on the other hand, looked like he might go mad right then and there.

"You? *You?!*" he spluttered.

The force of the punch was so powerful that it hadn't just pierced Wen Ning's chest, but also shattered part of his vocal cords. He couldn't even say a word before he toppled over—and he just so happened to fall directly on Jiang Cheng and Jin Ling. His body was temporarily immobile, but his eyes were still wide open as he stared unblinkingly at both of them.

Jin Ling had initially abhorred this murderer; this walking weapon that had driven a palm through his father's chest. Ever since he was a child, he'd sworn countless times that he'd cut Wei Ying and Wen Ning to a million pieces if he ever had the chance, one slice at a time. Later, he found he didn't want to hate Wei Wuxian, so he doubled his efforts to hate Wen Ning instead. But as he stared at this murderer, this weapon, who was sprawled before them with his chest similarly punched through, he couldn't even bring himself to shove Wen Ning away so that he wasn't leaning on them.

He knew full well that Wen Ning was a dead man. He would probably be fine even if he was cut in half at the waist—having a hole punched through his chest was nothing. But for some reason he couldn't understand, tears just kept flowing uncontrollably from his eyes.

With that single punch, Nie Mingjue's movements came to a standstill as well.

Lan Wangji and Lan Xichen played their instruments in unison, with the guqin flowing like an icy spring and the xiao howling like forbidding winds. The sounds they made were all ones that Nie Mingjue loathed, and the shrillness of the duet only increased exponentially. The music made him sluggish, as if someone had bound him from head to toe with an invisible rope. As the rope tightened around him, so too did his rage increase, until he finally went berserk and forcibly broke the shackles of the Eradication Tone.

He struck out at the one playing the guqin. Lan Wangji calmly spun to sidestep his attack. The sound of his guqin did not stall for even a moment.

Nie Mingjue's blow broke through the wall. He was just about to turn around when he suddenly heard two sprightly chirps. Withdrawing his fist from the wall, he looked in the direction of the sound instead.

Wei Wuxian whistled twice more and greeted him with a smile. "Hello, Chifeng-zun. Recognize me?"

Nie Mingjue's hideous white eyes locked on him.

"It's fine if you don't," he continued. "As long as you recognize this whistle."

LAN XICHEN REMOVED Liebing from his lips. "Wei-gongzi!"

He had intended to remind Wei Wuxian that his current body belonged to Mo Xuanyu, who was also related by blood to Jin Guangyao—and more closely than the latter was to Jin Ling. Things would only grow more fraught if Nie Mingjue identified him as a target for his vengeance.

But before Lan Xichen could say another word, Lan Wangji turned to him and shook his head, looking both calm and composed. Lan Xichen immediately understood what he meant. There was no need to worry—Lan Wangji believed Wei Wuxian would be fine.

Wei Wuxian whistled an easy tune, complementing his easy stride. The whistling was calming to the ear, but the idyllic melody sounded eerie against the backdrop of a Guanyin Temple littered with bodies in the middle of a raging storm. Wen Ning remained sprawled on Jiang Cheng and Jin Ling, but when he heard the song, an unusually powerful urge seemed to drive him to stand. He struggled a moment, then fell over again, perhaps because he'd managed to resist the compulsion, or because he hadn't yet regained his ability to move. Jiang Cheng and Jin Ling both unconsciously reached out to catch him, but they looked conflicted about it, as though they also wanted to drop him immediately.

Grinning, Wei Wuxian continued to whistle what sounded like a whimsical tune. He backed away at an unhurried pace, hands clasped behind his back. Nie Mingjue remained where he was. He seemed indifferent when Wei Wuxian took his first step back, and even the third did not move him. But by the seventh, it seemed he could no longer withstand the power of that compulsion, and took a step in the direction Wei Wuxian was heading—

Which was toward the magnificent, empty coffin in the temple's rear grounds.

As long as Nie Mingjue went in there, Wei Wuxian had a way of sealing him away.

The corrosive white smoke had long since dispersed and was no longer a threat. Nie Mingjue's expression was dark and steely as he was guided to the empty coffin, which seemed to instinctively repulse him. Everyone, especially Lan Wangji, watched with bated breath as Wei Wuxian circled around the coffin.

As he continued to whistle leisurely, Wei Wuxian tossed a look Lan Wangji's way. When their eyes met, he gave Lan Wangji a flirtatious wink.

A barely perceptible quiver rippled through the guqin music flowing from Lan Wangji's fingers, as if they'd been pricked by a small needle of sweetness. But the vacillation was instantly calmed. Wei Wuxian, feeling a bit smug, turned his head back to Nie Mingjue and patted the rim of the coffin.

Finally, moving at a painfully slow pace, Nie Mingjue leaned down. But just as he was about to lay half his body into the coffin, there came a sudden, horrid cry from behind Lan Xichen.

Nie Mingjue stopped mid-action and whipped his head around, as did everyone else. They saw Su She with Jin Guangyao on his back; one of his hands supporting Jin Guangyao's thigh and the other gripping a sword that dripped with blood. Nie Huaisang lay collapsed on the floor, clutching his leg and rolling around in pain.

At the sight of this, Lan Xichen used Shuoyue's sword qi to strike the hand with which Su She held his blade, leaving him stunned as the hilt slipped free of his grip. Nie Huaisang had already been wounded, and the air was tinged with the scent of blood.

Ruining my work at such a critical moment. Outrageous! Wei Wuxian berated him in his head.

Nie Huaisang and Nie Mingjue were half brothers, born of different mothers but sharing the same father. The smell of Nie Huaisang's blood wouldn't rouse Nie Mingjue's murderous intent, but it *would* rouse his curiosity. That curiosity would lure him into renewed proximity to Jin Guangyao, who would then regain his attention. If Jin Guangyao was killed, Nie Mingjue's ferocity would no doubt escalate—and thus make him all the harder to subdue!

Sure enough, Nie Mingjue growled as he moved away from the coffin. He instantly recognized who lay on Su She's back, and not even Wei Wuxian's whistling could restrain him any longer. Nie Mingjue hurtled over like a blast of wind, his grasping hand aiming for Jin Guangyao's head.

Su She swiftly sidestepped. With the tip of his foot, he kicked up the longsword that had previously been struck out of his hand, and gathered every last bit of spiritual power he had to aim the blade at Nie Mingjue's heart. Perhaps because it was a matter of life or death, the attack was miraculously fast and fierce. The sword was filled to the brim with his spiritual power, glowing with a stunning brilliance that put all his previous attacks to shame.

"Beautiful," said Wei Wuxian, unable to resist praising it.

The explosive attack forced Nie Mingjue to take a single large step back. But as soon as the spiritual light dimmed, he moved forward once more, relentlessly grabbing at Jin Guangyao. Su She flung Jin Guangyao to Lan Xichen with one hand while he slashed at Nie Mingjue's throat.

Even though Nie Mingjue's body was as impenetrable as iron, the thread sewn around his neck might not be. Had the attack landed, it might have at least bought them some time, even if it couldn't subdue Nie Mingjue. But the sword had just been infused with a sudden burst of spiritual power that was well beyond its capacity. Without warning, it shattered into pieces mid-swing. As for Nie Mingjue's strike...it landed squarely on Su She's chest.

Su She's brilliance had only lasted a moment. He didn't even have time to cough up blood or say any respectable or ruthless last words before the life in his eyes was instantly snuffed out.

Jin Guangyao, lying next to Lan Xichen in a heap, also witnessed this. A hint of tears glistened in his eyes, perhaps because of the immense pain and blood loss from his midriff and severed hand. There was no time for him to catch his breath or lick his wounds, however. Once Nie Mingjue withdrew his hand, he turned around and stared predatorily in Jin Guangyao's direction once more.

The set jaw, the aloof, stern and critical way he looked at him— it was exactly the same as when he was alive. It was the gaze that Jin Guangyao feared the most.

Jin Guangyao's tears ran dry due to sheer terror. "Er-ge..." he pleaded in a quivering voice.

Lan Xichen shifted the course of his sword, and Wei Wuxian and Lan Wangji also hastily changed their tune. But the whistling's control had already been broken previously, and renewing the effect using the same method would be much harder.

"Wei Wuxian," someone called suddenly.

"What?" Wei Wuxian answered immediately, realizing only after the fact that it was Jiang Cheng who'd spoken. He found the latter calling him a bit odd, but Jiang Cheng didn't say another word.

Instead, he retrieved something from his sleeve and hurled the item at Wei Wuxian, who caught it without a second thought.

When he looked down, he saw that it was a shining black flute with a bright red tassel fastened at the end.

The hell flute, Chenqing!

With that very familiar flute in his hand, Wei Wuxian abandoned his surprised expression, along with everything else. He raised it to his lips without hesitation.

"Lan Zhan!" he called.

Lan Wangji gave a slight nod. Nothing else needed to be said.

Guqin and flute began their duet. Icy spring water was the guqin, and the flute was like a bird in flight. One suppressed while the other lured. Under their combined efforts, Nie Mingjue's body swayed before he was finally half forced to move away from Jin Guangyao.

Under the duet's thrall, he moved stiffly toward the empty coffin once more, step by step. Wei Wuxian and Lan Wangji followed him closely, step by step. As he leapt into the casket, the two each kicked one end of the coffin cover at the same time. The hefty lid flew upward, then dropped into place. Moving fast, Wei Wuxian hopped agilely onto the head of the coffin, stuck Chenqing back into his waistband, and bit a finger on his right hand. Movements flowing like water, he drew the vibrant, bloody lines of a spell without a moment's faltering.

Only then did the beastly howling within the coffin gradually subside. Lan Wangji pressed down on his guqin's seven vibrating strings, halting the song flowing from his fingertips. Wei Wuxian softly blew out a long breath. He prudently waited to see if he could sense anything, and only stood up after ensuring there was no more power to be felt from beneath the lid.

"What a bad temper, no?"

Standing on top of the coffin, he was much taller than Lan Wangji. Lan Wangji put away his guqin and raised his head to look at him with his light eyes. Wei Wuxian leaned down, unable to resist giving that pristine face a little scratch. Maybe by accident, or maybe on purpose, his fingers left a few bloody red streaks in their wake. Lan Wangji didn't mind in the least.

"Come down now."

Wei Wuxian jumped, smiling, and he caught him perfectly.

Things were quieting down, but Nie Huaisang started crying in pain at the other end of the room.

"Xichen-ge!" he cried. "Quickly, come help me see if my leg's still connected to my body!"

Lan Xichen walked over and held him down. After his examination, he comforted him. "Huaisang, you are fine. No need to be so scared. Your leg is not broken, it was merely stabbed."

Nie Huaisang was horrified. "Stabbed?! How could I not be scared if I was stabbed! Was it pierced through? Xichen-ge, help me!"

Lan Xicheng was torn between laughing and crying. "It is not that serious."

But Nie Huaisang continued to roll around on the ground, hugging his leg. Knowing Nie Huaisang was terrified of pain, Lan Xichen retrieved a pill bottle from his breast pocket and placed it in his hands.

"To soothe your discomfort."

Nie Huaisang immediately took out a pill and swallowed it. "Why am I so unlucky? Getting randomly captured by Su Minshan on the road... He started out just trying make a break for it moments ago, too, but then turned around and stabbed me. If I was in his way, he could've just pushed me aside... Why use a weapon?"

Lan Xichen straightened up and looked back. Jin Guangyao was in an extremely sorry state, still sitting where he had fallen. His face was white as a sheet, his hair was slightly mussed, and cold sweat drenched his forehead. Perhaps because the pain of his severed hand was too great, he was unable to contain the soft groan that escaped his lips. He looked up to meet Lan Xichen's eyes. Although nothing was said, the sight he presented alone—protecting the stump that was now his wrist, wearing a most miserable expression—made it difficult not to feel sympathy.

Lan Xichen gazed at him for a bit, then sighed. In the end, he took out the medicinal remedies he carried on him.

"Sect Leader Lan," Wei Wuxian cautioned.

"Wei-gongzi, he...cannot do anything right now, considering the state he is in," Lan Xichen said. "He might die here and now if we do not tend to him. There are still many things that remain unclear, and will require further questioning."

"I understand, Sect Leader Lan," Wei Wuxian said. "I'm not telling you not to save him, I'm just cautioning you to be careful. Best to cast the silence spell, to keep him from speaking."

Lan Xichen gave a light nod and turned to Jin Guangyao. "As you hear, Sect Leader Jin. Please do not do anything unnecessary. In the event you make any sort of move, I will show no mercy..." He took a deep breath. "...in taking your life."

Jin Guangyao nodded, and said in a weak, quiet voice, "Thank you, Zewu-jun..."

Lan Xichen bent down and began to minister to Jin Guangyao's wrist with both care and caution as the latter shivered. Seeing the state his once-infinitely glorious sworn brother had been reduced to, Lan Xichen didn't know what to say. All he could do was sigh to himself.

Wei Wuxian and Lan Wangji went together to the corner where Wen Ning still lay awkwardly half collapsed over Jiang Cheng and Jin Ling. Wei Wuxian laid him flat on the floor and inspected the hole in his chest.

"Look at this... What am I gonna fill this with?" he griped, greatly chagrined.

"Gongzi, is my condition serious...?" Wen Ning asked.

"No," Wei Wuxian replied. "It's not like you need organs. But it's ugly."

"I don't need to look pretty, though..."

Jiang Cheng was silent, while Jin Ling looked like he was holding back what he wanted to say.

At the other end of the room, Lan Xichen had wanted to take this chance to issue a proper reprimand. Seeing Jin Guangyao on the verge of fainting from the pain of the treatment, however, he was unable to bear the sight. He turned his head to make a request of Nie Huaisang.

"Huaisang, pass me the bottle from earlier."

Nie Huaisang had tucked the pill bottle into his breast pocket after taking a few painkillers earlier. "Oh, okay," he replied quickly.

He began to rummage through his robes, trying to find the bottle for Lan Xichen. All of a sudden, his pupils contracted and he cried out, voice aghast.

"Xichen-ge, watch out behind you!"

Lan Xichen had never let down his guard around Jin Guangyao. He was tense as a taut string, and Nie Huaisang's expression, coupled with his cry, made his heart drop. He drew his sword without a second thought and stabbed behind him.

His blade pierced Jin Guangyao's chest. Shock and dismay were written on Jin Guangyao's face as his heart was run through.

The others were just as shocked by this sudden turn of events. Wei Wuxian shot to his feet.

"What happened?!"

Nie Huaisang stammered as he tried to explain himself. "I-I-I... I saw san-ge—no, I saw Sect Leader Jin reach behind his back, and I didn't know if he was going to..."

Jin Guangyao looked down at the sword that had penetrated him. His lips quivered. He clearly wanted to speak, but thanks to the silence spell, there was nothing he could say in his own defense. Wei Wuxian noticed something was off, but before he could raise any questions, Jin Guangyao coughed up a large mouthful of blood.

"Lan Xichen!" he cried in a raspy voice. Surprisingly, he had managed to break the silence spell by force.

Jin Guangyao was covered in injuries. His left hand had been burnt by the corrosive smoke, his right had been severed, and he was missing a chunk of his midriff. He was stained in blood from head to toe. Though he could barely sit up, he somehow managed to get to his feet, perhaps thanks to a sudden burst of his remaining strength.

"*Lan Xichen!*" he cried again, voice full of hate.

Lan Xichen looked both disappointed and despondent in equally severe measure.

"Sect Leader Jin, I said that I would not show mercy if you made another move."

Jin Guangyao scoffed brutally, then rebutted, "Yes! You said just that. But did I do anything at all?!"

He had always been gentle and graceful in front of others, but now wore a vulgar, savage face more suited to the streets. At the sight of this complete reversal, Lan Xichen also sensed something was wrong. He immediately turned to look at Nie Huaisang.

Jin Guangyao burst out laughing. "Enough! Why bother even looking at him?! What could you possibly detect? Even *I* didn't notice anything after all these years. Good one, Huaisang."

Nie Huaisang's mouth gaped open, as if he'd been scared mute by the sudden accusation.

"To think I'd fall like this, by *your* hand..." Jin Guangyao spat hatefully.

He forced himself to remain upright. He clearly wanted to walk over to Nie Huaisang, but there was still a sword piercing his heart. He took a single step and immediately grimaced in pain.

Unable to either deal him a finishing blow or recklessly pull the blade free, Lan Xichen could only blurt, "Don't move!"

Jin Guangyao couldn't move another step, regardless. He gripped the hilt of the blade protruding from his chest and remained where he stood. After coughing out another mouthful of blood, he began to speak.

"'Headshaker,' indeed! No wonder... Excellent work, concealing yourself for so many years!"

Nie Huaisang pleaded in a shuddering voice. "Xichen-ge, you have to believe me. I really did see him..."

"*You...!*" snarled Jin Guangyao with a scowl.

He lunged forward in an attempt to tackle Nie Huaisang, and the sword pushed another inch into his chest.

"Do not move!" Lan Xichen shouted.

He'd suffered so many losses at Jin Guangyao's hands, fallen for so many of his lies. He couldn't help but remain vigilant, afraid Jin Guangyao was attempting to distract him in a moment of desperation, going on the attack simply because Nie Huaisang had exposed what he was about to do behind Lan Xichen's back. Jin Guangyao understood the look in his eyes and laughed with sheer anger.

"Lan Xichen! All my life, I've lied to countless people and I've harmed countless others. It's just like you said. I killed my father, killed my brothers, killed my wife, killed my son, killed my teachers, killed my friends—I've committed every crime there is!"

He inhaled deeply, then rasped out, "But never have I ever wanted to hurt *you*!"

Lan Xichen was stunned.

Panting, Jin Guangyao gripped the hilt of Lan Xichen's sword and clenched his teeth.

"...Who saved you from disaster, back when the Cloud Recesses burned to the ground and you were on the run? And who put forth the utmost effort to provide assistance when the Lan Clan of Gusu was rebuilding their home? In all these years, have I ever wronged the Lan Clan? Was there ever an occasion when I didn't support you in every way?! Aside from temporarily sealing your spiritual powers tonight, when have I ever done wrong by you or your clan? When have I ever demanded you repay your debt?!"

His questions left Lan Xichen unable to bring himself to cast the silence spell again. And so Jin Guangyao continued.

"Su Minshan went this far to repay my kindness simply because I remembered his name. But you, Zewu-jun, Sect Leader Lan...just like Nie Mingjue, you cannot tolerate me... You won't even give me a way to live!"

When he was done speaking, Jin Guangyao abruptly backed away, forcibly drawing Shuoyue from his chest.

"Don't let him get away!" Jiang Cheng shouted.

Lan Xichen rushed forward, effortlessly seizing him again in a few steps. Jin Guangyao couldn't have gotten far in the state he was in, no matter how fast he ran. Even Jin Ling could have caught him with his eyes closed. He was wounded in numerous places and had been dealt a fatal strike to the heart. There was no need for them to take precautions.

It suddenly hit Wei Wuxian. "He's not trying to escape! Zewu-jun, get away from him!" he shouted.

It was already too late. Blood from Jin Guangyao's severed limb had dripped onto the coffin. It crawled over Wei Wuxian's drawings, ruining the spell and flowing beneath the lid and into the coffin itself.

Nie Mingjue burst through the coffin's seal.

The coffin lid shattered to pieces. One large, ghastly pale hand seized Jin Guangyao by the neck, and the other hand reached for Lan Xichen's throat.

Jin Guangyao wasn't trying to escape. With his last breath, he was trying to draw Lan Xichen to Nie Mingjue, so they could perish together!

Lan Wangji summoned Bichen with lightning speed, and it shot forth in their direction. But Nie Mingjue had no fear of such spiritual weapons. Even if Bichen struck him, it likely couldn't stop him from closing the minuscule distance between his hand and Lan Xichen's neck.

And yet, just when Nie Mingjue's hand was mere millimeters from its target, Jin Guangyao used his remaining left hand to shove Lan Xichen's chest—pushing him out of reach of Nie Mingjue's grasp.

In the same moment, Nie Mingjue dragged Jin Guangyao into the coffin by the neck, then raised him to dangle like a ragdoll. It was a horrifying tableau. Jin Guangyao was clawing at Nie Mingjue's iron-like grip, struggling and writhing from the pain. Ferocity flashed in his eyes as he fought, his hair loose and wild.

With all he had, he yelled, "*Nie Mingjue, you motherfucker!* You think I'm actually afraid of you?! I—"

With difficulty, he choked out a mouthful of blood. Everyone present heard an unusually cruel, loud *crack*.

A gagged whimper escaped Jin Guangyao's throat. Jin Ling's shoulders shuddered. He shut his eyes, covered his ears, afraid to listen or look any longer.

The push had sent Lan Xichen staggering back several steps. He had yet to realize what had happened during that split second.

Lan Wangji, on the other hand, smacked the back of the beautiful Guanyin statue. The impact shook the statue and sent it flying toward Nie Mingjue, who was still scrutinizing the crooked-necked corpse in his hands. The heavy Guanyin statue struck him so hard that he toppled back into the coffin.

Wei Wuxian leaped up and stood on the Guanyin statue's chest. The lid of the coffin had been cracked, so he had to use the statue in its place to seal the berserk Nie Mingjue, who struck the statue again and again with his palm in his attempts to get out from underneath. Wei Wuxian wobbled and swayed unsteadily with each strike, almost thrown off.

After teetering a few times, he realized there was no way he could draw a spell like this. "Lan Zhan, quick! Come up here with me so we have another person's weight. A few more blows and this Guanyin statue is gonna fall apart..."

Before he could finish, Wei Wuxian suddenly felt his body and line of sight slant.

Lan Wangji had grabbed one end of the coffin and lifted it. More specifically, he had raised the heavy, solid wood coffin off the floor using *only* his left hand—a coffin with two dead people inside, and a Guanyin statue and Wei Wuxian on top.

Wei Wuxian's jaw dropped.

Even if he had long known that Lan Wangji had astoundingly

strong arms, this was still...flabbergasting beyond belief!

Lan Wangji's expression remained unchanged as he brandished a silver guqin string. The string whirled itself around the coffin and the Guanyin statue dozens of times, firmly binding both together. A second and a third string followed. Once he determined that Nie Mingjue and Jin Guangyao had been securely sealed off, he hastily released his grip on one end of the coffin.

That end crashed to the ground with a thunderous noise. Wei Wuxian tilted with it, and Lan Wangji caught him before steadily setting him on the ground. The same hands that had just grappled with such a hefty weight held Wei Wuxian with the utmost gentleness.

Lan Xichen stared blankly at the coffin, which had been bound and sealed with seven guqin strings. He was still out of sorts. Nie Huaisang reached out a hand and waved it in front of him.

"...Xi...Xichen-ge," he called out, terrified. "Are you okay?"

"Huaisang," Lan Xichen began. "Was he really trying to sneak up on me earlier?"

"I think so..." Nie Huaisang said.

Hearing him stammer, Lan Xichen pressed him. "Think about it again, carefully."

"I can't be sure when you ask me like that..." Nie Huaisang said, "It really did look like it..."

"Stop dithering!" Lan Xichen snapped. "Was he or was he not?!"

Put on the spot, Nie Huaisang said, "...I don't know, I really don't know!"

Whenever Nie Huaisang was pushed into a corner, he would only repeat that phrase. Lan Xichen buried his head in his hands, looking like he had a splitting headache and did not want to speak any further.

"Huaisang-xiong," Wei Wuxian suddenly piped up.

"Huh?" Nie Huaisang said.

"How did Su She manage to stab you earlier?"

"He was fleeing with San-ge..." Nie Huaisang corrected himself. "...with Sect Leader Jin on his back, and I was in his way, so..."

"Really?" Wei Wuxian questioned. "As I recall, the spot where you stood wasn't in the path of their escape at all."

"Would I seriously have bumped into him to get stabbed on purpose?" Nie Huaisang said.

Wei Wuxian smiled. "I didn't say that."

"Then what *are* you trying to say, Wei-xiong?" Nie Huaisang asked.

"It's just that I've suddenly pieced together a few things," Wei Wuxian said.

"What things?" Nie Huaisang asked.

"Jin Guangyao said that someone sent him a letter, threatening to tell the world about everything he had done once seven days had passed," Wei Wuxian said. "If we assume he was telling the truth, that he wasn't lying, the letter writer was doing something unnecessary. If you wanted to expose someone's crimes, why not just expose them outright? Why make a point of notifying them that you had evidence of their guilt in your hands?"

"Didn't San-ge... Didn't Sect Leader Jin say that the letter writer wanted him to make the decision to confess and apologize for his crimes?"

"Please, wake up," Wei Wuxian said. "You don't have to be a genius to know that Jin Guangyao would never choose to confess or apologize. What would be the point? It seemed meaningless, on the surface. But would a person capable of digging up all of Jin Guangyao's dirty little secrets do something so pointless? There must have been a reason for that apparently needless act. They wanted to make something happen. They wanted the letter to provoke something."

"Provoke?" Lan Xichen asked blankly. "Provoke what?"

"Jin Guangyao's intent to kill," Lan Wangji replied in a low voice.

Zewu-jun would have realized this as well if he had been his usual self, but he was likely too preoccupied to consider the possibility right now.

"That's right," Wei Wuxian said. "It was the letter that catapulted Jin Guangyao's killing intent to an unprecedented level. Didn't it say he should wait for death to claim him in seven days? If that was the case, he'd make the first move within those seven days. He'd wipe out the main forces of the other clans at the Burial Mounds and see who'd be the one to die first."

"You are saying that was what the letter writer wanted?" Lan Xichen wondered. "It was all to spur him into taking action?"

"That's what I think," Wei Wuxian answered.

Lan Xichen shook his head. "...Then what was the letter writer trying to accomplish? Were they trying to expose Jin Guangyao? Massacre the other clans?"

"It's simple," Wei Wuxian said. "Look at what happened after the siege failed. Sisi and Bicao came calling at Lotus Pier, where everyone was assembled and emotions were running high. I don't think the arrival of those two witnesses was a coincidence. Things kept building up until they came to a head."

After a pause, he continued, "The letter writer didn't just want Jin Guangyao to lose his standing and fall from grace. They also wanted him to become public enemy number one. And it all had to happen in one single, critical hit. There could be absolutely no room for Jin Guangyao to turn the tide in his favor."

"Sounds like they've been plotting for a long time," Nie Huaisang commented.

Wei Wuxian looked at him, then suddenly asked a question. "Oh right, wasn't Chifeng-zun's body left with Sect Leader Nie for safekeeping?"

"It was in my custody at first," Nie Huaisang replied, "but I received news tonight that my da-ge's body had disappeared from Qinghe without a trace. Why else do you think I was rushing home? I even wound up being kidnapped by Su She on the way…"

"Sect Leader Nie, I heard you often travel between the Lan Clan of Gusu and the Jin Clan of Lanling. Is that true?" Wei Wuxian asked.

"Yeah," Nie Huaisang answered.

"Then do you really not know Mo Xuanyu?"

"Huh?"

"I remember the first time I met you after the sacrificial ritual succeeded," Wei Wuxian said. "You acted like you didn't know me at all. You even asked Hanguang-jun who I was. Mo Xuanyu had pestered Jin Guangyao a great deal in the past, and was even able to access the manuscripts in his collection. And you often went looking for Sect Leader Jin to pour out your woes. You might not have been well acquainted with Mo Xuanyu, but had you really never even seen him once?"

Nie Huaisang scratched his head. "Wei-xiong, Golden Carp Tower is so big. I couldn't possibly have met everyone there, and even if I had, I couldn't possibly remember them all. Besides…" He looked somewhat embarrassed as he continued, "You know what Mo Xuanyu was like. He was a little… The Jin Clan of Lanling did the best they could to hide him away. It isn't so strange that I'd never seen him before. Even Xichen-ge might not have met him."

"Oh, that's true," Wei Wuxian said. "Zewu-jun didn't know Mo Xuanyu either."

"Right?!" Nie Huaisang exclaimed. "And there's one thing I don't understand. Even if I *had* seen Mo Xuanyu before, why would I deliberately pretend to not know him? Why would I need to do that?"

Wei Wuxian smiled. "It's nothing. I just found it strange and wanted to ask."

Inwardly, he said, *To probe if this "Mo Xuanyu" was the* real *Mo Xuanyu, of course.*

How would Mo Xuanyu, who was said to be timid and weak-willed, have had the courage to offer up his body through suicide?

Why would Chifeng-zun's left arm have been tossed out into the world? Could Jin Guangyao have let it escape due to an oversight? And why did it just so happen to show up at *Mo Manor*, where the sacrificial ritual had been carried out and where a newly reborn Wei Wuxian would encounter it?

Chifeng-zun's corpse had been laid to rest by the Nie Clan of Qinghe. Had Nie Huaisang, who always respected his elder brother, really not noticed the corpse had been swapped for all those years?

Thus, Wei Wuxian was more inclined to believe in the following scenario:

Perhaps Nie Huaisang had really been a "head-shaker" before Nie Mingjue's passing. After Nie Mingjue's death, however, he went from knowing nothing to knowing everything—including the fact that Nie Mingjue's corpse had been swapped and the true colors of the san-ge he had once trusted.

He had attempted to find his elder brother's body, but after many years of hardship, all he could find was Nie Mingjue's left arm. He had been stuck, unable to find any clues to guide him to the next step. What's more, the left arm was unusually ferocious and difficult to subdue. Keeping it by his side would only lead to more bloodshed.

And then someone came to mind—a person who was most adept in dealing with these kinds of creatures and these kinds of problems.

The Yiling Patriarch.

But the Yiling Patriarch had been torn to shreds. What was he to do?

So yet another person came to mind. Mo Xuanyu, who had been banished from Golden Carp Tower.

In the past, Nie Huaisang might have chatted with Mo Xuanyu to glean information from him. From the mouth of the dejected Mo Xuanyu, Nie Huaisang had learned that he'd read one of Jin Guangyao's fragmented manuscripts of forbidden magic, in which an ancient, evil ritual was recorded. He had then incited Mo Xuanyu to exact revenge for the humiliation he'd suffered at the hands of his own clan members—to use the forbidden art of the sacrificial ritual to seek retribution.

And which malicious ghost should he invite in? The Yiling Patriarch, of course.

Unable to bear living any longer, Mo Xuanyu had finally activated the blood array, and Nie Huaisang had seized the opportunity to toss out the hot potato he could barely hold on to to begin with: Chifeng-zun's left arm.

The plan moved forward successfully after that. He no longer needed to go to the trouble of personally seeking Nie Mingjue's remaining limbs. Instead, he left everything dangerous or complicated to Wei Wuxian and Lan Wangji, needing only to keep a close watch on their movements.

The strange incidents involving murdered cats that Jin Ling, Lan Sizhui, Lan Jingyi, and the other juniors had encountered on their journey had clearly been the work of someone deliberately staging bizarre phenomena. Coupled with the non-existent "huntsman" at the nearby village who had given them directions, there was no doubt that the intent had been to lure the naive juniors into Yi City. After all, if Wei Wuxian and Lan Wangji had slipped up and failed to protect them, Jin Guangyao would likely be blamed for anything untoward that befell the juniors there.

In any case, the more chips there were in play to convict Jin Guangyao of his crimes, the better. The more mistakes he could tempt this prudent villain to make, the better the evidence to use against him. And the more tragic the fate that befell him, the better.

Lan Wangji used the tip of Bichen to turn over the black chest beside the coffin and glanced at the spell engraved on it.

"The head," he said to Wei Wuxian.

The chest had likely been used to contain Nie Mingjue's head. Jin Guangyao had probably buried it here after transferring it out of Golden Carp Tower.

Wei Wuxian nodded to him. "Sect Leader Nie, do you know what was originally contained in this coffin?"

"How would I know?" Nie Huaisang answered. "But given how San-ge...ah, no, how Sect Leader Jin looked, I guess it was probably something very important to him."

"Coffins are, of course, used to house the dead," Wei Wuxian said. "My guess is that the corpse that was buried here was Jin Guangyao's mother, Meng Shi. He came here tonight to retrieve her body and take it with him as he escaped to Dongying."

Lan Xichen was stunned speechless.

"Oh yeah, that makes sense!" Nie Huaisang exclaimed aloud as understanding dawned on him.

"What do you think they'll do with his mother's body, now that they've dug it up?" Wei Wuxian asked.

"Wei-xiong, why do you keep asking me?" Nie Huaisang said. "I don't know, and that's not going to change no matter how many times you ask!"

After a pause, he added, "However..."

Nie Huaisang slowly gathered up his hair, which had been drenched by the rainstorm.

"Since they hate Jin Guangyao so much, they'd probably be extraordinarily ruthless with something he valued as dearly as his life, right?"

"For example, dismembering the corpse and discarding the pieces in various places, just like what was done to Chifeng-zun?" Wei Wuxian asked.

Greatly shocked, Nie Huaisang took a few steps back. "Th-th-that's...much too vicious..."

Wei Wuxian stared at him for a while, but eventually averted his gaze.

Conjecture was only conjecture, after all. None of them had evidence.

Perhaps the blank, helpless expression on Nie Huaisang's face was a mask. He could be reluctant to admit that he treated others as his pawns, placed no value on their lives. Or maybe there was more to his plan, and he wanted to keep concealing his true colors so he could hatch more schemes, achieve greater goals.

Or maybe it wasn't that complicated at all. Maybe it was someone else who had delivered the letter, killed the cats, and sewed Nie Mingjue's head and body together. Maybe Nie Huaisang was simply a bona fide good-for-nothing. Maybe the last words Jin Guangyao had said were merely lies he devised after Nie Huaisang cried out and exposed his attempt to launch a sneak attack, all for the sake of throwing Lan Xichen's mind into turmoil so that Jin Guangyao could seize the opportunity to perish with him at his side. After all, Jin Guangyao was a professional liar and notorious for his misdeeds. No matter when he lied, or what he lied about, it would come as no surprise.

As for why he had changed his mind at the last second and shoved Lan Xichen away, who could ever know what he was really thinking?

Veins bulged on the back of the hand with which Lan Xichen clutched his head. "...What did he want?" he murmured. "I used to think I knew him very well. Later, I realized I did not. Before tonight, I thought I had renewed my understanding of him...but now I once again find myself at a loss."

No one could give him an answer. Lan Xichen repeated, "What exactly did he want?"

Lan Xichen was the one who had been closest to Jin Guangyao. If he did not know, the others were even less likely to.

After a moment of silence, Wei Wuxian said, "Let's stop standing around doing nothing. We'll pick a few people to go fetch help, and the rest will stay here to watch this thing. Those guqin strings won't be able to keep Chifeng-zun in the coffin for long."

As if to confirm his assessment, a wave of thunderous noise sounded from inside the coffin, indicating a nameless fury. Nie Huaisang shuddered.

Wei Wuxian cast a glance at him. "See? We have to replace it immediately with an even more secure and solid coffin, and rebury it in a deep pit where it cannot be unearthed for at least a century.

If it is opened, I guarantee the evil will persist, with endless trouble to follow..."

He had yet to finish his sentence when a clear, resounding bark rang out in the distance. Wei Wuxian's expression changed at once.

But Jin Ling managed to perk up a little. "Fairy!"

The claps of thunder had died down, and the downpour had dwindled to a drizzle. The darkest hours of the night had already passed, and dawn was breaking.

The soaking wet black-haired spirit dog pumped its legs as it dashed toward them like a gust of black wind. It pounced at Jin Ling and clung to its master's leg while standing on its hind limbs, whimpering all the while. Its round doggy eyes were damp.

Wei Wuxian saw its long red tongue flick out from between its sharp, snow-white fangs to lick Jin Ling's hand, and his face blanched equally white. Eyes blank and mouth agape, he felt as if his soul was about to turn into a wisp of smoke and take leave of his body to ascend to the heavens.

Lan Wangji silently stood in front of him to shield him and block his view of Fairy.

A moment later, hundreds of people surrounded the Guanyin Temple. Each wore a vigilant expression, swords drawn as if ready to start killing at any moment. But when those leading the charge into the temple got a clear look at the scene before them, they were stunned. There were dead bodies sprawled everywhere the eye could see, and anyone who wasn't dead could barely stand upright. The temple grounds were littered with corpses and wreckage.

Two people had led the charge, swords at the ready. The one on the left was the Jiang Clan of Yunmeng's chief of affairs, while the one on the right was, astonishingly, Lan Qiren. Surprise and bewilderment were written on his face. Before he could open his mouth to ask questions, the first thing he saw was Lan Wangji, stuck so close to Wei Wuxian that they were almost one person. In that instant, he forgot everything he had to say. Fury washed over his face. His long brows knitted, and his indignant huffing sent his beard quivering and bristling.

The chief of affairs hurried forward to support Jiang Cheng. "Sect Leader, are you all right..."

Lan Qiren raised his sword and bellowed, *"Wei—"*

He was cut off by several figures in white who rushed out from behind him, yelling.

"Hanguang-jun!"

"Wei-qianbei!"

"Patriarch-qianbei!"

The last boy bumped into Lan Qiren, almost causing him to fall over. Smoking with anger from his seven apertures, he barked, "No hurried walking! No clamoring!"

Other than Lan Wangji, who greeted him with "Shufu," no one else paid him any mind.

Lan Sizhui grabbed Lan Wangji's sleeve with one hand and Wei Wuxian's arm with the other. "This is great! Hanguang-jun, Wei-qianbei, you're both okay!" he said with delight. "We saw how anxious Fairy was and thought you might be in a tricky situation."

"Sizhui, are you confused or something?" Lan Jingyi said. "How could there ever be a situation Hanguang-jun can't resolve? I told you not to worry for nothing."

"Jingyi, wasn't it you who was worrying for nothing on the way here?"

"Go away! Don't blabber nonsense."

Lan Sizhui spotted Wen Ning, who had finally managed to crawl upright, out of the corner of his eye. He immediately grabbed him and pulled him into the circle of boys, who all began to talk over each other to recount what had happened.

After Fairy had bitten Su She, it had run until it found a clan affiliated with the Jiang Clan of Yunmeng that was stationed near the town. It had barked furiously at their door to sound the alarm. The junior head of the family had seen the special collar around its neck, marked with a golden motif, family crest, and other such things, and had immediately determined that this was a spirit dog of significance with a distinguished owner. Then he noticed the blood on its claws and fur. The dog had clearly been in a fight, most likely because its owner was in danger.

Not daring to dismiss the urgency of the situation, the man immediately took the dog and rode to Lotus Pier on his sword to notify the region's real boss—the Jiang Clan of Yunmeng. The chief of affairs instantly recognized it as Fairy, the spirit dog belonging to the little young master Jin Ling, and promptly sent reinforcements.

The cultivators of the Lan Clan of Gusu had been about to leave Lotus Pier right around then, but Fairy stopped Lan Qiren. It had leapt up and torn a thin strip of white fabric from the hem of Lan Sizhui's robes, then pulled it over its head with its paws, like it was trying to wrap it around its head. Then it lay down and played dead.

Lan Qiren had been baffled, but Lan Sizhui had a sudden flash of insight.

"Xiansheng, does it not look like it's imitating our clan's forehead ribbon? Is it trying to tell us that Hanguang-jun or another member of the Lan Clan is in danger?"

And so the Jiang Clan of Yunmeng, the Lan Clan of Gusu, and several other clans that had yet to leave Lotus Pier had all gathered their manpower and come here together to render assistance.

Lan Jingyi clicked his tongue. "We keep calling it 'Fairy, Fairy,' but who would have thought it really *is* a spirit dog?!" he praised in a wondering tone.

But no matter how spiritual or intelligent it might be, as far as Wei Wuxian was concerned, it was still a dog—the scariest creature in the world. Even with Lan Wangji standing in front of him, goosebumps spread all over his body.

Ever since the juniors from the Lan Clan came in, Jin Ling had been stealing glances in their direction, watching them clamor around Wei Wuxian and Lan Wangji. Seeing the color gradually leave Wei Wuxian's face, he patted Fairy on the butt and whispered, "Fairy, go outside."

Fairy wagged its tail and continued to lick him.

"Go out. Or are you disobeying me?" Jin Ling chided.

Fairy threw him a plaintive look, then obediently darted out of the temple with its tail wagging. Only then did Wei Wuxian heave a sigh of relief. Jin Ling wanted to go over, but embarrassment held him back.

As he continued to hesitate, Lan Sizhui suddenly saw something hanging at Wei Wuxian's waist. His entire body froze for a moment.

"...Wei-qianbei?"

"Hmm? What?" Wei Wuxian asked.

Lan Sizhui sounded like he was in a daze as he asked, "Can...can I take a look at your flute?"

Wei Wuxian grabbed it and offered it to him. "Something wrong with it?"

Lan Sizhui took the flute with both hands and frowned slightly, looking a little perplexed. Lan Wangji watched him, while Wei Wuxian looked at Lan Wangji.

"What's with your clan's Sizhui? Does he like my flute?"

"Huh? You finally discarded that lousy, out-of-tune flute of yours!" Lan Jingyi blurted in surprise. "This new flute looks pretty decent!"

He didn't know that this "decent" new flute was the very spiritual weapon he'd always been dying to catch a glimpse of—the legendary hell flute, Chenqing. He merely thought to himself with glee, *This is great! At least now when he and Hanguang-jun play duets, he won't look as much of a disgrace as he used to. Good god, that old flute was really ugly and horrible-sounding!*

"Sizhui," Lan Wangji called out.

Only then did Lan Sizhui snap back to his senses. He returned Chenqing to Wei Wuxian with both hands. "Wei-qianbei."

Wei Wuxian took the flute, then remembered Jiang Cheng was the one who had brought it here. He turned to Jiang Cheng.

"Thanks," Wei Wuxian casually said, then raised Chenqing. "I'll... keep this then?"

Jiang Cheng glanced at him. "It was yours to begin with."

After a moment of hesitation, his lips moved slightly—as if he still had something to say. But Wei Wuxian had already turned back to Lan Wangji, and seeing this, Jiang Cheng fell silent and said nothing else.

Some of the people present were cleaning up the scene, some were reinforcing the seal on the coffin, and some were discussing how to transport it safely.

Some, however, were angry.

"Xichen, what on earth is wrong with you?" Lan Qiren fumed.

Lan Xichen pressed his temple, face heavy with unspeakable melancholy. "...Shufu. Please, I beg you. Stop asking," he answered with audible weariness. "I really do not wish to speak right now."

Lan Qiren had raised Lan Xichen single-handedly, and he had never seen him look so agitated and restless, so undignified and unbecoming. He looked at him, then at Lan Wangji, who stood with Wei Wuxian, surrounded by the juniors. The more he looked, the more he fumed. Neither of these two previously flawless pupils would heed him anymore. Both were now sources of worry.

The coffin that held Nie Mingjue and Jin Guangyao wasn't just abnormally heavy, but also had to be treated with the utmost care. As such, several family heads volunteered to transport it.

One of those family heads saw the face of the Guanyin statue. He was taken aback at first, then directed the others to look at it too, as if he'd discovered something novel.

"Look at its face! Doesn't it look like Jin Guangyao?"

When the others saw it, they clicked their tongues in wonder.

"It really is his face! Why would Jin Guangyao make such a thing?"

"To arrogantly proclaim himself god, I wager," Sect Leader Yao stated.

"That *is* so very arrogant. Heh heh heh."

Not necessarily, Wei Wuxian thought.

Everyone regarded Jin Guangyao's mother as the lowliest of prostitutes. And so, he had insisted on carving this Guanyin statue in the likeness of his mother so she would be worshipped by millions of people, who would kowtow to her and offer her incense.

But there was no point in saying any of that now. Wei Wuxian knew better than anyone that nobody would believe it, or care. Anything involving Jin Guangyao would be met with only the most malicious of speculation, and gossip would spread that speculation across the land.

Not long after, the coffin would be sealed within an even larger and more secure one, then nailed shut with seventy-two peach-wood pegs and buried deep beneath some mountain to keep its evil suppressed. And there it would remain, accompanied by a stone tablet to warn passersby of the danger.

And those sealed within would also remain confined for eternity—reviled by all, never to be absolved.

Nie Huaisang leaned against the doorframe and watched as several heads of families lifted the coffin across the threshold of the Guanyin Temple. He lowered his head and patted the dirt from the front of his robes. He paused for a moment, as though he had seen something. Wei Wuxian looked over as well.

There was something left behind on the ground. It was Jin Guangyao's cap.

Nie Huaisang bent to pick it up before strolling out the door.

Fairy barked a few times as it waited anxiously for its master outside. Hearing it, Jin Ling suddenly remembered that Jin Guangyao had been the one who had given him Fairy, when it was still a clumsy puppy that didn't even reach his knees.

Jin Ling had only been so old at that time. He'd just had a fight with the other children in Golden Carp Tower, and though he'd won, he didn't find it gratifying at all. He had been in a frenzy, smashing things in his room and wailing at the top of his lungs. No maids or servants had dared to get close to him for fear they would be hit by flying objects.

But his little uncle had been all smiles when he poked his head into his room to ask him, "A-Ling, what's wrong?"

Jin Ling had immediately smashed five or six vases at Jin Guangyao's feet. "Oh goodness, so fierce. How scary," Jin Guangyao had replied. Then he had left, shaking his head and looking terribly scared.

Jin Ling had still been in a huff when the next day came, refusing to leave his room or eat. Jin Guangyao had hung around the entrance to his chamber.

Bracing his back against the door, Jin Ling had only just yelled "Leave me alone!" when a puppy's barks suddenly rang out.

He had opened the door, only to see Jin Guangyao crouching there, holding in his arms a tiny black-haired puppy with round, shining eyes. Jin Guangyao had looked up and smiled at him.

"I found this little thing, but I don't know what to call it. A-Ling, do you want to give it a name?"

That smile had been so gentle and sincere that Jin Ling refused to believe Jin Guangyao had been faking it.

All of a sudden, tears tumbled from his eyes once more.

Jin Ling had always thought that crying was a sign of weakness and incompetence, and scoffed at such behavior. But right now, he had no way to release the anguish and indignation in his heart other than shedding an ocean of tears.

Somehow, there didn't seem to be anyone he could blame or anyone he could hate. Wei Wuxian, Jin Guangyao, Wen Ning—he should hold every one of them responsible for his parents' deaths. He had good reason to loathe each of them. But they all seemed like they'd had *their* reasons, and it left him unable to hate them.

But if he didn't hate them, who *could* he hate? Had he deserved to lose both parents at such a young age? Was this how he would be forced to live—unable to seek revenge on his enemies, but also unable to loathe them without qualms?

He couldn't take this lying down. He couldn't help but feel aggrieved. How he yearned to perish with them and be done with it!

Sect Leader Yao saw him staring at the coffin, crying soundlessly. "Jin-xiao-gongzi, why are you crying? Are you crying over Jin Guangyao?"

When Jin Ling was silent, Sect Leader Yao began to chide him in a tone that elders used to reprove their own juniors. "Why are you crying? Stop those tears. A man like your uncle is not worth crying for. Xiao-gongzi, pardon me for saying this, but you can't be so weak. This is the softheartedness of a woman. You must know what is right and what is wrong. You should correct your—"

When the Jin Clan of Lanling's family head had still been the Cultivation Chief who oversaw all the clans, the other family heads would never have dared assume the air of an elder and lecture a Jin Clan junior. But Jin Guangyao was now dead, and there was no one in the Jin Clan of Lanling who could take his mantle. The Jin Clan's reputation was more or less ruined—they would likely never rise to the top again. And so, those who dared posture had already begun to come out of the woodwork.

Jin Ling was drowning in a sea of thoughts and emotions. Fury welled up within him to hear Sect Leader Yao rambling about his personal judgment on the matter while gesticulating here and there.

"So what if I wanna cry?!" he hollered. "Who are you? Who do you think you are? What do you care if I cry?!"

Sect Leader Yao had clearly not expected his lecture to be so thoroughly rebuffed, nor that he'd wind up being the one getting yelled at. He promptly pulled a long face.

"Forget it," the others advised him in hushed tones. "Don't bother yourself with children."

Only then was he able to rein in his rage at being humiliated. He snorted coldly. "That's for sure. Heh, why bother with a brat who's still wet behind the ears and can't tell right from wrong, or good from evil?"

Lan Qiren watched over the coffin as it was transported onto the wagon. He looked back and was dumbfounded. "Where's Wangji?" he asked.

He'd been planning to haul Lan Wangji back to the Cloud

Recesses and have a long heart-to-heart talk with him for a hundred and twenty days. Should that fail, he'd confine him again for a while. Who could have imagined Lan Wangji would vanish in the blink of an eye?

He circled the place a few times and raised his voice. "Where's Wangji?!"

Lan Jingyi spoke up. "Earlier, I said we'd brought Little Apple with us and tethered it outside the temple, so Hanguang-jun took... took...to see Little Apple together."

"And then?" Lan Qiren demanded.

What happened next was a foregone conclusion. There wasn't even a hint of Wei Wuxian, Lan Wangji, or Wen Ning's shadows to be seen outside the Guanyin Temple.

Lan Qiren looked at Lan Xichen, who lagged absentmindedly behind him, then heaved a heavy sigh and left with a flick of his sleeves.

Lan Jingyi looked around and exclaimed in surprise, "Sizhui? What's going on? When did Sizhui disappear too?"

When Jin Ling heard Wei Wuxian and Lan Wangji were gone, he dashed outside in a hurry, nearly tripping over the threshold of the Guanyin Temple in the process. But no matter how urgently he rushed, he couldn't even catch their shadows. Fairy happily circled around him, its tongue lolling as it panted.

Jiang Cheng was standing under a towering tree on the Guanyin Temple grounds. He glanced at him and said coldly, "Wipe your face."

Jin Ling rubbed his eyes hard and wiped his face. Running over to Jiang Cheng, he asked, "Where are they?"

"Gone," Jiang Cheng replied.

"And you just let them go?" Jin Ling blurted.

"What else was I supposed to do?" Jiang Cheng asked mockingly. "Keep them for dinner? Say 'thank you' and then 'sorry'?"

Agitated, Jin Ling pointed at him. "No wonder he wanted to leave. It's all because you're like this! Jiujiu, why are you so annoying?!"

Jiang Cheng glared at him angrily, raising his hand as he scolded, "Is that how you speak to your elders? You're asking for a beating!"

Jin Ling flinched back, and Fairy tucked its tail between its legs. Jiang Cheng's slap never did land on the back of Jin Ling's head. Instead, he weakly withdrew his hand.

"Shut up, Jin Ling. Just shut up," he said, irritated. "Let's go back. Everyone will return to their respective places."

Jin Ling was taken aback. After a moment of hesitation, he did as he was told and shut his mouth.

With his head drooping, he walked shoulder to shoulder with Jiang Cheng for a few steps before he looked up again. "Jiujiu, were you going to say something earlier?"

"What?" Jiang Cheng said. "No."

"Just now!" Jin Ling persisted. "I saw it. You were going to say something to Wei Wuxian, but you didn't."

After a long silence, Jiang Cheng shook his head. "There's nothing to say."

What *was* there to say?

Perhaps there was this:

"I didn't get caught by the Wen Clan because I insisted on returning to Lotus Pier to retrieve my parents' bodies.

"When you went to buy rations in that small town during our escape, a group of Wen cultivators caught up to us.

"I noticed them early and left the spot where I'd been sitting to hide in a corner of the street. I didn't get caught, but they were patrolling, and they would have surely bumped into you while you were getting us food.

"So I ran out and lured them away."

But just as the Wei Wuxian of the past who'd extracted his golden core for Jiang Cheng had been unable to tell him the truth, the Jiang Cheng of the present could no longer bring himself to speak up.

23
Wangxian: Forgetting Envy

THE SKY HAD YET TO LIGHTEN, and all was quiet on the long street. The only thing Wei Wuxian and Lan Wangji could hear was the soft clip-clopping of the little spotted donkey's hooves. Riding on the beast's back, Wei Wuxian patted its behind. The saddlebag was hard and stuffed full of apples that the Lan juniors had probably packed specifically for the donkey.

As he stared at Lan Wangji's attractive profile, Wei Wuxian fished an apple from the bag and raised it to his mouth. *Crunch.* The bite was unusually crisp. When Little Apple saw its apple so brazenly stolen, it angrily blew a heavy breath from its nostrils and kicked backward. Wei Wuxian, who had no time for that, slapped its behind a few more times before shoving the rest of the unfinished apple in its mouth.

"Lan Zhan, did you know? Apparently, Sisi was a friend of Jin Guangyao's mother."

"I did not," Lan Wangji replied.

Wei Wuxian didn't know whether to laugh or cry at the response. "That was a rhetorical question. I saw it during my session of Empathy with that vengeful female spirit back at the Guanyin Temple. Sisi took good care of the two of them back then, both mother and son."

After a brief silence, Lan Wangji said, "Surely that is why Jin Guangyao let her live."

"Probably," Wei Wuxian agreed. "I was afraid Zewu-jun would get softhearted again, so I didn't tell him the reason Jin Guangyao spared her. I don't think now is a good time to tell him either."

"Should he inquire in the future, I will inform him," Lan Wangji said.

"That's probably best." Wei Wuxian glanced back, then heaved a rare sigh of complaint. "I don't wanna deal with any more of these random messes," he groaned. "I guess it is what it is."

Lan Wangji nodded. He reined Little Apple in a bit and continued down the road.

Everyone had their own problems that no one but they could solve. Even when it came to blood-related brothers, there was nothing Lan Wangji could do right now to help Lan Xichen. Any consolation would be powerless to help, and anything he did would be in vain.

Lan Wangji paused for a moment, then said, "Wei Ying."

"What?" Wei Wuxian answered.

"There is something I never told you."

Wei Wuxian's heart skipped a beat. "What is it?"

Lan Wangji stopped to look him in the eyes. But just as he was about to speak, there came the sound of hurried running behind them.

"Goddammit, how have people caught up to us already?" Wei Wuxian griped.

Someone had indeed caught up, but fortunately, it wasn't anyone too awful. Lan Sizhui panted as he ran up to them.

"Han...Hanguang-jun, Wei-qianbei!"

Wei Wuxian propped his arms on the donkey's head. "Sizhui, my boy. I'm eloping with your clan's Hanguang-jun. What are you following us for? Aren't you scared of being yelled at by Lan-lao-xiansheng?"

Lan Sizhui blushed. "Wei-qianbei, don't be like that. I...I only came because I have a very important question to ask!"

"And what's that?" Wei Wuxian asked.

"I remembered some bits and pieces of my past, but I couldn't be sure, so...so I came here to confirm them with Hanguang-jun and Wei-qianbei."

Lan Wangji looked at him, then looked at Wen Ning. Wen Ning nodded.

"What is it?" Wei Wuxian asked.

Lan Sizhui squared his shoulders, puffed his chest, and drew in a deep breath.

"You call yourself an excellent cook, but everything you make burns both the eyes and the stomach."

Wei Wuxian was flabbergasted. "Huh?!"

"You buried me in the radish patch and told me that some sun and water would help make me grow faster and taller. And that more kids would sprout and play with me," Lan Sizhui added.

Wei Wuxian was speechless.

"You said you were going to treat Hanguang-jun to a meal, but in the end, you ran off without paying the bill," Lan Sizhui continued. "Hanguang-jun was still the one who paid."

Wei Wuxian's eyes widened. He was on the verge of falling off the donkey.

"You...you..."

Lan Sizhui stared squarely at Wei Wuxian and Lan Wangji. "Maybe I was too young back then. There are a lot of things I don't fully remember. But I am absolutely certain...that I used to be surnamed Wen."

"Surnamed Wen?" Wei Wuxian's voice was trembling. "Aren't you surnamed Lan? Lan Sizhui, Lan Yuan...Lan Yuan...Wen Yuan?"

Lan Sizhui gave a hard nod, his voice also shaking. "Wei-qianbei, I...I'm...I'm A-Yuan..."

Wei Wuxian had yet to wrap his head around it all. "A-Yuan..." he asked in a daze. "Didn't A-Yuan die? He wound up all alone on the Burial Mounds..."

He trailed off as Lan Xichen's words echoed in his ears. *"It has been said that he spent those years facing the wall in reflection. In truth, he was too injured to do any such thing. And even so, when he learned of your death, he had to go to the Burial Mounds to see for himself, forcibly dragging his body there in such a state..."*

He whipped his head around to face Lan Wangji. "Lan Zhan, was it you?!"

"Yes," Lan Wangji admitted. He gazed at Wei Wuxian. "That is what I never told you."

Wei Wuxian couldn't speak for the longest time.

Finally, Lan Sizhui couldn't hold back anymore and leapt over with a cry. He caught Wei Wuxian with one arm while his other caught Lan Wangji, and he pulled the three of them together into a tight hug. Wei Wuxian and Lan Wangji were both startled by the sudden embrace.

Lan Sizhui buried his head in their shoulders. "Hanguang-jun, Wei-qianbei, I...I..."

His voice was muffled. Wei Wuxian and Lan Wangji, who were only inches away from each other, exchanged a look. They both saw something very soft in each other's eyes.

Wei Wuxian pulled himself together and patted Lan Sizhui on the back. "All right, don't cry."

"I'm not... I'm just... I just suddenly feel so sad, but...so happy too...I don't know how to describe it..."

After a brief silence, Lan Wangji also patted him on the back.

"Then do not worry about it," he said.

"Yeah," Wei Wuxian agreed.

Lan Sizhui responded by hugging the two tighter.

It didn't take long before Wei Wuxian protested, "Hey, hey, hey. Child, why are your arms so strong? As I'd expect of someone taught by Hanguang-jun himself..."

Lan Wangji gave him a look. "You have taught him as well."

"No wonder he's so well brought up," Wei Wuxian commented.

However, Lan Sizhui disagreed. "No, Wei-qianbei never taught me."

"Says who?" Wei Wuxian protested. "You were too little, that's all. You forgot everything I taught you."

"I didn't. I remember it now. I think you did teach me in the past," Lan Sizhui said.

"See?"

"You taught me how to disguise erotica as regular books," Lan Sizhui said seriously.

"..."

Lan Wangji gave Wei Wuxian another look.

Lan Sizhui continued on. "You also taught me that when a beautiful girl walks by—"

"What a load of nonsense," Wei Wuxian interrupted. "Child, is that all you remember? Please. As if I'd teach that stuff to kids."

Lan Sizhui looked up. "Ning-shushu stands as my witness. He was also there when you taught me all that stuff."

"Witness to what? Nothing of the sort happened," Wei Wuxian insisted.

"I...I don't remember anything..." Wen Ning said.

Lan Sizhui turned to Lan Wangji. "Hanguang-jun, everything I said is true."

Lan Wangji gave a nod. "I know."

"Lan Zhan!" Wei Wuxian was about to make a scene and roll around on the donkey's back. But then he thought of something and instead asked, "Speaking of which, what triggered your memories, Sizhui?"

"I'm not sure," Lan Sizhui replied. "Just that when I saw Chenqing, it felt incredibly familiar."

Wei Wuxian suspected it had been Chenqing. "Of course you'd be familiar with that thing. You used to love chewing on it, always drooling all over it. There were times I couldn't even play it, thanks to you."

Lan Sizhui turned red at once. "Re...really...?"

Wei Wuxian grinned with glee. "Yeah. Why else would seeing it bring back your memories? Do you want to hear more stories from when you were little?"

He gestured with his hands, miming two butterflies. "Hanguang-jun, do you remember the time I treated you to food, and he was holding those two butterflies and muttering to himself, *'I like you,' 'I like you too'*..."

Lan Sizhui was blushing harder by the minute.

"Oh, yeah. You even called Hanguang-jun your daddy in public. Poor Hanguang-jun. An upstanding, chaste young man in the bloom of his youth became a father so suddenly..."

"Aaaahhhhh—!" Lan Sizhui blushed heavily as he cried, "Hanguang-jun, I'm sorry!"

Lan Wangji looked at the giggling Wei Wuxian and shook his head. There was nothing but softness in his expression.

"Oh yeah, Wen Ning. You knew about this already?" Wei Wuxian asked.

Wen Ning nodded.

Wei Wuxian was stunned. "Then why didn't you tell me?"

Wen Ning stole a glance at Lan Wangji before replying cautiously. "Lan-gongzi didn't say that I should tell you, so..."

Wei Wuxian was indignant. "Why are you so obedient to him? You're the Ghost General. Why is the Ghost General scared of Hanguang-jun? Isn't that embarrassing for me?!"

Lan Sizhui was still crying. "Hanguang-jun, I'm sorry!"

The four parted ways at the woods near the edge of Yunping City.

"Gongzi, we will be heading this way," Wen Ning said.

"Where to?" Wei Wuxian asked.

"Didn't you ask me what I'd do after everything was over?" Wen Ning said. "I discussed it with A-Yuan. We will go to Qishan and bury our family's ashes there. We were also thinking about searching the area to see if we can find anything that once belonged to my sister while she was alive, so we can build a cenotaph in her honor."

"I built one for the two of you at the Burial Mounds, but it was burnt down," Wei Wuxian said. "We'll make a trip to Qishan too."

He turned to Lan Wangji, but before he could ask for the latter's opinion, Wen Ning declined. "No, it's fine."

Taken aback, Wei Wuxian asked, "You don't want us to come with?"

Lan Sizhui quickly chimed in. "Wei-qianbei, just go with Hanguang-jun."

Wei Wuxian wanted to say more, but Wen Ning said, "Really, it's fine. Wei-gongzi, you have done enough."

After a brief pause, Wei Wuxian asked, "What will you do after you've finished all that?"

"Send A-Yuan back to the Cloud Recesses," Wen Ning replied.

"Then I can take my time pondering what to do next. As for what follows...let me go my own way."

Wei Wuxian nodded slowly. "...Just as well."

This was the first time in many years that Wen Ning would not be walking the same road as him. He had made up his own mind—perhaps, Wei Wuxian thought, he now had things he wanted to do.

It was the same thing Wei Wuxian had always wanted. Everyone had their own path to take.

Yet now that the day was finally here, it was a little saddening to watch Wen Ning and Lan Sizhui's backs gradually get farther and farther away until they disappeared.

The only person left at his side was Lan Wangji.

How very fortunate, then, that Lan Wangji was also the only person he wanted beside him.

"Lan Zhan," Wei Wuxian called.

"Mn."

"You've taught him well," Wei Wuxian remarked.

"There will be many more opportunities to meet in the future."

"I know."

"Once Wen Ning brings Sizhui back to the Cloud Recesses, we can settle nearby and see him regularly."

Wei Wuxian looked at him. "Lan Zhan, are you scared of me thanking you? It suddenly occurred to me that I said 'thank you' every time we parted ways in my past life. And each time we'd meet again, I would always be in a worse state than before."

The killing of Wen Chao and Wen Zhuliu at the post station, the encounter in Yunmeng at the flower-tossing terrace, their goodbye at the Yiling Burial Mounds. Each time, he'd used the phrase to draw a clear line between himself and Lan Wangji, and put greater distance between them.

Lan Wangji spoke after a long silence. "Between you and I, there is no need to say 'thank you' or 'sorry.'"

Wei Wuxian chuckled at that. "All right. Then let's say some other things. Like..."

He lowered his voice and gestured for Lan Wangji to come closer, as if he wanted to whisper in his ear. Sure enough, Lan Wangji approached. Unexpectedly, Wei Wuxian reached out and tilted his chin up before leaning down to press a kiss to his lips.

It was a long time before Wei Wuxian moved away slightly. His eyelashes brushed against Lan Wangji's own as he asked in a low voice, "How's that?"

"..."

"Give me a reaction, Hanguang-jun," Wei Wuxian prompted.

"..."

"So stoic. With the mood like this, shouldn't you be violently pinning me to the ground..."

Before he could finish, Lan Wangji circled his hand around the back of Wei Wuxian's neck and hooked him over in one rough movement to forcefully press the two of them together once more.

Little Apple was shaken. It even stopped chewing the apple in its mouth and froze as stiff as a wooden toy.

It wasn't long before the donkey could no longer carry Wei Wuxian. Lan Wangji wound one arm around his back, put the other under his knees, and in one swift movement, swept him off of the little spotted donkey.

Wei Wuxian was then pinned to the ground and brutally kissed by Lan Wangji, just like he wanted—but all of a sudden, he broke the kiss.

"Waitasec, hang on!"

"What?" Lan Wangji asked.

Wei Wuxian squinted. "I suddenly got the feeling that..."

The woods, the bushes, the wild grasses; the forceful action and the entangling tongues... It was like deja vu.

He thought for a moment, and the more he did so the more this felt familiar for some reason. He felt he had to ask, so he ventured carefully, "During the Siege Hunt at Mount Baifeng, the time I was blindfolded. Lan Zhan, did you...?"

He didn't finish his question. Nor did Lan Wangji answer—but his fingers curled slightly. The instant Wei Wuxian noticed the strangeness of his expression, he propped himself up and pressed his ear to Lan Wangji's chest. Sure enough, he heard wild, violent thumping.

Wei Wuxian was shocked to his core. "...Oh, it really *was* you?!"

Lan Wangji gulped nervously. "I..."

Wei Wuxian couldn't believe it. "Lan Zhan, you'd do something like that?! You really can't judge a book by its cover."

"..."

"Did you know? I always thought it was some shy female cultivator who had a secret crush but was too scared to tell me," Wei Wuxian added.

"..."

"You've harbored improper thoughts about me for that long?!" Wei Wuxian asked.

"...I... At the time, I was aware it was wrong of me. Very wrong of me," Lan Wangji mumbled.

Wei Wuxian remembered that Lan Wangji had been punching trees alone in the woods when he found him later. "So that's why you were so angry?"

And Wei Wuxian had thought he was mad at him! As it turned out, he was mad at himself—mad at his own momentary impulses, mad at his own inability to maintain self-control, mad that he had taken advantage of the situation. It was not how a gentleman should conduct himself, and more importantly, it went against his family's motto.

Seeing how low Lan Wangji hung his head, as if he'd started to reflect on his past behavior again, Wei Wuxian tickled him under his chin.

"Oh come on, why so conflicted? So you already kissed me long ago; I'm over the moon with happiness. That was my first kiss, you know. Congrats, Hanguang-jun."

Lan Wangji abruptly looked at him. "First kiss?"

"Yeah," Wei Wuxian replied. "Why, what did you think?"

Lan Wangji gazed at him unblinkingly with a strange, subtle shimmer in his eyes. "Then..."

"Then what?" Wei Wuxian prompted. "Hesitating over your words isn't your style, Lan Zhan."

"Then...you... At the time, why...why..." Lan Wangji asked haltingly.

Wei Wuxian was curious. "Why what?"

Lan Wangji moved his lips. "...Why did you not fight back?"

Wei Wuxian was taken aback.

"You...clearly did not know the other party, so why did you not fight back?" Lan Wangji grumbled. "And afterward, why did you tell me that..."

Tell him what?

Wei Wuxian finally remembered.

After Wei Wuxian had met Lan Wangji "by accident" at Mount Baifeng, he'd smugly boasted on and on about how he was *so* experienced, that no one would dare kiss Lan Wangji, and that there must be no one Lan Wangji would kiss either. He'd even said that Lan Wangji would never be able to give away his first kiss in this lifetime...

He burst out in wild, earth-shattering laughter, hugging his belly and pounding the ground with his fist. "Ha ha ha ha ha ha ha ha ha..." Lan Wangji was speechless.

Still roaring with laughter, Wei Wuxian hugged him and gave him a smacking kiss on the lips. "After all that fuss, what you were actually *angriest* about was that I'd apparently kissed someone else before? You're so silly, Lan Zhan. You really believe the fucking bullshit I spew? Only a little stick-in-the-mud like you would believe any of it, ha ha ha ha ha ha..."

His mocking was too loud, too excessive. Finally, unable to contain himself any longer, Lan Wangji pinned him to the ground again.

Leaving Little Apple where it was, the entwined couple stumbled behind a thicket.

The rain had only recently cleared up, and the water droplets still clinging to the grass dampened Lan Wangji's white robes. But those robes were quickly stripped away by Wei Wuxian.

"Don't move," he whispered.

The scent of fresh grass surrounded Wei Wuxian's neck and lips, while Lan Wangji emanated the cool fragrance of sandalwood. He kneeled between Lan Wangji's legs and pressed his lips to his forehead before tracing a path down with further kisses.

From between his eyebrows to the tip of his nose, his cheeks, his lips, his chin.

Downward to the curve of his throat, to the bend of his neck, to his heart.

With infinite veneration did he travel the highs and lows.

As his kisses reached Lan Wangji's toned abdomen and continued downward, strands of hair slipped past Wei Wuxian's shoulders. The locks of his hair, accompanied by the small puffs of his breath, brushed and teased this dangerous territory. Lan Wangji reached out to push his shoulders back, as if he could endure no more.

Wei Wuxian caught his wrist. "Hey, don't move. Like I said, allow me."

He tugged his hair ribbon loose, then re-tied his long hair before bending his head down again. Sensing what he was about to do, Lan Wangji grew a little flustered and objected quietly.

"No."

"Yes," Wei Wuxian countered, then gently captured Lan Wangji with his lips.

Mindful of his teeth, he carefully took him into his mouth. He swallowed as deep as he could, until he felt him hit the back of his throat, which was a little uncomfortable. Immediately sensing his discomfort, Lan Wangji made to push him away, worried that Wei Wuxian was forcing himself.

"Stop."

Wei Wuxian pushed his hand away and began to slowly bob up and down.

"You..." Lan Wangji started, but any further words quickly became caught in his throat.

The sum total of illustrated erotica Wei Wuxian had looked at over the years could fill an entire section of the Lan Clan's Room of Forbidden Books. Furthermore, he was also a very smart man. Extrapolating from what he'd read, he worked the hard, hot member in his mouth with his lips and tongue. To have the most sensitive part of him engulfed entirely within a warm, wet cavity, and lavished with such tender attention—it was sheer torture for Lan Wangji, who could barely keep himself from losing control and doing something violent.

When he heard Lan Wangji begin to heave increasingly harsh breaths, Wei Wuxian sped up. The fingers gripping his shoulder dug in harder. Just as his neck and jaw were starting to get sore from the effort, he finally felt a burst of something hot shoot down his throat.

The fluid was sticky, scalding, and had a thick musky flavor. The suddenness of it made Wei Wuxian choke violently for a second. He immediately spat out the huge member in his mouth and pulled back to cough. Lan Wangji patted his back, surprisingly at a loss for what to do.

"...Spit it out. Spit it out, quickly."

Pressing his hand over his mouth, Wei Wuxian shook his head. After a moment, he took his hand away and stuck his tongue out at Lan Wangji, then opened his mouth to show him.

"All swallowed."

The tip of his tongue was a vibrant red, and his lips were the same luscious hue. The smiling corners of his mouth were stained with traces of come. Lan Wangji stared at him in a daze, unable to utter a single word. He was the most ascetic of all distinguished cultivators, but his usual aloofness and composure had been shattered. He was dyed a blushing shade of peach from the corners of his eyes to the ends of his eyebrows, adding to his charm. He looked like he'd just been horribly bullied, and Wei Wuxian couldn't have loved this look more.

Arms still bare, he wrapped them around Lan Wangji's shoulders and dropped a light kiss at the corner of his mouth, then another on his brow.

"Good boy, don't let this scare you. Next time I'll let you blow me. Make sure you do it as well as I did, 'kay?"

His lips were still stained with come, which the kiss smeared on the corners of Lan Wangji's mouth too. Coupled with the dazed expression on his face, this made for a pitiful yet adorable image that tugged at Wei Wuxian's heart.

He gave him another smacking kiss on the lips and murmured, "God, I love you so much, Lan Zhan."

Lan Wangji slowly gazed at him.

Maybe it was his imagination, but Wei Wuxian thought his eyes were slightly red.

He had yet to notice the look of forced endurance in Lan Wangji's eyes—a sign that he was on the verge of losing control. Thinking perhaps he still hadn't had enough, Wei Wuxian cupped the growing heat on Lan Wangji's lower body and began to slowly stroke it up and down.

"Let's stay like this forever from now on, 'kay?"

All of a sudden, Lan Wangji tackled him and pinned him to the grass once more.

The world spun, and in an instant the two had switched positions. Feeling Lan Wangji biting at him again, Wei Wuxian moved to push his head away as he laughed. "Why so impatient? I said, next time you can..."

There was an abrupt jab of pain from his lower body that elicited an *"ah"* from his lips. He frowned slightly.

"Lan Zhan, what did you just shove in me?"

It was only a rhetorical question, since he could already tell it was a long, slender finger. He closed his legs reflexively, but the odd feeling of something foreign inside him grew stronger when a second finger followed.

Wei Wuxian had once been a hotblooded young man who'd read countless volumes of erotica—but he had never read anything *homoerotic*. He'd never imagined he'd wind up developing a taste for such things, and therefore had no urge to explore it. And so, he'd been under the impression that lovemaking between men basically involved some kissing, some hugging, and maybe some use of the mouth and hands. He'd never investigated further.

It was only now, being pinned to the ground by Lan Wangji and stretched bit by bit by his fingers, that he dimly realized their options might not be as limited as he'd thought. Aside from the minor discomfort, he felt shock tinged with amusement. But by the time a third finger joined in, he could not smile anymore.

He was already uncomfortably full, but three fingers were still far from that which he'd swallowed earlier.

Wei Wuxian rambled aloud, unable to stop himself. "Lan Zhan, Lan Zhan, um, can you—can you calm down for a sec? You're gonna stick it there? You sure you're not mistaken? Is that the right place? I think maybe it's not quite..."

But it didn't seem like Lan Wangji was able to hear a word he said anymore. He cut Wei Wuxian off with a rough kiss, lowered himself on top of him, and pushed inside.

It was only the head, but Wei Wuxian's eyes went unbelievably wide as his legs jerked upward and his knees bent. Their bodies were pressed tightly together. They were breathless, and their hearts beat like drums.

When Lan Wangji next spoke to apologize, his voice was shattered. "...Sorry...I couldn't hold back anymore."

Seeing how red his eyes had become after suffering so long under restraint, Wei Wuxian clenched his teeth. "If you can't, then don't... So...what do I do now?"

He was actually asking him for advice—a drowning man will clutch at straws.

"Relax..." Lan Wangji answered.

Wei Wuxian mumbled to himself. "Okay, relax, I'll relax..."

He'd only managed to loosen up a tiny bit before Lan Wangji tried to push inside. The muscles of Wei Wuxian's buttocks and abdomen tensed, and a broken moan escaped his throat.

"...Does it hurt very much?" Lan Wangji asked.

Wei Wuxian hugged him, his body shaking uncontrollably. Teary-eyed, he said, "Yeah, it hurts. It's my first time, of course it hurts."

As soon as he said that, he felt the thing inside him grow harder.

Something hard and foreign was penetrating his soft and vulnerable insides. It was easy to imagine how it felt. But Wei Wuxian snorted and laughed out loud when such a simple response made the self-possessed Hanguang-jun lose control of his body.

Being a man himself, he knew how awful Lan Wangji had to feel right now, being stuck like this. Despite his predicament, he was still being considerate of Wei Wuxian's comfort instead of just forcing himself all the way inside. Wei Wuxian's heart melted, and he reached out and hooked Lan Wangji's neck down to whisper in his ear.

"Lan Zhan, good Lan Zhan, er-gege, let *me* tell you what to do. Kiss me. Kiss me now and it won't hurt anymore..."

Lan Wangji's fair earlobe burned bright red.

"...Stop...stop calling me that," he gritted out with difficulty.

Wei Wuxian laughed at the stammer. "You don't like it? Then lemme change it up. Wangji-didi, Zhan-er, Hanguang, which one do you like? ...*Aaah-mmm*—!"

Lan Wangji bit Wei Wuxian's lips as he drove all the way inside. All of Wei Wuxian's cries were sealed in his throat. He gripped Lan Wangji's shoulders tightly, his brow furrowed deeply, tears trickling from the corners of his eyes. His legs were locked in place around Lan Wangji's waist, and he was afraid to move even a single limb.

Lan Wangji regained himself a little, heaving a few breaths before he apologized.

"Sorry."

Wei Wuxian shook his head and forced a smile. "Like you said, there's never any need to say that between us."

Lan Wangji tentatively leaned in to kiss him, somewhat clumsy in his movements. Wei Wuxian squinted with happiness, and opened his mouth to allow him deeper access. He hooked his tongue and intertwined it with Lan Wangji's.

Amidst this haze, his eyes traveled to the brand just beneath Lan Wangji's collarbone. He placed his hand over the scar, and his smile faded.

"Lan Zhan, tell me... Does this also have something to do with me?"

After a brief silence, Lan Wangji replied, "It is nothing. I was lost to drink at the time."

After escorting Wei Wuxian back to the Burial Mounds, what had awaited Lan Wangji was three years of confinement. However, during that period had come the news that what went around came around, that evil did not go unpunished—that the Yiling Patriarch was finally dead.

Dragging his horribly injured body, Lan Wangji had rushed to Yiling and searched the mountain for days. Although he had found the unconscious, feverish Wen Yuan tucked inside the hollow of a scorched tree, he had found nothing of Wei Wuxian. Not even a bone, a chunk of flesh, or a frail wisp of soul.

On his way back to the Lan Clan of Gusu, Lan Wangji had bought a jug of Emperor's Smile in Caiyi Town.

The liquor had been ambrosial and rich. It was clearly not heavily spiced, but it burned his throat all the same—burned all the way up to the rims of his eyes and down into the depths of his heart.

He hadn't liked the taste. But he had sort of understood why a certain person had liked it.

That night had been the very first time Lan Wangji had drunk alcohol—and likewise, the very first time he had gotten drunk. He had no memory of what he'd done in his inebriated state, but everyone in the Lan Clan had looked at him with disbelief for a long time afterward, whether they were juniors or sect disciples. Some had said that he'd smashed open an ancient room in the Cloud Recesses that night and rummaged through it, overturning everything in the chamber as if in search of something. When Lan Xichen had questioned him, he had been at a loss. Eyes blank, he had asked his brother for a flute.

Lan Xichen had found a fine flute made of white jade and brought it to him, but Lan Wangji had only hurled it aside in anger. It wasn't the one he wanted, and he couldn't find that one anywhere. Then, all of a sudden, he had spotted the iron branding rods which had been collected from the Wen Clan of Qishan and locked away.

When Lan Wangji had sobered up, his chest bore the same wound that Wei Wuxian had gained inside the Cave of the Xuanwu of Slaughter.

Lan Qiren had looked very sad and very angry, but in the end, he had not reprimanded him further. Reprimands, punishments— there had been enough of those. He had sighed and stopped fighting Lan Wangji's decision to keep Wen Yuan. Lan Wangji had bowed, assigned himself punishment of his own accord, and silently kneeled for one day and one night inside the Cloud Recesses.

He had drunk the liquor he had drunk; he had suffered the injury he had suffered.

By now, that wound had been scarred over for thirteen years.

Lan Wangji began to thrust in and out while Wei Wuxian shut his eyes and gasped for breath through his clenched teeth, adjusting his breathing to the rhythm of Lan Wangji's hips. When he had grown somewhat accustomed to the invasion of that foreign body, he unconsciously began to twist his waist. A sudden pleasure numbed his lower half as a tingling sensation crawled up his spine and spread throughout his entire body.

All of a sudden, Wei Wuxian discovered how to enjoy himself in this position.

His limbs, his body, his breath—every part of him had melted into a wanton puddle. Wei Wuxian dug his hands into Lan Wangji's long hair, which was drenched with sweat, and smiled as he toyed with his forehead ribbon.

"...Does it feel good? Inside me?" he cooed in a tender voice.

When it came to this sort of endeavor, Lan Wangji was a man of action, not a man of words. He had no idea how to flirt. He worked hard and spoke little, so he bit Wei Wuxian's bottom lip and redoubled his thrusting to answer the question. Wei Wuxian was sweating profusely from the power of his movements.

"Lan Zhan. Lan Zhan, Lan Zhan, Lan Zhan...I like you so much. I'm yours, only yours... Easy!" As they say, extreme joy begets tragedies, and he turned to begging. "Take it easy, that's a sensitive spot right there, don't pound so hard, you're too strong, you're gonna break me, I'm a little sore... Yeah...that's it..."

Wei Wuxian hooked his arms around Lan Wangji's shoulders, and his legs moved higher around his waist. His body rocked along with Lan Wangji's as his insides were rearranged. His skin rubbed against the wild grass, and he gave a soft whine. After he caught his breath with effort, he let his mouth run loose once more.

"Lan Zhan, you're so good. You're beautiful, you're gorgeous.

You're good at playing the guqin, good at calligraphy, strong in spiritual power and cultivation, and *so* incredible in bed. Why are you so good? Man, do I love you..."

Lan Wangji was speechless.

At a time like this, it was as though Wei Wuxian had been born without shame. And the more explicit his words, the more excited he became.

"You're the only one I'll let fuck me. You can go as deep as you want..." He spread his legs further apart with frank honesty. "Go on, put it all the way in. I'm all yours, inside and out. The deeper you are the more I like it, and you can come inside too...*mmph!*"

Wei Wuxian was babbling to the point of forgetting himself when Lan Wangji suddenly dove to a terrifyingly unprecedented depth. Wei Wuxian's eyes widened instantly. He hadn't thought Lan Wangji *could* actually go any deeper. After letting loose a horrible yelp, he slumped and groaned.

"*Wahh...waahhh*, help, no, not like that, that's too much."

He wanted to curl up and escape this pounding—not that Lan Wangji would let him. He stretched Wei Wuxian out and pinned him in a deadly hold to continue with what had to be done.

"You...get what you deserve!" he gasped, savage fury evident in his voice.

Wei Wuxian whimpered as he spread his legs obediently to get fucked. "Ge, er-gege, I'm gonna die, you're gonna fuck me dead. I was wrong, it's my bad, don't punish me like this. It's my first time—! Be nicer to me..."

Beads of sweat dripped from the tips of Lan Wangji's hair. A rare trace of shame colored the expression of this cool, aloof man who never faltered in the face of catastrophe. He was on the verge of losing it.

"Are you actually begging for mercy or are you...doing this on purpose... Your waist! Stop twisting!"

Wei Wuxian raised his head and cried at the top of his lungs, "Somebody help! Hanguang-jun, he...*ah!* Hanguang-jun...I don't dare anymore..."

Lan Wangji kissed away the tears his thrusts had forced out of Wei Wuxian, and gritted broken words through his teeth. "...Wei Ying, I'm...being serious. Stop it. I...I really...can't control myself. I'm scared I'll... I'm sorry."

He still knew to apologize, even in a situation as mortifying as this—his face was flushed and his brows knitted, making him the very picture of contrition. Listening to him made Wei Wuxian's heart so soft and weak that he was reduced to a complete mess.

"Why are you apologizing?" he murmured. "Even if you fuck me to pieces, I'll still be happy because you're the one who did it... *nngghaahh...*"

The two were damp and glistening from head to toe. Wei Wuxian was never one to learn his lesson; he'd just paid dearly for running his mouth, but it didn't take long for him to lose control again and start spewing nonsense in the midst of his gasps.

"Lan Zhan, hey...I suddenly realized. You're done for. We still haven't done our last wedding bow, so we're not married yet. Doing something like this before we're married—do you know what that's called? If your uncle finds out...*hah*...he'll dunk you in a pig's cage."[2]

Lan Wangji let out an almost ferocious growl. "...I was already done for!"

---

2   *Referring to an archaic punishment for adultery, in which both perpetrators are locked in a cage used for transporting pigs and then drowned in a river.*

Hit with another vicious thrust, Wei Wuxian threw his head back in both pain and pleasure, exposing his defenseless throat. Lan Wangji bit down.

The overwhelming power of the pleasure he felt drove Wei Wuxian to his peak. His mind went blank, and he remained disoriented for a moment after. In his daze, the only thing he could think was, *I can't believe I didn't fucking do this with Lan Zhan when we were fifteen. So much damn time wasted.*

At the same time, Lan Wangji embraced him tightly as he came deep inside him.

Wei Wuxian raised his slightly limp arm and hugged him back with equal vigor. They embraced each other quietly for a while. When Wei Wuxian regained a bit of energy, he smeared the come on Lan Wangji's body, feeling fully satisfied.

As he spread it around with his finger, he asked, "Lan-er-gongzi, when did you start to like me?"

It was a terrible time for what he was doing, and a terrible place for it too. An unnatural look began to return to Lan Wangji's face.

"If you've liked me for so long, why didn't you fuck me sooner? The mountain at the back of your Cloud Recesses is a pretty good spot. Back then, you could've tied me up and dragged me away while I was sneaking around all alone in the wild, and then you could've had your way with me on the grass just like this...*hiss*...easy..."

Lan Wangji hadn't even pulled out before he began to move again. Wei Wuxian could feel something hot flowing out of where they were joined. He still continued to spout a nonstop stream of filth in Lan Wangji's ear.

"You're so strong, I definitely wouldn't have been able to fight back. If I'd yelled, you could've silenced me. No one would have come to my rescue even if I lost my voice from screaming. Or—that

Library Pavilion of yours is pretty good too. We could've laid the books out like a bed, rolled around on them, and referenced all the positions from the erotica. Any position you would've liked. I'd have bullied you during the day, and you'd have bullied me at night. We'd close the door and fuck each other into the ground... Ge! Ge! Er-gege! Mercy! Mercy, let me go. Okay, okay, okay, I'll stop. You're incredible, you're too strong. I can't take it, I really can't, stop..."

Lan Wangji couldn't bear his teasing at a time like this. This fierce battering was going to turn Wei Wuxian inside out. He softened his tune and began to nicely beg for mercy, but that only made Lan Wangji all the more aggressive.

He crushed Wei Wuxian in this way for over an hour. They did not change position even once, even as Wei Wuxian's waist and hips began to go numb. When the numbness passed, he became sore and itchy instead, as if a million insects were gnawing on his bones. The pleasure of release gradually dispersed, and what slowly replaced it was a feeling of fullness and pain. At last, he reaped what he had sowed.

Wei Wuxian tried to coax his favor with kisses, while pleading without a shred of dignity. "Er-gege, please have heart, let me live, we've still got a whole life ahead of us. Um—you can fuck me again next time. You could hang me up and fuck me, how about that? Let this poor baby virgin go, please? Hanguang-jun is almighty, the Yiling Patriarch has lost completely. Please finish up inside me already, we'll fight this out again another day."

Veins bulged on Lan Wangji's forehead, and he replied with immense difficulty, enunciating each word clearly. "...If you really want this to stop...then...shut up and stop talking..."

"But I was born with a mouth to speak," Wei Wuxian said. "Lan Zhan, when I said I wanted to sleep with you every day, can you pretend you never heard me?"

"No," Lan Wangji said.

"How can you be like this?" Wei Wuxian sounded heartbroken. "You've never denied me anything before."

A small smile played on Lan Wangji's lips. "No."

The smile made Wei Wuxian's eyes light up in an instant. It made him feel like he was floating. For a moment, he forgot where he was—but in the next moment, he was forced to tears once more by the powerful movements that were jarringly different from that smile as bright as light reflecting off snow.

His hands gripped the grass as he cried at the top of his lungs, "*Then four days!* Can we change it to once every four days? If four days won't do, we could do every three days too!"

Lan Wangji's voice was both strong and resonant as he declared: "Every day means every day."

Three months later, a group of villagers slowly began to surround the dense woods at the top of a mountain in Guangling. They had torches raised in their hands and wielded farming tools like instruments of defense.

There was an abandoned gravesite on the mountain—one that hadn't been too peaceful in recent months. The villagers at the foot of the mountain had been constantly disturbed by the ghosts wandering out of those very graves. At last, unable to endure it any longer, they sought the help of passing cultivators and climbed the mountain to banish the hauntings once and for all.

Night was falling. Insects droned ceaselessly in the tall wild grass, their cries loud and clear. It was as though there were unknown creatures creeping within the brush, waiting to strike at any given moment—but whenever the group plucked up enough courage to tensely approach with their torches and push aside the grass, it always proved to be nothing but a false alarm.

Swords at the ready, the cultivators cautiously led the villagers across the meadow and into the forest proper.

The abandoned gravesite was in the woods. The tombs were crafted of stone and wood, all currently either slanting or collapsed from the toll neglect had taken. The air was thick with eerie, sinister energy. The cultivators traded looks with each other, then produced talismans to get down to the business of clearing out evil. Seeing them appear at ease, the villagers sighed a breath of relief—it seemed the situation was not too fraught.

Before they could fully exhale that breath, however, there suddenly came a loud crash. A mutilated corpse had fallen onto a burial mound ahead of them.

The villager closest to the mound let out a horrified scream and hurled his torch forward before running away, stumbling and crawling. Soon after, a second bloody corpse came crashing down, then a third, a fourth—it was as if the sky was raining corpses, surrounding them with the deafening, nonstop thuds of falling bodies. Screams instantly rang out all around. The cultivators had never witnessed something like this before. In their shock, their courage deserted them.

"Don't run away! Don't panic!" the leader of the cultivators barked. "It's nothing but a puny evil..."

His sentence came to an abrupt stop before he could finish, like he'd been seized by the throat.

He had spotted a tree.

There was a man sitting at the top of said tree. The black hem of his robe hung free and his long, slender leg, clad in a black boot, swayed gently back and forth with the utmost leisure. He seemed to be completely at ease.

A dark flute was tucked into the man's waistband. A tassel as red as fresh blood dangled from one end, swaying with the movement of his leg.

The cultivators' expressions changed instantly.

The villagers had been in a frenzy of panic and confusion until the head cultivator's cry brought them some peace of mind. But now, they could only watch as every last cultivator blanched and bolted in an instant, charging like a whirlwind out of the forest and down the mountain, leaving them to their fate. The villagers, deducing that there had to be some sort of great and formidable evil on the mountain that even the cultivators could do nothing about, were also scared witless. Everyone scattered like fleeing birds and beasts.

One of the villagers was slow in his escape. As he lagged behind, he tripped and fell. Left alone with nothing but a mouthful of dirt, he was sure he would be dead in moments. Instead, his eyes lit up as he saw a man dressed in white standing before him.

A longsword hung at this man's waist. He seemed awash in a hazy white glow. Surrounded by the dark and haunting forest, he looked like a transcendental being, quite unlike any inhabitant of the secular world.

The villager immediately begged for his help. "Gongzi! Gongzi! Help, there are ghosts! Hurry, get rid of the ev..."

Another dead body fell in front of him before he could finish. Its face, which was bleeding from every orifice, was staring right at him.

Just as the villager was about to faint from fright, the man said to him, "Go."

Although it was merely a single word, the villager felt inexplicably reassured, like he'd been granted reprieve from death. A sudden burst of energy filled him, and he crawled to his feet and ran away without looking back.

The white-clad man glanced at the bloody corpses crawling all over the forest, apparently at a loss for words. He gazed upward, and the black-clad vagabond sitting in the tree hopped down lightly. In the blink of an eye, the black-clad man flashed in front of him and pinned him against a tree.

"Hmm? Isn't this the incorruptible Hanguang-jun, Lan Wangji?" he breathed out. "What are you doing on my turf?"

The ground was littered with bloody corpses, all looking either confused or savage as they struggled to crawl around. The black-clad man extended an arm and propped it against the tree, trapping Lan Wangji between him and the trunk. Lan Wangji remained expressionless.

The black-clad man let out a sigh. "Since you've delivered yourself to my doorstep, then I'll...hey, hey, hey!"

With but a single hand, Lan Wangji caught and locked both his wrists.

The tables had turned. "Oh heavens," the now-restrained black-clad man exclaimed in feigned surprise. "Hanguang-jun, you're too amazing. Incredible, shocking, unbelievable—you were actually able to subdue me with but one hand. I couldn't fight back at all! What a terrifying man!"

Lan Wangji had no comment.

His hand unconsciously gripped harder, and the black-clad man's astonishment turned into horror. "Ahh, ouch. Let me go, Hanguang-jun. I won't do it again. Don't grab me like that. You *mustn't* tie me up either, and *absolutely* do not pin me to the ground..."

As his words and actions grew increasingly exaggerated, Lan Wangji's eyebrows twitched. He finally spoke to interrupt him. "...Enough playing around."

Wei Wuxian had been enjoying himself begging for mercy. "Why?" he exclaimed, astonished. "I'm not done begging, though."

Lan Wangji was momentarily speechless before he chided, "You have been begging for mercy every day. Enough."

Wei Wuxian leaned into him. "Isn't that what you wanted…?" he whispered. "Every day means every day."

His face was extremely close, almost as if he was going to kiss Lan Wangji, but he refused to press their lips together so easily. He teased, suggesting he might close the gap, but never breaching that paper-thin distance. He was like an amorous but mischievous butterfly, fluttering as soft as a wispy breath over a dignified petal—flirting with perching, flirting with the promise of a kiss.

At being teased like that, Lan Wangji's light eyes flashed. He moved like he had finally lost control of himself—the petal reaching out to touch the butterfly's wings, unable to resist the temptation. But Wei Wuxian raised his head at once, evading his lips.

"Call me gege," Wei Wuxian said, his eyebrows arching high.

"…"

"Call me gege," he prompted again. "Call me gege and I'll let you kiss me."

"…"

Lan Wangji's lips moved slightly. Never in his life had he ever called another by an address that had such soft, tender connotations. He had only ever addressed even Lan Xichen with a methodical *"xiongzhang."*

"C'mon, let me hear it," Wei Wuxian pressed, tempting him. "I've called you that so many times already. Once you say it and kiss me, you can do other things too."

The word was already on the tip of Lan Wangji's tongue. But the moment he heard that, he was defeated by Wei Wuxian's teasing, and the word never left his mouth in the end.

After trying to restrain himself, he hissed through his teeth, "...Shameless!"

"Aren't you tired, holding me with a single hand like this?" Wei Wuxian said. "How inconvenient to only have one hand left to do business."

Composing himself, Lan Wangji asked politely, "Then please enlighten me on what to do."

"Lemme give you some pointers," Wei Wuxian said. "Take off your forehead ribbon and tie my hands. Wouldn't it be much easier like that?"

Lan Wangji quietly watched him giggle to himself, then slowly removed his forehead ribbon and showed it to Wei Wuxian. Next, he tied both of Wei Wuxian's hands with lightning speed. He pressed them firmly in place over Wei Wuxian's head before burying his face in the crook of his neck.

Just then, a frightened shriek suddenly came from the brush.

The two immediately broke apart. Lan Wangji placed his hand on Bichen's hilt but didn't recklessly unsheathe the sword, as the cry had been quite crisp and delicate—obviously that of a child. It would be terrible if he hurt a passerby by accident.

The tall thicket rustled, and the signs of movement shifted farther and farther away. It appeared whoever had screamed was making an escape.

Wei Wuxian and Lan Wangji had only pursued the rustling trail for a few steps when they heard a woman's joyful voice from the bottom of the hill.

"Mianmian, are you all right?! How could you run off in a place like this? You scared Mom half to death!"

Wei Wuxian was taken aback. "Mianmian?"

Just as he was reflecting on the familiarity of that name—

he was sure he'd heard it somewhere before—a man's scolding voice joined in.

"We told you not to run off during Night Hunts, but you still charged ahead on your own. What would your mom and I do if you got eaten by a ghost?! ...Mianmian? What's wrong? Why do you l ook like that?" His next sentence must've been directed at the woman. "Qingyang, quick, take a look. Is something wrong with Mianmian? Why does she look like that? Did she see something she shouldn't have up there?"

Well, she certainly had...seen what she shouldn't have.

Lan Wangji shot a look at Wei Wuxian. Wei Wuxian returned an innocent look and mouthed, *"How sinful of us."*

He clearly felt not a single shred of guilt or contrition for having corrupted a child. Lan Wangji shook his head. The two left the gravesite together and made their way down the hill.

The family of three were both shocked and alarmed as they watched the two of them emerge from the brush. The man and woman were a married couple, both crouched on the ground. Between them stood a little girl. Her hair was coiffed in double buns, and she appeared to be about ten years of age. The woman was charmingly beautiful, and a sword hung from her waist. At the sight of Wei Wuxian, she immediately drew her weapon and pointed the blade at him.

"Who are you?!" she demanded.

"Whoever we may be, we're human," Wei Wuxian answered.

The woman was about to say something else when she noticed Lan Wangji standing behind Wei Wuxian. She was instantly taken aback. "Hanguang-jun?"

Surprisingly, Lan Wangji wasn't wearing his forehead ribbon, which meant she couldn't be certain it was him for a moment.

She might have doubted it even longer, had it not been for his unforgettable looks. When her gaze moved back to Wei Wuxian, her face went blank for a moment.

"Then...then you are...you are..."

News of the Yiling Patriarch's return had already spread. Wei Wuxian wasn't surprised to be recognized—of course the person at Lan Wangji's side must be him. He did notice she looked vaguely excited and that she also seemed somewhat familiar.

Could this lady know me? he wondered to himself. *Is there some grudge between us? Did I ever provoke her in the past? That can't be. I don't know any girl named Qingyang...ahh, Mianmian!*

It clicked in Wei Wuxian's mind. "You're Mianmian?"

The man glared. "For what reason are you addressing my daughter?"

As it turned out, the little girl who had been running around and accidentally got an eyeful was Mianmian's daughter, whose name was also Mianmian.

Wei Wuxian found this quite fun. "One big Mianmian, one little Mianmian."

Lan Wangji bowed his head in greeting toward the woman. "Miss Luo."

The woman tucked some stray strands of hair behind her ear and returned the courtesy. "Hanguang-jun." Then she turned her gaze to Wei Wuxian. "Wei-gongzi."

Wei Wuxian smiled at the woman. "Miss Luo. I finally figured out your real name."

Luo Qingyang gave a somewhat shy smile, seeming embarrassed to recall the past. She pulled the man over and introduced him. "This is my husband."

Realizing the two weren't criminals, the man relaxed.

After exchanging some pleasantries, Wei Wuxian casually asked him, "And to which clan or sect does the gentleman belong?"

"None," the man answered very directly.

Luo Qingyang gazed at her husband with a smile. "My husband isn't a cultivator. He used to be a merchant, but he's willing to come on Night Hunts with me..."

An ordinary person—and a man, at that—who was willing to give up his stable life to wander the world with his wife, unafraid of travel and of danger. A heart like that was an extremely rare and valuable thing, and Wei Wuxian couldn't help but feel respect for the man.

"Have you also come here to Night Hunt?" Wei Wuxian asked.

Luo Qingyang nodded. "Yes. I heard there is evil haunting the abandoned gravesite on the peak of this mountain, disturbing the locals' lives and causing them great misery. So I wanted to come see if there was anything I could do. The two of you have already cleaned up the place, I'm assuming?"

There was no need for others to interfere if Wei Wuxian and Lan Wangji had taken care of the situation. However, Wei Wuxian said, "Those villagers lied to you."

Luo Qingyang blinked. "What do you mean?"

"They told outsiders that evil forces were causing the random disturbances, but it was actually thanks to them robbing the graves and making a mess of the decedents' bones," Wei Wuxian said. "That's why the masters of the abandoned gravesite fought back."

"Really?" Luo Qingyang's husband asked doubtfully. "But even if it was in retaliation for a crime, there was no need for them to take lives."

Wei Wuxian and Lan Wangji exchanged a look before Wei Wuxian explained further.

"That was also a lie. Not a single life has been lost, as we found during our investigation. A few of the grave-robbing villagers lost some sleep as they cowered in their beds in fear of the spirits, and there was only one actual injury, a villager who broke his leg while he was fleeing in panic. There were no casualties. Any 'lost lives' were fabricated to sensationalize the problem."

"Is that true? How shameless!" Luo Qingyang's husband exclaimed.

Luo Qingyang sighed. "Oh, those people..." She shook her head like she had just remembered something from the past. "They're the same everywhere."

"I gave them a scare earlier," Wei Wuxian said. "After tonight, they probably won't dare rob graves again, and the spirits won't go looking for trouble without provocation. Problem solved."

"But they had asked other cultivators to come and help them suppress..." Luo Qingyang started.

Wei Wuxian flashed a smile. "I showed my face."

Luo Qingyang understood. The Yiling Patriarch had shown his face, which meant the cultivators who'd seen him would surely tell everyone they could. They would assume he had claimed this area as his territory—and who would be audacious enough to provoke his ire?

"I see," Luo Qingyang laughed. "And here I thought Mianmian had had a run-in with some sort of evil creature, she looked so scared. Please forgive us if she was rude in any way."

No, no, no. We were probably the uncivil ones, Wei Wuxian thought, though he appeared perfectly serious on the outside. "Please don't worry about it. And please forgive us as well for scaring Xiao-Mianmian."

Luo Qingyang's husband picked up his daughter. Mianmian sat on her father's arm and scowled at Wei Wuxian with her cheeks puffed out, indignant but too embarrassed to say anything. She wore a little light-red skirt, and her dark purple eyes gleamed in her fair, adorable face like a pair of glistening grapes. Wei Wuxian really wanted to pinch her cheek. Alas, her father was watching him with great vigilance, so he tucked one hand behind his back and settled for squeezing one of her little hanging braids.

"Mianmian looks so much like you when you were little, Miss Luo," he said with a merry grin.

Lan Wangji cast him a glance, but said nothing. Amused, Luo Qingyang pursed her lips in a smile.

"Wei-gongzi, how can you say that with a clear conscience? Do you really remember what I looked like when I was young?"

That pursed-lip smile seemed to overlap in his memory with the expression worn by the young lady of years gone by, dressed in a red gauze robe. Wei Wuxian didn't feel embarrassed in the least.

"Of course I remember! You haven't changed that much. Oh yeah, how old is she? I'll give her some evil-repelling money."[3]

Luo Qingyang and her husband hastily declined. "Oh no, it's okay."

Wei Wuxian smiled. "Oh yes, please. It's not my money anyway, ha ha."

The couple looked slightly confused, but before they understood what he meant, Lan Wangji had already handed something to Wei Wuxian. Wei Wuxian took the heavy coins and was adamant on giving them to Mianmian as an offering of evil-repelling money.

Seeing that they couldn't decline, Luo Qingyang said to her daughter, "Mianmian, thank Hanguang-jun and Wei-gongzi."

---

3   When meeting someone of importance for the first time, it is customary to give a gift. When meeting children, the gift is usually something simple like petty cash. The word Wei Wuxian used is the archaic term for 压岁钱 [Sui/Year-Suppressing Money], also known as "hongbao" (red pocket/packets). These are gifts that signify good fortune which are given during Lunar New Year to subdue and repel the evil Sui [Year Beast].

"Thank you, Hanguang-jun," Mianmian said.

"Mianmian, I'm the one who gave you the money. Why didn't you thank me?" Wei Wuxian teased.

Mianmian shot him an angry glare and refused to talk to him no matter how he teased. Instead, she tugged on a red string around her neck, pulling out an exquisite little perfume sachet. With careful concentration, she dropped the coins inside like they were treasure.

They soon descended the mountain. With some regret, Wei Wuxian had no choice but to bid them farewell, as his and Lan Wangji's journey would take them down a different road.

As they disappeared into the distance, Luo Qingyang admonished her daughter. "Mianmian, you were so rude. He saved Mom's life in the past."

Her husband was astonished. "Really?! Mianmian, you hear that? See how rude you were!"

Mianmian pouted. "I...I don't like him."

"Gosh, child," Luo Qingyang sighed. "If you didn't like him, you would've thrown that evil-repelling money away."

Mianmian buried her little blushing face in her father's chest and humphed. "He was doing a bad thing!"

Caught between tears and laughter, Luo Qingyang was about to speak when her husband said with amazement, "Qingyang, I've heard you mention Hanguang-jun before. I remember him being a major figure in a prominent clan. Why did he show up in a tiny village like this to hunt such petty prey?"

"Hanguang-jun is different from other distinguished cultivators," Luo Qingyang patiently explained to her husband. "He always appears where there is chaos. If anyone is being tormented by evil forces, he will come to their aid—no matter the level of the Night Hunt's prey, or the accolades he receives."

Her husband nodded. "A cultivator truly worthy of renown." He continued nervously, "Then what about Wei-gongzi? You said he saved your life, but how come I've never heard you mention him? When in the past was your life in danger?!"

Luo Qingyang took Mianmian into her arms. She smiled, an odd light shimmering in her eyes. "Well…"

Back on the other road, Wei Wuxian said to Lan Wangji, "To think a young lady from way back then has a daughter now, who's also a young lady!"

"Mn," Lan Wangji replied.

"But that's not fair," Wei Wuxian said. "She should've clearly seen that it was *you* doing a bad thing to *me*. How come she can't stand the sight of me?"

Lan Wangji didn't respond. Wei Wuxian spun around to face Lan Wangji and started walking backward.

"Oh, I get it," he said as he walked. "Deep down, she actually likes me. Just like a certain someone back then."

Lan Wangji brushed nonexistent dust from his sleeves and said calmly, "Please return my forehead ribbon, Wei Yuandao."[4]

Wei Wuxian paused when he heard that foreign name. It took a while for it to hit him, and then he clicked his tongue before beginning to snicker. "I knew it. Oh, Lan-er-gongzi. Jealous, are we?"

Lan Wangji lowered his eyes. Wei Wuxian walked in front of him and blocked his path. With one arm circled around Lan Wangji's waist and one hand tilting his chin up, he said seriously, "Be honest.

---

4   An allusion to the same historical poem from which Wei Wuxian originally derived Luo Qing-yang's "Mianmian" nickname, *Mianmian si yuandao.*

For how many years have you guzzled the vinegar of jealousy? You hid it so well I didn't even smell the sourness."

Lan Wangji obediently raised his head as he'd always done, but suddenly felt an unruly hand slip into his breast pocket. He looked down, but Wei Wuxian had already pilfered what had been tucked inside.

Wei Wuxian feigned surprise. "What's this?"

It was Lan Wangji's money pouch. Wei Wuxian spun the exquisite little sachet by its tassels while pointing at him accusingly.

"Hanguang-jun, oh Hanguang-jun. Taking without asking is called stealing. And what did they call you back then—the descendant of a prestigious sect, the role model of the clan's juniors? Role model, indeed. You were chugging vinegar in secret. You even stole the perfume sachet a young lady gave me to use as your own money pouch. No wonder I couldn't find it anywhere after I woke up. If this sachet wasn't exactly the same as the one Xiao-Mianmian had, I wouldn't even have remembered. Look at you, *tsk tsk*. Tell me. How'd you swipe it off me when I was unconscious? How long did you feel me up?"

A ripple of emotion flashed over Lan Wangji's face. He reached out to snatch the pouch back, but Wei Wuxian swung it away and dodged his hand. He backed up a couple of steps.

"Trying to snatch it back since you can't win the argument? What are you so shy for? Why be embarrassed over this? Now I finally know why I can be this shameless. We're a match made in heaven. All the shame I *should* have is stored with you, and you're keeping it for me."

Light pink colored Lan Wangji's earlobes, but his expression was still pulled tight. His hands moved quickly, but Wei Wuxian's feet were faster; Lan Wangji could see the pouch but not catch it.

"You're the one who gave the money pouch to me in the past, so why are you trying to take it back now? Look at yourself. Stealing things, engaging in fornication, and going back on your word to boot. You're bad to the bone."

Lan Wangji tackled him, finally capturing him in his arms. "We have done our three bows. We are...married. It is not fornication," he countered.

"Even as a married couple, you can't keep coming at me with such force. Always making me beg, not even stopping when I do beg. Look how you've changed. The ancestors of the Lan Clan of Gusu are gonna be vexed to death..."

Unable to endure this any longer, Lan Wangji brutally sealed his lips.

The day after encountering Luo Qingyang and her family, the two of them reached a small town in Guangling.

Wei Wuxian raised a hand to his brow and saw a tavern banner fluttering in the distance.

"Let's take a break up ahead," he said.

Lan Wangji nodded, and the two walked there side by side.

Since that night at the Guanyin Temple in Yunmeng, Wei Wuxian and Lan Wangji had traveled together, wandering all over with Little Apple in tow. They still "appeared wherever there was chaos"—wherever there was talk of hauntings and evil disrupting people's lives, they would go to lend a helping hand. They'd also sightsee while they were at it and learn about the local culture. They had spent three months this way, shutting out all news of the cultivation world and living a carefree life.

After entering the tavern, they took a seat in an inconspicuous corner, and the waiter came over to greet them. He saw the sword at Lan Wangji's waist, then the flute at Wei Wuxian's. Because of their appearance and bearing, he couldn't help but connect them to the pair who had been the subject of all the most heated talk recently. But after staring at them intently for a while, he noticed that the customer dressed in white was not wearing the Lan Clan's forehead ribbon. Ultimately, he was left unsure of their identities.

Wei Wuxian asked for liquor while Lan Wangji ordered a few dishes. With one hand propping up his cheek and the other toying with a snow-white forehead ribbon under the table, Wei Wuxian listened to his deep voice as he read off the dishes. A wide grin was plastered on his face.

Once the waiter was gone, he commented, "So many spicy dishes. Can you eat them?"

Lan Wangji picked up the teacup on the table and took a sip. "Sit properly," he said evenly.

"There's no tea in there," Wei Wuxian pointed out.

Lan Wangji filled the cup, then raised it to his lips again. After a while, he repeated, "...Sit properly."

"Am I not? It's not like I'm propping my feet up on the table like I used to," Wei Wuxian said.

Lan Wangji could no longer bear it. "Even so, do not put them elsewhere."

Wei Wuxian was confused. "Where did I put them?"

"..."

"Lan-er-gongzi has so many demands. Why don't you teach me how to sit properly?"

Lan Wangji put down the teacup and cast him a look. He was about to rise in a whirl of sleeves in order to teach him a very proper lesson indeed—but just then, a table at the center of the main hall burst into a chorus of roaring laughter.

"I just knew Jin Guangyao was going to fall sooner or later, considering his way of doing things," someone at the table gloated. "I've waited for this day for so long, and now it's all been exposed. Hmph! That's what you call karma!"

Wei Wuxian found the man's jeering almost endearing—if you just changed the name of the one being insulted, it was incredibly familiar. He couldn't help but listen closely.

One of the cultivators raised his chopsticks. "It's true what they've said all through history! People like him—the brighter they look on the surface, the nastier they are behind the scenes!"

"That's right. Not a single one of them is genuinely good. Who among the 'venerable' and the 'gentlemen' aren't filth wearing a saintly skin for the world to see?"

Another cultivator was chewing large mouthfuls of meat and gulping down liquor. He spat it all everywhere as he spoke. "Speaking of which, that Sisi woman was super popular in the brothels back in the day. She looks so old now that I didn't even recognize her. Fucking revolting. The way Jin Guangshan died was pretty tragic too, ha ha ha ha ha..."

"Amazing that Jin Guangyao came up with a method like that to kill his dad. How perfectly fitting. Impeccable."

"See, now I'm curious. Why didn't Jin Guangyao kill that old prostitute? Witnesses should be eliminated—was he that stupid?"

"How would *you* know if he was being stupid? He was Jin Guangshan's spawn, maybe he was promiscuous too. Maybe he had unique tastes. Maybe he had...heh, a special relationship with Sisi?"

"Ha! I agree, but don't the rumors say that Jin Guangyao was so frightened by his sinful fornication with his blood sister that he wound up with a certain...unspeakable affliction? Even if he had the intent, he didn't have the power, know what I'm sayin'? Ha ha ha..."

This baseless gossip was extremely familiar. Wei Wuxian recalled there being countless people back in the day who talked about how he'd kidnapped a thousand virgins and locked them away in his demonic lair, the Burial Mounds—committing licentious deeds day and night to cultivate some great and evil magic. It had been oddly hilarious to hear.

All right, he thought. *At least what they said about me back then was a little better than what they're saying about Jin Guangyao now.*

The comments were growing increasingly revolting to hear, and Lan Wangji's brow furrowed. Thankfully, the more normal folks at the table also couldn't take it anymore.

"Keep it down..." one of the cultivators said in a hushed voice. "It's not like any of that is pleasant to hear."

But the cultivators who were laughing boisterously didn't care. "What's there to be afraid of? No one here knows us."

"Yeah! Besides, so what if anyone overhears? What're they gonna do about it?"

"You think the Jin Clan of Lanling is what it used to be? Can they shut people up? If they've got what it takes, let them try to dominate everyone like they did in the past. If they don't like it, they can shove it!"

Someone finally derailed the subject. "All right, all right, why keep on this topic? Eat, eat. No matter how many waves Jin Guangyao made while alive, all he can do now is fight with Nie Mingjue in that coffin."

"I gotta say, it sucks. When enemies meet, their hate blazes twice as hot. Nie Mingjue has probably shattered his bones to pieces by now."

"You got that right! I went to the coffin-sealing ceremony, and the resentment surrounding the casket was so heavy that not a single blade of grass grew within a five-hundred-meter radius! I wonder if that coffin can really keep them sealed for a whole century?"

"Whether it can has nothing to do with you. It's those clans' problem. Either way, the Jin Clan of Lanling is over. The winds have changed completely, I say."

"Zewu-jun looked so upset at the coffin-sealing ceremony."

"How could he not? Those are his two sworn brothers inside the coffin. The juniors back at his home are running around everywhere with a fierce corpse—they even actually need that fierce corpse to help them out during Night Hunts! No wonder he's been shutting himself away in seclusion all day. If Lan Wangji doesn't go home soon, Lan Qiren will probably start cursing in the streets for all to hear..."

Lan Wangji had no comment. Wei Wuxian snorted a laugh. The comments continued.

"Speaking of which, the ceremony was managed really well, eh? I've got new respect for Nie Huaisang. When he asked to be the one to take on the task, I thought he was gonna mess up for sure, being the Headshaker and all."

"Me too! Who would've thought he could direct it just as well as Lan Qiren?"

Listening to their surprise, Wei Wuxian thought, *That's nothing. In the next few decades, the family head of the Nie Clan of Qinghe may reveal his genius and have many more surprises in store for the world.*

The dishes were served, as was the liquor. Wei Wuxian poured himself a cup and drank it slowly.

Suddenly, a young man's voice said, "So is the Yin Tiger Tally inside the coffin or not?"

The tavern fell quiet.

Shortly after, someone answered, "Who knows, maybe. If Jin Guangyao didn't have the Yin Tiger Tally with him, where else would he have put it?"

"But it's not a sure thing. Didn't they say the Yin Tiger Tally is just a piece of scrap metal now? That it's useless at this point?"

The young man who spoke sat alone at a table, holding a sword in his arms. "Is the coffin really sturdy enough? What if someone wants to see if the Yin Tiger Tally is inside? What'll happen?"

"Who would dare?!" someone shouted immediately.

"The Nie Clan of Qinghe, the Lan Clan of Gusu, and the Jiang Clan of Yunmeng have all sent people to guard the cemetery grounds. Who would be so audacious?"

The people voiced their agreement. The young man said no more, but picked up the bowl of tea on the table to take a sip instead, seeming to have given up on the argument.

However, the look in his eyes did not change.

Wei Wuxian had seen that look in many people's eyes. And he also knew it wouldn't be the last time he'd see it.

After they left the tavern, they continued on their way. Wei Wuxian still rode on Little Apple's back, and Lan Wangji held the reins.

Swaying leisurely back and forth on the little spotted donkey, Wei Wuxian took out his flute and raised it to his lips. The instrument's crisp sound shot into the sky like a bird taking flight. Lan Wangji stopped and listened quietly.

It was the song he had once sung for Wei Wuxian, back when they were trapped inside the Cave of the Xuanwu of Slaughter. It was also the one Wei Wuxian had been curiously compelled to play on Mount Dafan. The song that had allowed Lan Wangji to confirm his identity.

At the end of the song, Wei Wuxian gave Lan Wangji a wink. "How was it? Not bad, right?"

Lan Wangji slowly inclined his head. "For once."

Wei Wuxian, knowing that "for once" was directed at his memory, couldn't help but smile. "Stop being so peeved about that. I was wrong, okay? Besides, it's my mom's fault that I have a bad memory."

"How so?" Lan Wangji asked.

Wei Wuxian rested his arms on Little Apple's head and spun Chenqing in one hand.

"My mom once said, 'You have to remember the good things people have done for you, instead of remembering the bad. A person's heart shouldn't be burdened with so many memories. That's how you live freely.'"

This advice was one of the few memories he had of his parents.

Wei Wuxian's mind wandered for a moment, but he quickly pulled himself back down to earth. Seeing Lan Wangji staring at him, he continued, "My mom also said..."

When he was slow to finish his thought, Lan Wangji prompted him. "Said what?"

Wei Wuxian beckoned him close with a waggle of his finger, wearing a solemn expression. Lan Wangji moved closer.

Wei Wuxian leaned down and whispered into his ear, "...Said you're already mine."

Lan Wangji quirked his eyebrows, but just as he was about to open his mouth to speak, Wei Wuxian cut in.

"Shameless, flippant, frivolous, arrogant, crazy, spewing nonsense again—right? There, I said it all for you. It's always the same words, over and over. You really haven't changed a bit. I'm yours too, so we're even now, all right?"

Lan Wangji would never win against Wei Wuxian when it came to running his mouth. "Whatever you say," he replied calmly.

Wei Wuxian tugged at the donkey's reins. "Seriously though, I've come up with over eighty names now for that song. Is there not a single one you like?"

"No," Lan Wangji said with conviction.

"Why? I thought 'Lan Zhan and Wei Ying's Ballad of Love' was pretty good."

Lan Wangji didn't respond. Wei Wuxian began to spew nonsense once more.

"'Hanguang-Yiling Every Day Song' is good too. It's a name that obviously has a story behind it..."

"There already is," Lan Wangji finally said, as if not wanting to hear any more names.

"There's already what?" Wei Wuxian asked.

"A name," Lan Wangji said.

Wei Wuxian was astonished. "You already named it? If you did, you should've said so sooner. What's it called? You wouldn't tell me all this time. And there I was, spending all that time helping you come up with names—what a waste of my imagination and smarts."

After a brief silence, Lan Wangji said, "'Wangxian.'"

"Huh?"

"The name of the song is 'Wangxian,'" Lan Wangji repeated.

Wei Wuxian's eyes widened.

Then he burst out laughing, hugging his belly.

"Ha ha ha ha ha ha ha ha ha ha, no wonder you refused to tell me. It's because you sneakily titled it that—your intentions were clear. Good going, Lan Zhan. When did you come up with that? Ha ha ha ha ha ha ha ha ha..."

Lan Wangji seemed to have predicted this would be Wei Wuxian's reaction. He shook his head slightly as he watched him swaying forward and backward on Little Apple's back. He appeared resigned, but there was a subtle upward curve to his lips and an obscure look rippling in his eyes.

He reached out and set a hand on Wei Wuxian's waist to prevent him from tumbling off the donkey's back. When he'd finally had his fill of laughter, Wei Wuxian said seriously, "'Wangxian' is very good. Excellent! I like it. Yes, that's what it should be called."

"I like it too," Lan Wangji replied stoically.

"It sounds very elegant and righteous, very suited to the Lan Clan of Gusu," Wei Wuxian said. "I think it can go straight into your family's score collection, and we'll demand every Lan disciple learn it. If they ask you, 'Hanguang-jun, how should the title be interpreted?' you can tell them how the song came to be."

Seeing that he'd started spewing nonsense again, Lan Wangji gathered Little Apple's tether and carefully gripped the rope as they continued onward. Wei Wuxian continued to talk.

"So where are we going next? I haven't had Emperor's Smile in a long time. How about we go back to Gusu and make a trip to Caiyi Town?"

"Okay," Lan Wangji replied.

"It's been so long, the Waterborne Abyss must be cleaned out by now, right? If your uncle manages to work up the tolerance to meet me, we can hide my liquor jugs in your room. If he refuses to grant me an audience, we can go somewhere else. It sounds like Sizhui and the boys and Wen Ning are doing well on Night Hunts."

"Mn," Lan Wangji said.

"But apparently there's a new edition of the Lan Clan of Gusu's precepts? Seriously, is there even room left to write anything else on that Wall of Discipline near the front gates of your place...?"

A fresh breeze blew past, and their robes rippled with it like spring water.

Facing the wind, Wei Wuxian watched Lan Wangji's back as they went. He squinted his eyes, crossed his legs, and was astonished to find he could actually maintain his balance on Little Apple's back in such a quaint position.

It was such a boring, minor thing, but he was as eager to share it with Lan Wangji as if he'd discovered something new and interesting.

"Lan Zhan," he called. "Look at me. Quick, look at me!"

Wei Wuxian was calling to him with a smile on his lips. Just as he always had, Lan Wangji looked at him.

And forever after, his eyes could never move away from him again.

THE END

"**W**AIT FOR ME," said Lan Wangji to Wei Wuxian.

"Why don't I go in with you after all?" Wei Wuxian replied.

Lan Wangji shook his head. "His ire will only grow if you should come."

Wei Wuxian thought about it and realized he was right. Every time Lan Qiren saw him, the latter withered like a candle in the wind, as though on the verge of heart failure. Even his breathing would grow more labored than usual. The only compassionate thing to do would be to stay out of sight, out of mind.

Lan Wangji looked at him like he wanted to say something further.

"All right, I know," said Wei Wuxian, quickly. "No hurried walking, no clamoring, no whatever, right? Relax. I'll be more careful than ever, this time. I won't violate a single family precept on the Wall of Discipline...or I'll try, anyway."

"It is fine," answered Lan Wangji, reflexively. "Even if you were to break the rules..."

"Hmm?" Wei Wuxian said, catching on at once.

Lan Wangji seemed to realize how inappropriate what he had blurted out was. He turned his head away for a moment before glancing back. "...Nothing," he said sternly.

"What did you just say?" asked Wei Wuxian in feigned ignorance. "'Even if I were to break the rules,' what?"

Lan Wangji knew he was just teasing him. "Wait for me outside," he repeated with a stern look.

Wei Wuxian waved him off. "Fine, I'll wait. So mean. I'll go play with your bunnies."

And so Lan Wangji went alone to receive Lan Qiren's flying spittle, while Wei Wuxian was dragged by Little Apple into a mad dash across the Cloud Recesses. Little Apple had been particularly excited ever since they entered the Cloud Recesses and was full of bullish energy. Wei Wuxian couldn't rein it in no matter how he tried, but was forcibly dragged over to a meadow of lush green grass.

Over a hundred chubby snowballs quietly huddled there. Their pink noses twitched, and every so often, their long, pink-centered ears would twitch as well. With its head held high, Little Apple squeezed itself among them and soon found a place to rest.

Wei Wuxian crouched down and caught a rabbit. *Were there this many of them the last time I came?* he wondered as he tickled its tummy. *Is this one a male or a female? Oh... Male.*

It was then that Wei Wuxian realized that he'd never actually paid attention to whether Little Apple was a jack or a jenny. He couldn't help but cast a glance at the donkey, but didn't have a chance to solve that particular mystery before a sudden movement made him turn to look.

A petite young girl with a little basket stood there, hesitating about whether to approach. When she saw Wei Wuxian turn his head so abruptly to stare at her, she flushed bright red, clearly at a loss for what to do. She wore the Lan Clan of Gusu's uniform and had a plain white forehead ribbon without the rolling clouds properly fastened around her head.

Oh damn! *They do exist!*

This was a female cultivator. A female cultivator of the Lan Clan of Gusu.

The Lan Clan of Gusu was known for their rigid, conservative ways. Rules such as 'men and women are different' or 'men and women must not touch' were unquestioningly and unceasingly drilled into the ears of the disciples from the time they were young. The study halls and living quarters of male and female cultivators were all strictly separated; they were forbidden to take a single step across those boundaries and seldom left their own areas. Even Night Hunts were essentially divided by gender—parties consisted of either all men or all women. Instances where men and women mingled were virtually nonexistent. It was outrageously conservative.

When Wei Wuxian had studied at the Cloud Recesses all those years ago, he'd never seen any girls. He'd been deeply suspicious of whether there even *were* any girls in the Cloud Recesses. Every so often, he'd think he heard the sound of female cultivators reciting their lessons and attempt to hunt for them to satisfy his curiosity. Every time, he would be discovered immediately by a sharp-eyed and sharp-eared patrol, who would then call forth Lan Wangji. After experiencing this sequence enough times, Wei Wuxian lost interest and never ventured out in search of the ladies again.

But now he had run right into a real, live female cultivator here at the Cloud Recesses. A live! Female! Cultivator!

Wei Wuxian instantly straightened, eyes gleaming. He was about to move toward her, but Little Apple beat him to it—shoving itself to its feet, it practically knocked him out of the way as it rushed to the girl's side.

Wei Wuxian was baffled.

Little Apple pressed itself to the girl, then demurely delivered its donkey head and donkey ears under her hand of its own accord.

Wei Wuxian was absolutely flummoxed.

The girl looked flushed and a little stunned, and she stared at Wei Wuxian, tongue-tied. Wei Wuxian peered back at her, realizing she looked vaguely familiar. The memory came back all at once. Wasn't she the round-faced girl he had met briefly several times in passing, first on the road after he left the Mo Estate, then later at Mount Dafan?

He could immediately break the ice with playful banter with complete strangers, never mind a nice young lady he'd met several times before. He waved at her without hesitation.

"It's you!"

It seems he had left a strong impression, with or without makeup on his face. The girl dithered, twisting the basket in her hands.

"It's me…" she said at last, in a small voice.

Wei Wuxian tossed aside the rabbit—which was, as he'd determined, male—and took a couple steps toward the girl with his hands clasped behind him. Noticing the carrots and lettuce in her basket, he smiled. "Here to feed the rabbits?"

The girl nodded. There wasn't much to do with Lan Wangji gone, so Wei Wuxian's interest was piqued.

"Want some help?"

The girl didn't know what to do except, finally, just nod. Wei Wuxian took one of the carrots, and the two of them crouched among the rabbits. Little Apple stuck its head into the basket to rummage around. When it found no apples, it reluctantly settled for a carrot, mouthing it out of the basket and chomping it down.

The carrots in the basket were very fresh. Wei Wuxian took a bite of one himself before placing it next to a rabbit's mouth.

"Have you been the one feeding them this whole time?" he asked.

"No..." answered the girl. "I only started recently... When Hanguang-jun is around, he's the one who looks after them. When he's not around, Young Master Lan Sizhui and his group do it. If they're not around either, then we help..."

How does Lan Zhan feed rabbits? wondered Wei Wuxian. *How old was he when he started keeping them? Did he have a little basket too?*

He shooed away the ridiculously cute image in his head. "You're a disciple of the Lan Clan, now?"

"Yes," answered the girl, shyly.

"The Lan Clan is nice," Wei Wuxian said. "When did that happen?"

The girl stroked a white furry rabbit. "Not long after the incident at Mount Dafan—"

Just then, they both heard the soft sound of boots on grass. Wei Wuxian turned his head. Sure enough, Lan Wangji was making his way toward them.

Flustered, the girl quickly stood and bowed with the utmost respect.

"Hanguang-jun."

Lan Wangji nodded lightly in return. In contrast, Wei Wuxian remained sitting on the grass and watching him with a grin. The girl seemed awfully scared of Lan Wangji, which was perfectly normal—there wasn't a junior her age who wasn't scared of him.

She lifted her skirt and ran off in a panic.

"Miss! Little meimei!" Wei Wuxian called after her. "Your basket! Hey, Little Apple! Come back, Little Apple! Why are you running too?! Little Apple!"

He could stop neither girl nor donkey. Wei Wuxian flicked the carrots left in the basket. "Lan Zhan, you scared her off," he said.

If Lan Wangji had not wanted them to hear his footfalls, how could they have ever heard him coming?

Wei Wuxian grinned cheekily and offered him a carrot. "Want a bite? You feed the rabbits, and I'll feed you."

"...On your feet," said Lan Wangji, looking down at him imperiously.

Wei Wuxian tossed the carrot over his shoulder and extended his hand lazily.

"Pull me up."

After a brief pause, Lan Wangji reached out to take his hand. To his surprise, however, Wei Wuxian threw his weight back and pulled him down instead.

With their territory overtaken by some strange man, the bunnies behaved like they faced a great foe, running in frantic, aimless circles around the two people sprawled on the ground. The few that were particularly close with Lan Wangji actually stood up and clung to him, as if they were worried why their master would suddenly collapse. Lan Wangji gently shooed them away.

"The seventh rule upon the Wall of Discipline at the Cloud Recesses," he recited methodically. "Do not disturb the female cultivators."

"You said it's fine if I break the rules," Wei Wuxian said.

"I did not," Lan Wangji said.

"Why are you like this? Just because you didn't finish your sentence, it didn't count? What happened to the Hanguang-jun who always kept his word?"

"Every day," Lan Wangji stated.

Wei Wuxian stroked Lan Wangji's face. "Did your shufu yell at you earlier?" he asked pityingly. "Tell me all about it. Let gege comfort you."

The change of subject was quite blatant, but Lan Wangji didn't call him out. "No."

"Really? He didn't?" Wei Wuxian asked. "Then what *did* he say to you?"

Lan Wangji hugged him without batting an eyelid. "Not much. To gather the whole clan can be a trial. A family banquet will be held tomorrow."

"A family banquet?" echoed Wei Wuxian with a grin. "Good, good. I'll be on my best behavior and won't let you down." He suddenly thought of Lan Xichen. "What about your brother?"

There was a moment's silence. "I will go see him later," said Lan Wangji.

Zewu-jun had been perpetually in seclusion of late. Lan Wangji undoubtedly needed to have a long, heart-to-heart talk with him. Wei Wuxian put his arms around Lan Wangji and patted his back gently.

"Speaking of which," he said, after a while. "How come I didn't see Sizhui and the others when we got here?"

In the past, that group of juniors would have been at the mountain entrance as they arrived, waiting to crowd around them in a flurry of chatter. At the mention of Sizhui and the others, Lan Wangji's brow relaxed a little.

"I will take you to see them."

When he brought Wei Wuxian to visit Lan Sizhui, Lan Jingyi, and the others, the juniors could do little more than make the barest exclamations of delight. It wasn't that they didn't *want* to react more—just that they physically *couldn't*.

A dozen of them were doing handstands under the eaves. All of them had shed their outer robes, stripped down to their snow-white light shirts as they stood with their heads down and feet up. Several pieces of white paper and inkstones lay on the ground before them, and they each struggled to commit dense black characters to the pages with their right hands while balancing on their left.

As they couldn't let their forehead ribbons fall to the ground, they held the tail ends in their mouths as they sweated profusely, which also meant they couldn't speak. The so-called "barest exclamations of delight" were simply a series of bright-eyed, *"Mm, mm, mm!"*s.

As he surveyed the bodies teetering on the verge of collapse, Wei Wuxian had to ask, "Are the handstands necessary?"

"They are being punished," Lan Wangji answered.

"I know they're being punished," said Wei Wuxian. "I can see they're copying the Lan Clan's family precepts—heck, I can recite 'Standard Etiquette' from memory myself for the same reason. What did they do to be punished?"

"They did not return to the Cloud Recesses within the expected time," answered Lan Wangji coolly.

"Oh," said Wei Wuxian.

"They went on a Night Hunt with the Ghost General at their side," Lan Wangji added.

"Heh!" remarked Wei Wuxian. "You guys sure have guts."

"It was their third offense," added Lan Wangji.

Wei Wuxian stroked his chin. If that was the case, they couldn't blame Lan Qiren for punishing them like this. The man loathed wickedness in all forms. In fact, to be copying texts while doing handstands...they were getting off pretty light.

He squatted in front of Lan Sizhui. "Sizhui, why does your stack seem particularly thick? Am I hallucinating?"

"No..." Lan Sizhui said.

"He led the expedition," Lan Wangji explained.

Wei Wuxian wanted to pat Lan Sizhui's shoulder, but with the position the boy was in, there was nowhere for him to settle his hand. After a pause, he lowered his hand and patted him with an upward motion.

"I knew it," he said.

Lan Wangji walked along the line of boys, sparing them a few glances as he checked their work. "Your characters," he said to Lan Jingyi. "The strokes are not straight."

"Yes, Hanguang-jun," answered Lan Jingyi in a muffled voice—forehead ribbon in his teeth and tears in his eyes. "I'll recopy this sheet."

Those who had not been singled out all heaved a sigh of relief. They'd passed muster.

The two of them left the long corridor. Wei Wuxian recalled all the hard times when he himself had been forced to copy texts for punishment, and his heart went out to his fellow penitents. "It's already hard enough to maintain that position. Even I might not be able to write if you made me do it in a handstand. Heck, I can't even consistently write straight when I'm sitting down."

Lan Wangji glanced at him. "Indeed."

Wei Wuxian knew Lan Wangji remembered those days too—he'd kept close watch on him while he copied texts. "Was it like this when you had to copy texts for punishment as a child?"

"I never had to," Lan Wangji said.

That sounded about right. Ever since he was a child, Lan Wangji had been the role model for the juniors of the prominent clans. Every word he uttered and every action he took was incomparably precise and standard, like it had been measured with a ruler. So how could he err? And since he couldn't err, how could he be punished?

"And here I thought that was how you developed that terrifying arm strength of yours," Wei Wuxian said with a laugh.

"I was never punished," Lan Wangji said. "But that was how I trained."

"Why would you do handstands if you weren't being punished?" wondered Wei Wuxian.

"It calms the mind," answered Lan Wangji, looking straight ahead.

Wei Wuxian leaned in close to his ear. There was a lilt at the end of his words as he asked, "Then I wonder what it is that can *perturb* the mind of our cold-as-ice Hanguang-jun?"

Lan Wangji looked at him and said nothing. Pleased with himself, Wei Wuxian continued, "Going by what you said, that's how you trained your arms since you were little. Does that mean you can do anything upside down?"

"Mn."

Seeing him with his eyes downcast, almost shy in his answer, Wei Wuxian couldn't help but run his mouth. "Could you screw me upside down?"

"Let us try," Lan Wangji said.

Wei Wuxian laughed aloud. "Ha ha ha ha ha ha... Wait, what?"

"Let us try it tonight," Lan Wangji elaborated.

Wei Wuxian was dumbfounded.

That said, they did not immediately get the chance to "try it" that night. Lan Wangji first needed to have a heart-to-heart with Lan Xichen, who had been in seclusion for a long time.

Wei Wuxian had developed a strange habit lately—he liked to sleep *on* Lan Wangji, whether stacked atop him or cuddled face-down against his chest. Without his living mattress, he couldn't sleep. Instead, he brazenly rummaged around the Tranquility Room, turning up countless objects of interest.

Lan Wangji had been proper and rigid in all he did, ever since he was a child. Calligraphy he had practiced, paintings he had drawn, essays he had written—they were all neatly categorized and sorted by year. Wei Wuxian decided to look at the calligraphy sheets first, starting from when Lan Wangji was at his youngest. He chuckled with relish as he flipped through them. The sight of Lan Qiren's red-cinnabar-inked annotations made him wince, but Wei Wuxian found only one piece of paper with an erroneously written character in the thousands of sheets he flipped through. After making that mistake, Lan Wangji had studiously copied the incorrect character a hundred times on another piece of paper in the back. Seeing it nearly rendered Wei Wuxian speechless.

"Poor thing...he must have copied that word until he could barely recognize it anymore."

He was about to continue looking through the aged, faintly yellowed papers when a dim light flickered to life in the darkness of the night outside the Tranquility Room. Though he did not hear footsteps, Wei Wuxian rolled with practiced familiarity onto Lan Wangji's bed and pulled the blanket from his feet to his head. By the time Lan Wangji gently pushed the door open and entered, the facade that greeted him was the sight of a man sleeping soundly.

Lan Wangji was moving soundlessly to begin with, but seeing Wei Wuxian already "asleep," he reined in his breathing as he slowly shut the doors. After a moment of silence, he approached the bed.

Before he drew near, a blanket flew at his face and covered his upper body completely.

Lan Wangji was struck speechless.

Wei Wuxian jumped off the bed and wrapped his arms tightly around the still-covered Lan Wangji, then pushed him onto the bed. *"Rape!"*

Lan Wangji remained speechless.

Wei Wuxian crassly groped and tugged on every inch of Lan Wangji's body, but Lan Wangji lay there in silence like a dead man and simply let him do as he pleased. After a while, Wei Wuxian lost interest.

"Hanguang-jun, won't you resist even a little bit? Where's the fun if you just lay there like that?"

A muffled voice came through the blanket. "What would you most prefer I do?"

Wei Wuxian walked him patiently through the scenario, step by step. "When I hold you down, push back and don't let me pin you. Close your legs and struggle with all your might, and while you do so, scream for help at the top of your lungs..."

"Clamor is prohibited in the Cloud Recesses," Lan Wangji stated.

"Then scream for help quietly," Wei Wuxian said. "Also, when I tear off your clothes, do your very best to keep me at bay. Cover and protect your chest for dear life. Don't let me tear off anything."

There was momentary silence from under the blanket.

"That sounds complicated," said Lan Wangji, at last.

"*That's* complicated?!" Wei Wuxian blurted.

"Mn," Lan Wangji affirmed.

"Nothing for it, then," Wei Wuxian said. "Let's switch. You can rape me instead—"

He'd barely finished his sentence before the world was sent spinning and the blanket was sent flying. Lan Wangji had already pinned him to the bed.

Lan Wangji had been stuffed under the blanket for some time. His immaculately secured hair and forehead ribbons had been knocked askew, and a few tousled locks dangled free. His fair-as-jade cheeks were slightly flushed. Under the lamplight, he looked very much like a shy and timid beauty—unfortunately, this beauty was unbelievably strong and had a grip like a vise, which squeezed Wei Wuxian until he begged for mercy.

"Hanguang-jun, Hanguang-jun, a great man is magnanimous."

Lan Wangji's gaze didn't waver, but the blazing light reflected in his eyes quivered almost imperceptibly. Wearing an indifferent expression, he loftily answered, "Very well."

"'Very well' what?" asked Wei Wuxian. "Handstand? Rape? Hey! My clothes!"

"It is as you said yourself," said Lan Wangji.

With that, he planted himself between Wei Wuxian's legs and pressed against him. But though Wei Wuxian waited for a long time, he proceeded no further. "What's wrong?!"

Lan Wangji rose slightly. "Why did you not resist?" he asked.

Wei Wuxian clamped down on his waist with his legs and ground slowly against him, refusing to let him leave. He grinned cheekily and sighed. "What can I do? The moment you bear down on top of me, my legs can't help but spread on their own. I can't close them at all. Where would I find the strength to resist? It might be tough for you, but it's tough on me too... Hold on, hold on. Come, come. Here. Let me show you something." He fished a piece of paper out of his robes. "Lan Zhan, let me ask you something. How could you miswrite such a simple character? Were you really concentrating on your studies? Where was your head that day?"

Lan Wangji cast a glance at the paper and said nothing, but the meaning in his gaze was all too obvious. The nerve of Wei Wuxian—the King of Mistakes and Omissions, who wrote in wild cursive when he copied texts and cut corners whenever he could—to criticize him for writing one character wrong!

Wei Wuxian pretended he didn't understand that look. "Look at the day, month, and year you wrote on this piece. Let's see...you would've been fifteen or sixteen then, right? Fifteen or sixteen years old and still making a mistake like that. You..."

But when he considered the inscribed date a little more carefully, he realized that it fell within the three months he had spent studying in the Cloud Recesses.

Wei Wuxian was beside himself with joy. "Could it be that the young Lan-er-gege couldn't focus on his studies because he could think of nothing but me?" he wheedled deliberately.

Back when Wei Wuxian had been sentenced to copying texts in the Library Pavilion as punishment, he'd spent the whole day going buck wild, playing dead, harassing Lan Wangji in every imaginable way. He made such a fuss that Lan Wangji had had not a moment of peace—it would have been impossible for him to *not* think about Wei Wuxian, except they weren't the kind of thoughts Wei Wuxian was suggesting. The circumstances having been what they were, it was admirable that Lan Wangji had endured so much as he supervised him and come away with but a single error.

"Hey, why is it my fault again?" Wei Wuxian lamented. "Sure, *I'm* the one to blame."

"...Your fault!" Lan Wangji muttered.

His breathing stuttered as he grabbed for the page that was such a blemish on his life. Wei Wuxian loved seeing him forced to the point of being flustered. He shoved the paper down the front of his robes to hide it against his skin. "Come and get it, if you think you can."

Lan Wangji reached his hand down without hesitation.

And never bothered to take it out.

"Guess you can!" Wei Wuxian exclaimed.

They went on to spend more than half the evening messing around, and it was only much later in the night that they finally managed to have a proper conversation.

Wei Wuxian was sprawled atop Lan Wangji's body, his face buried in the crook of his neck, where the sandalwood scent grew all the more ambrosial. He felt languid from head to toe, his eyes squinted into crescents of contentment.

"How's your brother?" he asked.

Wrapping his arms around Wei Wuxian's bare back, Lan Wangji stroked along it over and over again. After a moment of silence, he answered, "Not well."

Both of them were damp with sweat. Lan Wangji's touch stirred up an itch that started in Wei Wuxian's skin and migrated to the very depths of his heart. Made somewhat uncomfortable by the sensation, he twisted and took Lan Wangji even deeper inside him.

"In my seclusion years ago, xiongzhang offered me an ear," Lan Wangji said in a low voice.

And now, their positions had been reversed.

As for what Lan Wangji did during his years in seclusion, Wei Wuxian no longer had to ask. He dropped a kiss on Lan Wangji's jade-white earlobe and drew the blanket up over them both.

Even so, Lan Wangji woke up promptly at mao time the next morning.

Living together these past few months, Lan Wangji had dedicated himself to correcting Wei Wuxian's daily habits. These efforts were invariably in vain.

He was already tidily dressed when a disciple brought warm water for bathing, and he pried a stark-naked Wei Wuxian from under the thin blanket and carried him to the bathtub. Wei Wuxian, however, could stay asleep even as he soaked in the water. As Lan Wangji nudged him gently, Wei Wuxian grabbed his hand, planted a few kisses upon its back and the center of its palm, nuzzled his cheek against it, and continued to doze. When the prodding began to annoy him, he grunted twice. With his eyes still closed, he pulled Lan Wangji down in order to cup his face and drop a few kisses there.

"Stop it, be a good boy," he mumbled. "Pleeease? I'll get up in a bit, m'kay?"

Then he yawned, leaned over the side of the bathtub, and went back to sleep.

Although he knew Wei Wuxian would probably just roll over and remain asleep even if the building was on fire, Lan Wangji still insisted on trying to wake him up every morning at mao time—and he received no less than sixty haphazard kisses in the process, all of which he accepted without batting an eye.

Lan Wangji brought breakfast back to the Tranquility Room and set it on the desk that had once held only brushes, papers, ink-sticks, and ink-slabs. Then he fished a still half-asleep Wei Wuxian from the wooden tub, wiped him clean, dressed him, and fastened his sash. Only after that did Lan Wangji take a book from the bookcase, flip to the page bookmarked by a dried flower, and then settle by the desk to read it slowly.

Sure enough, Wei Wuxian sat up straight toward the end of si time, as punctual as ever. He felt his way off the bed like a sleepwalker. Groping around for Lan Wangji before all else, he dragged him into his arms for a couple of caresses, then pinched his thigh out of habit. It was only after a quick wash that he was finally a little more awake. He felt his way over to the desk and chomped down on an apple, finishing it in a few bites. Seeing the meal box packed to the brim with food, the corner of Wei Wuxian's mouth twitched.

"Isn't there a family banquet today? Is it okay to eat so much ahead of time?"

Lan Wangji calmly straightened his hair and forehead ribbons, which Wei Wuxian had knocked askew earlier. "You must fill your stomach first."

Wei Wuxian had had the "pleasure" of sampling the food of the Cloud Recesses back in the day. Simple and bland, with vegetable dishes at the forefront, it was a never-ending expanse of green. Tree bark, grass roots, and various medicinal herbs—every dish was overwhelmingly bitter, with a bizarrely sweet aftertaste. If not for that, Wei Wuxian would never have toyed with the idea of roasting those two rabbits back in their school days. A Lan family banquet was unlikely to be filling or satisfying.

He knew the Lan Clan of Gusu attached great importance to these gatherings. Whether or not they allowed him to attend the family banquet would functionally indicate whether they acknowledged his status as Lan Wangji's cultivation partner. Lan Wangji must have pestered Lan Qiren for a long time, fighting for his right to attend.

Wei Wuxian sighed heavily and put on a smile. "Don't worry. I'll be on my best behavior and won't disgrace you."

While it might have been called a family "banquet," the Cloud Recesses' version of such an event was completely different from anything Wei Wuxian had once known.

For the Jiang Clan of Yunmeng's family banquets, over a dozen large square tables would be set up in Lotus Pier's open-air training grounds. Men and women, young and old—everyone sat together as they pleased, formality falling by the wayside. They would move the kitchen outside, lining up a row of pots and stoves. The flames would light up the sky, and the aroma of food would permeate the air. Anything they wanted to eat, they would go over and get themselves, and if there wasn't enough food, more would be cooked on the spot.

While he had never attended the family banquets of the Jin Clan of Lanling, the Jins had never demurred at sharing the details of their mind-boggling extravagance—sword dances by renowned experts to liven things up, ornamental topiaries and jade pools filled with liquor, fifty kilometers of red brocade paving the ground, and more.

In comparison, the family banquet of the Cloud Recesses was neither boisterous nor extravagant.

The education and upbringing of the Lan Clan of Gusu had always been terrifyingly strict, with countless rules—*"Food is taken in silence," "Rest is taken in silence,"* and so on. Even though the banquet had yet to start, no one in attendance said a word. Other than the hushed greetings and bows those who entered the hall gave their elders, almost no one spoke, let alone joked or laughed. The same white clothes, the same white cloud-patterned ribbons, the same stiff and solemn expressions—it was as if they had all been cast from the same mold.

Seeing the entire hall decked out in enough white for a full memorial procession, Wei Wuxian pretended not to notice the looks of astonishment and hostility from the other attendees as he grumbled inwardly, *Is this a family banquet? Why is it even more lifeless than a funeral?*

At that moment, Lan Xichen and Lan Qiren entered the banquet hall. Lan Wangji, who had been sitting quietly beside Wei Wuxian, finally moved as he saw them arrive.

Because Lan Qiren had a conniption every time he saw Wei Wuxian, he simply chose not to acknowledge his presence, keeping his eyes trained forward instead. Lan Xichen was as pleasant as ever, with a hint of a smile playing at the corners of his lips. Though the very sight of him made one feel warm and at ease, like basking in a spring breeze, Wei Wuxian couldn't help but wonder if seclusion had taken its toll—Zewu-jun seemed a lot thinner than before.

After the head of family took his seat, Lan Xichen spoke a few brief, polite words before the banquet commenced.

The first course served was soup.

Taking soup before a meal was traditional in the Lan Clan of Gusu. The bowl was a simple black lacquered cup that fit in the palm and was smooth to the touch. Wei Wuxian opened the tiny, exquisite lid and peeked inside. Sure enough, it was yet another heaping pile of bark, grass roots, and green and yellow leaves. Though just looking at it made his eyebrows twitch, he scooped a spoonful into his mouth.

He had mentally prepared himself beforehand, and still couldn't help but close his eyes and clutch his forehead. It was a long time before he finally recovered from that massive shock to his senses and was able to lever himself up onto his elbows, though with some difficulty.

...If the Lan Clan's ancestor was a monk, he must have been an ascetic monk.

He longed for a Jiang family banquet, for the big pot brimming with lotus root and pork ribs soup that was served on Lotus Pier's training grounds. The aroma of meat and lotus root would waft for five kilometers around, luring in the nearby children, who would lean over the courtyard wall to peek in, salivating. When they returned home, they would cry and yell that they were going to join the Jiang Clan of Yunmeng as disciples.

By comparison, Wei Wuxian didn't know who to pity more—himself, with a mouth full of bittersweetness, or Lan Wangji, who'd grown up eating this.

The rest of the Lan family had finished their medicinal soup without so much as batting an eye, their expressions and movements elegant, natural, and composed. Wei Wuxian couldn't help but feel sheepish to be the only one with so much left in his bowl. To make matters worse, he remembered there being some directives pertaining to mealtime etiquette among the four thousand family precepts—actually, no, who knew how many thousands more had been added by now. *"Picky eating is forbidden," "leaving food uneaten is forbidden," "eating more than three bowls of rice is forbidden,"* and so on. He found these family rules particularly mind-boggling, but he didn't want to be spurned by Lan Qiren again *that* quickly.

But just as Wei Wuxian was about to steel himself and down the odd soup in one gulp, he realized that the bowl in front of him was empty. Baffled, he picked up the exquisite little lacquered cup. *I clearly only drank a mouthful. Is there a leak in this thing?*

However, the dining table was spotless and shiny, no puddle of broth in sight. Wei Wuxian cast a sidelong glance at Lan Wangji just as he calmly finished the last mouthful of his own medicinal soup. Eyes lowered, he put the lid back on the bowl and patted the corner of his lips with a snowy-white square of napkin.

Wei Wuxian distinctly remembered that Lan Wangji had finished his cup much earlier. Furthermore, Lan Wangji's table seemed a lot closer than it had been before the banquet started, as if it'd been shifted toward Wei Wuxian's on the sly.

Stunned, Wei Wuxian arched an eyebrow. *"Hanguang-jun, you sure move fast, huh?"* he mouthed to Lan Wangji.

Lan Wangji set down the napkin and glanced at Wei Wuxian before calmly shifting his gaze forward once more.

The more serious he looked, the harder it was for Wei Wuxian to suppress the growing urge to make mischief. He tapped his finger gently on the small, black-lacquered cup, making a sound only the two of them could hear. On hearing it, Lan Wangji's eyes imperceptibly shifted a few centimeters toward him.

Wei Wuxian knew Lan Wangji would not miss a single movement he made, no matter how polite his line of sight might seem to onlookers. He raised the cup as though he was about to drink from it, then turned it in his hand and stopped at the spot from which Lan Wangji had just drunk. He then covered the edge of the cup with his lips.

The reaction was as he had anticipated: although Lan Wangji's hands remained properly placed on his legs, his fingers curled slightly beneath his white sleeves.

Wei Wuxian felt elated, like he was floating. Suddenly at ease, he was about to lean instinctively toward Lan Wangji when a stern cough rang out from Lan Qiren's direction. He quickly straightened up and resumed his upright posture.

After the soup, they waited in silence for a while before the main course was formally served. Every table received three side dishes, each on a tiny plate. If the food was not green, it was white—just like the meals served during Wei Wuxian's time studying here. Even all these years later, there was no change at all, save for an intensified bitterness.

Partly because of regional differences and partly because of his own nature, Wei Wuxian's tastes tended toward the stronger side—he adored spicy food and was displeased by a lack of meat. Faced with such simple fare, he really had no appetite. He powered through everything in a few bites, not registering what he ate at all. Lan Qiren swept his gaze over from time to time, ready to pin him with a ferocious glare. He was the same as he had been during lessons back in the day, always ready to single Wei Wuxian out by name and tell him to get lost. However, Wei Wuxian was so uncharacteristically well behaved that there was nothing he could do but let the matter drop.

After finishing the tasteless meal, the servants removed the dish-ware and tables. As was standard procedure, Lan Xichen began to review recent clan matters aloud—but after listening to him utter just a few sentences, Wei Wuxian thought he seemed distracted. Lan Xichen got the locations of two Night Hunts wrong without even realizing it and didn't catch his mistake. It caused Lan Qiren to look askance at him and huff, his goatee bristling. He listened for some more time, then was finally compelled to cut him off. With that, the family banquet was hastily concluded without further mishaps.

A depressing beginning, a depressing middle, and a depressing end.

Wei Wuxian had been forced to bear the gloom for nearly two hours. Not only was there no good food, there hadn't even been any entertainment to liven things up. He held himself in check until it felt like half a year's worth of accrued fleas were crawling up and down his back.

After the banquet ended, Lan Qiren sternly called Lan Xichen and Lan Wangji away—another lecture, from the looks of it. There was no one around whom he could act out with, so Wei Wuxian wandered until he found a gaggle of juniors walking together in twos and threes. He was about to call out to them, grab them, and head out to have some fun—but when Lan Sizhui, Lan Jingyi, and the others saw him, their expressions changed drastically and they turned to leave.

Wei Wuxian understood. He drifted to a part of the woods that was more secluded and waited. Eventually, the juniors furtively emerged.

"Wei-qianbei," Lan Jingyi said, "we weren't ignoring you on purpose, but xiansheng said that anyone who speaks to you will have to copy the Lan Clan's family precepts from beginning to end..."

"Xiansheng" was the standard honorific that all juniors and disciples of the Lan Clan of Gusu used for Lan Qiren, so any mention of "xiansheng" could only mean him.

"It's fine," said Wei Wuxian, a little smug. "I already knew that. It's not the first time your xiansheng has tried to guard against fires, burglars, and Wei Wuxian, but have you ever seen him succeed? He probably feels like his prize cabbage has been dug up by a pig, so it's only natural he'd be even more hot-tempered than usual, ha ha ha ha..."

Lan Jingyi was speechless.

Lan Sizhui could only chuckle weakly. "...Ha ha ha."

"By the way, I heard you guys were being punished because you went on Night Hunts with Wen Ning," said Wei Wuxian, once he was done laughing. He turned to Lan Sizhui and asked, "How is he now?"

"He's probably hiding in some corner of the mountain, waiting for us to look for him on our next Night Hunt," Lan Sizhui answered. After thinking for a moment, he added worriedly, "But Sect Leader Jiang still seemed very angry when we parted ways. I hope he didn't make things hard for him."

"Huh? Jiang Cheng? How did you run into him during a Night Hunt?" Wei Wuxian asked.

"We invited Jin-gongzi to go with us last time, so..." Lan Sizhui explained.

Wei Wuxian immediately understood.

He didn't need to guess what had happened. Wen Ning would naturally not remain idle when Lan Sizhui led the others on Night Hunts, but would follow them in secret to protect them and lend a helping hand if they encountered danger. Jiang Cheng also habitually followed Jin Ling in secret, for fear that something might happen to him. Thus, they had bumped into each other during said critical period when their aid was required.

After some probing, Wei Wuxian discovered this was indeed what had happened. Caught between laughter and tears, he paused, then asked, "How are Sect Leader Jiang and Jin Ling doing lately?"

After Jin Guangyao's death, the only legitimate heir left to lead the Jin Clan of Lanling was Jin Ling. However, there were many elders from the extended branches of the family eyeing the position from the sidelines, ready to seize any opportunity that arose. On the outside, the Jin Clan of Lanling was derided and spurned by the other clans. On the inside, it was a nest of deceit and ulterior motives. Jin Ling was only a teenager—how could he be expected to keep things under control?

In the end, it was only because Jiang Cheng descended on Golden Carp Tower with Zidian in hand that Jin Ling was able to temporarily secure his seat as the head of the family. As to whether that would change in the future, no one could say for sure.

Lan Jingyi pouted. "They seem to be doing well. Sect Leader Jiang is the same as ever, likes to go around cracking the whip. The Young Mistress's temper has gotten better, he used to talk back three times for each one of his jiujiu's reprimands, and now he manages to do it ten times."

"Jingyi, how can you call him that behind his back?" chided Lan Sizhui.

"I call him that to his face too," said Lan Jingyi, defensively.

Wei Wuxian heaved a small breath of relief on hearing this. He knew deep down that that wasn't actually what he wanted to ask, but there was really nothing more to say—Jiang Cheng and Jin Ling sounded like they were both doing all right.

He stood up and patted the hem of his robes. "All good, then. They can keep that up. You guys can go back to playing around, I've got something else to do."

"You never do anything in the Cloud Recesses," Lan Jingyi said disdainfully. "So what do you need to attend to?"

Without even looking back, Wei Wuxian answered, "Gnawing on cabbage!"

It was rare for him to wake this early, so when he returned to the Tranquility Room, he covered himself with a blanket and passed out. As a result of his messed-up sleep schedule, it was already dusk by the time he woke. He'd missed dinner, and there was nothing left for him to eat. Wei Wuxian did not feel hungry regardless, so he went back to rummaging through the chests and cupboards in search of Lan Wangji's past calligraphy and manuscripts as he waited. However, though he waited until nightfall, there was still no sign of his big cabbage.

By then, he had finally noticed his empty stomach. But by his estimation, the Cloud Recesses' curfew had already gone into effect. According to the family rules, unauthorized people were not permitted to wander the premises at night, much less climb over the wall and go outside. Back in the day, Wei Wuxian would not have cared what he was "not allowed" or "prohibited" to do—he would eat when hungry, sleep when sleepy, tease when bored, and flee when he stirred up trouble. However, his situation was different now. If he did not abide by the rules, the blame would fall squarely on Lan Wangji. No matter how hungry or bored he was, he could only heave a long sigh and endure it.

Suddenly, a soft noise echoed from outside the Tranquility Room and the door very gently slid open a sliver.

Lan Wangji had returned.

Wei Wuxian lay on the ground and played dead.

Very quietly, Lan Wangji walked over to the desk and set something on it, not speaking a word. Wei Wuxian would have continued to play dead, but then Lan Wangji opened something and a compelling spicy aroma instantly overpowered the scent of sandalwood that permeated the air in the Tranquility Room.

Wei Wuxian clambered up from the ground with all haste. "Er-gege! I'll be your slave for life!"

Without so much a ripple of change in his expression, Lan Wangji removed the dishes one by one from the meal box and placed them on the study desk. Wei Wuxian drifted over to him and saw the expanse of fiery red on five or six snowy-white plates, a sight which delighted him. His eyes gleamed hungrily.

"Hanguang-jun, you really are much too kind and considerate. Going out of your way to bring me food—from now on, just shout for me when you have anything that needs doing."

Lan Wangji produced a pair of ivory-white chopsticks and set them horizontally across the bowl. "Food is taken in silence," he said mildly.

"You also said that rest is taken in silence," Wei Wuxian said. "So why don't you stop me when I talk so much and scream so loudly every night?"

Lan Wangji glanced at him.

"Okay, okay, I'll shut up," said Wei Wuxian. "The two of us are already like this, and yet you're still so thin-skinned, getting all embarrassed at the tiniest things. That's what I like about you. Did you bring these from the Hunan cuisine restaurant in Caiyi Town?"

Lan Wangji neither confirmed nor denied this, so Wei Wuxian took it as tacit acknowledgment. He sat by the study desk. "I wonder if that Hunan cuisine restaurant is still open," he said. "We always used to eat there in the past. If I had to survive solely on your family's food, I wouldn't have lasted those few months. I mean, look at this—*this* is what I call a family banquet."

"We?" Lan Wangji echoed.

"Jiang Cheng and I," replied Wei Wuxian. "Occasionally, Nie Huaisang and the others too."

Casting a sidelong glance at Lan Wangji, he laughed. "Why are you looking at me like that? Hanguang-jun, don't forget that I invited you to come with us to that restaurant—invited you with enthusiasm and effort, even. You were the one who refused to go. I'd say a single word to you and you'd glare at me. Every time, your replies would start and end with 'no', and then you'd brush me off entirely. I still haven't settled the score with you, and yet you're the one sulking right now. Speaking of which..."

He nuzzled up to Lan Wangji. "I was worried about breaking the rules. That's why I held back from sneaking out. Instead, I behaved myself and waited for you here in our room. Who would've thought you'd break the rules on your own and sneak out to get me food? If your shufu finds out about your misbehavior, those heart problems of his are gonna act up again."

Lan Wangji lowered his head and wrapped his arms around Wei Wuxian's waist. He seemed quiet and still, but Wei Wuxian could feel his fingers subtly caressing his waist. His fingers were so hot that the heat penetrated his clothes to his skin. Wei Wuxian could feel their touch clearly and distinctly.

He hugged him back and whispered, "Hanguang-jun... I drank your family's medicinal soup, and now my whole mouth tastes bitter. I can't eat anything like this. What should I do?"

"A single mouthful," Lan Wangji said.

"Yes, I only drank a mouthful," Wei Wuxian said. "I don't know who concocted that stuff, but it had a seriously strong aftertaste. The bitterness slid right from the tip of my tongue down to the back of my throat. Quick, tell me, what should I do?"

"It must be neutralized at once," said Lan Wangji, after a moment of silence.

Wei Wuxian humbly asked for advice on the process. "How should I neutralize it?"

Lan Wangji raised his head.

A faint medicinal scent passed between their lips and teeth. The slight bitterness drew out this kiss, making it lingeringly long.

"Hanguang-jun, I just remembered that you drank two bowls of that soup," murmured Wei Wuxian when they finally parted. "The bitterness on your tongue must be much stronger than mine."

"Mn," Lan Wangji said.

"But you still taste pretty sweet," Wei Wuxian said. "How strange."

"...Have your meal first," said Lan Wangji. After a pause, he added, "We will do things when you are done eating."

"I'll have the cabbage first," said Wei Wuxian.

Lan Wangji frowned ever so slightly, as if puzzled why Wei Wuxian had suddenly mentioned cabbage. Wei Wuxian laughed out loud as he wrapped his arms around Lan Wangji's neck.

When all was said and done, a so-called family banquet was still best held behind closed doors.

WEI WUXIAN FOUND an old incense burner while rummaging through the Ancient Room inside the Cloud Recesses' Treasure Pavilion.

The body of the burner resembled that of a bear, the nose that of an elephant, the eyes that of a rhino, and the feet like that of a tiger. Its belly housed the burner, and light smoke blew from its mouth when the incense was lit.

Inside the Tranquility Room, Wei Wuxian asked, "This thing looks pretty fun. It doesn't have a murderous or hostile aura, so it must not be anything harmful. Lan Zhan, do you know what it's used for?"

Lan Wangji shook his head. Wei Wuxian took a whiff of the incense and determined there was nothing wrong with it either. Unable to make heads or tails of it, the two put the incense burner away to be examined further at a later date.

They had only just lain down that night when they were seized by heavy drowsiness and fell into a deep slumber.

Some time had passed before Wei Wuxian woke up and discovered that he and Lan Wangji were not in the Tranquility Room at the Cloud Recesses. Instead, they were somewhere in the wilderness.

He pulled himself upright from the ground, wondering, "What is this place?"

"This is not a place in the present," Lan Wangji answered.

"Not the present? No way," said Wei Wuxian. He shook his sleeves, and the feel of it was exceptionally real. "What is this if not the present?"

Lan Wangji didn't respond. Instead, he silently approached a stream and gestured for Wei Wuxian to look into it. After he walked over, Wei Wuxian was stunned by the reflection he saw in the water.

What the stream reflected was his face from his former life!

Wei Wuxian's head shot up. "Is this the incense burner's doing?"

Lan Wangji nodded. "I am afraid so."

Wei Wuxian stared at the face he'd not seen for a long time before moving his eyes away.

"It's fine. I tested that thing and sensed no resentment. It's definitely not an evil device. I figure it was probably the invention of some almighty immortal master, who created it to help with cultivation—or just recreation. Let's walk around and take stock of things."

Though they remained unsure whether this was an illusion or something else, the pair began to leisurely wander the woods. Not long after, they saw a small cottage.

When Wei Wuxian spotted it, he let out a soft *"huh?"*

"What is it?" Lan Wangji asked.

Wei Wuxian examined the little cottage. "This place looks a bit familiar."

The wooden cottage looked extremely ordinary, like any old farming house. As puzzled as he was, he couldn't be sure whether he'd actually encountered it before. Just then, they heard the creaking of a loom from within.

The two exchanged a look. Without needing to say a word, they approached the house together.

When they came to the door and looked in, they were both taken aback.

What was inside the cottage was an extreme departure from whatever terrors they had expected. There were no sinister scoundrels, no yao beasts or fierce corpses. There was only one man—and he was one they were both extremely familiar with.

Inside the wooden cottage, there sat a "Lan Wangji!"

That "Lan Wangji" looked just as tall and handsome as the one standing next to Wei Wuxian. His blue and white robes were plain, though not coarse, and he retained the transcendent air of a distinguished cultivator all the same. The loom beside him seemed to be driven by magic—it moved on its own, creaking as it wove fabric. Meanwhile, the man himself sat next to the machine with a book rolled up in his hand, which he read with great concentration.

The two of them were already at the door, and had made quite a bit of noise, but "Lan Wangji" didn't seem to notice at all. His expression was impassive as he flipped a page with a long, fair, slender finger.

Wei Wuxian looked at the Lan Wangji beside him, then looked at the "Lan Wangji" inside, then said with dawning understanding, "I see. I see!"

Lan Wangji's brows arched a little. This minuscule movement indicated that he was flabbergasted. "What?"

"This, this, this—this is my dream!" Wei Wuxian exclaimed.

Before he could say anything else, a black-clad figure came strolling over with airy steps. "Er-gege—I'm back!" he shouted, dragging out each syllable.

Lan Wangji fell even more silent at the sight of that lively "Wei Wuxian," who carried a hoe over his shoulder, a fish trap in his hand, and a stalk of grass between his lips.

If this was Wei Wuxian's dream, it was quite logical that inhabitants of the dreamscape couldn't see them.

Only then did the fabric-weaving "Lan Wangji" look up. Surprisingly, the corners of his lips hooked slightly upward on seeing "Wei Wuxian," then quickly flattened. He rose to his feet to welcome him and poured him a cup of water.

"Wei Wuxian" spat out the grass in his mouth and sat down by the small wooden table. He picked up the cup without a word and gulped it down in one go. Only after that did he begin to speak.

"The sun was too hot out there today. I'm scorched. I left the rest of the work in the fields, I give up. I'll see about going back if I've got the time."

"Lan Wangji" answered with a "Mn" and retrieved a snowy white cloth, which he handed to "Wei Wuxian." However, "Wei Wuxian" only grinned and leaned his face close, his intent obvious—he wanted "Lan Wangji" to wash his face for him.

"Lan Wangji" didn't seem to mind in the least and actually began to wipe his face with serious concentration. Although "Wei Wuxian" enjoyed the service, his mouth didn't take a break.

"I went and played in the river earlier, and caught two fish. Er-gege, make fish soup for me tonight!"

"Mn."

"How is carp usually cooked in Gusu? Lan Zhan, do you know how to make Sichuan fish with pickled greens? I like that dish. Absolutely do *not* make it sweet; I had it sweet once and almost threw up."

"Mn. I know how."

"It's been hotter and hotter these days. The bathwater doesn't have to be that hot tonight, so I only chopped half the regular amount of firewood."

"Mn. That is fine."

Lan Wangji watched the two casually chatting away about small household matters and asked, "...This is your dream?"

Wei Wuxian was laughing so hard he was going to sustain internal injuries.

"*Pfft*, ha ha ha ha ha ha ha ha... Uh, yeah. There was a period of time when I kept having dreams like this, for some reason. I dreamt that we'd retired and retreated from the world to live on some wild mountain. I'd go out to hunt and work the fields, while you would watch the house and weave cloth and cook for me. Oh yeah, and you'd manage the money too, and patch up my clothes at night. Every time I had the dream, I'd tell you to heat up the bathwater and we'd bathe together every evening... But every time, I'd wake up just before the clothes came off. What a shame. Ha ha ha ha ha ha ha ha ha..."

Wei Wuxian didn't find it at all embarrassing for Lan Wangji to have witnessed a dream like this; in fact, he was delighting in it. He was beside himself with glee, and Lan Wangji's eyes softened as he watched him.

"Just as well."

Wei Wuxian's dream was full of nothing but ordinary minutiae— they cooked, ate, fed the chickens, chopped firewood, and sure enough, the dream came to an abrupt end right as the bathwater was heated.

The two departed from the cottage and wandered the dreamscape for a little while before they found an elegant and tranquil pavilion. Outside the building was a magnolia tree. The blooms upon its outstretched branches diffused a faint, refreshing fragrance through the night air.

The dream had changed location to a place that the two of them recognized in a heartbeat—it was the Cloud Recesses' Library

Pavilion. There was light coming from a wooden window on the second floor and the faint sound of voices.

Wei Wuxian looked up. "Shall we go and take a peek?"

But for some reason, Lan Wangji wasn't acting like his usual self. He stopped in his tracks and stared contemplatively at that window, as if hesitant. Wei Wuxian found this strange. He couldn't think of any reason why Lan Wangji wouldn't want to go in.

"What's wrong?" he asked.

Lan Wangji shook his head slightly. He mulled it over for a moment, but just as he was about to speak, there was a sudden burst of uproarious laughter inside the Library Pavilion.

Wei Wuxian's eyes instantly lit up at the sound. He rushed inside, leaping up the stairs three steps at a time.

Naturally, Lan Wangji would not remain outside by himself, so he entered as well. As the pair approached the lamplit room, they did indeed see something very interesting.

A fifteen- or sixteen-year-old Wei Ying sat on a light-colored mat next to the desk reserved for transcription punishment. He was slapping the table and laughing uproariously.

"Ha ha ha ha ha ha ha ha ha ha ha ha ha ha ha!"

There was an erotic picture book on the floor, and a likewise fifteen- or sixteen-year-old Lan Zhan huddled in a corner of the room like he was evading a great venom. He was bellowing in rage. "Wei Ying—!"

The young Wei Ying was laughing so hard that he nearly rolled beneath the desk, and it was with great difficulty that he raised his hand. "Here! I'm here!"

Wei Wuxian was about to fall over laughing himself. Tugging at Lan Wangji beside him, he said, "This dream's good! I can't anymore, Lan Zhan—look at you, look at you back then, that face, ha ha ha ha ha ha…"

However, Lan Wangji's expression was growing increasingly odd. Wei Wuxian pulled him down to sit on a mat on the side of the room. With a hand propping up his cheek, he grinned as he watched their younger selves scuffle and quarrel.

On the other side of the room, the young Lan Zhan had already drawn Bichen. Wei Ying quickly grabbed Suibian and flashed a few centimeters of the blade from its sheath.

"Manners!" he reminded him. "Lan-er-gongzi! Watch your manners! I've brought a sword today too. If we start fighting, what's going to happen to your family's Library Pavilion?!"

Lan Zhan was outraged. "Wei Ying! You... What kind of person are you?!"

Wei Ying arched his brows. "What else can I be? A man!"

"...Shameless!" Lan Zhan rebuked.

"Do you need to feel shame over something like this? Don't tell me you've never seen that sort of thing. I don't believe it," Wei Ying said.

Having endured this for a while, Lan Zhan's face was frosty as he lunged with his sword.

"What, you're fighting for real?!" Shocked, Wei Ying also brandished his sword and struck back—and just like that, the two actually started trading blows inside the Library Pavilion.

Wei Wuxian made a noise of confusion at this turn of events. He turned to look at Lan Wangji. "Is that how it went? How come I remember we *didn't* actually fight at the time?"

Lan Wangji remained silent. Although Wei Wuxian looked at him, he was subtly evading his gaze. More and more, Wei Wuxian felt that he was acting strange tonight.

Just as he was about to ask about it, however, he heard the Little Wei Ying begin to tease as he fought.

"Very good, very good. You can release and retract, tense and relax at will—excellent swordplay! But Lan Zhan, oh Lan Zhan, look at you. You're so red in the face. Are you flushed because you're fighting with me, or are you blushing because you saw *something good* earlier?"

Little Lan Zhan wasn't blushing at all. He swung his sword. "Nonsense!"

Wei Ying bent backward, performing an extremely pliable iron board technique to dodge the attack, then straightened back up. With incredibly quick fingers, he pinched Lan Zhan's smooth, fair face.

"'Nonsense'? Why don't you feel your own face? It's so hot, ha ha!"

Lan Zhan's face blushed and blanched, and he raised a hand to smack away Wei Ying's claws. But Wei Ying had already withdrawn his hand, and Lan Zhan ended up smacking thin air and nearly hitting himself.

Wei Ying spun with skill and ease, and chided him leisurely. "Lan Zhan, oh Lan Zhan, I'm not trying to lecture you or anything, but look at everyone else your age—who gets red in the face as easily as you? You can't handle even a little stimulation. You're too tender."

This scene had never happened, nor was it anything Wei Wuxian had ever dreamed about happening. And so, this dream could only belong to Lan Wangji. He watched it play out with relish.

"Lan Zhan, you know me so well. That certainly is something I'd say," Wei Wuxian said.

However, he didn't notice that Lan Wangji now seemed almost restless.

From the other side of the room, Wei Ying continued, "It's pretty boring, transcribing books. Why don't I teach you about this stuff while I'm at it? Consider it my thanks for your supervision…"

After enduring his nonsense this long, Lan Zhan had finally had enough. Bichen shot over, the two swords crossed, and both were sent crashing out the window as a result of the clash. Seeing Suibian leave his hand, Wei Ying was slightly stunned.

"Hey, my sword!"

Shouting in dismay, he was about to leap out the window to grab for his sword when Lan Zhan pounced on him from behind and slammed him to the floor. Wei Ying's head knocked against the floor with the impact, and he fought to get up, flustered. After a few blows were traded back and forth, it devolved into a messy, tangled brawl. Wei Ying kicked in earnest and flung his arms out in every direction, but no matter how he tried, he couldn't prevent Lan Zhan from pinning all four of his limbs down. It was like he'd been trapped by an impenetrable iron net.

"Lan Zhan! Lan Zhan, what're you doing?! I was joking, joking! What are you doing, taking it so seriously?!

Lan Zhan seized both of Wei Ying's wrists and pressed them to his back. "What did you say you were going to teach me?" he asked darkly.

His tone sounded detached, but in his eyes lurked a volcano on the verge of eruption.

Their strength had been evenly matched to begin with, but Wei Ying's moment of carelessness had gotten him pinned firmly to the ground and seized by a vital point. He had no choice but to play dumb.

"I didn't say anything, what did I say?"

"Nothing?" Lan Zhan pressed.

"Nothing!" Wei Ying insisted self-righteously, then added, "Lan Zhan, don't be such a stick in the mud. Don't take everything I say so seriously, eh? You even believe me when I spout nonsense like this. What's there to be angry about? I'll shut up, okay? Let me go, I haven't finished copying today's book. I'm done playing."

Lan Zhan's expression relaxed somewhat, and he seemed to slacken his grip. But the moment Wei Ying pulled his wrists from Lan Zhan's clutches, his eyes squinted into crescents and darted from side to side—and he swung out with a smack at once.

Little did he know Lan Zhan was already prepared. He swiftly caught Wei Ying the moment he attacked and subdued him anew. This time, he used a heavier hand and twisted Wei Ying's wrist at an even more severe angle.

Wei Ying yelped incessantly. "I said I was joking! Lan Zhan! Can't you take a joke?!"

Dancing flames could be vaguely seen in Lan Zhan's eyes. Without another word, he yanked off his forehead ribbon and wound it three times around Wei Ying's hands before tying a dead knot to secure it.

Wei Wuxian, who hadn't expected such a development whatsoever, was left gaping at the sight. It took him a while before he could turn his head to look at Lan Wangji. When he did, he discovered that while there were no traces of red on Lan Wangji's perpetually snowy white complexion, his earlobes had turned pink.

Wei Wuxian scooted over slyly. "Lan-er-gege... This dream of yours doesn't seem quite right, eh?"

Lan Wangji was momentarily speechless before he suddenly moved to get up. "Do not watch anymore!"

Wei Wuxian immediately yanked on his sleeve to keep him from standing up. "Don't go! I wanna see what else happens in your dream. We haven't even gotten to the good part yet!"

Next to the desk inside the Library Pavilion, Wei Ying shrieked and howled as he was tied up. After he quieted down, he tried to reason with Lan Zhan.

"Lan Zhan, a gentleman uses his mouth, not his hands. You're being narrow-minded right now. Think about it; did I say anything bad about you?"

Lan Zhan huffed soundlessly and said, wholly aloof, "Think about what you said yourself."

"All I said was that you're tender and you don't understand certain things, that's all. Is that not the truth, though?" Wei Ying argued. "There really are some adult things you don't understand. Treating me like this just because I spoke the truth—isn't that narrow-minded?"

"Who said I do not understand?" Lan Zhan replied coolly.

Wei Ying quirked an eyebrow and laughed. "Oh...? Really? Don't be so stubborn. Like hell you do, ha ha ha ha ha ha—*Ah!*"

The sudden yelp of alarm was because Lan Zhan had suddenly grabbed a specific part of Wei Ying's lower body.

With a coldly handsome yet childish face, Lan Zhan repeated his question. "Who said I do not understand?"

Wei Wuxian was draped over Lan Wangji, practically whispering into his ear as he asked a question of his own. "Yeah, who said you don't understand? As the saying goes, 'You dream at night what you think in the day.' So 'fess up, *Lan Zhan*—did you desperately want to do this to me back then? Who would've thought...that you were like this, Hanguang-jun?"

While Lan Wangji remained expressionless, the smear of pink had crept down to his fair neck, and his fingers settled on his knees imperceptibly curled.

Over on the other side of the room, little Wei Ying lay slack on the floor and drew sharp breaths. Something quite precious to him had been seized, after all.

"What the hell are you doing, Lan Zhan? Have you gone mad?!"

Lan Zhan had already slotted himself between Wei Ying's legs, in a position that made Wei Ying feel quite threatened. Seeing how things were going awry, he quickly changed his tune.

"...No, no, no! No one said you didn't understand! Y-y-y-you let me go first, we can talk this out!"

He wrenched his hands wildly, but unfortunately, the Lan Clan forehead ribbon was made of a most exceptional material. No matter how he fought, he couldn't struggle free or untie the knot. He jerked another couple of times, then noticed a book that had fallen on the floor nearby. He quickly grabbed it and threw it at Lan Zhan, hoping to smack some sense back into him with words of wisdom.

"Come to your senses!"

The book slammed against Lan Zhan's chest, then dropped to the floor between Wei Ying's open legs, where it flipped open to display its pages. Lan Zhan looked down, and his eyes froze on the tableau on display.

Somehow, the book had just so happened to fall open on an erotic illustration that was particularly bold and explicit in nature. And furthermore—the two people in the piece were both men!

Wei Wuxian distinctly remembered the erotica he *had* shown Lan Wangji having nothing homosexual at all in it. It definitely hadn't contained a page like that. He was in awe, helpless to be anything but. This detailed addition to the scene in Lan Wangji's dream... It was just too rich for words. He really had to hand it to him!

Lan Zhan stared unblinkingly at that page. Wei Ying spotted the picture too and instantly felt a little awkward.

"...Um..."

He cried his grievances bitterly in his mind. In the end, he still felt fighting was more effective than arguing, and so he summoned all his might, pulled one leg free, and kicked. However, Lan Zhan spared a hand to grip him at the bend of his knee, then pried his legs apart into an even more splayed position. He yanked off Wei Ying's belt and trousers in two swift movements.

Wei Ying felt a sudden chill down below. When he looked down, his heart went cold as well. "Lan Zhan, what're you doing?!" he exclaimed in alarm.

Wei Wuxian, enthralled by the sight, was beside himself with excitement. "You! Duh!" he said in response, unable to resist.

With his trousers removed, the lower half of Wei Ying's body was completely naked. His long, slender, pearl-white legs kicked like mad. Lan Zhan pinned his legs down. Referencing the illustration in the erotica, his hand reached straight for the tightly closed spot of pink between Wei Ying's round white ass cheeks.

Wei Ying's bottom half was firmly and entirely subdued. Even with his private parts being violated, he had nowhere to run. Lan Zhan rubbed the pink spot with two fingers and Wei Ying shuddered. He forced away the flash of bashfulness that crossed his face, then resumed squirming and struggling.

The young man bearing down on him, however, had a dark look in his eyes. Lan Zhan's lips pursed tight, and his hand continued to rhythmically push against Wei Ying's private place. He gradually added force to his fingers until the little pink hole slowly softened and opened. Shyly, it swallowed a notch of the fair finger that rubbed it.

Grinning, Wei Wuxian looked at Lan Wangji askance. "No wonder you didn't want to come in here earlier, Hanguang-jun. You probably want to dig a hole to hide in—I caught you red-handed, doing things like this to me in your dreams..."

Although Lan Wangji remained poised and proper where he sat beside him, his eyes were downcast and his lashes seemed to tremble slightly.

Cheek still propped on his hand, Wei Wuxian continued to watch his younger self being forcibly opened up by the young Lan Zhan. He chuckled. "Hanguang-jun, if you've got the guts to dream about it after the fact, why didn't you have the guts to actually do it back then? I—"

Lan Wangji seized his hands before he could finish and pushed him down on the floor to seal his mouth. Wei Wuxian felt the hotness of Lan Wangji's cheeks, and the unusually frantic beating of his heart.

Amused, he murmured when their wet lips parted, "What? Feeling shy again?"

Lan Wangji's breathing was uncommonly harsh, and he didn't respond.

"Or are you...hard?" Wei Wuxian pushed further.

Over by the desk, a long wailing moan escaped Wei Ying's throat.

Lan Zhan was looming over him, their bodies seamlessly joined— clearly, he was in the process of penetration. At the feeling of the hard, foreign object invading his body bit by bit, Wei Ying was in so much discomfort that his legs curled in. But his hands were securely bound by the forehead ribbon. Unable to move, he could only bang the back of his head soundly against the floor to express his pain. Lan Zhan cradled his head with his hand while at the same time driving fully into Wei Ying's body.

The spot of pink had struggled to swallow even a single finger at first, but was now forced open and choking on a large, scalding hot and hard object. The folds at its entrance were stretched smooth. Wei Ying was still a little dazed, like he hadn't yet grasped the reality of things, but small whimpers unconsciously escaped his throat when Lan Zhan began to slowly rock his hips as per the instructions in the erotica.

"Lan Zhan, *you* might have been little at the time, but some parts of you weren't little at all," Wei Wuxian said to Lan Wangji. "I was a virgin back then, you know. That's gotta be rough on him."

As he spoke, he used his knees to deliberately rub between Lan Wangji's legs. Watching an erotic live show had piqued his interest, as was only natural, and he now wanted to feel just how rough that thing of Lan Wangji's could be.

He didn't need to rub for long before Lan Wangji tore off the bottom of his robe and his trousers without a word. Wei Wuxian instinctively spread his legs and wrapped them around his waist. Gripping his member, Lan Wangji rubbed its terrifyingly hard head against Wei Wuxian's entrance.

The two of them messed around and tangled with each other nearly every day, so Wei Wuxian was already in perfect concert with him, both body and mind. He hugged Lan Wangji's neck tightly and took a deep breath as he was breached, and Lan Wangji speared all the way inside.

The entry was smooth; he was soft inside, all hot and wet. The channel clenched hard around the massive invader in welcome, as if it had been made just to accept the man's intrusion. It didn't take long before the damp, sticky sound of flesh slapping against flesh came from the place where they were joined.

Lan Wangji was endowed with an impressive, heavyweight manhood. Its shaft was naturally curved at the head, and every time he thrust, he pressed against the most weak and sensitive spot inside Wei Wuxian with deadly accuracy. Overwhelming passion washed over both of them every time he dragged past that spot.

Lan Wangji's pounding was driving Wei Wuxian out of his mind. His insides contracted without rhythm as pleasure spread from the top of his head to the tips of his toes. He threw his head back in bliss, and at that arched angle, could see the teenage Wei Ying in Lan Wangji's dream being subjected to the same extreme pleasure and pain.

He lay there in a mess of scrolls and books, his wrists tightly bound and powerlessly fixed above his head. His black hair was loose and scattered, red ribbon lost in their scuffle. His eyes were half-lidded and hazy, wet and on the verge of tears.

He'd been pinned and fucked for a while now. Having determined that Wei Ying's legs weren't spread wide enough, Lan Zhan caught one and put it over his shoulder before resuming his violent pounding. The leg, unable to hold that position, quickly slipped down to rest in the crook of his arm. The smooth, beautiful lines of Wei Ying's calf and the muscles of his inner thigh convulsed slightly—the massive, curved, scalding thing inside him was thrusting in and out nonstop, driving him to the edge.

His first time had found him at a complete loss. He gripped Lan Zhan's shoulders like a drowning man, probably barely aware of where he was right now, much less able to remember that the unbearable torment was being inflicted by the one currently thrashing inside him.

As he watched his teen self being fucked by a teen Lan Zhan until he was flushed and shuddering, Wei Wuxian thought that this wasn't enough. It'd be even better if Little Lan Zhan were rougher, used more force, bullied Little Wei Ying within an inch of his life until he was bawling his eyes out. Right now, this was far from enough.

The Library Pavilion was small, but two of its corners were overflowing with boundless salacity. Wei Ying had been a little dazed earlier, but the wet, obscene slapping sounds seemed to have pulled him back to the present. He shuddered as he stared at the pavilion's ceiling, then looked down, seeming to want to peek at the situation playing out lower on his body, but lacking the courage.

After Lan Zhan had plowed away with lowered head for a while, he lifted both of Wei Ying's legs onto his shoulders before leaning back down. As he fucked him, Wei Ying's waist was bent into a pliable arch—an angle that let him see just what was happening down there through eyes blurred by tears.

The once perfectly clean little pink hole had been rubbed a deep ripe red by Lan Wangji's member, and its rim was pitifully swollen. The long, hot weapon still repeatedly thrust in and out, mixing the milky precome, the thin strings of vivid red blood, and a bit of unknown fluid into a mess where the two were joined. To his surprise, Wei Ying's own member was at half-mast and trickling precome.

This devastating sight completely stunned Wei Ying. It took him a good while before he somehow mustered the strength to suddenly struggle again. He broke free of Lan Zhan's hold, then flipped around and crawled away on his knees, wanting to escape.

After being pinned to the ground and so roughly fucked by Lan Zhan, he was already depleted of strength. His thighs and knees wobbled and trembled. He only managed to flop away for a short distance before his body gave out and he fell flat to the floor once more. The position hoisted his ripe snow-white ass cheeks into the air on display. A mess of come and blood flowed from the ravaged hole between his ass cheeks and wound down his thighs. His inner thighs were a shocking sight, a field of crisscrossing red and purple finger marks—just a single look would stir a powerful desire to abuse him further.

Lan Zhan had witnessed this whole display. Eyes bloodshot, he chased after him without a word. Wei Ying felt a tightening around his waist as he was pinned in a deadlock once more, and the place that was briefly empty was immediately and solidly filled to the brim.

He moaned and let out a weak protest. "No..."

After suffering this ravaging, his entrance was already wet, tender, and a complete mess. It easily took the cock that had just been violating him and swallowed it whole. Wei Ying kneeled on all fours on the mat, his body constantly inching forward with the force of the thrusts. Mortification was clear on his face. Wild beasts mated in this position—he had seen them on occasion when he went out to roam the woods. He couldn't help but feel even more embarrassed to be taken from behind like this, and he clenched tighter. Lan Zhan gripped his waist and also began to ram with increasing yet methodless force. The brutal pounding went on for a while until, at last, Wei Ying couldn't take it anymore.

Half of his face and his body were pressed to the floor, squished out of shape. He begged incoherently, "...M-mercy, mercy... Lan Zhan, Lan-er-gongzi, mercy *please*..."

A plea like that was useless, of course—aside from provoking deeper and faster penetration, that is. Wei Wuxian laughed aloud.

"Oh god, his squealing is making me hard. Don't show him mercy, fuck him to death, that's the way... *Ah*..."

Lan Wangji pulled Wei Wuxian up to straddle him. The weight of his body allowed him to swallow Lan Wangji's cock deeper, so deep that it made Wei Wuxian wince and slightly scrunch up his face. He quickly adjusted his position and regained his focus on riding Lan Wangji, no longer having the mind to spew filth.

As the wet slapping sound of flesh reached a crescendo, Wei Ying's cries were also becoming increasingly wretched.

"...Lan Zhan... Lan Zhan... You...you hear that...? *Ah*... Too deep... Don't go all the way in... My belly...hurts..."

Every time Lan Zhan entered him, it was as though he wanted to skewer him all the way through. Lan Zhan was rough and brutal, the force of his actions standing in stark contrast to the expression on his face. Wei Ying's ass was numb and red from the slamming; he'd practically lost feeling in his entire bottom half. Each time he struggled and tried to crawl away, he'd be yanked back and forced to take Lan Zhan's cock all the way in to the deepest parts of him.

This went on and on. "Li...listen to me," Wei Ying said with breathless, broken words, "there's, there's...there are people outside waiting for me. Jiang Cheng and the others...are still outside waiting for me...*Ah*!"

Hearing this, Lan Zhan abruptly pulled out of his body and flipped him over.

Wei Ying let out a sob and immediately shrank into a ball, trying to hide by curling like a shrimp. His member was almost at full mast and on the edge of climax. His crotch was a thrilling sight— a mess of flowing fluids. His entrance was red and swollen from being forcibly used for such a long time, but the rim clenched at irregular intervals, opening and closing. It sputtered out drops of white and red, as if unimaginably thirsty, loath to part with the cock that had just been fucking it.

Meanwhile, Wei Wuxian was bouncing up and down on Lan Wangji, who had his arms around his waist, grabbing his ass. Until now, Lan Wangji's face had maintained its facade of tranquil detachment. Aside from his slightly erratic breathing, nothing about his face would ever lead one to suspect what he was doing— certainly no one would ever suspect that his hands were kneading Wei Wuxian's ass with tremendous and unchecked strength, leaving bruising handprints on his full, round cheeks. He leaned down to take the red dot on Wei Wuxian's left breast into his mouth and lightly abuse it with his teeth. Wei Wuxian fucked himself with Lan Wangji's cock, its slick, dark-red length vanishing into the darkness between his cheeks again and again. The pleasure sent shivers down their spines.

Over on the other side of the room, Lan Zhan stared at the half-dead Wei Ying for a bit before suddenly ripping open his robes and pinching his left nipple hard. He then brutally buried himself within him again. Wei Ying had only just caught his breath, still hyper-sensitive all over and unable to handle such treatment. With a groan, he began to weep in earnest as both his entrance and his insides clamped down hard.

Lan Zhan almost seemed to be venting his fury on Wei Ying's nipples, twisting and kneading them until they swelled and peaked and turned red as blood. With every pinch, Wei Ying's inner walls clenched violently. The soft, wet heat relentlessly squeezed the weapon inside his body and perfectly outlined its shape.

"Lan Zhan, I was wrong, I was wrong, I shouldn't have said you were tender, I shouldn't have said you didn't understand anything, I don't dare teach you anymore," Wei Ying said through his weeping. "Lan Zhan, Lan Zhan did you hear me? Lan-er-gongzi, Lan-er-gege..."

Lan Zhan faltered at the last address that Wei Ying nasally babbled, and indeed softened his actions. With misty eyes, he leaned in and gently kissed Wei Ying's tearfully pleading lips.

The bottom half of Wei Ying's body felt like it'd been battered by a giant boulder. His insides were stinging and hot, his waist sore, and his belly both sore and distended. His nipples were incredibly abused, and his mind was in a daze. Suddenly, he realized that the weapon battering him had slowed its assault. The two gently pressed their foreheads together, and a pair of cool lips pressed close to his. They tasted faintly sweet. When he opened his eyes, Lan Zhan's long jet-black eyelashes were inches from his face.

Lan Zhan was kissing him with intent concentration, and Wei Ying seemed to take some comfort from it. And so, he opened his mouth and gently sucked on Lan Zhan's lips as he mumbled, "...More..."

He had meant more kisses, but Lan Zhan misunderstood and picked up the pace of his thrusts. Wei Ying hissed and drew two sharp breaths, then quickly wrapped his arms around Lan Zhan's neck and kissed him himself.

At first, Wei Ying had found it frightening to have his insides pounded by something so long, thick, and hard. But after taking so many blows, he had developed a taste for the sensations that came alongside the sore ache of stretching, and slowly began to enjoy it. Especially when Lan Zhan's slightly curved cock brutally pressed against a certain spot in his inner walls—a spot that sent pleasure coursing through his body like electricity and made him shudder. His member was getting harder and harder, and drooled with more precome. Unable to help himself, he began to twist at the waist. Sometimes, when Lan Zhan didn't hit the right spot, he'd even push himself against him to correct the trajectory. The cries coming out of his mouth also changed flavor.

"...Ge... Er-gege... Lan-er-gege... I...I beg you..." Wei Ying pleaded.

Lan Zhan exhaled a breath and asked in a deep voice, "What?"

Wei Ying cupped his face and littered it with kisses. "...Ram me right in that spot, right where you just did," he whispered. "Fuck me right there, won't you...?"

Wordlessly, Lan Zhan did as Wei Ying wished and bent at the waist to drive himself in. It was a particularly hard thrust, and Wei Ying gasped, his limbs suddenly tightly wrapping around Lan Zhan's body.

He cried, "Wha—"

But Lan Zhan had already sealed his lips with his, focused entirely on kissing him. Wei Wuxian also entangled his tongue with Lan Wangji's, using the tip to trace the shape of his lips as they intertwined.

When he heard the commotion on the other side of the room, Wei Wuxian commented, "Hanguang-jun, the you over there came."

A sweat-drenched Lan Zhan was holding an equally sweaty Wei Ying, and the two lay quietly on the now-wrinkled mat. Wei Ying's chest was heaving, his eyes a little unfocused. They were still joined together. Wei Ying's lower body still firmly gripped Lan Zhan's member, and the come that had been shot inside him was sealed in without a single drop leaking forth.

Wei Wuxian chuckled. "Do you think we should also...?"

Lan Wangji nodded and laid him flat on the mat. With a few steady rolls of his hips, he released inside Wei Wuxian.

Wei Wuxian breathed a sigh of relief. While the pleasure of the act was real, his waist and his ass weren't forged of iron. His energy was almost depleted after going at it for so long alongside the two kids. But unexpectedly, Lan Wangji didn't pull out. Instead, he readjusted Wei Wuxian's position while remaining inside.

Wei Wuxian looked at him questioningly. "Hanguang...jun?"

Lan Wangji gave a slight smile in response and softly whispered a few words into his ear.

"...Uhh, wait?" Wei Wuxian said. "When I said 'fuck to death,' I meant the little Lan Zhan in your dream should fuck the me inside the dream to death! I didn't mean... Lan Zhan? Er-ge...ge? *Mercy!*"

The next morning, most unexpectedly, Wei Wuxian woke up earlier than Lan Wangji. His legs shook the entire day.

They fished out the tapir incense burner once more and turned it over and over in their hands, flipping it this way and that. Wei Wuxian dismantled it, then put it back together exactly as it came, but they were unable to uncover any hidden secrets.

Wei Wuxian sat by the desk, his mind fixed on the problem at hand. "There's nothing wrong with the incense, so it must be the burner for sure. What an incredible object. Immersion that strong is functionally the same as Empathy. Your family's Library Pavilion has no record of this?"

Lan Wangji shook his head, which meant there really were no past records.

"That's all right," said Wei Wuxian. "The incense burner's effects have already worn off. We might as well put it well away so no one touches it by mistake. If any masters in the art of device forging come around in the future, we can ask about it then."

They both truly thought the effect of the incense burner had worn off. How could they have known things wouldn't go as they had anticipated?

Deep in the night, after Wei Wuxian and Lan Wangji had made love in the Tranquility Room as usual, they fell into slumber together. It didn't take long before Wei Wuxian opened his eyes and found himself lying under the magnolia tree outside the Library Pavilion.

Sunlight cascaded past the flowering branches and spilled upon his face. Wei Wuxian squinted, raising a hand to block out the sun as he slowly sat up. This time, Lan Wangji wasn't beside him.

Wei Wuxian cupped a hand by his mouth and shouted, "Lan Zhan!"

No one answered. Wei Wuxian found this strange.

It seems the incense burner's effects haven't actually worn off yet. But where did Lan Zhan go? Am I the only one still feeling the residual effects?

In front of the magnolia tree was a small path made of white stones. A bunch of white-clad, forehead ribbon-wearing Lan Clan juniors passed by in groups of two or three, carrying books in their hands. It seemed they were on their way to morning lessons, and not one spared a single glance Wei Wuxian's way—for they still couldn't see him.

Wei Wuxian went up to the Library Pavilion for a look, finding neither the big nor the little Lan Wangji inside. Thus, he went back down the stairs and aimlessly roamed around the Cloud Recesses.

Not long after, he caught the faint sound of two boys talking in hushed voices. When he approached, one of them sounded incredibly familiar.

"...There has never been anyone who kept animals in the Cloud Recesses. To do so would be against the rules."

After a brief silence, the other boy said in a sulky tone, "I am aware. However... I have already made a promise. I will not go back on my word."

Realization struck Wei Wuxian, and he secretly peered in on the conversation. Sure enough, two young men stood in a meadow, exchanging words—and they were Lan Xichen and Lan Wangji.

It was spring, and there was a gentle breeze. The young Twin Jades of Lan reflected each other like flawless examples of the stones for which they were named. Both wore plain robes as white as snow, and their expansive sleeves and forehead ribbons were aflutter in the wind. They looked like a painting.

The Lan Wangji of this time also seemed to be fifteen or sixteen years of age. His brow was slightly knitted, as though his mind was troubled. In his arms, he held a white rabbit that was twitching its pink nose. There was another white rabbit beside his feet, its long ears perked. It was standing on its hind legs and pawing at his boots, seeming to want to climb up.

"How could some joking comments between youths be considered a serious promise? Is that really the reason?"

Lan Wangji lowered his eyes and didn't speak.

Lan Xichen chuckled. "All right. If shufu asks, you will have to give him a proper explanation. You have spent a bit too much time on them of late."

Lan Wangji nodded solemnly. "Thank you, xiongzhang," he said, then added after a brief pause, "...This will not impact my studies."

"I know it will not, Wangji," Lan Xichen said. "However, you must not tell shufu who gave them to you. He would be furious, and do all he could to make you send them away."

At this warning, Lan Wangji seemed to hug the rabbit in his arms a little tighter. Lan Xichen smiled, then reached out and tickled the white rabbit's nose before strolling away.

Once he'd gone, Lan Wangji stood there contemplatively for a while. The white rabbit in the crook of his arm looked perfectly relaxed, flicking its ears every so often. The one next to his feet was pawing with increasing urgency. Lan Wangji glanced at it, then bent down to pick it up as well, cradling both rabbits in his arms. He stroked them softly, the gentleness of his hands a stark contrast to the cold expression on his face.

It was too tempting. Wei Wuxian walked out from behind the tree with the intent of getting closer to little Lan Wangji. To his surprise, Lan Wangji released both rabbits in his arms and whipped his head around, the aura around him changing drastically. When he saw who it was, however, he was taken aback. The stern glare had only lasted for an instant.

"...You?!"

He was shocked. Wei Wuxian was even more so.

"You can see me?" asked Wei Wuxian, curious.

Well, this was weird. A dream's inhabitants shouldn't be able to see him, as was logical. And yet Lan Wangji stared at him intently.

"Naturally. You are...Wei Ying?"

The man before him looked over twenty years of age—definitely older than fifteen. But at the same time, the face undoubtedly belonged to Wei Wuxian. Lan Wangji, having a hard time discerning the identity of this individual, was on high alert. If he'd been armed, Bichen would've probably been unsheathed by now.

Reacting with great speed, Wei Wuxian composed himself. "It's me!"

His response only made Lan Wangji more wary. He backed away from him.

"Lan Zhan, I went through hell and finally found you," said Wei Wuxian, in a wounded tone. "How can you treat me like this?"

"You...truly are Wei Ying?" Lan Wangji asked.

"Of course."

"Then why is your appearance different?"

"That's a long story," said Wei Wuxian. "It's like this: I really am Wei Wuxian, but from seven years in the future. Seven years from now, I'll discover an incredible spiritual device that can transport a person back in time. I was examining it in detail when I accidentally knocked it—and so here I am!"

This explanation was so absurd that it was near infantile. "How can you prove such a thing is true?" demanded Lan Wangji, coldly.

"How do you want me to prove it?" Wei Wuxian asked. "I know everything about you. Wasn't I the one who gave you the rabbit you were holding, as well as the one that was by your feet? You were so upset about taking them at the time, but now you're unhappy your gege won't let you keep them. Did they grow on you?"

Lan Wangji's expression changed a little at this. He was about to say something and then stopped. "I..."

Wei Wuxian took a couple more steps toward him, arms wide open. "You, what?" he asked, with a gleeful grin. "Feeling shy now?"

His strange action had Lan Wangji alarmed, as though he were about to face a great foe. He backed away further. Wei Wuxian, who hadn't seen Lan Wangji act like this in a long time, wheezed inwardly—though he feigned anger.

"What's the meaning of this? Why are you backing away? Lan Zhan, you jerk, we've been married for ten years! Don't turn around and pretend you don't know me!"

Lan Wangji's handsome, icy countenance instantly cracked the moment he heard this.

"You...me?" he said, unbelieving. "...Ten years? ...Married?!"

His sentence broke to pieces before it even got out of his mouth.

Wei Wuxian acted like something had just occurred to him. "Oh, I forgot. You don't know that right now. Estimating the time, we've only just met, right? Have I left the Cloud Recesses? That's okay, I'll tell you a secret. In another few years, we'll become cultivation partners."

"...Cultivation partners?" Lan Wangji echoed.

"Yeah!" Wei Wuxian replied, smugly. "The kind that practices dual cultivation every day. It was a formal and official wedding—we even did our three marriage bows."

Lan Wangji was infuriated. His chest heaved slightly as he fumed, and it took him some time to squeeze a word through his gritted teeth. "...Nonsense!"

"Let me tell you a few more things. You'll know I'm not talking nonsense," insisted Wei Wuxian. "You like to hold me tight when you sleep, and I have to be on top of you, or you can't nod off. Every time you kiss me, it goes on nearly forever, and when it's over, you like to bite my lip before we part. Oh, yeah, and you really like biting me in bed too, biting me while you do me. My body is covered with..."

The moment Wei Wuxian said "hold me tight," Lan Wangji looked like he couldn't bear to hear any more. His expression only worsened as he continued. He looked like he desperately wished he could cover his own ears to block out such filthy language. Finally, he struck out with his hand.

"Nonsense!"

Wei Wuxian dodged the attack and taunted him. "'Nonsense' again. Pick another word! Besides, how do you know if it's nonsense? Is that not how you kiss me?"

"I...have never kissed you even once... How would I know what I like when I...do that!" Lan Wangji clenched out through his teeth.

Wei Wuxian thought about it for a moment. "That's true. You haven't even kissed me at this age, so of course you don't know what you like. Why don't you give it a try then, right now?"

Lan Wangji was struck speechless. He was so angry he'd forgotten even to summon sect disciples to arrest this suspicious individual. He struck out without hesitation, going straight for the vital points on Wei Wuxian's inner wrists each time. Alas, he was simply too young— Wei Wuxian moved faster than him and easily dodged his every attack, all while appearing quite at ease. He waited for an opening, then pinched a point on Lan Wangji's arm. Lan Wangji faltered and Wei Wuxian seized the opportunity to plant a kiss on his cheek.

Lan Wangji was dumbstruck.

Wei Wuxian loosened his grip on Lan Wangji's arm after committing the deed, releasing him. But Lan Wangji stood stunned in place, unable to pull himself back together for the longest time. He'd been struck entirely speechless.

"Ha ha ha ha ha ha ha ha ha ha ha ha ha ha ha…"

Wei Wuxian woke up from the dream laughing.

He was laughing so hard he almost fell off the bed. Thankfully, Lan Wangji's arm was always locked firmly around his waist. Wei Wuxian's body continued to shake with laughter even now that he was awake, which roused Lan Wangji from his slumber as well. The two sat up. Lan Wangji bowed his head and raised a hand to gently rub his temple.

"Just now, I…"

"Did you have a dream just now? A dream where a fifteen-year-old you met a twenty-something me?" Wei Wuxian finished for him.

Lan Wangji stared straight at him. "…It was the incense burner."

Wei Wuxian nodded. "At first, I thought I'd entered that dream because the incense burner's residual effects were hitting me harder. Who would've thought *you* were the one worst affected?"

What had happened tonight was different from last time. The young Lan Zhan in the dreamscape was actually Lan Wangji himself. A dreamer is not often aware they are dreaming, and thus, Lan Wangji genuinely thought he was only fifteen years old while in the dream. It was a perfectly respectable dream—a morning lesson, taking a walk, raising rabbits—and yet it was crashed by Wei Wuxian, who had infiltrated it and given him a good round of teasing after catching him.

"I can't, Lan Zhan," Wei Wuxian continued. "The way you were holding that rabbit, refusing to let it go, scared that your gege and your shufu wouldn't let you keep them—man, I love it. Ha ha ha ha ha…"

"…The hour is late," Lan Wangji chided, helplessly. "Do not disturb others with your laughter."

"As if our nightly disturbances are quiet," Wei Wuxian countered. "Why did you wake up so quickly? You should've stayed asleep a little longer so I could drag you to the back mountain to do naughty stuff. Give little Lan-er-gege a little *introduction*, ha ha ha ha..."

Lan Wangji watched him roll around next to him, but ultimately didn't respond. He sat there for a long time, poised and unmoving, before he suddenly reached out and pinned Wei Wuxian to the bed, bearing down on him.

The two had thought the power of the incense burner would have dispersed after the second night. But unexpectedly, Wei Wuxian woke up in Lan Wangji's dream again on the third night.

Dressed all in black, he strolled leisurely down the small white-stone paths of the Cloud Recesses. Chenqing's red tassel swayed with each step. It didn't take long before the clear, sonorous sound of recitation came drifting through the air.

The voices came from the direction of the Orchid Room. Wei Wuxian sauntered over. As expected, there were many Lan Clan disciples inside for their evening lesson. Lan Qiren wasn't around; the one on supervisory duty was Lan Wangji.

Lan Wangji was still youthful in tonight's dream, but looked to be around seventeen or eighteen, the same age he'd been when Wei Wuxian encountered him inside the Cave of the Xuanwu of Slaughter. His features were handsome and his demeanor elegant; he already had the grace of a distinguished cultivator, though there was still a trace of youthful inexperience. He sat poised at the front of the hall, and looked to be concentrating on something. Whenever someone approached him with a question about their studies, he provided an answer with only a simple glance at the text. His stern expression was a powerful contrast to his youthful immaturity.

Wei Wuxian leaned against a pillar outside the Orchid Room and watched for a while before he soundlessly leapt onto the roof's eaves and placed Chenqing to his lips.

Inside the Orchid Room, Lan Wangji paused.

"What is it, gongzi?" asked one of the boys.

"Who is playing the flute now?" Lan Wangji questioned.

The boys traded looks of dismay. One of them slowly stated, "We do not hear the sound of a flute."

Lan Wangji's expression turned slightly hard at this, and he rose to his feet. Just as he left through the door with his sword in hand, Wei Wuxian tucked away his flute and leapt swiftly onto another part of the roof.

Lan Wangji detected the unusual movement. "Who goes there?!" he barked in a low voice.

Two clear and far-reaching whistling notes rolled from Wei Wuxian's tongue. He was already dozens of meters away as he yelled with a laugh, "Your husband!"

Lan Wangji's face changed at the sound of his voice. "Wei Ying?" he asked, uncertain.

Wei Wuxian didn't answer. Lan Wangji drew Bichen from his back and chased after him. After many leaps and bounds, Wei Wuxian had already landed on the very tall enclosure wall of the Cloud Recesses, straightening up to stand atop the black tiles, when Lan Wangji landed just five meters from him, wielding Bichen. His forehead ribbon, his sleeves, and the hems of his robes flapped in the night breeze. A sharp, transcendent air surrounded him.

Wei Wuxian grinned. "What handsome moves, what a handsome man! This scene, matched with this view... If only there was a handsome jug of Emperor's Smile. Then everything would be perfect."

Lan Wangji stared at him intently, and said after a moment,

"Wei Ying, might I inquire as to what you are doing here, visiting the Cloud Recesses uninvited at this late hour?"

"Guess?" Wei Wuxian asked.

"...Nonsensical!" exclaimed Lan Wangji.

Wei Wuxian easily dodged Bichen's approaching tip. While Lan Wangji was already an excellent fighter at age seventeen or eighteen, he was still unable to pose much of a threat to present-day Wei Wuxian. It only took a brief exchange of blows for Wei Wuxian to spot an opening and slap a talisman on Lan Wangji's chest. Lan Wangji froze in place, unable to move.

Wei Wuxian seized him and dashed to the back reaches of the Cloud Recesses' mountain with him in his arms. He found a thicket of eupatorium grass and settled Lan Wangji here, leaning him against a white rock.

"What are you doing?" Lan Wangji demanded.

Wei Wuxian pinched his cheek. "Rape," he replied, in a serious tone.

Lan Wangji blanched, unable to tell if he was joking. "Wei Ying," he said in warning. "You...cannot mess around."

Wei Wuxian laughed. "You know me. I like messing around."

He reached his hand inside Lan Wangji's many layers of firmly tucked white robes and gave the most notable part of his anatomy a squeeze.

The squeeze was delivered with extreme skill, the pressure was just right. Lan Wangji's expression turned odd in an instant. The corners of his lips twitched, and he pursed his lips tightly. At last, he reined in his expression and affected a forced calm. Unexpectedly, Wei Wuxian took the inch for a mile—untying his sash and stripping off his trousers in a few quick motions. He appraised the heavy cock that was so at odds with Lan Wangji's otherwise delicately handsome features, and offered the most heartfelt praise.

"Hanguang-jun, you really have been naturally well-endowed from a very young age."

He then lightly flicked the shaft. Lan Wangji looked as if he was about to spit blood and die from fury at the very idea that someone would toy with his privates in such a way—he didn't even have the mind to wonder who "Hanguang-jun" was.

"*Wei Ying!*" he barked.

"Go on, yell to your heart's content. No one will come save you, even if you scream yourself hoarse," Wei Wuxian said gleefully.

Lan Wangji was going to say more—but after the laughter ceased, he saw Wei Wuxian tuck a loose strand of hair behind his ear and bury his head in Lan Wangji's crotch to take his cock into his mouth.

Shock filled Lan Wangji's eyes. He couldn't believe this. His whole body went stiff.

A seventeen- or eighteen-year-old Lan Wangji still had the air of youth, but the size of his cock was not to be dismissed. Wei Wuxian slowly took it into his mouth, but he felt the slick head hit the back of his throat before he could swallow the whole length of it. The shaft was thick and hot; he could feel it throb in his throat, and his cheeks were stuffed to fullness with the foreign object. Difficult as it was to swallow, he remained patient, taking the last stretch of it down to deeper depths.

Wei Wuxian had considerable practice when it came to the subject of Lan Wangji's cock. He unleashed all his tricks, loudly sucking and licking and slurping like he was focused on savoring a gourmet delicacy. Even though Lan Wangji's snow-white face showed no blush, he was flushed from his ears down to his neck, and his breathing quickened.

Wei Wuxian took him in and out of his mouth for a good while, but though his cheeks were sore from sucking, there was still no release. He was quite confused—there was no way his mouth couldn't satisfy seventeen-year-old Lan Wangji. He stole an upward glance and saw Lan Wangji working hard to endure his ministrations. His cock was clearly hard as iron, but he was holding himself back by sheer force of will, as if he were trying to protect some vital principle.

Amused by this, Wei Wuxian felt the desire to prank him sprout within him once more. He licked the slit on the head of his massive cock repeatedly with his wet tongue, and took him deep into his throat a few more times. Finally, Lan Wangji could endure it no longer and came.

The spurts of come were thick, filling his throat with musk. Wei Wuxian straightened up, lightly cleared his throat a few times, and wiped his mouth with the back of his hand—swallowing the come completely, just as he'd always done. The rims of Lan Wangji's eyes were red, whether because of his body's reaction to climaxing or simply his deep embarrassment. He glared hard at Wei Wuxian without saying a word. He looked like he couldn't endure another moment of this humiliation... Wei Wuxian's heart melted at the sight. He left a light kiss on his cheek.

"All right," he said consolingly. "I was wrong, I shouldn't have bullied you."

As he spoke, he used two fingers to wipe Lan Wangji's softening cock, then retracted his hand and untied his own sash to remove his lower garments.

Wei Wuxian's legs were long and slender, and his thighs fair and luminous as jade, with graceful, powerful contours. His buttocks were perky, round, and full—quite a sight to behold. Lan Wangji, still leaning against the white rock, just so happened to be angled to receive the perfect view of the hidden spot between Wei Wuxian's cheeks.

Wei Wuxian knelt in the thicket of eupatorium grass and sprawled on all fours with his back to Lan Wangji. He moved his come-smeared fingers lower. The secret cave was hidden within the dark crevasse of his ass, the tiny pink spot only glimpsed when he spread his cheeks a little. The entrance was soft, demure, and primly shut tight at first, but when Wei Wuxian gently administered Lan Wangji's come with his long fingers, it opened a little to shyly swallow his fingertips. Wei Wuxian slowly but firmly pushed his fingers all the way inside, thrusting in and out. He did this for a while, slowly increasing the speed of his thrusting, and his cock gradually began to harden.

When the sounds turned wet, Wei Wuxian added a third finger. He panted lightly, as though he was reaching his limit. He slowed the pace of the fucking to what he could take.

In the dark of the night, it shouldn't have been easy to see every detail. But of course, all five of Lan Wangji's senses just had to be keen—especially his sight. He watched as this ridiculously obscene act played out just inches from him, unable to pull his eyes away.

When it came to making love, Wei Wuxian liked reaching climax together with Lan Wangji. To avoid coming too soon, he purposely avoided the most sensitive spot inside of him as he stretched himself out. But Lan Wangji had always taken such good care of that place that his body clenched particularly hard when it wasn't attended to, sucking inward again and again, as if displeased. When his fingers didn't touch that spot, his hips would unconsciously dip and deliver it to his fingers. Having brushed dangerously close to the spot many times, Wei Wuxian's inner thighs were weak and trembling. When he nearly fell out of his crouching position, he quickly withdrew his fingers to cool himself down for a moment. He turned his head and locked eyes with Lan Wangji without warning. Lan Wangji immediately closed his eyes.

"Hey, Lan Zhan, what're you doing? Reciting the Lan family precepts in your head?" Wei Wuxian laughed.

He'd hit the nail on the head. Lan Wangji's lashes quivered. He seemed to want to open his eyes, but managed to resist the urge, in the end.

"C'mon," Wei Wuxian beckoned in a languid tone. "Look at me. What're you afraid of? It's not like I'll do bad things to you."

His voice had always been pleasant to the ears. When he drawled those words, it was like a playful little hook with bait attached. However, Lan Wangji seemed determined not to look, to listen, or to speak—he was determined to remain unmoved.

"Will you really be so stone-hearted as to not even look at me?" asked Wei Wuxian.

No matter how he coaxed and cajoled, Lan Wangji refused to open his eyes. Wei Wuxian arched his brows.

"If that's the case, mind if I borrow Bichen for a little bit?"

True to his word, he grabbed the recently discarded Bichen off the ground.

Lan Wangji's eyes flew open at once. "What are you going to do?!" he barked sharply

"What do you think?"

"...I do not know!"

"Why are you so nervous if you don't know what I'm about to do?"

"I! I..."

Wei Wuxian looked at him, grinning, and waved Bichen in his hand. Then he lowered his gaze and dropped a light kiss to Bichen's hilt. What followed was a glimpse of a vibrantly red tongue as he began to carefully lick the hilt.

Bichen's blade was like ice and snow, translucent and crystalline. Its hilt was forged of pure silver, using a secret method. It was exceptionally heavy, its carvings dignified and ancient in design. It presented a wicked and bewitching sight.

Like he'd been set ablaze, Lan Wangji exclaimed, "Let go of Bichen!"

"Why?" Wei Wuxian asked.

"That is my sword!" said Lan Wangji. "You can't use it to...to..."

"I know it's yours," said Wei Wuxian in an inquisitive tone. "I just sort of like it, so I was playing with it. What did you think I was gonna do?"

Lan Wangji was momentarily stumped.

Wei Wuxian hugged his middle and laughed. "Ha ha ha ha ha ha ha ha! Lan Zhan, what were you thinking? How perverted!"

Having his accusation not just denied, but turned back on him, Lan Wangji's face flushed a thrilling array of colors. Wei Wuxian teased him to his heart's content before he said, "If you want me to not touch your sword, then swap it for yourself. How's that? Okay?"

Lan Wangji couldn't say "okay." Nor could he allow Wei Wuxian to profane his sword. He was stumped, unable to answer. Wei Wuxian knelt in front of him, his back as straight as a brush, then shuffled over on his knees and straddled him.

"Give me the okay and I'll return your sword," he coaxed. "Then you and I can do fun things together. Okay?"

It took Lan Wangji some time before a word escaped through his gritted teeth. "...No!"

Wei Wuxian quirked an eyebrow. "M'kay. You said it."

He backed down from his position atop Lan Wangji and sat in front of him. Snickering, he opened his legs.

"Watch me and Bichen play, then."

With his legs splayed wide in such an utterly shameless position, Lan Wangji had a full view of Wei Wuxian's lower body. Two fair cheeks spread from his opened legs, revealing the hidden pink hole. Its rim was already slightly red and swollen from his earlier ministrations, and the dampness made it appear even more tender.

Wei Wuxian turned Bichen around and aimed the hilt toward his entrance. He drew in a small breath, then pushed. The delicate folds were instantly stretched. The end of Bichen's hilt was pulled in, and nearly half of it entered at once.

Bichen's hilt was as icy as a piece of unyielding iron, and Wei Wuxian shuddered at the temperature. The flexing of his insides grew more intense from the cold, and a small stretch of the hilt slid out. He promptly gripped the sword and pushed it in harder, slowly fucking himself with it.

His inner walls wrapped tight around the hilt, which was engraved with exquisite ancient patterns that raised and dipped. The feeling of it bumping his inner walls was fit to drive him insane. When it rubbed a certain spot, Wei Wuxian let out a quiet moan and drew his legs together a little. A wave of vertigo and tingling tumbled from his head down his spine, and his cock stirred, standing tall and erect.

From Lan Wangji's perspective, the sight was obscene beyond measure. Wei Wuxian, lying in front of him with his legs wide open, his ass taking Bichen. The hilt of the sword was hard and cold, and the tender entrance was almost pitifully red and swollen from being fucked so hard. Even so, Wei Wuxian kept going, moving it in and out, faster and faster, until he was fucking himself smoothly along its length. He gazed at him with damp eyes, panting softly.

"Lan Zhan…" he called. "Lan Zhan…"

His nasal voice seemed to plead with him. Or perhaps the words had simply been slurred out in the throes of passion. Whatever the case, it was enough to enrapture a man and make him lose himself. Lan Wangji had no way to close his eyes or look away. He stared intently at Wei Wuxian's face like he'd been bewitched, stared as he struggled and twisted under Bichen's assault. He watched, knuckles white and cracking, as Wei Wuxian fucked himself to a trembling mess.

Wei Wuxian was unaware of the change, as Bichen was giving him a hell of a time. His legs kept closing of their own volition, firmly pushing the hilt inside him as his cheeks pressed closed. As the hilt was pulled in deeper, Wei Wuxian exhaled deeply, feeling his arms and legs going weak. He lay down on his side with the intent to take a short break, but something suddenly seized the bend of his knees. Wei Wuxian found his legs forced open once more, captured in a grip as strong as iron shackles.

Wei Wuxian opened his eyes and met Lan Wangji's gaze squarely. His eyes were terrifyingly bloodshot, filled with an unknown flame. He grabbed Bichen and pulled it out, flinging it far away. Wei Wuxian moaned as the hilt left his body, as though displeased by the loss.

"*Shameless!*" Lan Wangji bellowed furiously.

He crushed Wei Wuxian to the ground, and shoved inside him with his furious cock—so hard it was flushed a deep red. Once fully sheathed, he began to pound Wei Wuxian without a moment's pause.

When Lan Wangji entered him, Wei Wuxian's legs automatically wrapped themselves around his waist. He wound his arms around his neck most agreeably, putting himself in a position to cater to him. But after taking a few thrusts, he felt he couldn't take any more—Lan Wangji's movements were too rough, and every motion felt like it'd send him flying from the impact. He was so deep inside that Wei Wuxian's ass cheeks and tailbone ached.

"Lighter!" Wei Wuxian shouted. "Er-gege, go easy..."

He had forgotten he was older than Lan Wangji in this dream, and that was his downfall. When he blurted out "er-gege," not only did Lan Wangji not restrain himself, he pounded him harder—as though his sole purpose in life was to split Wei Wuxian's buttocks into eight pieces in retribution. Wei Wuxian threw his head back and drew a labored breath in the thick of the thrashing, storm-like battering.

"So...hot!"

Bichen emanated coldness. When the hilt had been seated inside him, it left Wei Wuxian's insides soft but slightly chilled. Lan Wangji's cock was thicker and hotter, and so every time he drove in, it was like a ball of fire blazing through Wei Wuxian's abdomen, burning so hot that it made him want to roll across the ground.

But his body had gone limp and malleable, thanks to how thoroughly he'd played with himself, and now thanks to Lan Wangji's roughness. All he could do was shiver through Lan Wangji's lashing. No matter how much higher his cultivation may have been, he had no way to retaliate. When he couldn't take the heat any longer, he tried to squirm away incessantly, rolling his hips in an attempt to escape. Lan Wangji only pinned him by the waist and drove deeper, slamming the voice out of him.

Lan Wangji growled in his ear. "Who is the husband?!"

Wei Wuxian was still dazed and confused, so Lan Wangji repeated the question, punctuated with a thrust so hard that Wei Wuxian's body and soul were both almost sent flying to the heavens.

"You! You!" he quickly answered. "It's you, you're the husband..."

He'd brought it on himself.

He clenched his teeth and suffered another round of fucking without complaint. As his frozen insides were warmed by the grinding, he gradually began to feel better. The head of Lan Wangji's cock was well defined, and fucked him with wild abandon. Wei Wuxian's insides were wet and slick, and drew him in with unceasing entanglement. Lan Wangji's cock was also slightly curved at the end, which let it rub Wei Wuxian's most sensitive spots again and again. It felt so good that Wei Wuxian was on the verge of losing his mind. And yet he couldn't help but put on a feeble act, as if he couldn't endure being fucked so hard.

He caught Lan Wangji's arms and cried pitifully as he rocked up and down with Lan Wangji's powerful thrusts. "...Er-gege... Lan Zhan... Go easier, won't you? This hurts... I think I'm bleeding..."

It certainly was slick where the two were joined, and the wet squelching grew louder. Lan Wangji immediately looked down between them, and was slightly taken aback.

Wei Wuxian humphed. "Am I bleeding?" he whined.

Lan Wangji breathed out harshly. "No."

"No? Then what is it?" Wei Wuxian asked.

"You're wet," said Lan Wangji, in a low voice.

Although he hadn't noticed until now, Wei Wuxian's inner thighs were drenched. Lan Wangji's hard, flushed cock was also glistening. The wetness could have only come from Wei Wuxian's body.

"Really? Really?" Wei Wuxian asked.

Feigning disbelief, he caught Lan Wangji's hand and brought it to touch where they were joined. Lan Wangji's cock was thick, strong, and lined with throbbing veins, stretching Wei Wuxian's narrow entrance to its limit. Lan Wangji felt the slippery wetness, and the spot where they came together. His hand recoiled as if he'd been pricked by a needle. But when he looked down, the fluid was clear—it wasn't blood, after all.

Wei Wuxian and Lan Wangji's bodies matched perfectly, and in the thick of passion, their bodies reacted naturally as well. Wei Wuxian had been trying to tease him. Seeing the hint of a grin, Lan Wangji knew he'd been deceived. He put his head down and renewed his attack.

Breath broken by the next round of thrusts, Wei Wuxian quickly cut in, "...Lan Zhan, Lan Zhan, let me top. Let me be on top, okay?"

Lan Wangji hesitated, as though he didn't understand what "top" meant. Holding on to him, Wei Wuxian flipped them around with great effort, reversing their positions.

Now Lan Wangji lay on the ground while Wei Wuxian straddled him, ass and crotch still tightly joined. That hot, thick cock remained buried deep inside Wei Wuxian without a moment of separation. It subtly rubbed Wei Wuxian's insides during the switch. He scrunched his eyes in contentment from the sensation, lost in a daze once more.

He looked down. Though it might have been his imagination, he kept thinking his flat abdomen was slightly distended by Lan Wangji's cock. He couldn't help but feel his own belly, but didn't touch it for long before Lan Wangji grabbed his ass and forced him to move again.

Wei Wuxian rose up and down with the force of Lan Wangji's grip. When he rose, only the hard, defined head would remain in his body; when he sank back down, he would take his cock to the deepest depths of him, so deep that his brows knit together in concentration. The up and down was extremely fast, leaving almost no time to breathe.

Wei Wuxian riding Lan Wangji was always one of their favorite positions when having sex, if only because it allowed for the deepest penetration, which Wei Wuxian loved. As it turned out, there could be too much of a good thing—Lan Wangji was penetrating him a bit *too* deeply.

The young, seventeen-year-old Lan Wangji in this dream had been tantalized to the point of madness and couldn't control his strength at all. Wei Wuxian was being fucked until his legs trembled and he couldn't stand up, much less find the energy to struggle free. He was in a terrible plight. All he could do was brace himself with both hands on Lan Wangji's firm abdomen and take shaky breaths.

Wei Wuxian was born with a thin waist and narrow hips, but his ass cheeks were plenty meaty. Lan Wangji sank his fingers deeply into his skin and kneaded with powerful force, bruising him all over in no time at all. The kneading made Wei Wuxian itch all over. His ass hurt, and he couldn't help but pry off one of the hands. Unexpectedly, Lan Wangji seemed deeply upset by having his hand removed. His brows knitted and his expression darkened.

With one loud clap, Wei Wuxian's ass was brutally spanked. The sound of the slap was clear and crisp.

Wei Wuxian was instantly stunned by the strike.

Not many people in his life had hit him there. Even when he was little and mischievous and Madam Yu punished him with the whip, he'd only ever been lashed on his back and palms. Jiang Fengmian and Jiang Yanli couldn't bear to hit him at all. When Wei Wuxian saw other children spanked for being naughty, he thought it shameful and humiliating, and was proud of the fact he'd never been subjected to it. Yet now Lan Wangji had gone and broken his streak—a seventeen-year-old Lan Wangji, to boot.

Wei Wuxian's face alternated between flushing and blanching. For the first time he'd experienced during sex, he discovered an irrepressible sense of shame surfacing within him.

The more he dwelled on it, the more he couldn't bear the thought. One of his ass cheeks was still stinging. "Stop! I'm not doing this anymore!" he cried hastily. Then he rolled to the side and off of Lan Wangji. Dragging his two weak legs behind him, he tried crawling away to go find his trousers.

The sex had Lan Wangji all worked up. An unspeakable fire had been suppressed in his chest for a good while—earlier, Wei Wuxian had squeezed and pinched and flicked him, kissing and touching and threateningly teasing him. Now that he'd suddenly discovered that Wei Wuxian was particularly scared of being spanked, why would he let this go?

With a casual wave of his hand, the trousers Wei Wuxian had just tugged up to his knees were instantly shredded to pieces. Lan Wangji flipped him over and seized both his wrists with one hand, locking them behind his back. The other hand gave Wei Wuxian's snow-white ass another hard spank.

Pa! Wei Wuxian's whole body jerked from the strike, and he cried pitifully. *"Ow!"*

It didn't actually hurt. It was just extremely, unbearably embarrassing. Wei Wuxian never tried to suppress his moans during sex, so his voice always wound up raspy at the halfway point. His cry, therefore, didn't sound like one of pain—it sounded a bit like a sweet moan, instead. Lan Wangji paused at the sound, his gaze lowered.

Beneath his hand were two plush ass cheeks. His two slaps had left a light blush coloring the fair skin, which was crisscrossed with all manner of violent fingerprints. Thanks to all this rough treatment, the cheeks were slightly parted and Wei Wuxian's timidly contracting entrance peeked between them, now even more delicately tender and flushed. It was a wonder how it had managed to swallow both Bichen's hilt and this terrifyingly massive cock. Slickness still flowed wildly around the summit of Wei Wuxian's cheeks as well as his inner thighs.

Lan Wangji's eyes grew increasingly dark at the sight of it.

As for the restrained Wei Wuxian, scared that he'd be spanked again, he quickly clenched his ass and made the small hole open and close to distract Lan Wangji in hopes that he would return to business instead of delivering another lash to his rear. Sure enough, Lan Wangji's breath turned harsh. He flipped Wei Wuxian over, penetrating him anew. The entry was incredibly smooth. Having been filled to fullness again, Wei Wuxian sighed a breath of relief.

Yet before he could fully exhale, Lan Wangji struck out again, slapping his ass. Wei Wuxian shuddered from the strike and his hole unconsciously squeezed as well, which caused the head of Lan Wangji's cock to bump his most sensitive spot. Wei Wuxian's cock grew harder, trickling with precome.

After that, Lan Wangji began to spank him on the hip with every thrust, so Wei Wuxian's insides would squeeze the hardest when the head of Lan Wangji's cock hit his most critical point. His own cock stood higher and higher. The three overlapping sensations made him feel like he was being tossed by surging waves.

"Don't be like this..." he whimpered. "Lan Zhan... Stop... Don't spank me anymore... Wake up! Lan Zhan, wake up..."

He knew Lan Wangji had always been inclined to roughness during sex, and Wei Wuxian had always enjoyed being roughed up. But he'd never been pushed to the edge like this.

Having been spanked a dozen times, Wei Wuxian's perfectly fine ass was beaten red, hot, and slightly swollen. It stung much he couldn't bear to be touched, and the rest of his body grew increasingly sensitive in turn. When Lan Wangji pushed into the deepest part of him once more, he leaned down and captured his lips. Sapped of energy, Wei Wuxian hugged his shoulders tight and deepened the kiss. He reached his climax at the point of exhaustion.

A streak of milky white splashed both of their abdomens. Following close behind, Lan Wangji spilled inside him abundantly.

Wei Wuxian held him quietly for a bit before complaining with a raspy voice. "*...Ow...*"

Lan Wangji seemed to have regained some calm and some sense after the second climax. "...Where does it hurt?" he asked, sounding somewhat at a loss for what to do. His weight was still crushing him.

It wasn't like Wei Wuxian could say *"My ass."* So after a pause, he said instead, voice low, "...Lan Zhan, quickly, kiss me..."

His downcast eyes and unusually demure manner had Lan Wangji's earlobes turning pink. He held him as tight as he had requested, and captured his lips, kissing him with the utmost care.

When they parted, Lan Wangji did indeed nip Wei Wuxian's lip.

And then the two woke up.

Lying there on the wooden bed inside the Tranquility Room, the two of them stared at each other for a moment before Lan Wangji pulled Wei Wuxian into his arms once more.

After being kissed in his embrace for a long time, Wei Wuxian seemed quite satiated, if bleary-eyed. "Lan Zhan... I've got a question for you. You come inside me every time...is that because you want me to bear a little Lan-gongzi for you?"

In the dream, his teasing had failed and he'd been fucked within an inch of his life. When he woke up to the sight of Lan Wangji, he couldn't help babbling nonsense again.

But Lan Wangji wasn't as easily provoked as he was in the past, and his only response was, "How might you bear a child?"

Wei Wuxian worked out his sore arms, then pillowed his head on them and sighed. "If I could, we'd have a bunch of them running around already, considering the way you screw me day and night."

Lan Wangji couldn't bear to listen to such filth. "Enough of that."

Wei Wuxian propped up a leg and snickered. "Shy again? I—"

Before he could finish his sentence, he suddenly felt Lan Wangji land a soft pat on his hip. Wei Wuxian nearly tumbled off the bed.

"What are you doing?!"

"Checking," Lan Wangji said.

Wei Wuxian climbed to his feet in one quick motion despite his shaky legs.

"No thanks. Lan Zhan, I remember what *fine things* you did in the dream. No one's ever treated me like that! You're not allowed to do that from now on. Fuck me all you want, I'll open my legs and let you have your way with me, but no more spanking!"

Lan Wangji pulled him back to bed. "I will not."

Wei Wuxian relaxed, assured of his promise. "You said it, Hanguang-jun."

"Mn."

The past three nights had been crazy. A wave of drowsiness washed over Wei Wuxian, and he couldn't hang on any longer. He curled back into Lan Wangji's arms, grumbling.

"No one's ever treated me like that..."

Lan Wangji stroked his hair and dropped a kiss on his forehead. He shook his head and smiled.

X UE YANG SAT at a wooden table near a roadside stall. He had one bent leg propped on the long bench where he lounged as he ate a bowl of tangyuan—glutinous rice balls in sweet broth. He clinked and clanked his spoon in the bowl while eating, making a racket. Though initially satisfied with his meal, he suddenly realized toward the end that the tangyuan were way too sticky and the rice wine was not sweet enough.

And so, Xue Yang stood up and kicked over the stall.

The stall owner, who had been bustling around, was stunned by his actions. He looked on helplessly as the boy suddenly went on a rampage and then turned and left with a grin on his face—without so much as a word once he was done.

It took quite a while for the peddler to react, but he belatedly caught up to him and raged, "What are you doing?!"

"Wrecking your stall," Xue Yang answered.

The peddler was infuriated. "You're sick! Insane!"

Xue Yang remained unmoved. The stall owner continued to curse him, one finger pointed at Xue Yang's nose.

"You little bastard! Instead of paying me after eating my food, you have the nerve to wreck my stall?! I..."

Xue Yang's right thumb twitched, and the sword at his waist left its sheath. He patted the peddler's face with the tip of his sword, its glint sinister and ominous. The movement was ever so light and gentle.

"The tangyuan were yummy," he said in a saccharine tone. "Add more sugar next time."

Having said that, he turned around and swaggered on his way.

The stall owner was both terrified and petrified. Livid, he could only choke with silent fury as he helplessly watched Xue Yang walk a good distance away. Then all of a sudden, his frustration and indignation boiled over, and he let loose a furious bellow.

"How can you do this in broad daylight, with no rhyme or reason? Who are you to do this?!"

Xue Yang waved without even looking back. "Meh, many things in the world happen without rhyme or reason. They're called unexpected disasters. Bye!"

He briskly skipped along, passing by a few streets. After a while, a person approached from behind him. His walk was easy and unhurried as he kept pace with Xue Yang, and his hands were tucked politely behind his back.

Jin Guangyao sighed. "I turn around for just a moment and you cause such a mess. I start out paying for just a bowl of tangyuan, but now must pay for no less than the tables, chairs, benches, pots, bowls, and pans."

"You short on that bit of money?" asked Xue Yang.

"No," answered Jin Guangyao.

"Then what are you sighing about?"

"I don't think you're short on money either. Can't you try to be a regular customer once in a while?"

"Back in Kui Prefecture I never needed money to get the things I wanted," said Xue Yang. "Like so."

As he spoke, he casually swiped a skewer of candied hawthorns from the pole of a roadside peddler. The peddler gaped, dumbfounded.

It was probably the first time he had encountered such a shameless person.

Xue Yang bit a candied hawthorn off the stick. "And besides, it's not like you can't sort out some measly stall being wrecked."

"You little hooligan," Jin Guangyao said with a laugh. "Wreck stalls if that's what you want. You can burn down the entire street, for all I care, as long as you mind two things—don't wear the Sparks Amidst Snow uniform, and keep your face hidden. Don't let anyone find the culprit and put me on the spot."

He tossed money to that particular peddler.

Xue Yang spat out a hawthorn pit. Out of the corner of his eye, he saw a small patch of purple and blue that wasn't well concealed at Jin Guangyao's temple. He laughed. "How'd you get that?"

Jin Guangyao shot him a slightly reproachful glance and straightened his cap to hide the bruise. "It's a long story."

"Nie Mingjue hit you?" Xue Yang asked.

"Do you think I'd be standing here talking to you now if he had been the one to hit me?" answered Jin Guangyao.

Xue Yang had to agree with that.

The two of them left Lanling City and traveled to a strange complex of buildings, located out in the wilderness.

It was not a particularly impressive sight to behold. A row of dark, grim houses lay beyond the tall perimeter wall. There was a square in front of the houses, enclosed by a chest-high metal fence plastered with red and yellow talismans. At the center of the square was a collection of peculiar equipment, such as metal cages, guillotines, and boards studded with nails. Some shabbily dressed "people" were also lumbering around.

These "people" had ashen skin and empty gazes. They milled

about aimlessly in the open square, bumping into one another from time to time. Their strange rasping breaths sounded like leaking wind.

This was the Corpse Refinery.

Jin Guangshan desperately coveted the Yin Tiger Tally. No matter how many covert attempts he made, no matter what tactics he employed, Wei Wuxian had yielded to neither the carrot or the stick, leaving Jin Guangshan to slam into brick walls every single time. And so, Jin Guangshan had thought, *Since you can do it, why can't others? Wei Ying, I refuse to believe you're the only person in the whole world with the skill to create a device like that. The day will come when you're surpassed, trampled underfoot, and mocked by future generations. Let's see if you can still be so arrogant when the time comes.*

And so, Jin Guangshan brazenly recruited deviant cultivators who pursued the demonic path in imitation of Wei Wuxian and put them to use for his own aims. He invested massive sums of money and resources into these people, ordering them to clandestinely analyze the structure of the Yin Tiger Tally in order to replicate and restore it. Very few of them made any headway in their research. The one who made it the furthest turned out to be the youngest of them—Xue Yang, whom Jin Guangyao had personally recommended.

Overjoyed by his results, Jin Guangshan designated Xue Yang a guest cultivator and accorded him significant privileges and freedom. The Corpse Refinery was a piece of land Jin Guangyao had specially requested to allow Xue Yang to conduct his independent research in secrecy—in other words, to allow him to fool around as brazenly as he wished.

When they arrived at the Corpse Refinery, two of the fierce corpses were fighting in the square. These two were completely unlike the other walking corpses—they were well dressed, the whites of their eyes were visible, and they held weapons in their hands. Sparks flew everywhere as the swords clashed.

There were two chairs in front of the metal fence. Jin Guangyao and Xue Yang took their seats at the same time. As Jin Guangyao adjusted his collar, a walking corpse shuffled unsteadily over to present a tray.

"Tea," Xue Yang said.

Jin Guangyao glanced at it. A strange purplish-red object lay at the bottom of the teacup, bloated from soaking. Who could say what it was?

He pushed the teacup away with a smile. "Thanks."

Xue Yang pushed the teacup back and said warmly, "This is my secret blend, which I made personally. Why won't you drink it?"

Jin Guangyao pushed the teacup away again and replied amicably, "It's precisely *because* it's your secret blend that I don't dare to drink it."

Xue Yang raised an eyebrow, then turned his head to watch the fierce corpses fight.

The battle was growing increasingly heated and intense. Swords and claws slashed, blood and flesh flew everywhere—and yet, the boredom on Xue Yang's face deepened. After a while, he snapped his fingers and made a gesture. Both fierce corpses instantly began to convulse, then turned their swords on themselves and sliced off their own heads. The headless bodies flopped to the ground, still spasming.

"Wasn't the fight going well?" asked Jin Guangyao.

"Too slow," said Xue Yang.

"They were a lot faster than the two I saw last time," remarked Jin Guangyao.

Xue Yang held out his black-gloved hand and extended out a finger. Waggling it, he said, "It depends on what they're compared against. Those two wouldn't even last long against the ordinary fierce corpses that Wei Wuxian summoned to action with his flute, much less Wen Ning."

"What's your rush?" Jin Guangyao said with a smile. "I'm certainly in no hurry. Take your time and tell me if there's anything you need. Ah, yes…"

He took something out of his sleeve and handed it to Xue Yang. "Maybe you need this?"

Xue Yang flipped through it. All of a sudden, he straightened up in his seat. "Wei Wuxian's manuscripts?"

"That's right," said Jin Guangyao.

Xue Yang lowered his head and looked through it with eyes shining. A moment later, he raised his head. "Are these really his handwritten manuscripts? The ones he wrote when he was nineteen?"

"Of course," said Jin Guangyao. "Everyone fought tooth and nail to get their hands on these. It took me quite a lot of effort to gather them all."

Xue Yang cursed under his breath. The excitement in his eyes grew increasingly brighter. After flipping through them, he remarked, "It's incomplete."

"Given the raging fire and intense battle at the Burial Mounds, you should count your lucky stars that I could even find these remnants. Use them wisely."

"How about that flute of his?" Xue Yang asked. "Can't you get me Chenqing?"

Jin Guangyao spread his hands in a gesture of helplessness. "Not Chenqing. Jiang Wanyin took it."

"Doesn't he hate Wei Wuxian the most?" Xue Yang wondered. "What does he need Chenqing for? Didn't you also get your hands on Wei Wuxian's sword? Give him the sword in exchange for the flute. Wei Wuxian gave up on using Suibian a long time ago. It even sealed itself off—no one can pull it out of its sheath. What's the damn use of keeping it, other than as a display piece?"

"Xue-gongzi really is adept at imposing the impossible on others," Jin Guangyao said. "Do you think I never tried? Not everything is that simple. Jiang Wanyin is obsessed to the point of madness. He thinks Wei Wuxian is still alive. If Wei Wuxian *does* return, he might not come for his sword, but he'd definitely come for Chenqing. And so, Jiang Wanyin absolutely will not hand it over. If I said so much as another word on the subject, he'd snap."

Xue Yang snorted twice with laughter. "Mad dog."

Just then, two disciples from the Jin Clan of Lanling dragged over a cultivator with disheveled hair.

"Weren't you going to refine a new set of fierce corpses?" Jin Guangyao said. "As it happens, I've brought materials for you."

The cultivator's eyes were red with fury. They seemed to burn as the man glared at Jin Guangyao and struggled with all his might.

"Who's he?" Xue Yang asked.

Without batting an eyelid, Jin Guangyao answered, "Everyone I send you is a sinner, of course."

Hearing this, the cultivator lunged with all his might, somehow spitting out the ball of cloth that gagged him, along with a mouthful of blood. "Jin Guangyao! You heinous, inhumane scum. The nerve of you to call me a sinner! What sin have I committed?!"

He said this slowly and clearly, each word forming a barrage of sharp nails he wanted all too badly to drive into Jin Guangyao.

Xue Yang snorted a laugh. "What's going on?"

The person behind the cultivator yanked at him as if pulling at a dog's leash. Jin Guangyao waved his hand. "Gag him."

But Xue Yang said, "Whatever for? Let me hear him. I wanna know why you're heinous, inhumane scum. I can't make out what he's saying when he barks like a dog."

"He Su-gongzi is a renowned cultivator," Jin Guangyao said in a slightly reproachful tone. "How can you address him with such disrespect?"

The cultivator gave a grim laugh. "I'm already in your clutches, at your mercy. Why keep up the act?"

"You don't have to look at me like that," said Jin Guangyao, amiably. "I had no choice in the matter either. The election of a cultivation chief is only par for the course, given the way the situation has developed. Why must you fan the flames and stir up conflict? I warned you repeatedly, but you insisted on ignoring me. Now that we're at this impasse, there's no turning back. I do regret that it came to this, and it pains me—"

"What do you mean, 'par for the course' and 'fanning the flames'?" asked He Su. "Jin Guangshan only wants to establish the position of cultivation chief to emulate the Wen Clan of Qishan and reign supreme over all the other clans. Do you think the rest of the world is too ignorant to see that? You set me up only because I spoke the truth!"

Jin Guangyao smiled and said nothing.

"When you people get your way, all the cultivation clans will see the Jin Clan of Lanling's true colors," He Su continued. "Do you think you can rest easy simply by killing me? Big mistake! The He Clan of Tingshan has many talented people. From now on, we will work as one against you. We will never submit to you Wen dogs in disguise!"

On hearing this, Jin Guangyao narrowed his eyes slightly, while the corners of his lips curved up. It was the same gentle, affable expression he usually wore, but He Su's heart dropped at the sight of it. There was suddenly a commotion outside the Corpse Refinery, with the cries of women and children audible among the noise.

He Su snapped his head back, only to see a bunch of cultivators from the Jin Clan of Lanling in the process of hauling sixty or seventy people inside the complex. All of them wore the same uniform. There were men and women, elders and youngsters, each of them terrified and panicked. Some were already wailing their hearts out. A young girl and boy, both trussed with rope, kneeled on the ground and shouted miserably to He Su.

"Ge!"

He Su was stunned. His face blanched white as paper. "Jin Guangyao! What do you mean by this?! You can just kill me. Why implicate my entire clan?!"

Jin Guangyao looked down and straightened the cuffs of his sleeves. He beamed as he explained, "Didn't you just remind me that I won't rest easy if I only kill you? That the He Clan of Tingshan has many talented people who will work as one from now on, and never submit to me? The prospect terrifies me so much that, after thinking it over, I'm left with no choice but to do this."

It was as if a fist had been shoved down He Su's throat, rendering him speechless. After a long silence, he raged, "You're massacring my clan for no reason! Do you really not fear public condemnation?! Do you not fear what Chifeng-zun will do when he finds out?!"

At the mention of Nie Mingjue, Jin Guangyao arched his brow. Xue Yang laughed so hard he almost toppled over in his chair.

Jin Guangyao shot him a glance, then turned back around and said in an even-tempered tone, "You can't say that. The He Clan of

Tingshan used the full force of its power to start an uprising and plot to assassinate Sect Leader Jin. All of you were caught red-handed. How can you call this 'no reason'?"

A number of the captives cried out, "Ge! He's lying! We didn't. We really didn't!"

"What a crock of shit!" He Su spat. "Open your damn eyes and take a good look around! There's a nine-year-old child here, and elders who can't even walk! What uprising could they start?! And why would they assassinate your father out of the blue?!"

"Because they refused to accept that He Su-gongzi made a grave mistake, of course—a mistake for which he was declared guilty of the crime of murder by Golden Carp Tower," Jin Guangyao said.

It was then He Su remembered the charges that had brought him to this eerie, hellish place. "This is a setup! I didn't kill that cultivator from the Jin Clan of Lanling! I'd never even seen him before! It remains to be seen if he's even a cultivator from your clan! I...I..."

He was stumped for a long while before he broke down in despair. "I...I don't know what happened! I have no idea at all!"

However, no one here would listen to his defense. Sitting before him were two vicious villains who already considered him a dead man and were enjoying the sight of his last-ditch struggle. Jin Guangyao leaned back with a smile and waved.

"Gag him. Go on, gag him."

Knowing he could not escape death, a look of despair came over He Su's face. He clenched his teeth and howled, "*Jin Guangyao! You'll get what you deserve one day! Your father will rot to death among the whores sooner or later, and you, son of a whore, will end up no better than him!*"

Xue Yang was all chuckles and laughter as he listened with relish.

Suddenly, a black shadow and a silver glare flashed through the air. He Su covered his mouth and let loose a blood-curdling scream.

Blood splattered all over the ground. He Su's clan members cried and cursed, erupting into complete chaos, but remained firmly restrained despite of their struggles.

Xue Yang stood before He Su, who had fallen to the ground. He picked up a bloody object, which he tossed around in his hands. Then he snapped his fingers at two walking corpses on the sidelines and commanded, "Lock him up in the cage."

"Alive?" Jin Guangyao asked.

Xue Yang looked back and lifted a corner of his mouth into a smirk. "Wei Wuxian never used living humans to refine corpses. I, on the other hand, would like to give it a try."

Heeding his order, the two walking corpses dragged a still-screaming He Su by the legs and threw him into the metal cage at the center of the Corpse Refinery. Seeing their elder brother frantically banging his head against the metal bars, the boys and girls threw themselves at the cage and wailed. The cries were shrill and jarring to the ears, and Jin Guangyao raised a hand to massage his temple. He looked like he might pick up the cup of tea and take a sip to calm himself, but then saw the bloated purplish-red object at the bottom of the cup again as he lowered his head. He looked up again to see Xue Yang jovially juggling that chunk of tongue.

After considering it for a moment, it suddenly hit him. "You use *that* to brew tea?"

"I have a whole jar of 'em," Xue Yang said. "Want some?"

Jin Guangyao was dumbstruck. "...No, thank you. Clean yourself up a little and follow me to collect someone. We will go elsewhere for tea afterward."

As if just remembering something, he straightened his cap and accidentally touched the concealed bruise on his forehead.

"What's with that lump on your head?" Xue Yang asked again, gloating.

"As I said, it's a long story," Jin Guangyao replied.

Jin Guangshan always dumped all his work on Jin Guangyao so he could leave home to go indulge in women and drink all through the night. And Madam Jin would always rage all through Golden Carp Tower, infuriated by her husband's behavior. Jin Zixuan had once mediated between his parents, but now that he was gone, the two of them were past the point of reconciliation.

Every time Jin Guangshan went out to fool around with women, he would have Jin Guangyao cover up his activities and make excuses for him. Unable to get at Jin Guangshan, Madam Jin would instead turn her fury on Jin Guangyao, smashing an incense burner on him today and splashing a cup of tea at him tomorrow. To survive a few more days at Golden Carp Tower, Jin Guangyao had to personally search the various brothels, collect Jin Guangshan, and escort him back in a timely manner.

Having done this kind of thing many times, Jin Guangyao already knew where he was most likely to find Jin Guangshan. His search led him to a small, resplendent building, where he strode inside with his hands tucked politely behind his back. The floor manager of the main hall came over with an ingratiating smile to greet him, but Jin Guangyao raised his hand to indicate that service was not necessary.

Xue Yang swiped an apple from a customer's table and slowly followed Jin Guangyao up the stairs, during which he wiped the fruit on his chest before crunching down on it. Not long after, the sound of Jin Guangshan's laughter and the coquettish giggles of women—several of them—wafted near. Their voices chirped melodiously.

"Sect Leader, what do you think of this? Does this flower look real when I paint it on my body?"

"What's so great about knowing how to paint? Sect Leader, look at my calligraphy. What do you think of it?"

Jin Guangyao had long grown accustomed to this. He knew when he should appear and when he should not. He gestured to Xue Yang and stopped in his tracks.

Xue Yang clicked his tongue, his expression one of impatience. Just as he was about to head downstairs to wait, he suddenly heard Jin Guangshan say in a gruff voice, "Isn't it enough for girls to play with flowers and plants? To powder and doll themselves up? Why practice calligraphy? What a mood killer."

The women had intended to please Jin Guangshan, but his sudden statement turned the atmosphere awkward for a moment. Jin Guangyao froze a little too.

Not long after, someone said with a laugh, "But I heard there was once a renowned courtesan in Yunmeng who captivated the masses with her talents in the Four Forms and the Four Arts!"

Jin Guangshan was apparently dead drunk, as evidenced by his stumbling words.

"You can't put it...that way," he slurred. "I realize now that women should steer clear of that nonsense. Women who have read a little always think they're a cut above other women. They have a lot of demands and the most unrealistic fantasies. It's most bothersome."

Xue Yang leaned back against the window behind him and propped his arm on the windowpane. He ate his apple and turned his head to look at the scenery outside. On the other hand,

Jin Guangyao's face seemed to have taken root. It was firm and unmoved, his eyes remaining crescents.

The women in the loft were all smiles as they chimed in agreement.

Jin Guangshan seemed to be remembering the past, as he mumbled to himself, "If I bought her freedom and she found her way to Lanling, who knows if she'd continue to pester me? She could have been popular for a few more years if she knew her place and stayed put, and she wouldn't have needed to worry about her daily expenses for the rest of her life. Why did she have to give birth to a son? What was she hoping to achieve by counting on the son of a prostitute…"

"Sect Leader Jin, who are you talking about?" asked a woman. "What son?"

"Son?" answered Jin Guangshan, his voice light and airy. "*Hah*, forget him."

"Sure! We won't talk about it!"

"Since Sect Leader Jin doesn't like us to write and paint, we won't. How about we play with something else?"

Jin Guangyao stood in the stairwell for an incense time. Xue Yang watched the scenery for an incense time as well, until the merry laughter upstairs gradually quieted down.

After a while, Jin Guangyao turned around and started to walk slowly downstairs, wearing a calm and composed expression. Seeing this, Xue Yang casually tossed the apple core out of the window and sauntered down as well.

Both of them walked down the street for a while. A moment later, Xue Yang suddenly burst into outright laughter.

"Ha ha ha ha ha ha, fuck me, ha ha ha ha ha ha …"

Jin Guangyao halted in his tracks and asked in a frosty tone, "What are you laughing at?"

Doubling over with laughter, Xue Yang said, "You really should have found a mirror and looked at your face earlier. That was a *horrible* smile. It was so disgustingly fucking fake."

Jin Guangyao humphed. "What does a little hooligan like you know? I have to smile, no matter how fake or disgusting it comes out."

"You asked for this," Xue Yang said lazily. "If anyone dared to say I was raised by a whore, I'd go find *his* old hag and fuck her a few hundred times, then drag her to a brothel for others to fuck her a few hundred more times. Then we'd see who's the son of a whore. Easy-peasy."

Jin Guangyao laughed too. "I don't have such leisurely pursuits."

"You don't, but I do, and I don't mind standing in for you," Xue Yang said. "Just say the word and I'll help you fuck 'em. Ha ha ha ha ha ha..."

"That's not necessary," Jin Guangyao said. "Xue-gongzi should just save his energy. Are you free in a few days?"

"Whether I'm free or not, I'll still have to do it, no?" Xue Yang quipped.

"Go to Yunmeng on my behalf," Jin Guangyao said. "Clean up a place for me, and be thorough."

"As the saying goes, even fowl and dogs aren't spared when Xue Yang strikes," Xue Yang said. "How do you still have misgivings about whether I'll be thorough?"

Jin Guangyao glanced at him. "I don't seem to have heard that saying before."

Night had already fallen, and their surroundings were silent, with few pedestrians around. As the two of them walked and talked, they passed a roadside stall. The peddler was in the midst of listlessly cleaning up the small table when he looked up and suddenly yelled, jumping back.

The shout and jump were so startling that even Jin Guangyao froze slightly in shock. His hand swiftly moved to the hilt of Hensheng, which was around his waist. When he saw it was just an ordinary peddler, he paid him no heed, but Xue Yang went forward and kicked over the stall without another word.

The peddler was shocked and terrified. "You again?! Why?!"

"Didn't I tell you before? There's no 'why,'" Xue Yang answered with a smile.

He was about to kick again when he felt a sharp pain in the back of his hand. Pupils shrinking, he swiftly backed up a few steps. He raised his hand, saw several bloody lashes on the back of it, then looked up. A Daoist cultivator dressed in black was giving him a frosty glare as he retracted his horsetail whisk.

The cultivator was tall and slender, his features handsome with an air of cool detachment. He held a horsetail whisk in his hand and carried a long sword on his back. The tassel of the sword fluttered slightly in the night breeze.

Killing intent flashed in Xue Yang's eyes. He struck a palm out to attack, and the Daoist cultivator in black brandished his horsetail whisk, intending to repel the blow. But Xue Yang's strike was bizarre and unfathomable; the trajectory of his hand suddenly veered toward the black-clad cultivator's heart. The man frowned slightly and sidestepped the blow, but Xue Yang's palm grazed his left arm. Though clearly not physically hurt, the cultivator's expression suddenly frosted over with intense revulsion.

This subtle change of expression did not escape Xue Yang's eyes. He let out a grim laugh and was about to make another move when a figure dressed in snow-white robes joined the fray. Jin Guangyao came forward and stood between the brawling parties.

"Song Zichen-daozhang, please stay your hand on my account."

The peddler had long fled. "Lianfang-zun?" asked the Daoist cultivator in black.

"I am indeed that humble servant," Jin Guangyao said.

"Why is Lianfang-zun defending this overbearing and unreasonable person?" Song Zichen asked.

Jin Guangyao gave a pained smile, looking as if he had no choice in the matter. "Song-daozhang, he is a guest cultivator of our Jin Clan of Lanling."

"If he is a guest cultivator, why does he act in a manner unbefitting his position?" Song Zichen asked.

Jin Guangyao coughed. "Song-daozhang, you may be unaware, but he's...eccentric, and young as well. Please do not hold it against him."

Just then, a clear, gentle voice rang out, "Indeed, he's quite young."

Like a sliver of moonlight piercing the night, a Daoist cultivator in white silently appeared beside the trio. He carried a horsetail whisk over his arm and a long sword on his back. He was slim and graceful, and walked like he was stepping across floating clouds, his sleeves and sword tassel fluttering behind.

"Xiao Xingchen-daozhang," Jin Guangyao greeted.

Xiao Xingchen returned the greeting and said with a smile, "I didn't expect Lianfang-zun to remember me. We last met many months ago."

"Xiao Xingchen-daozhang's Shuanghua is a sword that shakes the world," said Jin Guangyao. "It would be stranger if I didn't remember, wouldn't it?"

Xiao Xingchen smiled, seemingly well aware that it was in Jin Guangyao's nature to speak in an ingratiating way. "Lianfang-zun speaks too highly of me." His gaze then turned to Xue Yang. "He may be young, but since he ranks among the guest cultivators, he must still exercise self-discipline and restraint. The Jin Clan of

Lanling is distinguished, after all, and should strive to set an example in many aspects."

His black eyes shone, bright and gentle, and his gaze held no hint of reproach as he looked at Xue Yang. Even though he was giving advice, no offense was intended.

Jin Guangyao immediately and calmly took the out he had been provided. "Of course."

Xue Yang snorted. Xiao Xingchen did not lose his temper on hearing his derisive scoff, but sized him up for a while. After some thought, he said, "Come to think of it, it seems to me that the way this boy strikes is rather..."

"Vicious," Song Zichen finished for him in a frosty tone.

Hearing this, Xue Yang laughed out loud. "You say I'm still young, but how much older than me are you? You say my blows are vicious, but who was the one who lashed out at me first with his horsetail whisk? The way you two try to lecture others is really absurd."

As he spoke, he held up the hand with the streaks of blood and shook it to demonstrate. He was clearly the one who'd first moved to wreck the stall, but was now distorting the truth and acting with self-righteous confidence.

Jin Guangyao looked like he was caught between tears and laughter as he said to the two Daoist cultivators, "Gentlemen, this..."

Xiao Xingchen couldn't help but smile. "He's truly..."

Xue Yang narrowed his eyes. "Truly what? Spit it out?"

"Chengmei,[5] shut up," Jin Guangyao said mildly.

On hearing that name, Xue Yang's face promptly grew dark.

"Gentlemen, I am sorry about today," Jin Guangyao continued. "For my sake, please do not hold it against him."

---

5   "Xue Chengmei" is Xue Yang's courtesy name. It is derived from a Confucian proverb describing the conduct of the ideal gentleman: 成人之美 / cheng ren zhi mei – "help others accomplish good works."

Song Zichen shook his head. Xiao Xingchen patted him on the shoulder and said, "Zichen, let's go."

Song Zichen glanced at him and gave a slight nod of his head. Both of them bade Jin Guangyao farewell in unison and left, shoulder to shoulder.

Xue Yang stared at their backs with a sinister gaze and clenched his teeth into a smile. "...Fucking foul cultivators."

"They didn't do anything to you," Jin Guangyao commented curiously. "Why are you so resentful?"

"Their breed of self-righteous hypocrisy disgusts me the most," Xue Yang spat. "Xiao Xingchen clearly isn't that much older than me, but he's a nosy busybody—how annoying. And he even lectured me. Then there's that Song guy," he sneered. "All I did was graze him with my palm. What was with that stink eye he was giving me? One of these days, I'm gonna gouge out his eyes and crush his heart. We'll see what he can do about it."

"That's where you're wrong," said Jin Guangyao. "Song-daozhang has a fixation with cleanliness and doesn't like physical contact with others. He's not targeting you specifically."

"Who are those two foul cultivators?" Xue Yang asked.

"After all that fuss, you don't even know who they are?" Jin Guangyao asked. "Those two are at the height of their popularity right now. 'Xiao Xingchen, bright moon, cool breeze, ever distant; Song Zichen, dauntlessly scorns the snow and frost.' Haven't you heard that phrase?"

"Never," Xue Yang said. "Don't get it. The hell does that mean?"

"Never mind if you never heard of it or don't understand it," said Jin Guangyao. "Either way, they are two virtuous gentlemen. Just don't provoke them."

"Why?" Xue Yang asked.

"As the saying goes," Jin Guangyao said, "it's better to offend a petty villain than a virtuous gentleman."

Xue Yang looked at him. "Is there really any such saying?" he asked, dubious.

"Of course," Jin Guangyao said. "When you offend a petty villain, you can simply kill them outright to avoid future trouble; the world will even applaud and celebrate you for it. But when you offend a virtuous gentleman, it gets trickier. Their kind is the most trouble-some of all—they will chase you relentlessly and refuse to let it go. If you so much as lay a finger on them, you'll be condemned by the masses. So keep your distance from them. Fortunately, they thought you were just a little cocky due to your young age. They don't know what you've been doing all day long. If they did, there would be no end to it."

Xue Yang scoffed. "Playing it so safe. I'm not afraid of people like that."

"You're not, but I am," said Jin Guangyao. "Better to save yourself trouble than create it for yourself. Let's go."

After only a few more steps, the two arrived at a fork in the road. The path on the right led to Golden Carp Tower, while the one on the left led to the Corpse Refinery.

They smiled at each other and parted company.

I T ALL STARTED on one particular night, three days ago.

That night, a tired and drunk Young Master Qin had returned to his residence after a social engagement. He'd been settling down to rest when he suddenly heard banging. Someone was pounding on the main doors of the Qin residence—or rather, smashing their fist against them.

The servant keeping the gate had groggily acknowledged the guest and gotten up to take a look, a lantern in hand. But just as he was about to ask who it was, whoever was knocking suddenly went into a frenzy, slamming into the doors as if they had gone mad.

Literally *slamming*—the bolt holding the door shut had creaked with the force. And then came a noise like ten metal claws raking away at the door panels.

The commotion was so loud that the courtyard quickly became crowded with servants who had been startled awake. They raised their oil lamps and clubs and lanterns, trading looks with one another as they waited for their master to appear—which he finally did, sword in hand and draped in only an outer robe.

Young Master Qin drew his sword with an echoing *sching* and bellowed, "Who's there?!"

The scratching on the doors immediately grew louder.

Young Master Qin pointed to a servant huddled in a corner with a broom raised.

"You...climb up and take a look outside," Young Master Qin ordered.

The servant didn't dare defy him. Ashen-faced, he slowly climbed the wall, looking beseechingly back at Young Master Qin all the while. The only response he got was more impatient urging.

Finally, he set both hands on the tiled eaves and poked his head over with fear and trepidation. He had taken only one look before he plunged headfirst to the ground.

"He said the thing knocking at the doors was a monster in funeral clothes, completely drenched in blood, with disheveled hair," Young Master Qin finished recounting. "It wasn't a living person."

Wei Wuxian and Lan Wangji exchanged a look, while Lan Sizhui asked, "Young Master Qin, do you have a more detailed description?"

Young Master Qin was not part of the cultivation world and had found the right people purely by accident. He knew that the gentlemen before him were cultivators, but not who they were. All the same, Lan Wangji's frosty demeanor gave him an extraordinary, otherworldly air, and Wei Wuxian looked quick-witted, as if he had everything worked out. And while Lan Sizhui was young, there was a touch of class and elegance to his bearing. As such, Young Master Qin did not dare snub him.

"No. That servant is an idiot and a coward. He passed out after taking a single look, and I had to pinch his philtrum for a while before he came back around. Do you think I could count on *him* to get a clearer look at the thing?"

"Allow me to ask a question," Wei Wuxian said.

"Please," Young Master Qin answered.

"It seems you had someone else look on your behalf. Didn't you look for yourself?" Wei Wuxian asked.

"No."

"A pity."

"What about it is a pity?"

"From what you've told us, that was probably a fierce corpse knocking on your door. When a fierce corpse comes calling, nine times out of ten it's there for a particular person," Wei Wuxian explained. "If you had taken a look with your own eyes, you might have recognized it as an old acquaintance."

"Perhaps I'm that one person out of ten," Young Master Qin said. "And besides, even if it was there for a particular person, that person might not necessarily be me. Right?"

Wei Wuxian nodded and said with a smile, "Sure."

"The creature clawed at the door until daybreak," Young Master Qin continued. "When I went out early in the morning to take a look, the door was already mangled beyond recognition."

Wei Wuxian and Lan Wangji circled around to the entrance of the complex, and Lan Sizhui followed them, observing carefully. The main doors of the Qin residence were covered in hundreds of harrowing scratch marks. Each swipe had left five ghastly streaks in its wake, ranging from a few centimeters to a meter or so. The door was indeed mangled beyond recognition.

The marks had undoubtedly been made by human hands. But no matter how you looked at it, the gouges hardly resembled anything that could be accomplished by a living human's fingernails.

"To get back on topic," Young Master Qin said, "since both gongzi are men of the cultivation world, do you have a way to drive away this evil creature?"

However, Wei Wuxian answered, "That's not necessary."

Lan Sizhui found his response strange, but didn't speak out of turn. Young Master Qin found it strange as well and parroted him.

"Not necessary?"

"Not necessary," Wei Wuxian confirmed. "The moment a residence is constructed and comes under someone's ownership, it attains the inherent purpose of sheltering inhabitants and repelling outsiders. The entrance is a natural barrier. It can not only keep out humans, but also ward off non-humans. You're the rightful master of this place, so evil spirits can't invade as long as you don't invite them in with your words or actions. Judging by the residual evil qi on the front door, the fierce corpse or malicious ghost that came calling on your residence wasn't rare or special. One set of doors will be enough to keep it out."

Young Master Qin was still skeptical. "Is this 'barrier' really that powerful?"

"Yes," Lan Wangji answered.

Wei Wuxian set one boot on the threshold. "It is. Furthermore, a residence's threshold forms another barrier. Reanimated corpses have stagnant blood that doesn't circulate, and their tendons are rigid. All they can do is hop stiffly around. Unless that walking corpse had amazingly strong legs in life and could leap a meter into the air, it couldn't get over the threshold even if you left the doors wide open."

Still not reassured, Young Master Qin asked, "Is there nothing else I need to buy—residence protection talismans, exorcism swords, and so on? I'm willing to pay a high price—money is no problem."

"Replace the door bolt with a new one," Lan Wangji said.

Young Master Qin did not know what to say to that. His skeptical expression seemed to indicate he thought this suggestion had been made purely to placate him, so Wei Wuxian added, "It's up to you whether you replace it. Do as you see fit, Young Master Qin. Please feel free to consult us again if there are any further developments."

Upon leaving the Qin residence, they walked for a while. Wei Wuxian and Lan Wangji strolled side by side, peppering in snippets of conversation every now and then.

One could say they had somewhat pulled away from the cultivation world. If they had nothing of importance to attend to, they would roam aimlessly for a few days, half a month, a whole month. Wei Wuxian had long known Lan Wangji's reputation for "appearing where there is chaos" and hadn't thought it would be a tough job. But now that he was tagging along, he realized it was a test of patience—not because it was tough, but rather, it was too *easy*.

When he had gone on Night Hunts in the past, he'd favored strange and dangerous locations where he could experience a variety of adventures that were naturally full of turns and twists. However, Lan Wangji was not picky—he did what he ought to do, and it inevitably ended with some commonplace Night Hunt target that was unremarkable by Wei Wuxian's standards. Case in point, this fierce corpse that had come knocking. Compared to the creatures Wei Wuxian used to hunt, it was boring indeed. Even other cultivators might consider dealing with it to be a waste of time and talent.

But even if the case itself wasn't enticing, Wei Wuxian was with Lan Wangji. It was relaxing and idyllic to enjoy each other's company.

Lan Sizhui quietly followed them, leading Little Apple by the reins. After much pondering, he couldn't help but ask, "Hanguang-jun, Wei-qianbei—is it okay to just leave Young Master Qin's house like that?"

"It is fine," Lan Wangji said.

Wei Wuxian laughed. "Sizhui, do you think I was just spouting nonsense to trick people?"

Lan Sizhui quickly denied it and coughed to clear his throat. "Not at all! That's not what I meant. What I'm trying to say is...

a residence's door might indeed be able to keep evil out, but *that* residence's door is about to fall apart. Is it really all right to not even give him a single talisman?"

Wei Wuxian gave him a weird look. "Well, duh?"

"Oh..." Lan Sizhui said.

"Of course it's not all right," Wei Wuxian said.

"Huh? Then why...?" Lan Sizhui wondered.

"Because," Wei Wuxian explained, "Young Master Qin was lying."

Lan Wangji nodded slightly. On the other hand, Lan Sizhui was somewhat astonished.

"How could Wei-qianbei tell?"

"I've only met Young Master Qin once, so I can't say for sure, but that guy is..."

"Intransigent and coldhearted," Lan Wangji finished.

Wei Wuxian made a noise of agreement. "More or less. In any case, he's no coward. The situation that night was bizarre, but based on what he described, not bizarre enough to frighten someone out of their mind. Would it have been that hard for him to climb up on the eaves and take a look outside?"

Although he acknowledged the point, Lan Sizhui said, "But he kept insisting that he didn't take a single look..."

"Exactly," Wei Wuxian said. "If someone was pounding like crazy on your doors in the middle of the night, it'd be normal to sneak a peek. Everyone's born curious, and that guy isn't the timid type— but he insists he didn't see anything. Isn't that strange?"

"Wholly agreed," Lan Wangji said.

"As they say, great minds think alike!" Wei Wuxian smiled and stroked his chin as he continued speaking. "Besides, even though the claw marks the fierce corpse left on the front door looked scary, the evil qi and scent of blood weren't all that strong. It definitely didn't come to kill for revenge—of that much I can be sure. What's *really* going on remains to be seen."

"In that case, why doesn't Wei-qianbei summon the fierce corpse to ask it directly?" Lan Sizhui asked.

"Nah."

"Huh?"

"Can you draw a Spirit-Attraction Flag without letting blood? I'm too weak and frail," Wei Wuxian stated with self-righteous confidence.

"Wei-qianbei, you can use my blood," Lan Sizhui assured him, thinking he genuinely couldn't be bothered to shed some blood.

To his surprise, Wei Wuxian only sputtered a laugh in response. "Sizhui," he said. "That's not actually the problem. We brought you with us to gain experience, right?"

Lan Sizhui was momentarily taken aback. "Of course *I* can call the fierce corpse right over and tell it to get lost," Wei Wuxian continued. "But could you do the same?"

When he heard this explanation, Lan Sizhui promptly understood.

He and the other juniors of the Lan Clan of Gusu had become too dependent on Wei Wuxian after everything they'd gone through together. Summoning a corpse and asking it questions while it was under one's command might be the quickest method, but not everyone could manage it. And Lan Sizhui did not cultivate the demonic path, making it inadvisable for him to learn too much about its arts. What experience did he stand to gain if Wei Wuxian simply used his usual methods to deftly and easily resolve the issue, as he always did?

This time, Wei Wuxian and Lan Wangji meant to lead him through a more standard investigative process, teaching him how cases like these should be resolved.

"So," Lan Sizhui said, "what Hanguang-jun and Wei-qianbei mean is—since Young Master Qin refused to tell the truth, we should simply leave him for the time being in order to give him a good scare?"

"That's right," Wei Wuxian affirmed. "Just wait and see. The door bolt can last another two days or so. Your clan's Hanguang-jun told him to replace it with a new one, which was a very conscientious suggestion, but Young Master Qin doesn't seem to care. Then again, if he's really hiding something important, even replacing it with ten new bolts will do no good. The creature will come again, sooner or later."

Surprisingly enough, the bolt didn't even last one night. The next day, a glum-looking Young Master Qin called on Wei Wuxian and Lan Wangji once more.

Prominent clans in the cultivation world owned many estates across the land. The three of them were currently staying in a small, elegant building owned by the Lan Clan of Gusu, which was called the Little Bamboo Abode. Young Master Qin had arrived very early in the morning and come upon Lan Sizhui pulling a donkey by the reins. Poor Lan Sizhui was trying his very hardest to drag Little Apple away and prevent it from gnawing on the bamboo. The moment he turned around, he saw Young Master Qin looking at him, the corners of his mouth twitching.

Lan Sizhui's face went red as he tossed the rope aside and invited Young Master Qin into the house. He gingerly knocked on the two seniors' bedroom door to inform them of the guest's arrival. Upon seeing a neatly dressed Lan Wangji quietly open the door and shake his head, Lan Sizhui knew Wei-qianbei would not be waking any time soon.

Lan Sizhui was in a bind. In the end, he steeled himself to break the clan rule that forbade lying and claimed that his senior wasn't feeling well and was still resting. He couldn't possibly tell Young Master Qin the truth, which was "Wei-qianbei wants to sleep, so Hanguang-jun told you to wait..."

Wei Wuxian slept until it was late in the morning, and when he woke, he could only force himself to get out of bed after receiving a multitude of caresses and embraces from Lan Wangji. Eyes still closed as he washed up, he put on Lan Wangji's inner robe by mistake. Its sleeves were a few centimeters longer than those of the outer robe, and had been rolled up several times, making for quite an unbecoming sight. Fortunately, Young Master Qin was too preoccupied to notice as he dragged the trio away.

The Qin residence's entrance doors were tightly shut. Young Master Qin stepped up, rapped the door knocker, and discarded pleasantries to get straight to the point.

"I felt a little more at ease after your advice yesterday, but I still couldn't sleep last night. And so I read for a while in the main hall with the doors shut, keeping an ear open for movement outside."

Shortly after, a servant opened the front doors and welcomed the trio into the courtyard. As soon as they took the steps down, Wei Wuxian was slightly taken aback by the shocking sight they beheld.

Large, vivid red footsteps were scattered all over the courtyard.

"That thing came again last night," Young Master Qin continued gloomily. "It clawed and slammed against the front door again for almost an hour, making quite a racket. I was growing more and more irritated at the commotion, but then I heard a sudden crack—its banging had broken the bolt."

The hair on Young Master Qin's neck had stood on end at the sound of the bolt snapping. He'd rushed over and peeped through a crack in the main hall's wooden door.

The front door across the courtyard had been flung open. Lit by dim moonlight, he had seen a figure jumping around before the entrance of the Qin residence, like a log fitted with a spring underfoot.

It hopped like that for a while, but never managed to hop inside. Young Master Qin heaved a small sigh of relief, thinking the creature really was like how Wei Wuxian had described it during the day—lacking functional tendons and circulation, stiff all over. It couldn't bend its legs, so it would never be able to jump across the high threshold of his front doors.

But before he could fully exhale, he saw the figure bounding around the entrance suddenly spring high into the air. In a flash, it had leapt through the front door!

Young Master Qin had whirled around and pressed his back against the door of the main hall. The evil creature, having crossed the threshold and entered the courtyard, continued to hop straight ahead.

Thump, thump.

Thump, thump.

In no time, it had thrown itself at the doors of the main hall. Young Master Qin had felt the impact through the wood pressed against his back. Realizing with a start that there was only a single door between him and the creature, he had hastily scrambled away.

"The moonlight cast the evil creature's shadow on the paper windows," Young Master Qin said. "It couldn't come in, so it circled around the hall, leaving behind all these footprints in the courtyard! Gentlemen, it's not that I doubt you, but you clearly said that thing couldn't jump in."

Wei Wuxian stepped on the threshold. "Generally speaking, a corpse certainly couldn't manage such a jump once rigor mortis set in. With no working tendons or blood circulation, the dead can't bend their legs. You can ask any of the other cultivation clans, and they'll all tell you the same thing."

Young Master Qin opened his arms wide, as if to show him the red footprints all over the courtyard. "Then how do you explain this?"

"There's only one possible explanation—it wasn't an ordinary creature that entered your residence," Wei Wuxian said. "Think back for a moment. Did you notice anything odd when you took a look at that fierce corpse last night?"

Looking upset, Young Master Qin thought about it for a while before saying, "Now that I think about it, there *was* something strange about the thing's posture when it jumped."

"How so?" Wei Wuxian asked.

"It seemed like..." Young Master Qin trailed off in hesitation.

Lan Wangji, who had already done a lap of the courtyard, provided an answer in a mild tone as he walked back to Wei Wuxian's side. "It had a limp."

"That's right!" Young Master Qin promptly confirmed, but then immediately grew dubious. "How did you know that?"

Lan Sizhui had been wondering the same thing, but he'd always understood there was nothing Hanguang-jun didn't know. Rather than reacting with doubt, he waited with quiet curiosity for the answer.

"The footprints on the ground," Lan Wangji said.

Wei Wuxian bent, and Lan Sizhui followed suit, squatting with him to scrutinize the marks. A couple of glances was enough for Wei Wuxian. He looked up at Lan Wangji.

"A one-legged corpse?"

Lan Wangji nodded, and Wei Wuxian stood up. "No wonder it was able to jump over the threshold. These footprints are uneven and of varying depths. The walking corpse has one broken leg."

He thought for a moment, then continued, "Do you think it was broken before or after his death?"

"Before," Lan Wangji answered.

"Mmm," Wei Wuxian hummed in agreement. "If it had been after, it wouldn't matter which body parts were broken."

They were freely discussing the matter now, but Lan Sizhui couldn't keep up. He was quickly forced to call for a time-out.

"Hold on, Hanguang-jun, Wei-qianbei—let me sort this out. You're saying that because this fierce corpse has a broken leg and walks with a limp, it's far easier for it to jump over the threshold than it would be for a two-legged...uh, intact fierce corpse?"

Young Master Qin was obviously thinking the same thing. "Did I hear that right?"

"Yes," Lan Wangji answered.

Young Master Qin looked like he found the idea absurd. "Isn't that like saying a person with one leg can run faster than a person with two?"

The couple were involved in their discussion, but Wei Wuxian spared a moment to answer with a smile.

"You've got it wrong, but maybe you'll understand if I put it another way. Some people are blind in one eye, so they take extra care of their remaining eye. Despite being partially blind, their eyesight might not necessarily be worse than that of someone with two working eyes—in fact, it might even be *better*. Similarly, if someone lost the use of their left arm, their right might develop extraordinary strength in the long run. Maybe even to the point that their right arm possessed twice the strength of an ordinary person's."

Lan Sizhui understood now. "And because the fierce corpse had broken its leg while it was alive, it hops constantly on one leg after death. Therefore, it wound up able to jump much higher than walking corpses with two legs."

"Precisely," Wei Wuxian said cheerfully.

Lan Sizhui made a mental note of this, finding it rather interesting.

"It's all my fault for quarreling with my wife yesterday," Young Master Qin said irritably. "Dealing with those domestic affairs took up most of the day and went on well into the night, and I didn't have the time to repair the main doors. I'll reinforce them now and make them as impregnable as an iron fortress!"

However, Lan Wangji shook his head. "That will be of no use. 'Precedent must not be set.'"

Young Master Qin startled, as that did not sound like an auspicious statement. "What do you mean by that?"

"It's trade jargon," said Wei Wuxian. "It means some defensive measures can only be used once against evil spirits. They won't work a second time. If you had rushed to repair the doors yesterday, they would've held up a while. But if a creature manages to get through once, its path will be unimpeded in the future."

Young Master Qin was both shocked and regretful. "Then...what should I do?!"

"Simply sit tight," Lan Wangji said.

"No need to panic," Wei Wuxian reassured. "It might be able to enter through the main entrance, but it won't be able to get through the second gate. Your mansion's like a city—only the first gate has been breached right now, and there are still two more after that."

"Two more? Which two?"

"The door of socialization. The door of privacy," Lan Wangji said.

"Your main hall and your bedroom," Wei Wuxian clarified.

The group had long since crossed the courtyard as they continued their discussion. They strode into the main hall and took their seats, but even after a long time had passed, no one came to serve tea. For some reason, all the servants were gone. Young Master Qin shouted for a while before someone finally came, but he was quick to kick the person away as soon as they arrived. Having indulged that opportunity to vent his anger, he brightened a little.

Unwilling to give up, he pressed, "Can't you give me some talisman to suppress it? Don't worry, gentlemen—payment really isn't a problem."

Of course, he was unaware these three never cared about payment when they went on Night Hunts.

"That depends on how you want to suppress it," Wei Wuxian said.

"What do you mean?"

And so Wei Wuxian began his spiel.

"Suppression," he began, "only treats the symptoms, not the root cause. If you want to stop an evil creature from entering through the door, just change the talisman twice a month and you'll be fine. But it'll still be able to approach your house and claw your door. I reckon you'll eventually be changing front doors even faster than talismans. If you want the evil spirit to back off and stay away for good, the high-caliber talismans you'd need are complex to draw and expensive to make, and you'd have to change them every seven days. On top of that, its resentment will only grow more powerful the longer it's suppressed..."

Lan Wangji sat in silence and listened as Wei Wuxian spouted nonsense.

It was true that suppression was not a good strategy in the long-term, but suppression and expulsion talismans were not as complex and laborious to produce or utilize as Wei Wuxian was making them out to be. But when it came to the art of making up nonsense, no one could rival Wei Wuxian's eloquence. Lan Sizhui was a brilliant student, and even he was dumbfounded by his speech—and was nearly led to believe him.

Young Master Qin couldn't help but grumble inwardly as he listened to how troublesome Wei Wuxian was making suppression out to be, as if he'd have no end of trouble if he opted for it. He kept glancing over at Lan Wangji, who sat drinking his tea with his head lowered. But Lan Wangji's expression didn't seem to suggest Wei Wuxian was only exaggerating things to frighten him, so Young Master Qin had no choice but to believe.

"Isn't there a way to resolve this once and for all?!"

Wei Wuxian jumped on this opportunity at once. "That depends on you, Young Master Qin."

"Why?" Young Master Qin asked.

"I *can* make you a specially tailored talisman," Wei Wuxian said, "but whether I *will* do so depends on whether you're willing to answer my question truthfully."

"What question?"

"Did you know that fierce corpse when it was alive?" Wei Wuxian asked.

After a long silence, Young Master Qin finally answered, "Yes."

The couple exchanged a look, while Lan Sizhui perked up.

"Please elaborate," Wei Wuxian said.

It was only after some contemplation that Young Master Qin slowly said, "There isn't really much to explain. I don't know much about him. I grew up in my grandmother's house, in a mountainous village in a faraway province. He was one of the household's servants. Because we were similar in age, we played together growing up."

"That's called a childhood friend," Wei Wuxian said. "How can you 'not know much about him'?"

"Because we drifted apart when we got older," Young Master Qin said.

"Think back," Wei Wuxian urged. "Did you ever do anything that offended that servant in any way?"

"There was one instance," Young Master Qin answered, "but I don't know how badly I offended him."

"Tell us," Lan Wangji said.

"The servant had served year-round at my grandmother's side," Young Master Qin began. "He was efficient and similar in age to me, her grandson, so my grandmother liked him and often praised him for his intelligence. For that reason, he grew a bit arrogant. He often tagged along behind our clan's juniors with no understanding of the distinction between master and servant. Later, my grandmother even let him attend school with us.

"One day, the teacher had given us a difficult assignment. Someone came up with an answer during discussion, and everyone in class was praising it when that servant suddenly said it was wrong. He'd only been attending class for a month or two at the time, while the clan juniors had been studying for two or three years. Naturally, there was no need to discuss who was right or wrong, so someone promptly dismissed him. But he was stubborn—adamant that the previous person was wrong, wanting to show us how he had achieved his conclusion. Eventually, the dispute annoyed everyone in class, and we all booted him out."

At this point, Lan Sizhui couldn't help but say, "Young Master Qin, even if he had annoyed the rest of you, he hadn't done anything unreasonable... Why boot him out?"

"It sounds like a bunch of juniors from your clan provoked him," Wei Wuxian commented. "Did you play a special role? Otherwise, he'd have sought out the entire group, not just you."

"I was the first to tell him to get out," Young Master Qin answered. "It was just an offhand comment, but everyone had long been unhappy with him, and the situation got out of hand. That guy had quite a temper too. After he returned home, he told my grandmother he wouldn't be attending school anymore, and true to his word, he never went again."

"I'll ask two more questions, and you must answer them truthfully," Wei Wuxian said.

"Go ahead," Young Master Qin said.

"First question," said Wei Wuxian with a particularly bright glint in his eyes. "You said that 'someone came up with an answer.' Was that someone you?"

After a pause, Young Master Qin asked, "Is that information relevant?"

"Well then. Second question—whose answer was right, and whose was wrong?"

Looking sour, Young Master Qin shook out his sleeves and answered dispassionately. "It's an old story from years ago, please excuse me for not remembering everything vividly. But in all fairness, who has never let their feelings get the better of them in their youth—or done inexplicable things, or met strange people? Let us not dwell on it. I merely wish to settle this case once and for all, and as soon as possible."

"Sure thing," Wei Wuxian answered with a happy smile. "I get it, I get it."

"When did that person pass away?" Lan Wangji asked.

"About two years ago, I guess," Young Master Qin replied.

"Two years?" Wei Wuxian parroted. "Not too bad. It's not an old corpse, but not a fresh one either. How did he die? Suicide?"

"No. I heard he'd been out drinking and was running around in the middle of the night. He didn't watch his footing and fell to his death."

"Not suicide, then. That makes the situation slightly better. Young Master Qin, is that all?"

"Yes."

"In that case, please head back inside. The talismans will be delivered to your residence later. Please keep us in the loop if you remember anything else."

After the three of them had returned to the Little Bamboo Abode, Lan Sizhui shut the door behind him and turned around to expel a breath. "Young Master Qin...is honestly...honestly..."

"Two years," said Lan Wangji all of a sudden.

"Yeah, two years is a little strange," Wei Wuxian agreed.

"Strange?" Lan Sizhui repeated.

Wei Wuxian retrieved a blank sheet of talisman paper from his sleeve. "Hate-fueled evil spirits that want to seek vengeance for the grievances they've suffered usually start haunting on the night of the seventh day after their death. Ones that wait a bit longer and start haunting within a year are fairly common too. Since he'd already turned into a fierce corpse, why drag his feet for two years before coming?"

Lan Sizhui ventured a guess. "Perhaps it hadn't managed to find Young Master Qin's address after he moved?"

He felt a slight chill run down his spine as he imagined the corpse knocking on the doors of one household after another every night, peeping inside to see if it was the home of Young Master Qin.

But Wei Wuxian said, "That couldn't be the case. The fierce corpse and Young Master Qin are old acquaintances, it could easily find him by following his scent. Plus, if things went down like you suggested, it would've hit up at least a few wrong houses in its search for Young Master Qin—and there would've been more than one strange report of a fierce corpse banging on doors. Lan Zhan, you're better read than I am and have a better memory. Have you come across any similar accounts over the past two years?"

"There has been nothing related," Lan Wangji stated as Wei Wuxian entered the study.

"Exactly," said Wei Wuxian, taking out a brush. "...Lan Zhan, I can't find the cinnabar ink. I even used it last night! Have any of you seen it around?"

Lan Wangji entered the room as well and found the ink. Wei Wuxian dipped the tip of his brush twice in the fine little dish, then poured himself a cup of tea and sat by the table. With tea in his left hand and a brush in his right, he drew wild, bold strokes on the talisman paper in one motion without looking, speaking to Lan Wangji as he worked.

"If *you* don't remember, there must not be any such incidents. So there must be another reason why it didn't lay its hands on Young Master Qin for two years. There, the drawing's done."

The talisman's cinnabar ink was still wet when he handed it to Lan Sizhui. "Go deliver this to him."

Lan Sizhui took the talisman and looked it over, but he couldn't decipher a single word. He had never seen such a frenzied, chaotic, and arbitrary spell in any book, so he couldn't help but ask. "Wei-qianbei, this...couldn't be something you just randomly scrawled out, could it?"

"Of course it is," Wei Wuxian answered.

Lan Sizhui was struck speechless.

"I never look when I draw talismans."

" "
...

Wei Wuxian laughed. "Don't worry, it'll definitely work. Speaking of which, Sizhui—you don't like Young Master Qin, do you?"

Lan Sizhui considered this question for a moment. "I don't know," he said honestly. "He hasn't done anything evil or heinous, but perhaps I have a harder time getting along with people with temperaments like his. I didn't really like his tone when he said 'servant'..."

He paused, but Wei Wuxian was completely unaware of his hesitation. "That's common," he said. "Most people look down on servants. Even servants sometimes look down on themselves... Why are you two looking at me like that?"

He had to stop midway through his sentence, torn between laughter and tears. "Hold it, have you two misunderstood? Is this even a comparable situation? Lotus Pier wasn't your regular household. I hit Jiang Cheng way more than he hit me when we were kids!"

Lan Wangji made no comment, but instead gave him a silent squeeze. Wei Wuxian couldn't suppress a smile as he returned the hug, stroking down his back.

Lan Sizhui cleared his throat, relieved to see Wei Wuxian so calm. He didn't seem at all sensitive about the word "servant," as he'd expected.

"But he'll likely come back," Wei Wuxian continued.

Lan Sizhui was taken aback. "It won't be resolved tonight?"

"He did not tell us the full story," Lan Wangji stated.

"Yeah," Wei Wuxian said, "and that's not the first time he's pulled that. There's nothing we can do—people like that, you just have to unearth the story bit by bit. Let's see if he'll spit it out after tonight."

As expected, Young Master Qin came again the next day while Lan Sizhui was training with his sword in the Little Bamboo Abode's courtyard.

The moment he arrived, he shouted right in Lan Sizhui's face, "I don't care!"

"Please wait, Young Master Qin," Lan Sizhui hurriedly said. "Both of my seniors are sleep...cultivating! They are at a critical juncture and must not be disturbed!"

Hearing this, Young Master Qin did not forcibly barge inside, but instead took all his pent-up resentment out on Lan Sizhui. "I don't want to hear about treating the symptoms, or the root cause! I want this thing to never come looking for me again!"

Young Master Qin had still been unable to sleep last night, so he'd hung up a lantern in the main hall and done some night reading. Not long after, the fierce corpse—that one servant—had come as usual. Still unable to enter the house, it had jumped here and there outside the door, slamming into it from time to time. Surprisingly, the wooden windows and paper had held up against its blows without falling apart. Not long later, the commotion receded into the distance.

Young Master Qin hadn't gotten a good night's sleep for a few days in a row. Unable to hang on any longer, fatigue washed over him in an unguarded moment. His head drooped, and he fell sound asleep, still seated.

He'd drifted off for an unknown length of time when he suddenly heard three clear, crisp knocks on the door. His whole body had tensed, and he straightened his back as he was startled awake.

"My lord," a woman's voice called out from outside the door.

Young Master Qin had only just woken and was still so disoriented that he wouldn't have recognized his own father. When he'd heard Madam Qin's voice, he got up and moved to open the door—but he had only taken a few steps before he suddenly recalled something. Madam Qin had been tearfully arguing with him over the past few days. Just a day ago, she had packed her things and left for her parents' house, declaring she couldn't live like this anymore. Since her fear had only just propelled her to leave, how would she have found the courage to come back alone in the middle of the night?

The graceful womanly shadow on the paper window did indeed resemble his wife's silhouette, but Young Master Qin didn't dare act hastily. He silently drew his sword.

"My lady, why have you returned? You're not angry anymore?"

"I'm back," the woman outside the door had replied in a flat tone. "I'm not angry. Open the door."

Young Master Qin didn't dare do so without careful consideration. He pointed his sword at the door. "My lady, it's safer for you to return to your father's place. What if the creature has not left yet, but is lurking around here?"

There was a long stretch of silence outside the door. Young Master Qin's hand was slick with cold sweat as he gripped his sword.

All of a sudden, the woman shrieked at the top of her lungs.

"Open the door now! There's a ghost here! Let me in!"

The thing outside the door that called itself Madam Qin had clawed at the paper windows as it screamed. Young Master Qin had felt a chill run down his back. Gripping the talisman Wei Wuxian had delivered to him, he felt a sudden burst of courage and charged out the door with sword in hand—

"And then a bunch of things smashed into my face and knocked me out," Young Master Qin finished.

"What knocked you out?" Wei Wuxian asked.

Young Master Qin pointed a finger at the table. Wei Wuxian looked and was beside himself with amusement.

"Why was it fruit?"

Young Master Qin fumed. "How would I know?!"

"Of course you do. No one knows except you," Wei Wuxian said. "Evil spirits are very vindictive. Did you ever fling fruit at him?"

Young Master Qin looked glum and said nothing. Seeing his expression, Wei Wuxian knew his guess wasn't far off. However, he also knew he'd be reluctant to admit to it if he'd been in Young Master Qin's shoes, so he didn't pry any further.

As expected, Young Master Qin changed the topic when he opened his mouth again. "I sent someone to my father-in-law's place to make an inquiry, and my wife did not leave their house last night."

"That creature was one with the specific power to break the protective barriers of human residences," Wei Wuxian explained. "It's been only rarely documented in the notes of our forebears and ancient books. It doesn't harm humans directly, but it can imitate the voices and shapes of people close to the residence's owner. It usually works with evil spirits that are unable to step through the door on their own, helping them dupe you into inviting them in. That fierce corpse sure found itself a good helper."

"Whatever it is, the details are pointless to me," Young Master Qin said. "Gongzi, the second door has been breached, and this thing has entered my residence's main hall. Dare I ask whether you still plan to declare that nothing needs to be done?"

"Young Master Qin, let's be reasonable here," Wei Wuxian said. "*You* were the one who opened the second door. Had it not been for that talisman I gave you, I don't dare comment on what state you'd be in today."

Young Master Qin was momentarily struck dumb, then flew into a rage. "If this continues, am I going to see that thing standing at the head of my bed the next time I wake up?!"

"If you really want to have a good night's sleep, you'd better hurry and think about whether there's anything else you forgot to tell us," Wei Wuxian said. "This time, you mustn't hold anything back. You have to know that tonight...ha ha ha, I'm not trying to scare you, but tonight it'll come calling at your bedroom door."

Left with no choice, Young Master Qin could only tell them about another incident.

"The last time I saw that person was when I'd returned to my hometown to perform memorial rituals for my parents and ancestors. When I returned to my former family residence to offer my respects, I had been wearing a jade pendant. He had recognized it as something my grandmother owned while she was alive, and asked to borrow it to take a look. I handed it over, assuming he probably wanted to reminisce about my grandmother. Before long, it was gone."

"Gone, meaning...?" Wei Wuxian asked. "Did he lose it? Or did he sell it?"

Young Master Qin hesitated for a moment. "I don't know. I had initially thought he sold it and was lying about losing it when he returned, but..."

When he didn't continue, Wei Wuxian patiently probed, "But what?"

Lan Wangji's expression remained apathetic throughout. "Please speak your mind."

"But now that I think about it, he wouldn't have sold my grandmother's belongings," Young Master Qin said. "Later, I heard that he loved to drink. It was probably lost or stolen when he went out drinking at night. Either way, I was so furious that I lashed out at him."

"Wait a minute," Wei Wuxian spoke up. "You can't be vague with your words when it comes to matters of life and death. A 'lashing' can be trivial or serious. There's quite a range of potential severity there. What exactly do you mean by 'lashed out at him'?"

Young Master Qin's eyebrows twitched. "I remember that I gave him a light beating."

Wei Wuxian blinked. "Uh... Were you the one who broke his leg?"

After a pause, Young Master Qin continued as if nothing was amiss. "...I don't know about that, and I don't know how heavy-handed the servants were with their blows. But he was a former servant of our household, after all, so I never intended to do any real harm. If he decided to bottle up his anger and hate me in secret, there was nothing I could've done about it."

Listening from the side, Lan Sizhui could not help but blurt his thoughts. "Young Master Qin, this...this is...poles apart from what you said in the beginning. Why did you hold so much back when my two seniors asked you to make things clear?"

"I thought peace would return to my household as long as I had some talismans and a treasured sword," Young Master Qin said. "How could I know that I'd have to describe some irrelevant old nonsense?"

Wei Wuxian's tone rose and fell as he explained the issue. "No, no, no, that wasn't irrelevant old nonsense. The situation is serious right now, Young Master Qin! Think about it—you scolded him and beat him when he was alive, and you might have even broken his leg. If he really didn't sell that jade pendant, he died a wrongful death. Who is he supposed to go looking for, if not you?"

Young Master Qin immediately refuted the accusation. "I wasn't the one who killed him! And he didn't commit suicide either! Why must he come looking for me?"

"Eh? How do *you* know he didn't commit suicide?" Wei Wuxian said. "Maybe he did kill himself in a fit of anger, and everyone else just thought it an accident. That'd be even worse."

"He was a grown man," Young Master Qin said. "How could he kill himself out of anger over a trifle like this?"

"In our trade, making assumptions is the most taboo thing of all," Wei Wuxian said. "Every person has a different mindset and temperament; it's hard to say whether a man would kill himself out of anger over a 'trifle.' You have to understand that there can be a variety of reasons why a corpse would reanimate itself. It could have been provoked by someone kidnapping their wife and killing their son, or by something as trivial as someone not inviting them to play in the mud when they were kids."

"It definitely wasn't suicide!" Young Master Qin stubbornly insisted. "If a man wanted to kill himself, he could put a noose around his neck or take poison. Why would he choose rolling down a slope as the method? He couldn't even guarantee it would kill him. It's definitely not suicide."

"What you say also makes sense," Wei Wuxian said. "But Young Master Qin, have you ever considered that he only rolled down the mountain and fell to his death because *you* crippled his leg and impaired his mobility? If that's the case, then it's no different from you actually killing him, once you get down to it. Isn't that even worse?"

"What do you mean by that?! If that was actually what happened, it'd still be considered an accident!" Young Master Qin said with exasperated anger.

"Are you sure you want to try and convince someone who died such a tragic death that it was an 'accident'?" Wei Wuxian said. "Since he returned, it means *someone* has to take responsibility for the 'accident.'"

Every statement Young Master Qin made, Wei Wuxian refuted. Young Master Qin was clammy with cold sweat and his face was ashen.

"But there's no need to despair," Wei Wuxian continued. "I'll tell you one last method you can use to save your life. Do this for now."

"What's the method?!" Young Master Qin demanded.

Lan Wangji only had to look at Wei Wuxian to know that he was planning to spout nonsense again. He shook his head.

"Listen carefully," Wei Wuxian said. "You have to open the doors to the residence and the main hall that have already been breached. Ensure that they are kept unobstructed. Even if you don't open them, you can't stop that thing anyway."

"Okay!" Young Master Qin said.

"Dismiss all uninvolved people from the house." Wei Wuxian continued. "Take care not to hurt the innocent."

"They've pretty much all left!" Young Master Qin said.

"Good," Wei Wuxian said. "Then find a virgin boy brimming with yang energy to sit on a long bench positioned in front of your bedroom. Have him keep guard at midnight and take the necessary measures for which the situation calls."

"That's all?"

"That's all," Wei Wuxian said. "The virgin boy is already here. As for the rest, Young Master Qin can ignore it and just wait for daybreak with peace of mind."

Wei Wuxian was referring to Lan Sizhui. The corners of Young Master Qin's mouth twitched when he heard the last statement, and he swept a glance at the gentle, delicate-looking boy.

"If he's keeping guard outside, what about both of you?"

"We will be keeping guard inside with you, of course," Wei Wuxian said. "We'll make a backup plan if the outside defense can't hold up and the fierce corpse fights his way in."

Young Master Qin really couldn't hold back anymore. "Can't we just ask this gentleman to keep guard outside?"

He was referring to Lan Wangji, and thus Wei Wuxian was dumbstruck.

"Who? Him?" He almost fell over laughing. "Ha ha ha ha ha ha ha ha ha ha ha ha ha ha ha ha!"

The only reason Wei Wuxian didn't actually hit the ground was because Lan Wangji wrapped an arm around his shoulder.

"No," Lan Wangji answered.

Young Master Qin was rather displeased by this terse refusal. "Why not?"

"You forgot what I just said," Wei Wuxian replied solemnly. "It has to be a virgin."

Young Master Qin didn't believe it. "...What? He isn't one?!"

Long after Lan Sizhui saw Young Master Qin out of the Little Bamboo Abode, Wei Wuxian was still bowled over with laughter. Lan Wangji glanced at Wei Wuxian and suddenly scooped him onto his lap.

"Are you done laughing?" Lan Wangji asked mildly.

"Nope!" Wei Wuxian answered.

Perched on Lan Wangji's lap, he said, "Hanguang-jun, your looks are really deceiving. Everyone says you're a man who is open and aboveboard, ascetic and chaste. I feel very wronged."

Lan Wangji hauled him further up his lap so the two were closer together. "Wronged?"

"It's really outrageous," Wei Wuxian said. "See, you're obviously no longer a virgin, but everyone assumes it when they see your face. I'd never even touched a girl's hand in my former life, except for when I was in the process of saving her life—but not one person believed I was still a virgin." He started counting his fingers, one at a time. "At school and on Night Hunts! Everyone always said I was a playboy. At the Burial Mounds! Everyone always said I was a mad sex fiend. I'm suffering in silence even now, and have no way to lodge a formal complaint."

Without batting an eyelid, Lan Wangji firmly covered one of Wei Wuxian's hands with his own. A barely perceptible hint of a smile rippled through his eyes.

"And yet you still smile," Wei Wuxian accused. "You are a cold and heartless man who lacks compassion. For what it's worth, I was still ranked fourth on the list of the cultivation clans' top young masters. But it turns out that I only kissed *one* person in that lifetime. I always thought it was some beautiful female cultivator who was smitten with me—that, at least, made me feel like I, Wei Ying, hadn't lived in vain. Who would have thought it would end up being you..."

Hearing this comment, Lan Wangji couldn't sit still anymore. He pinned Wei Wuxian to the bed. "Is it a bad thing that it was me?!"

"What are you so nervous for?! Ha ha ha ha ha ha ha ha ha..."

When the appointed hour came around, Lan Sizhui had been waiting in the courtyard with Little Apple's reins in hand for quite a while before Wei Wuxian and Lan Wangji finally slowly emerged from the house.

He initially wanted to remind them, *"Wei-qianbei, you're wearing Hanguang-jun's clothes by mistake again."* But upon reflection, he silently swallowed back the words.

After all, Wei-qianbei made that same "mistake" every two or three days. Lan Sizhui would surely exhaust himself to death if he had to remind him each time. What was more, Wei-qianbei would just *keep* wearing Hanguang-jun's clothes because he considered it too much trouble to go change. Deciding it was pointless to remind him, Lan Sizhui feigned obliviousness.

Wei Wuxian settled himself onto Little Apple, then fished an apple from the saddlebag and took a crisp bite.

Lan Sizhui stared at the apple, finding it awfully familiar. After a moment's hesitation, he asked, "Wei-qianbei, isn't that one of the fruits that Young Master Qin brought over?"

"That's right," Wei Wuxian confirmed.

Lan Sizhui felt the need to press the topic. "...Fruit that had originally been brought by a fierce corpse?"

"It certainly was."

"Is it okay to eat?" Lan Sizhui wondered.

"It's fine. It just fell on the ground. Give it a wash and it can be eaten."

"Would an apple from a fierce corpse be toxic...?" Lan Sizhui asked.

"I can answer that question: nope," Wei Wuxian responded.

"How would qianbei know?"

And Wei Wuxian replied, "Because I've already fed five or six of 'em to Little Apple... Little Apple, stop it! Don't buck! Lan Zhan, *save me!*"

Lan Wangji grabbed the reins of the furious Little Apple and took the apple from Wei Wuxian's mouth with his other hand. "Do not eat these anymore. We will buy some tomorrow."

Holding Lan Wangji's shoulder for support, Wei Wuxian finally managed to settle back into his seat. "I was just trying to save some money for Hanguang-jun."

"You will never need to do so," Lan Wangji said.

Wei Wuxian beamed as he tickled the underside of Lan Wangji's chin. Suddenly, he seemed to remember something and casually asked, "Oh, right. Sizhui, are you a virgin?"

He asked the question with such ease, but Lan Sizhui promptly spat out his water: an action very unbecoming of a Lan. Noticing Lan Wangji glancing at him, Lan Sizhui hurriedly composed himself.

"Don't be nervous," Wei Wuxian said. "I was babbling nonsense to Young Master Qin earlier. It's true you sometimes need a virgin when casting spells or performing a ritual, but since you're using a sword to slay that fierce corpse, it makes no difference if you're a virgin or not. But I'd be very shocked if you aren't—"

He hadn't even finished his sentence when a red-eared and red-faced Lan Sizhui cut in. "O-o-o-of course I am!"

The empty Qin residence really had its doors wide open in the middle of the night, as expected. Young Master Qin had already been waiting for several hours.

Lan Sizhui stood before Young Master Qin's bedroom door. Despite not wearing any armor or even a helmet, he still looked very coolheaded and dependable. Seeing the air of youthful fearlessness that surrounded him, like a newborn calf that feared no tiger, Young Master Qin's frown relaxed a little. But he still couldn't rest easy. After entering his bedroom, he closed the door behind him and turned around.

"Is it really okay to have that young master guard the door? What if the exorcism fails and I end up with another life on my hands..."

The couple had already taken their seats on the other side of the room.

"No lives will be lost," Wei Wuxian said. "Young Master Qin, think about how many days that fierce corpse has been making a commotion at your residence. Has there been a single life lost in that time?"

Young Master Qin sat down as well. Wei Wuxian put one of the pears thrown by the fierce corpse on the table. "Have some fruit to calm your nerves."

Thanks to the stress of the past few days, Young Master Qin was in a daze. He picked up the pear and brought it to his mouth. Just as he was about to speak, he heard strange sounds.

Thump, thump.

Thump, thump.

In that instant, a cold gust swept into the room. The candle flame on the table flickered.

The pear tumbled from Young Master Qin's hand and rolled away. He gripped the hilt of his sword once more.

Thump.

Thump.

Thump.

The strange sounds grew increasingly louder and closer. Each time, the candle flame quivered as if it was afraid.

The sound of a longsword leaving its sheath rang out from the other side of the door, and a faint black shadow flitted past the paper window. The strange thumping sound instantly vanished, replaced by the sounds of soaring and flapping, and the thunderous crash of wooden furniture being smashed to pieces.

Young Master Qin's face was ashen. "What's going on outside?!"

"It's just a fight," Wei Wuxian said. "Don't mind it."

Lan Wangji listened for a moment, then commented, "Excessive."

Wei Wuxian understood what he meant. Judging by the sound of his sword and footsteps, Lan Sizhui's strikes were swift, but that ferocity came at the expense of focus and his blows weren't decisive. Although his attacks weren't weak, they weren't consistent with the principles of the Lan Clan of Gusu's sword techniques. If his spirit, qi, and mind could not be unified, or if he used a mishmash of styles, he might stray from the path and hit a dead end when trying to cultivate to a higher level.

"He's already pretty good," Wei Wuxian said. "Sizhui is still young and doesn't have full control of his attacks yet. Once he gets a little older and spars with more people, he'll figure it out."

Lan Wangji shook his head and listened for a moment before he suddenly looked at Wei Wuxian, who was astonished as well. Wei Wuxian could tell that a few of Lan Sizhui's attacks had not used techniques from the Lan Clan of Gusu but rather from the Jiang Clan of Yunmeng. However, he had never taught the Lan Clan of Gusu's juniors any such things.

"Sizhui and the others often go on Night Hunts with Jin Ling. He probably picked it up unconsciously while blows were exchanged," he hazarded a guess.

"Inappropriate," Lan Wangji stated.

"Are you going to punish him when you get back, then?"

"Yes."

"What are you two talking about?" Young Master Qin wondered.

Wei Wuxian picked up the pear from the ground and set it beside Young Master Qin's hand again. "Nothing. Eat something to calm your nerves. Don't be so nervous." Then he said to Lan Wangji with a smile, "But Hanguang-jun, you're truly impressive. It's one thing for me to identify sword techniques from the Jiang Clan of Yunmeng, but how can *you* tell?"

Lan Wangji seemed to be stumped for a moment before he answered, "I remembered them from the many times we have sparred."

"That's why I said you're impressive," Wei Wuxian said. "I've only traded blows with you using the Jiang Clan of Yunmeng's style a few times, and that was over a decade ago. And yet you can remember the techniques and identify them from sound alone. Isn't that impressive?"

As he spoke, he pushed the candle flame over to Lan Wangji in order to see if his earlobes had gone red. However, Lan Wangji saw through his wicked intent and grasped Wei Wuxian's hand, pushing the candle back toward him. The candle flame wavered like it was drunk as it was pushed to and fro, its light flickering across Wei Wuxian's smiling eyes and curved lips. The sight made Lan Wangji swallow hard.

Suddenly, they both froze for a moment, and Wei Wuxian made a surprised noise.

Looking as if he was about to face a formidable foe, Young Master Qin asked, "What's wrong? Is there a problem with the candle?"

Wei Wuxian was only speechless for a moment. "No. The candle's decent—though it'd be better if it was a bit brighter." However, he whispered to Lan Wangji, "Those last couple moves Sizhui used were pretty slick, but they didn't sound like your family's sword techniques, or mine."

After a while, Lan Wangji said with a frown, "Perhaps they were Wen techniques."

Understanding dawned on Wei Wuxian. "Wen Ning taught him, most likely. Just as well."

As they spoke, the thunderous noise outside persisted, crashing and banging louder and louder. Young Master Qin's face grew more and more ashen, and even Wei Wuxian was starting to find it a little ludicrous.

"Sizhui, we've been chatting for a while in here," he called out. "Even if you're tearing the house down, shouldn't you be finished by now?"

Lan Sizhui responded from where he was outside. "Wei-qianbei, this fierce corpse is very good at dodging. It keeps avoiding me!"

"Is it afraid of you?" Wei Wuxian asked.

"No," Lan Sizhui answered. "It can fight, but it doesn't seem interested in fighting me."

"It doesn't want to hurt a bystander?" Wei Wuxian wondered in surprise before commenting to Lan Wangji, "This is interesting. It's been ages since I last saw a fierce corpse this reasonable."

Young Master Qin, on the other hand, fretted restlessly. "Can he do it? Why hasn't he defeated it yet?"

Wei Wuxian had yet to say a word when Lan Sizhui called out, "Hanguang-jun, Wei-qianbei! This fierce corpse's left hand is curled into a claw, but its right hand is balled into a fist. It seems to be grasping something!"

On hearing this, Wei Wuxian and Lan Wangji exchanged a glance. Wei Wuxian gave a slight nod of his head, and Lan Wangji stated, "Sizhui, put away your sword."

"Hanguang-jun?" Lan Sizhui said in astonishment. "I still haven't gotten whatever's in its hand..."

Wei Wuxian stood up. "It's fine! Put away your sword. There's no need to keep fighting."

"No need to keep fighting?" Young Master Qin parroted.

"Affirmative!" Lan Sizhui acknowledged from outside the room. Sure enough, he sheathed his sword and leapt aside.

"What is this all about?" Young Master Qin said. "That thing is still outside!"

Wei Wuxian rose. "There's no need to keep fighting. The matter is more or less resolved—only one last step remains."

"What step?" Young Master Qin asked.

Wei Wuxian kicked the door open. "This step!"

The wooden door panels sprang open with a *bang*. A dark figure stood rigidly before the door. Its hair was disheveled, its face filthy, and its white eyes uncommonly savage.

On seeing the corpse's face, Young Master Qin's expression changed drastically. He drew his sword as he beat a swift retreat, but the fierce corpse assailed him like a gust of black wind and grabbed him by the neck.

Lan Sizhui, stunned at the scene that awaited him upon his

entry to the room, was about to rush to the rescue when Wei Wuxian stopped him. Although Young Master Qin was unyielding and unlikeable by nature, Lan Sizhui did not think his crime was heinous enough that he deserved to die. However, he knew that his two seniors wouldn't simply sit back and watch the fierce corpse kill the man, so he composed himself a little.

The dead servant's fingers were like an iron hoop around Young Master Qin's neck, choking him until his face turned purple and his veins bulged. Although he stabbed the fierce corpse again and again, it was like stabbing a piece of paper. The corpse showed no reaction. Instead, it slowly raised its right fist toward Young Master Qin's face as if it planned to punch his brain out of his skull. The others in the room stared at the scene playing out. Lan Sizhui could barely hold down his sword-bearing hand.

Just as it seemed Young Master Qin's head was about to explode, Lan Sizhui saw the fierce corpse loosen its grip. An oval object slid from between the fingers of its right hand. A black string dangled from one end, which the fierce corpse attempted to place over Young Master Qin's head.

Young Master Qin was speechless.

So was Lan Sizhui.

After three attempts, the corpse managed with some difficulty to loop the string over Young Master Qin's head. The struggle was so excessively clumsy and rigid that it was truly...hard to find threatening. It did not deal a killing blow, and it did not look like it was planning on strangling Young Master Qin to death with that thin string. And so, Lan Sizhui and Young Master Qin simultaneously heaved a sigh of relief.

But they had yet to fully release that breath when the fierce corpse threw out an unexpected punch at lighting speed. The blow was powerful and brutal, and Young Master Qin managed only to yelp before it knocked him out cold. He fell to the ground with blood flowing from his mouth and nose.

After the fierce corpse was done hitting him, it turned around and set out to leave. Lan Sizhui, watching the scene unfold with his mouth agape, gripped the hilt of his sword. But he found the situation inexplicably absurd, and somehow, it seemed it would be made even more ludicrous if he reacted *too* seriously. Thus, he was torn on whether he should make a move.

However, Wei Wuxian was laughing his ass off. He waved at Lan Sizhui. "Don't bother. Let it leave as it wishes."

The fierce corpse turned and glanced at him. With a nod of its head, it hobbled along, dragging its broken leg, and jumped out the door.

Lan Sizhui blanked out for a moment as he gazed at its fleeing back. "Wei-qianbei, this... Is it okay to just let it go?"

Lan Wangji leaned down to check on Young Master Qin, whose face had been beaten bloody. "It's fine."

Lan Sizhui's attention shifted back to Young Master Qin. Only then did he have the presence of mind to look closely at the object hanging from his neck—a jade pendant.

The red string that secured the jade pendant looked as if it had been rolling around in the soil for many years, turned black by filth. However, the jade itself was still a lustrous white.

"This..."

"It's now been returned to its rightful owner," Wei Wuxian said.

Once Lan Wangji had made sure that Young Master Qin was just unconscious and in no danger of losing his life, the two left the Qin residence with Lan Sizhui in tow. Before leaving, Wei Wuxian thoughtfully closed the three doors for Young Master Qin.

"He didn't have it easy," Lan Sizhui said.

Wei Wuxian got on Little Apple. "What? Are you talking about Young Master Qin? Just one punch from the fierce corpse, and it was all over for good. That's already very easy, okay?!"

"I'm not talking about Young Master Qin. I'm talking about the fierce corpse," Lan Sizhui explained. "In the records that I've seen regarding malicious ghosts and fierce corpses avenging a grievance, most of the feuds stemmed from a kindness that was taken for granted in life. When they die, they go on to kill people, and they're feral when they're wreaking havoc. But that fierce corpse..."

Lan Sizhui stood in front of the disfigured main doors and glanced back at the claw marks, still finding the situation incredible. "After it turned into a fierce corpse, it searched the mountain for two years for the jade pendant it lost while it was still alive. This is the first time I've ever seen a fierce corpse transforming to do something like this, instead of coming back to kill and seek revenge."

Wei Wuxian fished out another apple from the saddlebag. "That's why I said I hadn't seen such a reasonable evil spirit in a long time. Had he been slightly more vindictive, it wouldn't have been unusual for it to sever one of Young Master Qin's legs—or even worse, massacre his entire family."

Lan Sizhui thought for a moment. "Qianbei, I still have an unanswered concern. Did Young Master Qin break the man's leg? And did that directly cause him to lose his footing and fall to his death?"

"Whatever the truth may be, the guy doesn't hold Young Master Qin accountable, at any rate," Wei Wuxian said.

"Mn," Lan Sizhui said. "So it was really satisfied with just one punch?"

"By the looks of it, yes," Lan Wangji replied.

There was a loud, clear crunch as Wei Wuxian took a bite of the apple. "Right? As the saying goes, people will strive to prove their worth and vindicate themselves. If someone can't rest in peace, it's because they're suppressing something in their heart. He pelted him with some fruit, returned the jade pendant, and knocked his block off. He let off some steam, and is no longer suppressing anything."

"If only every evil spirit was so reasonable," Lan Sizhui lamented.

Hearing this, Wei Wuxian laughed. "Oh, you silly child. Even human beings are unreasonable when they bear someone a grudge. You expect evil spirits to be amenable to reason? You must understand something—everyone in the world feels like they've been treated unjustly."

Lan Wangji tugged Little Apple's reins and commented in a mild tone, "He is lucky."

Wei Wuxian agreed. "Indeed. Young Master Qin is really very lucky."

Lan Sizhui had held this back for a long time, but he could finally no longer help himself. He said, in all earnestness, "But I somehow feel just one punch is letting him off lightly..."

"Ha ha ha ha ha ha ha ha ha..."

Whether it was because he was still out cold from the fierce corpse's punch, or because he'd completely lost faith in Wei Wuxian, Young Master Qin never again came calling on them.

But seven days later, news of him reached their ears.

The gossip went like this: one morning, they found a young man's corpse on the side of the main road. It had been half-decayed, dressed in tattered funeral garb, and stank to the high heavens. They had been discussing whether they should roll him up in a mat and dig a pit somewhere to bury him, but in a massive act of kindness, Young Master Qin had forked over the money needed to collect the remains and hold a proper burial. He was unanimously lauded for it for a long time after.

Lan Wangji and Wei Wuxian passed the Qin residence as they were leaving the city. It had long since repaired its main entrance and boasted two new imposing jet-black doors. People came and went, sweeping away the grim atmosphere and bleak desolation of the days before. It was, once again, the very picture of a thriving house.

THE BAI RESIDENCE'S infamous local reputation could largely be attributed to the White Chamber.

As for why it was called the White Chamber, the first reason was naturally because it was white. When it was first built, the walls had been covered with white mortar. The owner had planned to add some color with decorations. Construction went very smoothly in the rest of the residence, but strange things began to happen when it reached the chamber in the western courtyard, leaving them no choice but to shelve their renovation plans.

To date, the White Chamber remained incongruous with the rest of the magnificently ornamented Bai residence. It was such a stark white that it made one's skin crawl.

"The room is secured with three locks and three bolts. No matter how sweltering the summer day might be, its vicinity is as cold as an ice cellar. According to the current master of the Bai family, when his father was a child, there was a day when the ball he was playing with rolled all the way to the room's entrance. When he went to pick it up, he was unable to restrain his curiosity and snuck a peek through the slit in the door."

When a straight-faced Jin Ling got to this point in the story, he saw Wei Wuxian, who was standing off to the side, reach his hand into a coffin to peel open the corpse's eyelids. The words that would have followed got caught in Jin Ling's throat, choking him off.

Hearing the lull in his story, Wei Wuxian turned to look at him. "Snuck a peek through the slit in the door?"

The group of Lan Clan juniors behind Jin Ling shifted their gazes toward Jin Ling in unison. After a pause, Jin Ling continued.

"...Snuck a peek through the slit in the door, then stood there blankly, unable to move even after a long time. When his family found him and dragged him away, he fainted. He was struck with a fever that burned so hot he became delirious, and later, couldn't remember a thing. From then on, he never dared go near the place again.

"No one is allowed to leave their room after midnight, and they are not allowed to go near the White Chamber in particular. This is one of the family's unbreakable rules. At a certain time after midnight, they can hear the creaking of the old wooden floorboards inside the chamber, even though there's clearly no one inside. And they can also hear..."

Jin Ling clenched his hands into fists and made a murderous gesture.

"...the sound of hemp rope slowly tightening, like there's something being strangled to death."

Many days ago, a servant of the Bai residence had passed by the White Chamber while doing his morning sweeping. He discovered a small hole the size of a finger poked in the thin paper window of the White Chamber's wooden door.

And a man had been prone on the ground at its entrance.

He was a stranger, unknown to anyone from the residence. He was about forty years old, veins bulging on his ashen face and fingers clutching at his chest. He was long dead.

The servant had been terrified, as was the master of the house. After much deliberation, the authorities had concluded that he was an unlucky night burglar who just happened to barge, of all places, into the forbidden area of the Bai residence. It was there he had seen something that triggered a heart attack, causing him to die of fright right then and there. As for what that "something" was, they had torn down all the locks and paper seals in the White Chamber in their investigation, only to remain baffled.

But now that someone had died, the master of the Bai family knew they could no longer pretend there was nothing in the White Chamber. If this evil was not eradicated, there would be no end to the trouble it would cause them in the future. So he had gritted his teeth, plucked up his courage, and traveled to Golden Carp Tower, where he presented a huge sum of money to implore the Jin Clan of Lanling to call on his house for a Night Hunt.

That concluded the backstory of this incident.

Lan Jingyi was on the verge of a breakdown as he held up the coffin lid and said despairingly, "Wei-qianbei, are you done...? This person's been dead for so many days... Even a walking corpse doesn't stink this bad..."

Lan Sizhui, who was helping him hold the lid open, hovered between laughter and tears. "The coffin is simple and crude, and this rundown charitable mortuary is exposed to the elements with no one to care for it. It's inevitable, given the coffin has been here for a few days. Hang in there a bit longer. We still need to take notes."

Jin Ling humphed. "It's more than enough to give a burglar a proper burial. Don't tell me we should worship him like he's the Buddha."

After prodding the corpse for half a day, Wei Wuxian finally lifted his face out of the coffin. He took off his gloves and tossed them away. "Have you all had a look?"

"Yes!"

"Good. In that case, what's our next step?" Wei Wuxian asked.

"Summon his soul!" answered Lan Jingyi.

"Duh," Jin Ling scoffed. "I've already tried that."

"And?" Wei Wuxian probed.

"He's not powerfully obsessed with anything, and his soul's too weak. What's more, he was frightened to death. More than seven days have passed since he died, so his soul has completely dissipated. There's no way to summon it back," Jin Ling answered.

"An attempt like that is no different from not attempting at all..." Lan Jingyi lamented.

"Then let's go take a look at the White Chamber," Lan Sizhui quickly cut in. "Let's go, let's go. Jin-gongzi, please lead the way." As he spoke, he pushed Lan Jingyi out of the door, successfully nipping a new round of meaningless arguments in the bud.

The group of boys strode across the threshold, several of them jumping over it, their steps brisk and spry. Although Jin Ling was supposed to lead the way, he trailed behind them.

"Have there been any instances of unnatural deaths or unsolved cases in the Bai residence before?" Lan Sizhui asked Jin Ling.

"The master of the family insists there are none," Jin Ling answered. "The few elders who have passed did so naturally, of old age. There are no conflicts among the household's members either."

"Oh no," Lan Jingyi said. "I have a bad feeling about this. Usually when someone says that, there's definitely some kind of conflict and they're just covering it up."

"In any case, I've repeatedly confirmed it with them," Jin Ling said. "But nothing came of questioning them, and there was nothing unusual about what I turned up. You can try again, though."

As he had already done his homework beforehand and repeatedly investigated the White Chamber, he did not enter the Bai residence with them this time. Instead, he found a roadside tea stall outside and took a seat.

A black shadow drifted over not long later. Wei Wuxian sat across from him. "Jin Ling."

Two dashing characters sitting at the same tiny tea stall were indeed a tad conspicuous, so much so that the woman serving tea kept looking back, despite how busy she was.

This was the first time Wei Wuxian had seen Jing Lin face-to-face after they had parted at the Guanyin Temple, and he had only now managed to get a chance to speak to him alone.

Jin Ling paused for a moment, his expression unreadable. "What?"

"How are you doing at Golden Carp Tower nowadays?" Wei Wuxian asked.

"Same old," Jin Ling answered.

As it happened, there had been many twists and turns on the journey that the master of the Bai family had taken to request Golden Carp Tower initiate a hunt.

Had it been a few years earlier, when the Jin Clan of Lanling was at the peak of their power like the sun at high noon, even offering ten times as large a reward might not have made it possible for him to request the assistance of a scion of the Jin Clan of Lanling. In fact, a common merchant household like the Bai—wealthy but lacking in power and prestige—could never have called on the Jins for even a social visit, let alone pled with them to hunt down some evil creature.

But the cultivation world was no longer what it used to be. Although the common folks didn't know the details of this dramatic change, they had heard some vague rumors, and that was what encouraged the master of the Bai family to give it a try. He had approached the main gate with some trepidation, presented his name card,[6] and explained his intentions. The guard had taken his bribe and reluctantly left to report his arrival. When he returned, however, he was suddenly hostile, claiming the head of the family had turned down the request. He moved to drive the Bai family head away.

The Bai family head, who had never really expected to secure the Jin Clan's help, was fine with leaving. However, he grew annoyed with the guard for being so nasty to him after accepting his bribe and demanded his money back. As they argued back and forth, a handsome young man wearing a Sparks Amidst Snow uniform emerged from the vermilion doors with bow in hand. Seeing this unbecoming scene, he instantly frowned and asked about the situation.

The guard had started stammering. The master of the Bai family observed that despite being but a child, this young man was likely of quite high status. He hurriedly told him everything. To his surprise, the moment the young man heard his story, he flew into a rage and sent the guard rolling down Golden Carp Tower's steps with a strike of his palm.

"The 'head of the family' said to drive him away?!" the young man yelled. "Why didn't I hear anything about that?!" He had then turned to the master of the Bai family and said, "You're from the Bai family? The ones who live ten kilometers west of the city? I got it. Go back now. Someone will go find you in a few days."

The master of the Bai family returned home in utter bewilderment. A group of juniors from prominent cultivation clans had indeed arrived at his door a few days later, but he had no idea

---

6   名帖 (also 拜帖) / name card (visitation card): A paper or wooden badge that indicates a person's name, position, and so on. They were commonly used by officials, nobles, or other distinguished people to notify another party of their visit.

that one of the young men was, in fact, the head of the Jin Clan of Lanling himself.

Of course, he couldn't have known that the Jin Clan of Lanling was currently in a state of total disarray. The guard hadn't reported to Jin Ling, who was the real head of the family. Instead, he had gone to inform an elder of the Jin Clan of Lanling. When that elder heard even the most common of merchants now dared set foot on the Jin Clan of Lanling's golden steps, he had promptly flown into a rage and ordered the guard to throw the man out. Who would have thought he would run into Jin Ling, on his way to the hunting grounds, by complete coincidence?

Jin Ling knew all the clan elders put on airs, priding themselves on being a prominent clan with a century of history. They refused to lower themselves, no matter what, and refused to give audience to anyone who wasn't distinguished or eminent. Jin Ling had always detested such behavior. He was furious with the guard for treating him like a nobody and going over his head to report to someone else, and it also occurred to him that no disciples or guest cultivators would have dared accept bribes while Jin Guangyao was still alive. The more he dwelled on it, the angrier he became.

It just so happened that he had made plans with Lan Sizhui, Lan Jingyi, and the others to go on a series of Night Hunts that month. And so, they made a trip to the Bai residence together.

If he was honest with himself, Wei Wuxian's presence wasn't a complete surprise. Jin Ling might not have been willing to tell others of his struggles, but many eyes were watching Golden Carp Tower, and many mouths had nothing better to do than gossip. News had long since spread to Wei Wuxian and Lan Wangji.

Wei Wuxian knew Jin Ling wasn't willing to show weakness, so he said, "Go to your uncle more often if something's wrong."

"It's not like he's a Jin," Jin Ling answered coldly.

Wei Wuxian was taken aback when he heard this, but then understanding hit him. Caught between laughter and tears, he raised a hand and smacked Jin Ling on the back of his head. "Talk sense!"

Jin Ling let loose an *"Ow!"* His forced composure finally cracked. The slap might not have hurt, but he felt as if he had suffered a great humiliation, which deepened even further when he heard the girlish giggle of the woman serving tea at the side.

Covering his head, he hollered, "Why did you hit me?!"

"I hit you to remind you to think of your uncle," Wei Wuxian said. "He's not a busybody who likes meddling in other people's affairs, but for your sake, he goes to other people's houses to throw his weight around. In turn, he gets fingers pointed at him. And *you* write him off as 'not a Jin.' Surely he'd be bitterly disappointed to hear that."

Jin Ling was stunned for a moment, then began to rage. "I didn't mean it that way! I—"

"Then what *did* you mean?" Wei Wuxian replied.

"I!" Jin Ling said. "I..."

The first "I" was full of bluster, while the second "I" was deflated.

"I, I, I. *I* will help you say what you mean," Wei Wuxian said. "Jiang Cheng may be your uncle, but he's still an outsider to the Jin Clan of Lanling. He's already intervened a few times to help you, but if he continues to overstep his authority in other people's domains, it will become an excuse for others to denounce him in the future, which will cause him trouble. Am I right?"

Jin Ling fumed. "Duh! So you *do* understand! Then why did you hit me?!"

Wei Wuxian backhandedly smacked him again. "That *is* why I'm hitting you! Can't you just come out with whatever you have to say?

How does such a nice sentiment sound so offensive when it comes from your mouth?!"

"It's just like you to start hitting me when Lan Wangji isn't around!" Jin Ling hollered as he covered his head.

"If he were here, do you think he wouldn't help me hit you if I told him to?" Wei Wuxian said.

"I'm the head of a family!" Jin Ling blurted in disbelief.

Wei Wuxian scoffed, smiling scornfully. "I've beaten up at least eighty family heads, if not a hundred."

Jin Ling leapt to his feet and made to dash out of the tea stall. "Hit me again and I'll leave!"

"Come back!" Wei Wuxian yanked him by the back of his collar like he was lifting a baby chick. He gave the stool a slap. "I'll stop. Sit properly."

Jin Ling was wary. It was only when he saw Wei Wuxian indeed showed no intent to hit him again that he very reluctantly sat down. Seeing the commotion finally draw to a close, the woman from the tea stall came over, a hand covering her smile, to refill their water.

Wei Wuxian picked up the teacup and took a sip. All of a sudden, he said, "A-Ling."

Jin Ling shot him a glare. "What?"

But Wei Wuxian simply smiled. "You've grown a lot."

Jin Ling was stunned.

Wei Wuxian stroked his chin. "You seem, mmm...a lot more dependable now. I'm really happy, but I'm also... How should I put it? You were pretty adorable back when you were silly and naive."

Jin Ling started fidgeting in his seat again.

Out of the blue, Wei Wuxian reached out to wrap an arm around Jin Ling's shoulders and tousle his hair. "But no matter what, I'm really happy to see you, ya brat! Ha ha!"

Disregarding his messy hair, Jin Ling leapt up from the bench in another attempt to rush out. Wei Wuxian smacked him back down again.

"Where are you going?"

Jin Ling's neck was already red. "I'm going to see the White Chamber!" he answered gruffly.

"Didn't you already see it?" Wei Wuxian asked.

"I! Am! Going! To! See! It! Again!" Jin Ling said.

"You've seen it several times now. I doubt a few more looks will turn up anything new. Why not help me investigate something else?"

Jin Ling was afraid he was going to say more sappy, cringe-worthy stuff. He'd rather be slapped hard than get used to someone patting him on the head and saying nice things to him with an arm around his shoulders. There was really no way to predict what would come out of this man's mouth, especially considering how he had even gone so far as to shout in public about wanting to bed Hanguang-jun.

And so Jin Ling hurriedly said, "Sure! What do you want to investigate?"

"I want to look into whether there's this strange person in the area," said Wei Wuxian. "Someone with dozens of slashes on their face. Their eyelids and lips are also cut off."

Jin Ling could tell that he wasn't talking nonsense. "That I can do, but why do you want to investigate such a—"

Out of the blue, the woman refilling the water piped up. "You're talking about Hookhand, right?"

Wei Wuxian turned his head. "Hookhand?"

"Yeah." The tea lady had probably been eavesdropping for amusement. As soon as she had the opportunity, she butted in. "No mouth, no eyelids. Isn't that who you're talking about? Gongzi, from your accent, you don't seem to be a local. I'm surprised you actually know about him."

"I'm a local, and I've never heard of him," Jin Ling said.

"That's because you're young," said the tea lady. "It's no surprise you've never heard of him. But he used to be quite well known."

"Well known?" echoed Wei Wuxian. "In what way?"

"Not in a good way," the tea lady answered. "When I was a child, I heard the story from my grand-aunt's mama. You can imagine just how long ago this took place. I don't know what Hookhand's real name was, but he was once a small-time blacksmith. Although he was poor, his workmanship was excellent, and he was pretty good-looking to boot. He was also an honest and diligent man. He had a wife who was really, really beautiful, and he was very good to her. His wife, however, was not very good to him. She took a lover outside the marriage, and then, not wanting her husband anymore, she...killed him!"

The tea lady had obviously grown up blighted by this tale and was vivid and dramatic when inflicting it on others. Her tone and facial expressions as she narrated were on point—so much so that listening to her put Jin Ling on edge as well.

The most vicious be the heart of a woman, indeed! he thought.

Wei Wuxian, on the other hand, dealt with fierce corpses and evil spirits for years on end. He had heard at least eight hundred similar stories, if not a thousand; the trope wasn't just old, it was dead and rotted. He merely propped his chin on his hand and listened expressionlessly as the tea lady continued.

"The wife was afraid people would recognize the corpse was her husband's, so she cut off his eyelids and slashed his face dozens of times. And then she spotted a newly forged iron hook laying nearby. Because she was afraid he would lodge a complaint against her to the Judges of the Underworld, she grabbed it and used it to hook his tongue and tear it from his mouth—"

All of a sudden, someone blurted out, "How could his wife do that?! I can't believe she'd kill and mutilate her own husband in such a depraved way!"

Jin Ling had been listening to the story with fascination, and the voice startled him so bad he nearly jumped out of his skin. He looked back, realizing that Lan Sizhui, Lan Jingyi, and the rest had already emerged from the Bai residence. They had crowded together behind him and were listening with rapt attention. The one who'd spoken up was Lan Jingyi.

"Alas," said the tea lady. "There's only so much we can learn from tales of the relationships between men and women. When our protagonists despise the poor and curry favor with the rich, or abandon an old flame for the new lover, it's not something any bystander could ever understand. In any case, the blacksmith became a specter that looked neither human nor ghost. He was on the verge of death when his vicious wife secretly threw him into the grave mound to the west of the city. Crows love to eat corpses and rotting meat, but they didn't even dare peck at his flesh when they saw that face of his..."

Lan Jingyi was easily moved and became absorbed in any story he heard. He was the perfect audience. "...She's too much...too much! Didn't she get her comeuppance for killing him?"

"She did! How could she not?" said the tea lady. "Although the blacksmith was horribly injured, he somehow survived. One night, he crawled from his grave and returned home. While his wife was sleeping like nothing was wrong, he used the hook to—" She made a gesture. "*Slash* her throat to shreds."

The juniors' expressions were complicated. They could feel their hair standing on end, but at the same time, they wanted to breathe a sigh of relief.

"After he killed his wife, he slashed her face to bits and ripped out her tongue too," the tea lady continued. "But his resentment was not appeased. From then on, he started killing any beautiful woman he came across!"

Lan Jingyi was stunned. The last sentence had hit him hard. "That's not right! It's one thing to take revenge, but what did the other beautiful women do to him?"

"Indeed," the tea lady replied. "But he didn't really care. His face was now hideous, and every time he saw a beautiful woman, it reminded him of his wife. What could you expect him to do, with all that hatred in his heart? Anyway, for a long time afterward, no young women dared walk alone once the sky darkened. If they didn't go out, those who stayed home without a father, brother, or husband present also didn't dare sleep. And that's because every so often, a female corpse with its tongue ripped out would be found discarded on the side of the road..."

"Didn't anyone manage to catch him?" Jin Ling asked.

"They couldn't," the tea lady answered. "After this blacksmith killed his wife, he disappeared. He abandoned his former home and appeared and disappeared mysteriously, moving so dexterously he seemed possessed. How could the average person catch him? Anyway, I heard it took several years for him to finally be subdued. With the matter resolved, everyone was able to sleep in peace! Amitabha Buddha, thank heavens!"

After leaving the tea stall and returning to the mortuary, Lan Sizhui said, "Wei-qianbei, is the Hookhand you thought to investigate related to the evil spirit at the Bai residence?"

"Of course," Wei Wuxian answered.

Jin Ling had more or less guessed this, but still asked what needed to be asked. "How are they related?"

Wei Wuxian opened the coffin lid again. "In the corpse of this burglar."

The boys covered their noses.

"I've already examined the burglar's corpse several times," Jin Ling said.

Wei Wuxian dragged him over. "Evidently, you didn't look *closely* enough."

He patted Jin Ling's shoulder and suddenly pressed down on it. The moment Jin Ling's head went down, he came face-to-face with that ashen-faced bulging-eyed corpse in the coffin. The stench hit him head-on.

"Look at his eyes," Wei Wuxian said.

Jin Ling narrowed his eyes and stared at the dull, lifeless eyes of the corpse. One glance was enough to make him go cold from head to toe. Knowing there was something amiss, Lan Sizhui immediately bent over for a look too.

The figure reflected in the corpse's black eyes wasn't his own.

It was an unfamiliar face that almost filled the entire iris—a face missing its eyelids and lips, with patchy skin covered in slashing scars.

Lan Jingyi hopped a couple times behind them, seemingly wanting to look but not daring to. "Sizhui, what...what did you see?"

Lan Sizhui waved his hand. "Don't come over."

"Oh!" Lan Jingyi hurriedly took several big steps back.

Lan Sizhui raised his head. "Speaking of which, I've heard folktales like this. Sometimes, the eyes will 'record' what a person sees before they die. I didn't expect it to be true."

"It only happens occasionally," Wei Wuxian said. "The burglar was scared to death. No matter what he saw, it probably made a deep and indelible impression on him. That's why it worked. Under different circumstances, nothing might have been recorded. We probably won't be able to see it anymore once the corpse decays completely in a few days."

Jin Ling voiced his doubt. "Is this really a credible lead? Since it's based on a folktale, and an inconsistent one at that?"

"Credible or not, let's investigate it before we come to a decision," said Wei Wuxian. "It's better than being stuck here."

At least they were making progress. Lan Sizhui decided to head to the grave mound west of the city to search for clues, and Wei Wuxian declared that he would accompany him. Meanwhile, the rest of them would investigate Hookhand. After all, it would be hard to accomplish what they'd set out to do by relying only on hearsay—the more information they could gather, the better.

Jin Ling wasn't fond of Lan Jingyi and also felt like the place Wei Wuxian was going would be more conducive to gaining experience. But then he remembered the others weren't familiar with Lanling and might run into issues without him to lead them, so he promptly agreed without complaint.

The group agreed to rendezvous at the Bai residence in the evening. The information they obtained after making a few rounds of inquiries was essentially the same as what the tea lady had said earlier that day. Presumably, her account matched the version in wide circulation. And so, Jin Ling and the others returned to the Bai residence first.

As dusk fell, Jin Ling paced back and forth in the main hall of the Bai residence. Wei Wuxian and Lan Sizhui had yet to return, even after he'd gone a few rounds of bickering with Lan Jingyi. Just as he was about to head west of the city to search for them, someone suddenly slammed the main door open with a loud *bang*.

The first one to barge through the door was Lan Sizhui. He was struggling to hold onto a scalding hot object. The moment he stepped through the door, the object slipped from his grasp and fell to the ground. It was palm-sized and wrapped in layers of yellow talisman paper. Damp scarlet blood seeped through and stained the surface of the paper.

Wei Wuxian followed him in, strolling leisurely across the threshold. Seeing the others crowding over excitedly, he quickly shooed them away. "Spread out and stay away! Danger, beware!"

And thus, the crowd dispersed just as excitedly. The object seemed to be corrosive, slowly eating away the talisman paper on the surface of the bundle to reveal what was within:

A rusty iron hook!

It wasn't just rusty. The brightness of the blood staining it made it seem like it had just been dislodged from a hunk of human flesh.

"The iron hook of Hookhand?" Jin Ling asked.

Burn marks and bloodstains covered Lan Sizhui's uniform. He gasped slightly for breath, his face slightly flushed as he answered, "Yes! Something has possessed it. Don't touch it with your bare hands!"

The iron hook began to shake violently.

"Close the door!" Lan Sizhui commanded. "Don't let it escape! If it gets away, I don't know if I can catch it again!"

Lan Jingyi was the first to rush forward and slam the main door shut with another *bang*. Bracing his back against the door, he yelled, "Talisman! Guys, hit it with your talismans!"

All at once, it was slapped with hundreds of talismans. If everyone from the Bai residence hadn't already hidden themselves in the eastern courtyard at Jin Ling's behest, they would surely have been shocked by the sight of the blazing flames and sizzling lightning.

The boys exhausted their supply of talismans in short order, but before they could breathe a sigh of relief, the iron hook began to bleed again.

They couldn't stop for even a moment!

Lan Sizhui could find no more talismans in reserve. Suddenly, he heard Lan Jingyi shout, "Kitchen! Into the kitchen! Salt, salt, salt! Bring the salt!"

At his reminder, the boys dashed into the kitchen to grab the salt jar. They hurled a handful of snowy grains to scatter all over the iron hook. The result was incredible—the rusty iron hook started to sizzle and splutter white foam and steam, as if it was being deep-fried in a wok full of oil.

A wave of stench permeated the main hall, like the smell of rotten meat being charred. The fresh blood on the iron hook looked like it was gradually being absorbed by the grains of salt.

One of the boys said, "We're almost out of salt! What should we do next?!"

The hook was about to bleed again. This was clearly not a long-term solution. So Lan Jingyi said, "If worse comes to worst, we'll smelt it!"

"We can't smelt it!" Jin Ling objected.

But Lan Sizhui said, "Okay, we'll smelt it!"

He immediately took off his outer robe, threw it over the iron hook, rolled it up, and dashed into the kitchen to fling the whole bundle into the stove.

Seeing this play out, Jin Ling's eyes blazed with fury. "Lan Sizhui! It's one thing for Lan Jingyi to be silly, but why are you being silly too?! You're gonna try to smelt it with just that tiny bit of fire?!"

"Who are *you* calling silly?!" Lan Jingyi fumed. "And what do you mean it's one thing for *me* to be silly?!"

Lan Sizhui cut in. "If there's not enough fire, we'll make more!"

He made a hand seal with his fingers, and the flames instantly erupted, sending forth a wave of searing heat. Understanding immediately dawned on the others, who all followed suit. Even Jin Ling and Lan Jingyi were too preoccupied to continue their argument as they concentrated on maintaining their hand seals. The fire underneath abruptly flared, and the flames burned so red that they cast a crimson hue over their faces.

They waited like that for a long time, as though they were locked in a battle against a formidable foe. Finally, the iron hook gradually disappeared into the scorching flames.

Seeing nothing strange ultimately happen, Lan Jingyi asked tensely, "Is it done? Did we succeed?"

Lan Sizhui exhaled. After a while, he stepped forward to check, then turned around. "The iron hook is gone," he declared.

With the possessed object gone, the resentful energy should naturally have dispersed as well. Everyone heaved a sigh of relief— especially Lan Jingyi, who was the happiest of all.

"I told you it could be smelted. It worked, you see? Ha ha ha ha..."

Although Lan Jingyi was happy, Jin Ling was feeling down. He hadn't been much help during the Night Hunt, leaving him without much gained from the experience either. Deep down, he was chagrined. He should have insisted on going with Wei Wuxian and Lan Sizhui to look for Hookhand during the daytime. He'd never do any of the grunt work again.

Unexpectedly, Wei Wuxian said, "You were too sloppy with your wrap-up. How can you be so confident that the matter's been settled? Don't you need to verify it?"

On hearing this, Jin Ling perked up. "How do we verify it?"

"Have someone spend the night in that room," said Wei Wuxian. There was silence all around.

"Once you've spent a night in there and can come out of it safe and sound, without experiencing anything abnormal—that's when you can pat yourself on the back and guarantee that the matter has been thoroughly resolved. Right?" Wei Wuxian continued.

"Who do you think is gonna do a thing like that...?" wondered Lan Jingyi.

"I'll do it!" Jin Ling immediately chimed in.

Wei Wuxian didn't even have to look at him to know what he was thinking. He patted his head and said with a smile, "Do your best if the chance presents itself."

"Don't touch my head," said Jin Ling, displeased. "Haven't you heard that men's heads should not be touched?"

"Your uncle must've been the one who told you that," said Wei Wuxian. "It doesn't matter if you listen to him or not."

"Hey!" Jin Ling was shocked. "Who told me earlier to go to him if something's wrong?!"

The Bai family had arranged for everyone's food and lodging, so the group stayed in the eastern courtyard for the evening while Jin Ling went to the western courtyard alone.

The juniors of the Lan Clan of Gusu, who still strictly followed their daily work and rest routine while on the road, woke early the next morning. Lan Sizhui had been instructed by Lan Wangji to wake Wei Wuxian up for breakfast before he left, so he spent nearly an hour doing all he could to finally drag Wei Wuxian downstairs. When they arrived in the main hall, Lan Jingyi was helping the servants of the Bai residence distribute congee. Lan Sizhui was about to go over to help as well when he saw Jin Ling trudge in with two dark circles under his eyes.

The circle of people gazed at him in silence. Jin Ling sat down at Wei Wuxian's left, and Wei Wuxian greeted him.

"Good morning."

Jin Ling nodded in reply, wearing an expression of forced calm. "Good morning."

The others nodded too. "Good morning."

Seeing that he had no intention to speak even after some time had elapsed, Wei Wuxian pointed to his own eyes. "You're looking a bit..."

After ensuring that he still looked coolly indifferent, Jin Ling spoke up. "As expected, the wrap-up was sloppy."

The crowd tensed.

After Jin Ling entered the White Chamber last night, he had surveyed his surroundings. The room was extremely simple, with barely any furniture except for a dusty bed resting against the wall. Jin Ling touched it once and couldn't stand it another moment. No servant dared approach the room, and there was no way he could lie down with so much dust everywhere. Left with no other choice, he fetched water and cleaned the place up himself before managing with some difficulty to lie down...

...with his face to the wall and his back to the room, and a mirror hidden in the palm of his hand. By turning the mirror, he could get a general view of the room behind him.

Jin Ling had waited for over half the night. All the mirror reflected was endless darkness, so he twirled it in his hand. Just as he was about to amuse himself by doing it again, a dazzling white figure suddenly glinted across the mirror's surface.

His heart had lurched. He composed himself, then slowly turned the mirror around.

Something had finally appeared on its surface.

Hearing this, Lan Jingyi said in a trembling voice, "What was in the mirror? Hookhand...?"

"No," said Jin Ling. "It was a chair."

Lan Jingyi was about to breathe a sigh of relief when he thought on it further, and his hair instantly stood on end. How could a chair's appearance merit a sigh of relief? Jin Ling had clearly said that the room's furnishings were extremely simple, with nothing but a dusty bed against the wall.

If that was the case...

...then where did the chair come from?!

"The chair was close, right by my bed," Jin Ling said. "At first it was empty, but after a while, a figure in black suddenly appeared in it."

Jin Ling had wanted to get a clear look at her, but the woman had her head lowered, and half her long hair hung loose, obscuring her face. From head to toe, the only visible part of her was a pair of snow-white hands, which were settled on the armrests.

He quietly adjusted the position of the mirror, but had only just moved his wrist when the woman slowly raised her head, as if sensing something. Her face was covered in dozens of bloody slashes.

Wei Wuxian was not at all surprised, but the other juniors were dumbfounded by what they heard.

"Wait a minute." Lan Jingyi set a bowl of congee before Jin Ling. "A female ghost? How could it be a female ghost? You couldn't have been scared so silly that you started seeing things..."

Jin Ling smacked him. "Anyone can call me silly except for you. I couldn't get a clear look at her because of all that blood and hair, but her hairstyle and clothing were that of a young woman, so there's definitely no mistake. We were looking in the wrong direction." After a pause, he continued, "There *was* resentful energy lingering on the iron hook, but the one haunting the White Chamber is probably not Hookhand."

"Why didn't you spend more time looking at her appearance...?" asked Lan Jingyi. "Who knows? We might even determine her identity based on some distinctive facial features, like a mole or birthmark."

Jin Ling huffed. "You think I didn't want to? I meant to, but the female spirit noticed the moonlight reflected by the mirror and immediately looked in my direction. The mirror reflected her eyes, and I locked gazes with her in a momentary lapse of attention."

If an evil spirit caught him spying, he couldn't possibly keep looking at them. He had to set down the mirror at once and close his eyes, pretending to be sound asleep. If he hadn't, it would have provoked the evil being and intensified its killing intent.

"What a close call..." Lan Jingyi said.

Everyone at the table started speaking at once.

"But there was no woman in the burglar's eyes."

"Just because he didn't see one doesn't mean that there *wasn't* one. Perhaps the burglar's position was off..."

"That's not it. A female ghost—why is it a female ghost? Who is she?!"

"The woman's face had been slashed dozens of times," said Lan Sizhui. "So she's very likely one of Hookhand's many victims. What Jin Ling saw must be a residual imprint of her resentful energy."

A residual imprint was a constant reenactment of the point in an evil spirit's life when its resentment ran deepest. Usually, it was the moment before its death or an event that had earned the bulk of its hatred.

"Mmm." Jin Ling made a noise of acknowledgment. "The White Chamber in the mirror I saw last night had completely different furnishings—it looked like an inn. There probably used to be an inn here before the Bai residence was built, and the woman was murdered there."

"Ooooh," Lan Jingyi said. "That's true. Come to think of it, when we were gathering information, someone mentioned that Hookhand could easily pry open the lock on the inn's door. He often snuck in at night and targeted women who were staying there alone!"

"And the room in which the girl or madam was killed just so happened to be in the same location as the White Chamber when the Bai residence was built!" Lan Sizhui concluded.

No wonder the master of the Bai family kept insisting there were no unsolved murders in the Bai residence and that no one had died an unnatural death. It wasn't that they were deliberately trying to cover up the truth, but that they were truly innocent—this really had nothing to do with them at all!

Jin Ling picked up the congee and drank a mouthful. "I've long known that this case wouldn't be simple," he said, feigning composure. "It's just as well. We have to solve it, anyway."

"Jin Ling, go catch up on your sleep in a bit," said Wei Wuxian. "We still have work to do tonight."

Lan Jingyi glanced at Wei Wuxian's bowl. "Wei-qianbei, you didn't finish your food. Don't leave any leftovers."

"I'm done eating," said Wei Wuxian. "But you should eat some more, Jingyi. You'll be taking the lead tonight."

Startled, Lan Jingyi nearly dropped the bowl he was holding. "Huh? Me? T-take what lead?!"

"Jin Ling didn't see everything last night, right?" Wei Wuxian said. "This time, we'll watch to the end and find out what's going on. You take the lead."

The color drained from Lan Jingyi's face. "Wei-qianbei, are you sure this isn't a mistake? Why me?"

"No mistake about it," Wei Wuxian said. "It's all part of gaining experience. Everyone will have an opportunity, and everyone will need to have a go at it. Sizhui and Jin Ling had their turns, so you're next."

"Why me...?"

Of course, Wei Wuxian would not say outright that Lan Jingyi's name was the only one he remembered out of this group of kids, aside from Lan Sizhui's and Jin Ling's. He merely patted Lan Jingyi's shoulder encouragingly.

"It's a good thing! Look at the others! See how much they want to have a turn?"

"What others? Everyone's fled!"

No matter how Lan Jingyi protested, he was still shoved to the very front of the White Chamber when midnight came around. A few rows of long benches had been set up outside the White Chamber, currently filled with seated people. Someone poked a hole in the paper covering the window. A moment later, it was riddled with holes, presenting a wretched sight.

Feels like...this can no longer be called "peeping," thought Lan Sizhui, poking his own peephole with his finger. *The way we're poking holes in it, we might as well tear down the whole window...*

Sure enough, Lan Jingyi was hauled by Wei Wuxian into a seat at the front of the group. From this spot, he would have the most complete and clearest view. Had this been a play they were watching, it would have been a prime seat that not even money could buy. It was a pity Lan Jingyi did not want this privilege in the least.

Sandwiched between Jin Ling and Lan Sizhui, he asked with trepidation, "Can I sit somewhere else...?"

"No," said Wei Wuxian, pacing back and forth off to the side.

When the others heard him, they all felt like Wei Wuxian's tone bore the true essence of Lan Wangji's influence. Someone even snickered.

"Good attitude there," Wei Wuxian said. "So relaxed. Good, good."

Lan Sizhui, who couldn't help himself earlier, hurriedly schooled his expression.

"Look, I don't even have a seat," said Wei Wuxian to Lan Jingyi. "So count your blessings."

"Qianbei, I can give you my seat…" Lan Jingyi offered.

"You cannot."

"Then what *can* I do?"

"You can ask questions."

Left without a choice, Lan Jingyi could only say to Lan Sizhui, "Sizhui, if I pass out, y-you have to let me copy your notes."

Torn between laughter and tears, Lan Sizhui said, "All right."

Lan Jingyi breathed a sigh of relief. "Then I can rest assured."

"Don't worry, Jingyi. You will definitely persevere," Lan Sizhui encouraged him.

Just as a grateful expression crossed Lan Jingyi's face, Jin Ling patted him on his shoulder, looking very dependable indeed. "That's right, don't worry. If you pass out, I'll wake you up right away."

Greatly alarmed, Lan Jingyi smacked at his hand. "Begone with you. Who knows what method *you'd* use to wake me up?!"

Just as they were chattering amongst themselves, a bloodred light glowed from behind the paper window, as if someone had suddenly lit a crimson lamp in the pitch-dark room.

The group immediately shut up and held their breath in rapt attention. The red light seeped through the tiny holes in the windows, making each peeping eye look utterly bloodshot.

Lan Jingyi raised a trembling hand. "Qianbei...w-why does the room look so red? I-I've never seen such a bloodred residual imprint. Could it be that there was a red lamp lit in the room at the time of the incident?"

"Not a red lamp," Lan Sizhui whispered. "It's because the person—"

"Had blood in their eyes," Jin Ling finished.

Something suddenly appeared under the room's red light. It was a chair, with a "person" sitting on it.

"Jin Ling, is this what you saw last night?" asked Wei Wuxian.

Jin Ling nodded. "But I didn't look carefully enough. She wasn't sitting on the chair...she was tied to the chair."

Just as he said, the woman's hands were tightly bound to the armrests with hemp rope. The crowd was about to take a closer look when a black shadow suddenly flashed past, bringing the figure count in the room up to two.

To think yet another "person" was part of this imprint... The second person's eyelids and lips were missing, so he could neither blink nor close his mouth. With his bloodshot eyeballs and bright red gums exposed, he was a thousand times more terrifying than suggested in the legend.

"Hookhand!" Lan Jingyi involuntarily blurted out.

"What's happening? Didn't we already smelt the iron hook? Why is Hookhand still here?"

"So there are actually two evil spirits in the room?!"

On hearing this, Wei Wuxian spoke up. "Is it two? How many evil spirits are in this room, precisely? Can someone clarify?"

"One," answered Lan Sizhui.

"One," Jin Ling said as well. "The Hookhand in the White Chamber is not a real malicious spirit, but a residual imprint of the scene right before the woman's death, which is playing out because of her resentful energy."

"It may be a residual imprint," said Lan Jingyi, "but it's just as creepy and terrifying as the real thing!"

As they spoke, the face slowly moved toward the door. The closer it got, the clearer and more hideous it became. Even though the boys knew that this was merely a residual imprint, that they had destroyed the iron hook hosting Hookhand's lingering resentment and this phantom image would never really come through the door, the spine-chilling fear that they had been discovered still haunted them.

If that unfortunate burglar had seen this scene when he crept into the White Chamber in the middle of the night, then it was little wonder he had suffered a shock bad enough to trigger a heart attack.

When that hideous face was less than thirty centimeters from the paper window, it paused for a moment, then turned around and strode toward the chair.

The boys started to breathe again.

Hookhand paced back and forth inside the room, and the old wooden boards creaked under his feet. Outside, however, Jin Ling suddenly started to wonder about something.

"There's one thing that's been bothering me," he said.

"What?" Lan Sizhui asked.

"The residual imprint formed by resentful energy must be showing the scene of the woman's death—no doubt about it. But would an average person be so calm when faced with such a homicidal maniac, making no sound at all? In other words... That woman was clearly conscious, so why didn't she scream for help?"

"Scared out of her wits, perhaps?" Lan Jingyi suggested.

"Not to the extent she wouldn't even make a single peep," Jin Ling argued. "She's not even crying. Don't women usually cry when they're extremely frightened?"

"Does she still have her tongue?" Lan Sizhui asked.

"No blood at the corners of her mouth, so she should still have it," Jin Ling replied. "And besides, it's not like she couldn't make a sound at *all* with no tongue, even if she couldn't speak clearly."

Sandwiched between them, Lan Jingyi looked as if he was about to die right then and there. "Can you two not casually discuss such a frightening thing right in my ear...?"

"Could this inn have been abandoned or deserted?" one of the boys asked. "And so she knows screaming is pointless, and she might as well save her breath?"

Lan Jingyi, who had the clearest look of them all, finally had something to offer. "It can't be that. Look at the residual imprint. There's no dust on the furnishings, so they've clearly been in use. And it can't be deserted, or she wouldn't have stayed here."

"Looks like you're not *that* incurably stupid, after all," said Jin Ling. "Whether it's deserted or not is one thing, and whether she'd scream or not is quite another. If someone was hunting you down in the wilderness, fear would make you scream for help even if you knew there was no one around to save you, wouldn't it?"

Wei Wuxian applauded him softly. "Oh my. As expected of Sect Leader Jin," he whispered.

Jin Ling blushed and fumed. "What are you doing? Don't distract me like that, okay?!"

"If you can be distracted that easily, you still need to work on your focus," said Wei Wuxian. "Hurry up and look. Hookhand seems to be making his move!"

The boys hurriedly turned their heads to look, only to see

Hookhand take out a bundle of hemp rope. He wound it around the woman's neck, then began to tighten it.

The sound of hemp rope being tightened! So this was the source of the strange sound that the master of the Bai family had said he heard every night in the White Chamber.

The slash wounds on the woman's face bled profusely as the pressure of the rope tightened, but she still did not make a sound. The boys had their hearts in their throats at the sight, and someone couldn't help but urge in a small voice, "Go on, scream. Scream for help!"

Contrary to their expectations, the victim didn't move, but the murderer did. Hookhand abruptly released his grip on the rope and pulled a sharpened iron hook from behind him. The boys outside were so anxious their hair stood on end. They itched to jump into the room and scream wildly on the woman's behalf—they wanted to wake the entire city with their howls.

Hookhand's back blocked their line of sight as he reached out with one hand. From where the boys were, they could only see the back of a hand resting on the armrest. All of a sudden, veins bulged on the back of that hand.

Even at this stage, the woman still didn't make a sound!

Jin Ling couldn't help but wonder, "Is she weak in the head?"

"What do you mean by 'weak in the head'?"

"Like...dim-witted."

Silence descended on the room.

Saying she was dim-witted sounded quite rude, but considering the situation, it really seemed the most plausible explanation. How else would a normal person still not have reacted?

Watching this was making Lan Jingyi's brain hurt, so he turned his face away. Wei Wuxian, however, said, "Watch carefully."

Looking like he couldn't bear another moment of the scene before him, Lan Jingyi begged, "Qianbei, I...I really can't watch anymore."

"There are hundreds and thousands of things in the world more tragic than this," said Wei Wuxian. "If you don't dare face this one directly, you can forget about the rest."

Hearing that, Lan Jingyi composed himself. He gritted his teeth and turned his head to continue watching, face miserable. But none of them could have expected what happened next.

The woman opened her mouth and bit down on the iron hook!

The bite startled the rows of boys outside, and they all jumped. Inside the room, Hookhand also seemed greatly startled. He tried to retract his hand, but even as he yanked, he couldn't pull the iron hook from the vise of the woman's teeth. Instead, the woman lunged forward with the chair in tow. Somehow, the iron hook that Hookhand had intended to use to rip out her tongue had slashed open his own stomach!

The boys broke out in a flurry of exclamations. They practically clung to the doorframe, desperately wishing they could stuff their eyeballs through the holes in the windows to get a closer look into the White Chamber.

Hookhand's injured hand was clearly in pain. He suddenly froze, as if remembering something. With his right hand, he grabbed for the woman's chest like he wanted to gouge out her heart. The woman rolled to the side to dodge the attack, chair and all, but he had grabbed the robes at her chest and they tore with a loud ripping sound.

Given the situation, the boys were too distracted to dwell on little things like indecent exposure. What made their jaws drop was that the "woman's" chest was flat and broad.

How was this a woman? The would-be victim was a man in disguise!

Hookhand pounced and seized the man's neck with his bare hands, forgetting his hook was still in the man's mouth. The man instantly jerked his head to the side, and the iron hook cut into Hookhand's wrist. One man was doing all he could to break the other's neck, while the other was determined to drain the first man of blood. For a moment, both of them were locked in a stalemate.

It was only when a rooster's crowing heralded the arrival of daybreak that the red light in the room disappeared and the residual imprint faded.

The circle of boys outside the White Chamber were completely dumbfounded by what they had just seen.

It was a long time later when Lan Jingyi stammered, "Th-th-these... two..."

Everyone was thinking the same thing: *In the end, it's likely neither of them survived...*

No one could have imagined that the evil spirit haunting and disrupting the peace of the Bai residence for decades was not Hookhand, but the hero who had eliminated Hookhand.

The juniors' discussion was in full swing.

"That was totally unexpected. To think that's how Hookhand was defeated..."

"Come to think of it, that was the only way it could've happened, wasn't it? After all, Hookhand came and went like the wind, and no one knew where he was hiding. If he didn't disguise himself as a woman to lure Hookhand out, no one would ever have caught him."

"But that was so dangerous!"

"It was indeed. Look, didn't the hero fall for his trap and end up tied to a chair? He was already at a disadvantage right from the start. Would he have wound up in such a bad situation if they had confronted each other head-on?"

"Yeah, and he couldn't even shout for help. Hookhand killed so many people; cruelty comes naturally to him. Even if ordinary folk answered the hero's shouts, they'd be delivering themselves to their deaths..."

"That's why he wouldn't try to call for help!"

"They perished together..."

"I can't believe there wasn't a single mention of that valiant hero's righteous deeds in the rumors! It's really puzzling."

"That's only to be expected. Everyone finds the legend of a homicidal maniac more interesting than that of a hero."

Jin Ling considered it. "A departed soul that's reluctant to move on to the next life must have some unfinished business or unfulfilled wish. When the departed's corpse is incomplete, the reluctance is always because they have yet to find those missing pieces. That must be his true reason for haunting the Bai residence."

It could be unbearable to part with a superfluous object one had carried with them for decades, let alone a piece of flesh from one's mouth.

Lan Jingyi listened with reverent awe. "Then we must find his tongue as soon as possible and burn it in his name so he can move on to the next life!"

Eager to get started, they all abruptly stood. "That's right! How can we let a hero like that die without a complete corpse?!"

"Let's find it! We'll start searching in the grave mound west of the city. We'll do the graveyard and the entire Bai residence, as well as the house Hookhand formerly lived in. Don't miss any of them."

The boys were full of determination as they flowed out the door. But before leaving, Jin Ling looked back at Wei Wuxian.

"What's wrong?" Wei Wuxian asked.

Wei Wuxian had remained noncommittal during their discussion, staying out of the conversation. It made Jin Ling uneasy. He wondered if they had made a mistake somewhere, but after careful consideration, felt they hadn't missed any key points.

So Jin Ling answered, "Nothing."

Wei Wuxian smiled. "Then go on with your search. Be patient."

And so Jin Ling left, valiant and spirited.

It was only days later that Jin Ling realized what Wei Wuxian had meant when he told him to be patient. Wei Wuxian had led Lan Sizhui on the search for the iron hook, which had taken them a grand total of an hour to find. But Wei Wuxian did not interfere in their quest for the tongue, leaving them to search on their own for a full five days.

The others were ready to collapse from exhaustion by the time Lan Jingyi sprang up, holding an object over his head.

Despite having searched among the wild graves until they were a wretched, unkempt, smelly sight, they were elated, for Wei Wuxian seriously told them the honest truth when he heard about their findings—that successfully completing their search in five days, using only their own abilities, was very impressive. Many cultivators would fail to find their objective in ten days or half a month and simply give up, empty-handed.

The boys were beyond excited as they huddled around the dead man's tongue. It was said that objects with malevolent energy glowed green, but this tongue was so dark that it was black and jarringly hard to the touch. It was impossible to tell it was once a piece of human flesh. It emanated a hostile aura, and if not for that energy, it would have decayed long ago.

After performing an exorcism, they burned the tongue. It seemed this major case had finally been closed. Now that they'd come so far and done so much, it *should* have been over with, no matter what. As far as Night Hunts went, Jin Ling was pretty satisfied with this one.

Who could have imagined that his satisfaction wouldn't even last a few days? The master of the Bai family came to Golden Carp Tower again. As it turned out, all had indeed been peaceful for two days after they burned that hero's tongue...but only for those two days.

On the third night, a strange sound suddenly rang out from the Bai residence again, growing louder and louder by the day. By the fifth night, the entire Bai residence was completely unable to sleep because of the din. This time, it bore down on them with such menace that their fear was even greater than before. The strange sound was not the sound of rope being tightened, or flesh being cut—it was now a human voice!

According to the master of the Bai family, the voice was extremely hoarse, as if it was moving a heavy tongue that had not been in use for many years. Although the words were indecipherable, it was clearly a man screaming in agony.

After he was done screaming, he wept bitterly. His cries were feeble at first, but gradually grew louder, until they were almost hysterical. It was both pitiful and terrifying to hear. Even neighbors three streets away from the Bai residence could hear it. It made passersby's hair stand on end and scared them out of their minds.

It left Jin Ling in a bind. He was too busy at the end of the year to deal with it personally, so he sent a few sect disciples to check. They reported upon their return that though the screaming was indeed very tragic, there was no other harm done.

Being a public nuisance did not count.

As he handed in his Night Hunt notes, Lan Sizhui recounted this matter to Lan Wangji and Wei Wuxian. Wei Wuxian heard him out, then took a pastry from Lan Wangji's desk and ate it.

"Oh, that's nothing to worry about."

"Nothing to worry about...even with the way he's screaming?" Lan Sizhui said. "By all logic, the deceased's soul should have been delivered once its obsession was dealt with."

"It's true that a soul can be delivered once its obsession is resolved," Wei Wuxian said. "But did it ever occur to all of you that the hero's real obsession might not be to retrieve his tongue and be reincarnated?"

Lan Jingyi had finally got a jia grade and was so happy he was inwardly shedding tears at the thought that he wouldn't have to copy passages as punishment this time. He couldn't help but wonder aloud, "Then what could it be? Don't tell me it's to howl every night so others can't sleep?"

Unexpectedly, Wei Wuxian nodded. "That's exactly it."

Lan Sizhui was astonished. "Wei-qianbei, what's the explanation for this?"

"Didn't you figure out earlier that this valiant hero didn't want to endanger the lives of innocent bystanders? And therefore did his best to endure Hookhand's torture, refusing to scream?" Wei Wuxian said.

"That's right," said Lan Sizhui, sitting upright. "What's wrong with that?"

"Nothing wrong with it, but let me ask you a question," Wei Wuxian said. "If a homicidal maniac waves a knife at you, bleeds you dry, slashes your face, wrings your neck, and rips out your tongue, wouldn't that be scary? Wouldn't you be afraid? What would you want to cry out?"

Lan Jingyi thought for a moment, and his face paled. *"Help!"*

Lan Sizhui, on the other hand, said in all seriousness, "The family precepts state that even in the face of danger..."

"Sizhui, don't try that with me," Wei Wuxian said. "I'm asking if you would be afraid. Give it to me straight."

Lan Sizhui's face reddened, and his back straightened even more. "I would not..."

"Would not?" Wei Wuxian repeated.

Lan Sizhui looked entirely honest as he cleared his throat and continued. "...Would not be able to say I would not be afraid."

Having said that, he cast an apprehensive glance at Lan Wangji.

Wei Wuxian was highly amused. "What are you ashamed of? People feel fear in the face of pain and terror. They want someone to save them, and they want to scream and shout and cry and make a scene. Isn't that only human? Am I right? Hanguang-jun, look at your clan's Lan Sizhui. He's sneaking peeks at you. Say yes, quick. Once you say yes, it means you agree with me and you won't punish him."

He gently elbowed Lan Wangji in the stomach, who sat prim and proper as he wrote comments on the juniors' notes.

"Yes," said Lan Wangji, without batting an eye.

Having said that, he wrapped an arm around Wei Wuxian's waist, locking him in place so that he couldn't move as he pleased, and continued to look over the notes that had been submitted.

Lan Sizhui blushed even harder.

Unable to free himself after two attempts, Wei Wuxian maintained this posture and continued. "Since he resisted the urge to scream, he truly had a hero's backbone. But it's also true that doing so goes against human nature and instinct."

Lan Sizhui tried his best to ignore the way they were positioned. After giving it some thought, his heart went out to that hero.

"Is Jin Ling still bothered by this?" Wei Wuxian asked.

"Yeah," Lan Jingyi said. "Little Miss...uh, Jin-gongzi doesn't know what went wrong either."

"Since that's the case," Lan Sizhui said, "how should we handle an evil spirit such as this?"

"Let him scream," Wei Wuxian said.

Silence descended for a moment.

"Just...let him scream?" Lan Sizhui repeated.

"That's right," Wei Wuxian confirmed. "Once he's done screaming, he'll naturally leave."

The other half of Lan Sizhui's heart went out to the entirety of the Bai residence.

Fortunately, despite the hero's pent-up grievances, he had no intent to harm others. The strange sounds from the White Chamber persisted for several months before they gradually subsided. Presumably, the hero had finally had his fill of all the screams he had been unable to vent when he was alive. Content at last, he left to be reincarnated.

Pitiful were the people of the Bai residence, however, who tossed and turned in agony for many long, sleepless nights. Once again, the White Chamber's reputation spread far and wide.

O UTSIDE LOTUS PIER'S SWORD HALL, the cicadas chirped noisily in the Yunmeng summer air. Inside, bodies were strewn across the ground, presenting quite the ugly sight. A dozen or so bare-chested boys were glued to the hall's wooden floorboards, occasionally turning over, like sizzling pancakes emitting dying moans.

"Hot..."

"So hot..."

Wei Wuxian squinted his eyes. *If only it was as cool here as it is in the Cloud Recesses,* he vaguely thought.

The wooden floorboards under him had absorbed his body heat, so he turned over. Coincidentally, Jiang Cheng turned over too, and they brushed against each other, arm on leg.

"Jiang Cheng, move your arm away," said Wei Wuxian at once. "You feel like a hot coal."

"Move your leg away." Jiang Cheng retorted.

"Arms are lighter than legs," said Wei Wuxian. "Takes more effort to move my leg. Move your arm instead."

And now Jiang Cheng was pissed off. "Wei Wuxian, I'm warning you, don't go too far. Shut up and don't say a word. The more you talk, the hotter it gets!"

"Can you guys stop fighting?" Liu-shidi said. "I feel hot just listening to you. I'm sweating even harder now!"

Blows and kicks were already being traded between them.

"Get lost!"

"*You* get lost!"

"No, no, no, please. *You* get lost!"

"No need to be so polite. You first!"

Cries of complaint rose from the various shidi.

"Go outside if you guys wanna fight!"

"Can both of you get lost together?! Please, I'm begging you!"

"Heard that?" Wei Wuxian piped. "Everyone's telling you to get out. You... Let go of my leg, it's gonna break, man!"

The veins on Jiang Cheng's forehead bulged. "They were clearly telling *you* to get out... Let go of my arm first!"

Suddenly, they heard the rustling of skirts on the wooden walkway outside. Both of them parted in a flash. Soon after, the bamboo blind lifted.

Jiang Yanli poked her head in to take a peek. "Oh, so this is where you've all been hiding."

Everyone greeted her.

"Shijie!"

"Hi, shijie!"

Some of the more bashful disciples couldn't help but cover their chests with their arms. They slunk away to hide in the corner.

"Why are you lazing around today instead of training with your swords?" Jiang Yanli wondered.

"The weather's sweltering, and it's unbearably hot at the training ground," groused Wei Wuxian. "We'd burn off a whole layer of skin if we tried to train. Shijie, please don't tell anyone."

Jiang Yanli looked between him and Jiang Cheng for a moment. "Did you two fight again?"

"Nope!" Wei Wuxian answered.

Jiang Yanli made her way inside, carrying a loaded tray. "Then whose footprint is it on A-Cheng's chest?"

Hearing that he had left evidence of his crime, Wei Wuxian hurriedly turned to look. Sure enough, there it was. But no one cared if the two of them had been fighting or not, for Jiang Yanli was carrying a huge tray of sliced watermelons. The boys swarmed over, divvied up the slices in no time, and sat facing each other on the ground to munch on them. Not long after, a small mountain of watermelon rinds piled on the tray.

Wei Wuxian and Jiang Cheng always had to compete in everything they did, and eating watermelons was no exception. They attempted to seize each other's melons by force, trading a never-ending stream of underhanded blows that the others—unable to dodge in time—scrambled away from, clearing out an open space for them.

At first, Wei Wuxian spared no effort in devouring his watermelon. But as he ate, he suddenly burst into laughter.

Jiang Cheng eyed him warily. "What are you scheming now?"

Wei Wuxian took another slice. "Nah! Don't misunderstand. I'm not scheming anything. I just thought of someone."

"Who?" asked Jiang Cheng.

"Lan Zhan," answered Wei Wuxian.

"Why are you thinking of him out of the blue?" asked Jiang Cheng. "Don't tell me you miss those transcription punishments."

Wei Wuxian spat out the seeds. "Just thinking about how funny he is, that's all. You have no idea how interesting he can be. One time I told him, 'Your family's food tastes so bad, I'd rather eat fried watermelon rind. If you have time, come have fun at Lotus Pier...'"

He had yet to finish talking when Jiang Cheng smacked his watermelon askew. "Are you nuts? Did you invite him to Lotus Pier to torture yourself?"

"What're you getting antsy for? My watermelon nearly went flying!" Wei Wuxian said. "I was just saying it. Of course he's not going to come. Have you ever heard of him going out just to have fun?"

"Let me make it clear," said Jiang Cheng, sternly. "I refuse to allow him to visit us. Don't invite people as you please."

"I didn't realize you disliked him that much," said Wei Wuxian.

"I have nothing against Lan Wangji," said Jiang Cheng. "But if he visits and my mom starts comparing her children to a guy like that, you can forget about having it easy either."

"It's fine. There's nothing to be scared of, even if he visits," Wei Wuxian said. "If he really does, tell Jiang-shushu to have him sleep with me. I guarantee I'll be able to drive him bonkers in less than a month."

Jiang Cheng scoffed. "You want to bunk with him for a month? If you ask me, he'll stab you to death in less than seven days."

Wei Wuxian thought otherwise. "I'm not scared of him. If we really came to blows, he might not be a match for me."

The others cheered him approvingly. While Jiang Cheng jeered at him for being thick-skinned, he knew deep down that Wei Wuxian spoke the truth. He wasn't just tooting his own horn.

Jiang Yanli sat down between them. "Who are you two talking about?" she asked. "A friend you made at Gusu?"

"Yeah!" Wei Wuxian answered happily.

"You have the cheek to call yourself his 'friend'?" Jiang Cheng said. "Ask Lan Wangji about that, see if he's willing to accept you as one."

"Screw off. If he doesn't, I'll just pester him—we'll see if he caves." Turning to Jiang Yanli, Wei Wuxian asked, "Shijie, do you know Lan Wangji?"

"Yes," Jiang Yanli said. "He's the second young master of the Lan Clan, the one everyone says is very handsome and capable, right? Is he really very handsome?"

"Very!" Wei Wuxian gushed.

"Compared to you?" Jiang Yanli probed.

Wei Wuxian thought for a moment. "Perhaps just a *tiny* bit more handsome than me."

He held two of his fingers a tiny distance apart to demonstrate. As Jiang Yanli collected the plates, she smiled.

"Then he must be really very handsome. It's a good thing to make new friends. You guys can drop in on each other to have some fun in the future, when you have nothing to do."

Jiang Cheng spat out his watermelon on hearing that. Wei Wuxian waved dismissively.

"Forget it, forget it. The food's bad and they have so many rules. I'm not going there again."

"Then you can bring him over instead," said Jiang Yanli. "This is a good opportunity. Why don't you invite your friend to stay at Lotus Pier for a while?"

"A-Jie, don't you listen to his nonsense," Jiang Cheng piped up. "No one likes him at Gusu. Lan Wangji would never be willing to come with him."

"What are you talking about?!" Wei Wuxian shot back. "He would."

"Wake up," said Jiang Cheng. "Lan Wangji told you to get lost, didn't you hear? Remember?"

"What do you know?! Even though he told me to get lost, I know deep down, he must want to come play with me in Yunmeng. And he wants it badly."

"I ask myself the same question every day—where in the world did all your self-confidence come from?" Jiang Cheng asked.

"Stop thinking about it," Wei Wuxian said. "If I'd been asking the same question for so many years without getting an answer, I'd have given up long ago."

Jiang Cheng shook his head. Just as he was about to fling his watermelon, he suddenly heard swift, fierce footsteps approaching and a woman's frosty voice.

"I wondered where everyone disappeared to. Just as I expected..."

The boys' expressions changed dramatically. They dashed through the blinds just in time to run into Madam Yu as she turned the corner of the long corridor. Her purple robes fluttered as she bore down on them with truly terrifying murderous intent in her eyes.

Madam Yu's face contorted at the unbecoming sight the group of bare-chested, bare-footed boys presented. Her slender eyebrows raised so high they almost flew off her face.

Shit! Everyone thought. Frightened out of their wits, they took to their heels and ran.

Seeing this, Madam Yu finally reacted. "Jiang Cheng!" she raged. "Put your clothes on right now! Look at yourself, naked as a barbarian! If others were to see you, how could I ever show myself again?!"

Jiang Cheng's clothes were tied around his waist. Hearing his mother's scolding, he hastily fumbled to put them on.

Madam Yu continued with her scolding. "You boys! Can't you see A-Li is here? Who taught you brats to strip like this in front of a girl?!"

Of course, there was no question at all about who had taken the lead. So Madam Yu's next sentence was, most predictably, "Wei Ying! Seems to me like you have a death wish!"

"Sorry!" said Wei Wuxian loudly. "I didn't know shijie would come! I'll go look for my clothes right now!"

Madam Yu was even more incensed. "You dare run from me?! Get the hell back here and kneel!"

As she spoke, she cracked her whip. A searing pain spread down Wei Wuxian's back.

"*Yowch!*" he exclaimed aloud. The pain was so intense it almost sent him rolling on the ground.

Just then, Madam Yu heard a soft voice ask, "Mom, do you want some watermelon...?"

Jiang Yanli's sudden appearance startled Madam Yu. With this delay, the group of little brats had vanished without a trace. Madam Yu was so infuriated she turned to pinch Jiang Yanli's cheeks.

"Eat, eat, eat. That's all you know!"

The pinch made Jiang Yanli's eyes water. Vaguely, she said, "Mom. A-Xian and the rest were hiding here to cool off. I came looking for them on my own, so don't blame them... Do...do you want some watermelons...? I don't know who sent them over, but they're very sweet. Eating watermelon in summer can relieve the heat and quench your fire. They're sweet and juicy. I'll slice some for you..."

The more Madam Yu stewed on it, the more infuriated she became—and she actually did want to eat some watermelon, as the summer heat had made her thirsty. It only made her angrier.

Meanwhile, the group of boys had finally managed to flee from Lotus Pier, dashing toward the docks and leaping onto a small boat. Only after some time had passed with no sign of pursuit did Wei Wuxian finally relax. He tried to push himself, paddling twice with the oar, but his back still hurt. He threw the oar to the others and sat down to touch the stinging flesh.

"This is clearly an injustice. Let's be reasonable here, obviously no one was wearing clothes, so why scold and hit me and only me?"

"Must be because you were the biggest eyesore with no clothes on," Jiang Cheng quipped.

Wei Wuxian threw him a look. All of a sudden, he dove into the water. The others all entered the water as well, as if responding to his call. In no time at all, only Jiang Cheng was left on the boat.

Jiang Cheng sensed something amiss. "What the heck are you doing?!"

Wei Wuxian slid over to the side of the boat and smacked it hard with his palm. The entire boat overturned and bobbed heavily in the water with its belly up. Wei Wuxian laughed out loud, hopped onto the bottom of the boat, and sat on it with his legs crossed.

He shouted at the spot where Jiang Cheng had fallen, "Eyes still sore? Jiang Cheng? Answer me. Hey, hello!"

No one responded even after he had shouted a few times. Only a string of gurgling bubbles broke through the water's surface.

Wei Wuxian wiped his face and wondered, "Why is he taking so long to come up?"

Liu-shidi swam over and blurted out in shock, "He couldn't have drowned, could he?!"

"How is that possible?!" asked Wei Wuxian.

He was just about to dive in to give Jiang Cheng a hand when he suddenly heard a loud howl behind him. He shouted in surprise as someone pushed him into the water from behind. The boat turned back upright. Apparently, Jiang Cheng had remained underwater after he was thrown off the boat and circled up behind Wei Wuxian.

Having each succeeded in their surprise attacks, both boys began to circle the boat vigilantly. The others splashed around in the water and spread out in the lake to watch the show.

"What do you think you're doing, grabbing a weapon?" Wei Wuxian called out across the boat. "Put down the oar if you're worth your salt. We'll fight with our bare fists."

"You think I'm a fool?" asked Jiang Cheng with a sardonic smile. "The moment I let go, you'll grab it!" He swung the oar like the wind, forcing Wei Wuxian to back off repeatedly. The various shidi cheered him on.

Wei Wuxian had to find some breathing space from this distraction in order to defend himself. "Am I *that* shameless?!"

Jeers erupted all around him. "Da-shixiong, you've got some nerve!"

What ensued was a truly chaotic water fight. Disciples pulled out all their special moves—from the Merciful Club to the Venomous Grass to the Life-Taking Water-Spouting Arrow. Wei Wuxian threw a kick at Jiang Cheng and finally sprawled across the boat. He spat out a mouthful of lake water and raised his hand.

"Enough. Cease fire!"

Everyone wore lush clumps of water weeds on their heads, and they were having an absolute blast fighting. "Why?" they asked immediately. "Begging for mercy now that you're at a disadvantage?"

"Who said I'm begging for mercy?" Wei Wuxian retorted. "We'll fight later. I'm just too hungry to fight now. Let's grab a bite to eat."

"Then are we going back?" asked Liu-shidi. "We can eat a few more watermelons before dinner."

"Go back now and there'll be nothing for you other than a lashing," said Jiang Cheng.

But Wei Wuxian already had an idea. "We're not going back," he announced. "We're going to pick lotus seed pods!"

"You mean 'steal,'" Jiang Cheng mocked.

"It's not like we don't pay up every time!" said Wei Wuxian.

The Jiang Clan of Yunmeng took care of the nearby households in the area and eliminated water ghosts without asking for compensation. People for dozens of kilometers around were more than happy to partition out a portion of their lakes to plant lotus seed pods for them to consume, and were unlikely to quibble over a stolen few.

Every time the boys went out to eat someone else's melons, catch someone else's chickens, or drug someone else's dog, Jiang Fengmian would send someone to compensate them after the fact. As for why they insisted on stealing food—it wasn't because they were hoodlums, but because they were simply boys with playful hearts who wanted the thrill of being laughed at and cursed at, being chased and beaten up.

The boys got on the boat and rowed for a while before arriving at a lotus lake.

It was a large lotus lake, green and verdant. Emerald leaves overlapped one another, the smallest the size of plates and the biggest as large as umbrellas. The ones at the periphery were lower and sparser as they spread out flat across the water's surface, while the ones further in were taller and crowded together, enough to hide the boats ferrying people. But one only needed to see a cluster of lotus leaves rustling shoulder to shoulder to know that someone was up to something inside.

The little boat from Lotus Pier glided through the lush, verdant world. They were surrounded by large and plump hanging seed pods. One person punted the boat, while the others began grabbing the seed pods. The big-headed pods grew on tall and slender stems riddled with tiny, harmless thorns. The smooth green shafts broke easily with just a snap. The boys broke off the seed pods along with a long section of the stem, which would allow them to stick them in a vase of water upon their return. It was said doing that would keep the seed pods fresh and tender for a few more days...or so Wei Wuxian had heard, at any rate. He didn't know if it was true or not, but he relayed the fact to others in all seriousness.

He broke off a few and peeled one that was full of seeds. He popped them into his mouth, finding them tender and juicy. As he ate, he hummed off-handedly. "I'll treat you to lotus seed pods; what will you treat me to?"

Jiang Cheng heard him. "Who are you treating?"

"Ha ha, not you in any case!" Wei Wuxian answered. He was about to pluck a lotus seed pod to throw at his face, but then suddenly hushed everyone around him instead. "Oh shoot! The old man is here today!"

The "old man" was the farmer who had planted the lotuses in this stretch of water. As for how old he actually was, Wei Wuxian had no idea. Jiang Fengmian was "shushu" to him, at any rate, and anyone older than Jiang Fengmian surely must be an old man.

This man had worked this lotus lake for as long as Wei Wuxian could remember, and he would hit them if he caught them when they came to steal lotus seed pods in the summer. Wei Wuxian often suspected that this old man was the reincarnation of a lotus spirit, because he knew the seed pods in his lake like the back of his hand and always knew exactly how many were missing. The number stolen would be exactly how many times he would hit them in retribution. After all, bamboo punt-poles were easier to use than oars when getting around the lotus lake by boat.

Thud, thud, thud! Each blow to the body hurt like hell.

All the boys had taken a few beatings from him before. *"Run, run!"* they hissed in hushed tones. They quickly grabbed the oars and fled, rowing out of the lotus lake in a flurry. Their guilty consciences made them glance back. The old man's boat had already made its way out of the layers and layers of lotus leaves and was gliding in open water.

Wei Wuxian cocked his head and squinted. "Weird!" he blurted out.

Jiang Cheng stood up too. "Why's that boat going so fast?"

All the boys looked. The old man had his back to them, counting the lotus seed pods on the boat one at a time. The bamboo punt-pole had been set off to the side and wasn't moving. But the boat still moved steadily and swiftly, so much so that it was even faster than their own.

Everyone was on guard. "Row back over, row back over," Wei Wuxian prompted.

Once the boats drifted close, the boys could make out a faint white shadow wandering under the water next to the old man's boat!

Wei Wuxian looked back and pressed his index finger against his lips, signaling for the others to be cautious and not alarm the old man or the water ghost beneath him. Jiang Cheng nodded. He rowed with soundless movements, leaving waves of silent ripples in his wake. When the two boats were about ten meters apart, an ashen, dripping wet hand rose out of the water and stealthily grabbed one of the lotus seed pods from the heap on the old man's boat before retreating soundlessly below the lake.

After a moment, two lotus seed pod shells floated to the water's surface.

The boys were struck dumb by the sight. "Oh, wow, even the water ghost steals lotus seed pods!"

The old man finally noticed someone behind him. With one hand holding a large lotus seed pod, he grabbed the bamboo punt-pole with his other hand and spun around. This movement startled the water ghost, and with a slithering sound, the white figure vanished without a trace.

"Where do you think you're running?" the boys hurriedly cried.

Wei Wuxian lunged into the water and dove beneath the surface. In no time, he dragged something back up. "Caught it!"

He lifted a water ghost in his hand. Its skin was pale and it looked like it was once a child of about twelve or thirteen. It was so terrified it almost shrank into a ball under the boys' gaze.

The old man swung the pole at them and shouted, "Here to mess around again, ya bratty little ghouls?!"

Wei Wuxian's back, which had just received a lashing, took another strike. He yelped in pain and almost lost his grip.

Jiang Cheng fumed. "Be nice to us! Why lash out at us?! You're mistaking our goodwill for ill intent!"

"It's fine, it's fine," Wei Wuxian said hurriedly. "Old ma...erm, uncle, please take a good look. We're not ghouls. *This* is the ghoul."

"Obviously," the old man said. "I'm old, not blind. Let it go!"

Wei Wuxian was stupefied. But then, he saw the little water ghost he had caught was repeatedly bowing to him with tearful eyes. It was quite the pitiful sight. The ghost was still grasping the large lotus seed pod it had stolen earlier, loath to part with it. The seed pod had been pried open—it seemed like it had only managed to eat a couple of seeds before Wei Wuxian hauled it out.

Finding the old man unreasonable, Jiang Cheng said to Wei Wuxian, "Don't let it go. We'll bring it back with us."

Hearing this, the old man lifted his bamboo punt-pole again.

"Don't! Don't hit me! I'll put it down," said Wei Wuxian, quickly.

"Don't let it go!" said Jiang Cheng. "What if it kills someone else?"

"It doesn't stink of blood," said Wei Wuxian. "It's too young to leave this stretch of water, and there hasn't been news of any deaths in this area. It probably hasn't harmed anyone."

Jiang Cheng continued to argue. "Even if it hasn't yet, that doesn't mean it won't in the future—"

He hadn't so much as finished his sentence when the bamboo punt-pole came down on him. Jiang Cheng bristled at the blow. "Can't you tell good from bad, old man?! Aren't you afraid it will harm you, knowing that it's a ghost?!"

"Why would someone with one foot in the grave be afraid of a ghost?" the old man answered with self-righteous confidence.

It's not like it can run very far, Wei Wuxian reasoned. "Stop hitting me! I'm letting go now!" he said.

And then he really did let it go. The water ghost leapt behind the old man's boat, as if afraid to come out again.

Wei Wuxian climbed onto their boat, soaking wet. The old man picked a lotus seed pod from his boat and tossed it into the water, which the water ghost ignored. The old man then selected a larger one and tossed it into the water, where it bobbed on the surface for a time. All at once, half a pale head peeked out. Like a giant white fish, the water ghost dragged the two green lotus seed pods underwater with its mouth. A moment later, a splotch of white materialized on the water's surface. Exposing its shoulders and hands, the water ghost shrank back behind the boat and lowered its head to crunch noisily on its catch.

As it ate with gusto, the boys watched, puzzled.

Seeing the old man toss another lotus seed pod into the water, Wei Wuxian stroked his chin. Feeling a little hard done by, he asked, "Uncle, why is it that you let it steal your lotus seed pods, and even give it more to eat, but when we do it, we just get smacked?"

"It helps me propel the boat, so what's wrong with giving it a few lotus seed pods to eat?" asked the old man. "You little ghouls, though—how many did you steal today?"

The boys felt embarrassed. Wei Wuxian glanced out the corner of his eye at the pile of lotus seed pods in the middle of the boat. Sensing things did not bode well for them, he hurriedly called out, "Let's go!"

The boys immediately grabbed their oars. The old man brandished his bamboo punt-pole as he came charging toward them, his boat fast as the wind. The boys felt a chill run down their spines, as if that pole would come down on them any minute. They pumped their limbs and paddled like crazy.

The two boats made two full laps around the lake. The distance between them was closing, and Wei Wuxian had already taken a few hits. Realizing that the pole was only aiming for him, he covered his head.

"That's unfair!" he yelled. "Why are you only hitting me? Why are you only hitting me *again*?!"

"Shixiong, hang in there!" the group of shidi called out. "We're all counting on you!"

Jiang Cheng, too, piped up. "Yeah, hang in there."

Wei Wuxian fumed. "Bah! I can't anymore!" He grabbed a lotus seed pod stalk from the boat and tossed it out. "Catch!"

It was quite a big seed pod, landing in the lake with a splash. Sure enough, the old man's boat stalled for a moment as the water ghost merrily swam over to fish up the seed pod to eat.

Seizing their opportunity, the boat from Lotus Pier took the opportunity to beat a quick retreat.

"Da-shixiong, can ghosts taste things?" asked one shidi while they made their way back.

"Typically not, I guess," said Wei Wuxian. "But I think that little ghost probably...*ah...ah-choo!*"

The sun had set and a breeze rolled in, bringing a break from the heat. With it, the air had grown chilly.

Wei Wuxian sneezed and rubbed his face. "It probably didn't get to eat lotus seed pods while it was alive. When it snuck in to steal them, it fell into the lake and drowned. So...*ah*...*ah*..."

"So by eating lotus seed pods, it's fulfilling its wish," said Jiang Cheng. "It gets a sense of satisfaction from it."

"Uh, yeah," Wei Wuxian said. He felt his back, which was lined with old and new welts. He couldn't help but ask the question he'd been dwelling on. "Really, this must be the greatest injustice in all of history. Why am I always the only one getting hit whenever something happens?"

"You're the most handsome," said one of the shidi.

"Your cultivation is the highest," offered another.

And yet another piped up, "You look the best without clothes on."

The boys all nodded.

"Thank you for the praise," said Wei Wuxian. "I'm getting goosebumps."

"You're welcome, da-shixiong," a shidi said. "You stand before us to shield us every time. You deserve even more!"

"Oh? There's more?" Wei Wuxian asked in astonishment. "Let's hear it."

Jiang Cheng couldn't stand it anymore. "All of you, shut up! Talk sense, or I'll stab through the bottom of the boat and we can all die together."

They were passing through a stretch of water with farmland on both sides and several petite farm girls working the fields. Seeing their little boat passing through, the girls ran to the edge of the water and greeted them from afar.

"Hey—!"

The boys "hey"-ed in response and nudged Wei Wuxian. "Shixiong, they're calling you!"

Wei Wuxian looked over. Sure enough, these were girls he'd introduced them to before. The gloom in his heart cleared immediately, and he stood up to wave in greeting.

"What's up?" he called out with a grin.

The little boat drifted with the current, and the farm girls followed along on the riverbank, chatting as they walked.

"Did you all go stealing lotus seed pods again?"

"Quick, tell us how many blows you took!"

"Or did you go drugging someone else's dog again?"

After the first few remarks, Jiang Cheng longed to kick Wei Wuxian off the boat. "That notoriety of yours really is a disgrace to our family," he said bitterly.

"They said 'you all,'" said Wei Wuxian in his defense. "We're a gang, okay? If I'm a disgrace, then we're disgraces together."

The two were still bickering when one farm girl yelled out, "Was it tasty?"

Wei Wuxian took a moment to shout back, "What?"

"The watermelon we brought," said the farm girl. "Was it tasty?"

Understanding dawned on Wei Wuxian. "So you were the ones who brought the watermelon. It *was* tasty! Why didn't you come in to sit with us? We could have treated you to tea!"

The farm girl smiled sweetly. "You weren't all around when we brought it, so we left it and went on our way. We wouldn't dare come in. Glad you liked it!"

"Thank you!" Wei Wuxian said as he fished several large seed pods from the bottom of the boat. "I'll treat you girls to lotus seed pods. Next time, come inside and watch me train with my sword!"

Jiang Cheng scoffed. "What's there to watch about you training?"

Wei Wuxian tossed the seed pods to the riverbank. It was quite the distance, but they landed lightly in the girls' hands. He grabbed a few seed pods and shoved them into Jiang Cheng's arms. "What are you standing there blankly for? Hurry up."

Jiang Cheng had no choice but to take the pods after two shoves. "Hurry up and what?"

"You ate the watermelon too," Wei Wuxian said, "so you have to give them a gift in return. Come on, don't be shy, start throwing, go on."

Jiang Cheng snorted. "What a joke. What's there to be shy about?"

But for all his bluster, he still didn't move—not even when the entire boatful of shidi began throwing seed pods with gusto.

"Then throw 'em," Wei Wuxian said again. "Throw 'em now, and you can ask *them* if the pods are tasty next time. It's an excuse to talk to them again!"

The shidi were now enlightened. "So that's your method. What an eye-opener. Shixiong is really an old hand at this!"

"You can tell he does this all the time!"

"You think too highly of me, ha ha ha ha..."

Jiang Cheng snapped to his senses upon hearing this. He'd been about to throw the pods too, but finding it deeply embarrassing now, he peeled one open instead and started eating it himself.

The boat glided through the water, and the girls trotted after it along the bank, catching the verdant lotus seed pods that the boys on the boat threw to them, laughing as they ran.

Wei Wuxian held his hand to his brow and gazed at the sight as they went, smiling. Then suddenly, he sighed.

"What's wrong, da-shixiong?" the boys all wondered aloud.

"You're sighing, even with all these chicks chasing after you?"

Wei Wuxian hoisted the oar over his shoulder and chuckled. "It's nothing. I just thought about how I so sincerely invited Lan Zhan to Yunmeng, but he actually had the nerve to turn me down."

"Wow! As expected of Lan Wangji!" The various shidi gave a thumbs-up.

"Shut up!" Wei Wuxian said, in high spirits nonetheless. "One of these days, I'll drag him here and kick him off the boat. I'll trick him into stealing lotus seed pods so that the old man will rap him with the bamboo pole and make him run after me, ha ha ha ha…"

After hooting with laughter for a while, he looked back at Jiang Cheng, who was eating lotus seeds with a straight face. His smile gradually faded, and he sighed. "Truly an unteachable child."

Jiang Cheng raged. "So what if I just want to eat them myself?!"

"Oh, you," Wei Wuxian sighed. "Never mind, you're beyond hope, Jiang Cheng. Enjoy eating 'em alone for the rest of your life!"

Nevertheless, the little boat that had endeavored to steal lotus seed pods had, once again, returned with a full load.

Outside the Cloud Recesses, the remote mountain's summer air was sweltering. Inside, it was a world of tranquility and coolness.

Two straight-backed figures in white were present on the long walkway outside the Orchid Room. Their white robes fluttered lightly as the wind brushed by, but both figures remained still.

Lan Xichen and Lan Wangji were indeed very straight-backed. And upside down.

Neither said a word, seeming to have entered a meditative state. The murmur of the flowing spring and the wings of chirping birds were the only sounds to be heard. Contrary to what one might expect, this made the place seem even quieter.

After a while, Lan Wangji suddenly spoke up. "Xiongzhang."

Lan Xichen unhurriedly emerged from his mediation. "Yes?" he asked without looking at him.

There was a long moment of silence before Lan Wangji asked, "Have you ever picked lotus seed pods before?"

Lan Xichen turned his head to the side. "...No."

Naturally, if juniors of the Lan Clan of Gusu wished to eat lotus seed pods, they had no need to go pick them themselves.

Lan Wangji nodded. "Xiongzhang, did you know?"

"What?" asked Lan Xichen.

"The ones with stems are tastier than those without," said Lan Wangji.

"Oh? I have never heard that before," Lan Xichen said. "Why did you bring this up all of a sudden?"

"No reason," said Lan Wangji. "Time is up. Swap over to the other hand."

Both of them switched the hand that supported them from right to left, their movements soundless, steady, and in sync.

Lan Xichen was about to ask more questions when he spotted something. He smiled. "Wangji, you have a guest."

From the edge of the wooden walkway, a fluffy white rabbit slowly crept over. It nuzzled against the side of Lan Wangji's left hand and twitched its pink nose.

"Why did it find its way here?" Lan Xichen wondered.

"Go back," Lan Wangji said to the rabbit.

But the rabbit did not heed his words. It bit down on the tail of Lan Wangji's forehead ribbon and tugged at it hard, as if wanting to drag Lan Wangji away.

"It probably wants you to come with it," said Lan Xichen, unbothered.

Unable to move him, the rabbit circled them in exasperation. Finding the sight interesting, Lan Xichen remarked, "Is this the boisterous one?"

"Excessively boisterous," said Lan Wangji.

"It is fine if so. It is adorable, after all," said Lan Xichen. "I seem to remember there were two. Are they not usually together? Why did only one come? Is the other one unwilling to come out because it prefers the quiet?"

"It will come," said Lan Wangji.

As expected, it didn't take long for another snowy white head to peek above the edge of the wooden walkway. The other rabbit had come in search of its companion.

The two snowballs chased each other about for a while, eventually cuddling up together while leaning against Lan Wangji's left hand. They snuggled and nuzzled each other—a most adorable sight, even witnessed upside down.

"What are their names?" asked Lan Xichen.

Lan Wangji shook his head. It was unclear if they had no names or if he refused to say them.

Lan Xichen, however, pressed on. "I have heard you call their names before."

There was only silence from Lan Wangji.

"They are good names," Lan Xichen said in all sincerity.

Lan Wangji swapped to the other hand.

"It is not yet time," Lan Xichen said.

Lan Wangji quietly swapped back.

They ended their training an incense time later. Finishing their handstands, they returned to the Elegance Room, where they sat in silence.

A servant presented chilled fruits to ward off the summer heat.

The watermelon had been sliced, its flesh cut into neat pieces, and arranged on a jade plate. It looked very pretty, all red and translucent.

The two brothers sat on their heels on the mats and exchanged a few words in hushed tones, trading insights from yesterday's studies before they began to eat.

Lan Xichen took a watermelon slice. Seeing Lan Wangji stare at the jade plate with an unreadable expression, he instinctively paused.

Sure enough, Lan Wangji spoke. "Xiongzhang."

"What is it?" Lan Xichen asked.

"Have you ever eaten the rinds?" Lan Wangji wondered.

"...Can watermelon rinds be eaten?" Lan Xichen answered with a question of his own.

After a moment of silence, Lan Wangji replied, "I have heard they can be stir-fried."

"Perhaps," Lan Xichen said.

"I have heard that the taste is excellent," Lan Wangji said.

"I have never tried them before."

"Nor I."

"Umm..." said Lan Xichen. "Do you want to have someone try to stir-fry some?"

Lan Wangji thought about it, then shook his head with a solemn expression. Lan Xichen heaved a sigh of relief.

As for who Lan Wangji might have heard that from, Lan Xichen had a feeling he needn't ask...

The next day, Lan Wangji went down the mountain alone.

Leaving the mountain was hardly an uncommon occurrence for him, but he seldom visited the bustling marketplace by himself.

People came and went, went and came. There were never so many people to be seen in a cultivation clan's territory or a mountainous hunting ground. Even when large numbers of people gathered to attend symposiums, they were organized and methodical, never this kind of jostling, shoving crowd. It was practically a given that someone would step on another's foot or carriages would bump into each other while passing through.

Lan Wangji had never been fond of physical contact with others. He hesitated when faced with this situation, not because he wanted to withdraw—but rather, because he wanted to find someone to ask for directions. Despite searching for some time, however, he couldn't find a single person to ask.

Only then did Lan Wangji realize: he wasn't the only one steering clear of the crowd—the crowd steered clear of him, in turn.

He was truly at odds with the hustle and bustle of the market. He was too austere, and he carried a sword on his back. The vendors, farmers, and idle passersby seldom saw young masters of this caliber. They all scrambled to avoid him, either fearing he was the wastrel son of an affluent house, one whom they didn't dare risk offending, or fearing his cold and stern expression.

After all, even Lan Xichen had once joked that the land in a two-meter radius around Lan Wangji was a frozen tundra where not even a blade of grass grew.

The women in the market did not dare to look at Lan Wangji when he walked near, despite wanting very much to do so. They pretended to be busy, peeking at him with their heads lowered. When he passed by, they gathered in a group behind him and giggled.

Lan Wangji had walked for a long time before he saw an old woman sweeping the floor at the entrance of a house.

"Excuse me, where is the nearest lotus lake?" he asked.

The old woman had poor eyesight, and on top of that, there was dust blurring her vision. "There's a family about four kilometers or so from here," she panted, unable to see him clearly. "They've planted a few hectares."

"Thank you," Lan Wangji said with a nod.

"Young master, they don't allow anyone to enter that lotus lake at night," the old woman added. "If you plan to go there for fun, better go quick, while there's still daylight."

"Thank you," Lan Wangji said again.

As he turned to leave, he saw the old woman reach out with her long, thin bamboo pole, trying in vain to knock down a withered branch stuck on the eaves. With a twitch of his finger, he struck down the withered branch with his sword qi. Only then did he depart.

Four kilometers was not terribly far for him, given his walking speed. Lan Wangji followed the old woman's directions, never once breaking stride.

After five hundred meters, he had left the market behind. One kilometer away, signs of human habitation faded. When he passed two kilometers, all he could see along the road were green hills, fields, and crossroads. Occasionally, he'd spot a crooked cottage with spirals of smoke rising from its chimney. Several muddy toddlers with their hair pulled up into tight little topknots squatted in the ridges of earth between fields, playing with the mud as they laughed merrily and smeared each other with it.

There was such a rustic charm to the scenery that Lan Wangji stopped to look, but he had only been watching a short while when they noticed him. The children were all young and scared of strangers, so they soon fled. Only then did Lan Wangji continue on his way.

When he hit the two-and-a-half kilometer mark, he felt a chill on his face—a drizzle, brought on by a breeze.

He looked at the sky. Sure enough, the rolling, overcast clouds were bearing down on him. He quickened his pace, but the rain soon overtook him.

Just then, he saw five or six people standing on the ridge between fields ahead of him. The drizzle had already turned into rain, but these people neither held umbrellas nor shielded themselves from the weather. They seemed to be crowded around something, too preoccupied to pay attention to anything else.

As Lan Wangji approached, he saw a farmer on the ground, moaning in pain. He listened quietly to a couple of remarks, piecing together what had happened. While this farmer had been working the fields, a bull belonging to another farming household had rammed him. The others weren't sure if he had hurt his back or broken his leg, but whatever the case, he couldn't get up. The bull, the undisputed guilty party, had been chased to the far end of the field. It stood with its head lowered and tail swinging, not daring to approach.

The owner of the bull had run off to call for a doctor, and the remaining farmers didn't dare to risk moving the injured farmer, lest it cause further injury. All they dared do was to keep an eye on him. Unfortunately, the weather was bad, and it had begun to rain. It was just a drizzle at first, which was tolerable, but was now coming down harder.

Seeing the rain grow heavier, one of the farmers had gone to fetch some umbrellas, but he lived some distance away and wouldn't be back any time soon. The remaining people were anxious. Together, they raised their hands to shield the injured farmer as much as they could from the rain, but it was hardly a long-term solution. Even if they had umbrellas, there would only be so many to go around. How could they possibly let only one or two people be shielded while the rest got drenched?

"What the hell. Pouring like this out of the blue," one of the farmers cursed under his breath.

"Let's hold that shed up for as long as we can," said another farmer.

There was an old, abandoned shed not far away. The roof had been propped up with four wooden logs. One log was crooked, while another had rotted after being exposed to the elements for years on end.

"We can't move him, right?" asked someone, hesitantly.

"A...a few steps should be fine."

They quickly but carefully carried the injured farmer to the shed. Two farmers went to hold the roof up, as it was half-collapsed, but to their surprise, they couldn't even lift it. The others urged them on and they mustered all their strength, but even as their faces flushed from exertion, it wouldn't move at all. Two more people joined in, but still it wouldn't budge!

The roof of the wooden shed had been built with wooden cross-beams and was stacked with tiles, thatch, and layers of dust. While it shouldn't have been light, it seemed impossible that four farmers, men who tilled the land all year round, couldn't lift it.

Lan Wangji knew what was going on without even getting close. He walked over to the wooden shed, bent down, and grabbed a corner of the roof. He lifted it with one hand.

The farmers were dumbstruck. Four farmers had not been able to lift the shed's roof, yet this boy had done so with just one hand!

After a long, stunned moment, one farmer spoke in a hushed tone to the others. Needing no further prompting, they swiftly carried the injured farmer over. As they entered the wooden shed, they glanced at Lan Wangji. Lan Wangji, however, continued to stare straight ahead.

After setting the injured man down, two others approached him. "You...young master, you can put it down now. We'll take over."

Lan Wangji shook his head.

"You're just a kid. You won't be able to keep that up for long," the two farmers insisted.

They raised their hands to help him brace the roof. Lan Wangji cast a glance at them. Wordlessly, he withdrew a fraction of his strength. The color promptly drained from the two farmers' faces.

Lan Wangji looked away and reapplied his original strength. The two farmers retreated, hunched in embarrassment. The wooden shed was even heavier than they had expected. Without that boy's efforts, they couldn't hope to hold it up.

One farmer shivered. "Strange. Why is it even colder in here?"

None of them could see the shabbily dressed figure hanging from the roof's central rafter. It had dry, brittle hair and a long drooping tongue. As the rain raged outside, the figure swayed, stirring up a gust of ominous wind.

That evil spirit had made the shed so unusually heavy that no ordinary people could lift it, no matter what they did.

Lan Wangji had not brought the tools required for exorcism when he ventured out. Since this evil spirit had no interest in harming humans, he naturally could not disperse and indiscriminately scatter its soul. It also seemed there was temporarily no way to convince it to come down, leaving him with no choice but to continue bracing the roof. He would report it later so someone could return and deal with it.

As the wind blew, the hanging evil spirit swung to and fro behind Lan Wangji.

"It's soo cold…" it complained.

"…" Lan Wangji ignored it.

The evil spirit looked left and right, then found a farmer to lean against, as if trying to warm itself up. The farmer shivered, and Lan Wangji shot the spirit a cold, stern look out of the corner of his eye.

The evil spirit shivered as well. It recoiled, much aggrieved, but still lolled out its long tongue and grumbled, "Such heavy, pouring rain, and it's all open ground here... I'm really soo cold..."

"..." Lan Wangji continued to ignore him.

Even when the doctor arrived, the farmers didn't dare speak with Lan Wangji. Once the rain stopped, they moved the injured farmer out of the wooden shed. Lan Wangji set the roof down and left without a word.

It was already sunset by the time he reached the lotus lake. He was about to go down to the water when a small boat came over from the opposite end.

"Hey, hey, hey! What are you doing?" a middle-aged woman called from the boat.

"Picking lotus seed pods," said Lan Wangji.

"The sun has already set," the woman said. "No visitors after dark. No more entry today. Come back another time!"

"I promise I will not stay long," Lan Wangji said. "I will leave after a short time."

"No means no," said the woman. "That's the rule, and I don't make 'em. Go ask the owner."

"Where can I find the owner of the lake?" Lan Wangji asked.

"He left already," the lotus-picker woman said. "So it's pointless to ask me. If I let you in, the lake's owner will be on my case. Don't get me in trouble."

Upon hearing this, Lan Wangji did not force the issue further. He nodded. "My apologies for having bothered you."

Although his expression was calm, the hint of disappointment was visible.

Seeing his snow-white robes partially soaked by the rain and his white boots smeared with mud, the lotus-picker woman softened her tone. "You're too late today, but come earlier tomorrow. Where are you from? It was raining so heavily earlier. Child, you didn't run here in the rain, did you? Why didn't you use an umbrella? How far is your house from here?"

"Seventeen kilometers," Lan Wangji answered honestly.

Hearing this, the lotus-picker woman was momentarily struck dumb. "So far! It must have taken you a long time to get here. If you really have a craving for lotus seed pods, buy them on the streets. There are plenty."

Lan Wangji was just about to turn around when he heard this. He paused. "The lotus seed pods from the streets do not have stems."

"Do you really *need* the ones with the stems?" asked the lotus-picker woman, curious. "It's not like there's any difference in taste."

"There is," Lan Wangji said.

"There isn't!"

"There is," Lan Wangji insisted stubbornly. "Someone told me that there is."

The lotus-picker woman puffed out a laugh. "Who told you that? What an obstinate young master. You must have been bewitched!"

Without saying a word, Lan Wangji lowered his head and turned around to leave.

The lotus-picker woman shouted again, "Is your house really that far?"

"Mn," answered Lan Wangji.

"How about...you don't go back today?" the lotus-picker woman suggested. "Find a place to stay nearby and come back tomorrow."

"We have a curfew to obey, and lessons to attend first thing in the morning," Lan Wangji answered.

The lotus-picker woman scratched her head, agonizing over her dilemma. "...All right," she said, at last. "I'll let you in, but just for a short time. A *very* short time. If you want to pick them, hurry up so no one sees you and rats me out to the owner. Someone my age doesn't need a scolding."

The magnolias in the Cloud Recesses were particularly fresh and dainty after the rain. The sight filled Lan Xichen with fondness— so much so that he spread paper on his desk to paint by the window.

Through the engraved lattice, he saw a figure in white slowly approach. Without setting down his brush, Lan Xichen called out to him. "Wangji."

Lan Wangji walked over and greeted him from the other side of the window. "Xiongzhang."

"You mentioned lotus seed pods yesterday," Lan Xichen said, "and it just so happens that shufu had some brought up the mountain. Would you like to try them?"

"I have already eaten some of my own," answered Lan Wangji, standing outside.

"You have?" Lan Xichen felt a little surprised.

"Mn," Lan Wangji affirmed.

After a few more brief words, Lan Wangji returned to the Tranquility Room.

When Lan Xichen finished his painting, he regarded it for a short while before casually setting it aside, where it was soon out of mind. He took out Liebing and headed over to the spot where he practiced Purification Tone every day.

Surrounding the little cottage were clusters of purple gentians, each adorned with twinkling droplets of morning dew. Lan Xichen walked along the narrow path and passed through the gates. When he raised his eyes, he was slightly taken aback.

On the wooden veranda before the entrance of the building was a white jade vase, filled with several lotus seed pods of varying heights. The vase was long and slender, as were the stems of the pods, arranged in a careful manner most pleasing to the eye.

Lan Xichen put Liebing away and sat on the veranda, facing the jade vase. He tilted his head to look at it for a moment, greatly conflicted.

It took every ounce of restraint he had, but in the end, he did not sneakily peel one for himself, as much as he wanted to see whether or not there was really a difference in the taste of the lotus seed pods with stems.

Since Wangji looked so happy, it must have been truly delicious.

B Y THE TIME LAN WANGJI returned, Wei Wuxian had
already counted to one thousand three hundred-something.

"One thousand three hundred and sixty-nine, one thousand three hundred and seventy, one thousand three hundred and seventy-one..."

He alternated legs as he kicked a colorful shuttlecock, which bounced between his feet. The shuttlecock shot to the sky and steadily drifted down, then flew even higher before leisurely falling. It was as if it'd been tethered by an invisible thread that ensured it could never escape from Wei Wuxian.

At the same time, there appeared to be another invisible thread that tethered and guided the rapt attention of the many children gathered around him.

Wei Wuxian continued his count. "One thousand three hundred and seventy-two, one thousand three hundred and eighty-one..."

Lan Wangji was speechless. "..."

And thus did Wei Wuxian blatantly cheat as he basked in the admiration of the crowd of children. This huge number had caused the snot-nosed children to lose their sense of judgment; not one of them had actually noticed anything amiss.

With his own ears, Lan Wangji had heard Wei Wuxian skip from seventy-two to eighty-one, and then from eighty-one to ninety. Wei Wuxian spotted him just as he was about to make his next leap in numbers. His eyes lit up. He looked as if he was about to call out to him, but then miscalculated the amount of force his foot exerted. The brightly colored shuttlecock was sent flying over his head and tumbled behind him.

Seeing that he was about to drop it, Wei Wuxian hurriedly kicked backward and saved it with his heel—and this last kick sent it flying higher than ever before. A loud and clear "One thousand six hundred!" followed right after, causing the children to exclaim in surprise and clap with all their might.

With the outcome a foregone conclusion, a little girl squealed, "One thousand six hundred! He won. All of you lost!"

Not in the least bit ashamed, Wei Wuxian accepted his victory with high spirits and no qualms.

Clap, clap, clap. Lan Wangji also provided some dry, scattered applause.

A boy with a furrowed brow chewed on his finger, commenting, "I...don't think that's right."

"What do you mean?" Wei Wuxian asked.

"How did you suddenly go from ninety to a hundred?" the boy said. "Your counting was definitely wrong."

The group of children seemed to be divided into two groups. One group, obviously completely under Wei Wuxian's spell, berated the skeptics.

"How could it be wrong? Don't be a sore loser."

"Why would a hundred not come after ninety?" Wei Wuxian argued too. "Count it yourself. What comes after nine?"

With some difficulty, the boy slowly counted on his fingers. "... Seven, eight, nine, ten..."

"See, ten comes after nine," Wei Wuxian immediately commented. "So it's definitely a hundred after ninety."

The boy was still skeptical. "...Really? No way."

"Why not?" Wei Wuxian said. "If you don't believe me, we can ask someone passing by." He scanned around and then slapped his thigh. "Oh look, I found one. You sir, the gongzi over there who looks very reliable. Please stop for a moment!"

Lan Wangji remained speechless, but stayed where he was nonetheless. "What is the matter?"

"Might I ask you a question?" Wei Wuxian asked.

"You may," Lan Wangji replied.

So Wei Wuxian asked, "What number comes after ninety?"

"One hundred," Lan Wangji answered.

Wei Wuxian cupped his hands in a gesture of gratitude. "Thank you."

Lan Wangji nodded. "You are welcome."

Wearing a happy smile, Wei Wuxian nodded and turned to say to the boy, "Told ya."

The boy didn't really believe Wei Wuxian, whose face now bore a wicked smirk, but a sense of awe unconsciously filled his heart at the sight of Lan Wangji. This young master was dressed in snow-like white robes, and a jade pendant hung from his sword. His face was so handsome that he didn't feel real. It was like he was a divine being. The boy's wavering mind was immediately convinced.

"Is that how counting works...?" he mumbled to himself.

"One thousand six hundred against three hundred," the children chattered in chorus. "You lost!"

"Okay, okay," the boy said reluctantly as he handed the skewer of candied hawthorns in his hand to Wei Wuxian. "You win! Here, take it!"

After the group of children left, Wei Wuxian addressed Lan Wangji around the candied hawthorn stuffed in his mouth.

"Hanguang-jun, you really do give me face."

Only then did Lan Wangji walk over to him. "Sorry to have kept you waiting."

Wei Wuxian shook his head. "It wasn't long at all. You were gone for just a little while. I only kicked that shuttlecock about three hundred or so times."

"One thousand six hundred times," Lan Wangji corrected him.

Wei Wuxian laughed out loud and bit down on a hawthorn. Lan Wangji was about to speak again, but he felt a chill on his lips and sweetness on his tongue. Wei Wuxian had stuffed the skewer of candied hawthorns into his mouth.

Noticing his odd expression, Wei Wuxian asked, "Do you like sweets?"

Lan Wangji was unable to speak as he held the skewer in his mouth, neither taking a bite nor spitting it out.

"If you don't, give it to me," Wei Wuxian said.

He grabbed the thin stick, intending to take it back, but failed to pull it out after several attempts. It appeared Lan Wangji had bitten down on it.

"So are you eating it or not?" Wei Wuxian wondered with a grin.

"Yes." Lan Wangji bit a hawthorn off the skewer as well.

"That's more like it," Wei Wuxian said. "If you want it, just say so. You've been like this since you were little. You keep your jaw clamped on whatever it is you want and refuse to say a word."

After Wei Wuxian had laughed at him for a bit, they strolled into town.

Ever since he was a child, Wei Wuxian had always been playful and greedy while shopping on the streets. He ran everywhere and wanted everything. He had to squeeze every little trinket he came across, and whenever he smelled anything delicious wafting over from the roadside, he had to try a bite.

At Wei Wuxian's urging, Lan Wangji also tried some snacks that he would otherwise never have touched in the past. Each time Wei Wuxian watched him finish his food, he had to ask, "How was it? How was it?" Sometimes, Lan Wangji would answer, "Passable," and sometimes he would answer, "Very good," but more often he would reply with, "Strange." And each time the last happened, Wei Wuxian would snatch the item back with a roaring laugh and refuse to let him keep eating it.

They had originally planned to find a place for lunch, but Wei Wuxian had eaten his way from west to east and stuffed himself so full that his stride became increasingly indolent. And so, the pair sat down inside a clean and decent-looking soup restaurant.

Wei Wuxian nibbled and played with the radish slice between his chopsticks as he waited for the lotus root and pork rib soup he had ordered. When Lan Wangji stood up, he asked in surprise, "Where are you going?"

"Please wait," Lan Wangji said. "I will return shortly."

Sure enough, he returned shortly—right as the lotus root and pork rib soup just so happened to be served. Wei Wuxian drank a mouthful, then waited until the waiter left to quietly comment to Lan Wangji, "It's not good."

Lan Wangji took a small taste with a spoon. "How so?"

Wei Wuxian stirred his bowl with his own spoon. "You can't use lotus roots that are too tough. The pinker ones are good. This shop is too conservative with their seasoning, and it hasn't been simmered long enough to bring out the flavor. Anyway, it's not as tasty as the stuff my shijie used to make."

He was just casually chatting, expecting Lan Wangji to only listen attentively, and at most make noises of acknowledgment. Who would have thought he wouldn't just listen but even ask questions?

"Then how does one choose the right ingredients? What should be done for the flavor to emerge?"

Finally sensing something was up, Wei Wuxian wondered aloud, "Hanguang-jun. You're not thinking of making lotus root and pork rib soup for me, are you? Did you just sneak away to observe the process?"

Before Lan Wangji could answer, Wei Wuxian was already laughing at him. "Ha ha, Hanguang-jun. Not that I'm looking down on you, but no one in your clan would ever deign to enter the kitchen. Plus, growing up eating like *that* has made you develop certain tastes. Nothing you make would even be fit for the eyes."

Lan Wangji drank another mouthful of the soup, neither affirming nor denying his accusations. Wei Wuxian waited for him to continue the thread of conversation, but Lan Wangji remained as steadfast as a rock. Eventually, he couldn't wait anymore.

"Lan Zhan," he asked without a shred of shame, "do you really mean to cook for me?"

Lan Wangji was surprisingly able to keep his composure. He did not answer, even with a simple "Yes" or "No."

Wei Wuxian grew a little impatient. He shot to his feet and leaned his hands on the edge of the table. "Gimme an 'Mn' or something!"

"Mn," Lan Wangji said.

"So is that a yes or no?" Wei Wuxian probed. "My dear Lan Zhan, everything I said was just teasing. If you really wanna cook for me, then you could burn right through the pan until the whole stove is nothing but a smoking crater, and I'd still eat it all up, pan and all, just to show you."

A momentary silence.

"That is not necessary," Lan Wangji stated.

Wei Wuxian was close to jumping on him to plead for an answer. "So are you doing it or not? Do it, come on, Hanguang-jun, I'll eat it!"

Without batting an eyelid, Lan Wangji held Wei Wuxian's waist steady. "Manners."

"Er-gege," Wei Wuxian warned him. "You can't be like this with me."

Lan Wangji finally could no longer withstand his pestering. He held Wei Wuxian's hand and told him, "I have already done so."

"Huh?" Wei Wuxian was taken aback. "You already did? When? What did you cook? Why don't I remember?"

"During the family banquet," Lan Wangji said.

"...So that night, those dishes I thought you'd bought from the Hunan restaurant in Caiyi Town were all personally made by you?" Wei Wuxian probed.

"Mn," Lan Wangji answered.

Wei Wuxian was shocked. "You made all that? Do kitchens even exist in the Cloud Recesses?"

"...Naturally."

"So you washed and chopped the vegetables? You put the oil and the food into the pan? You mixed in the spices?"

"Mn."

"You...you..."

Wei Wuxian was so shocked he could no longer form words. Eventually, he grabbed Lan Wangji's collar with one hand, grasped Lan Wangji's neck with the other, and hauled him in to kiss him hard.

Fortunately, the two of them always picked the most inconspicuous and secluded spots against the wall to sit. Lan Wangji wrapped his arms around him and turned, ensuring the other patrons could only see his back and one of Wei Wuxian's arms hooked around his neck.

Seeing that Lan Wangji wasn't blushing or gasping for breath, Wei Wuxian reached out and seized something to confirm. Sure enough, his hand came into contact with scalding heat.

Lan Wangji caught his restless hand. "Wei Ying," he warned.

"I'm already on your lap, aren't I?" Wei Wuxian said. "What are you calling me for?"

Lan Wangji had no answer to that. "..."

"Sorry," Wei Wuxian apologized solemnly. "I was just too happy. Lan Zhan, how are you so amazing at everything you do? Even the cooking!"

His praise was unbelievably sincere. Growing up, Lan Wangji had been the recipient of countless compliments, but not a single one had ever made it this hard for him to keep the corners of his lips from arching into a smile.

He could only give a mild reply. "It was nothing difficult."

"No, it's very difficult," Wei Wuxian said. "You have no idea how many times I've gotten booted out of the kitchen since I was little."

"...Have you ever burnt through the bottom of a pan?" Lan Wangji asked.

"Just once," Wei Wuxian answered. "I'd forgotten to add water, and the pan caught fire. Don't look at me like that. It really was just once."

"What did you put in the pan?" Lan Wangji asked.

Wei Wuxian thought for a moment, then answered with a smile, "That was so many years ago, how would I remember? Don't bring it up again."

Although Lan Wangji made no comment, he arched an eyebrow slightly. Wei Wuxian pretended to not notice the minuscule expression. All of a sudden, something came back to him, and he threw his hands up in remorse.

"But why didn't you tell me you'd made those dishes? What a fool I was. I didn't have more than a few bites of the food that night."

"It is fine," Lan Wangji said, "I will make them again when we return."

Wei Wuxian, who had been pestering him all this time specifically to hear that one statement, instantly beamed with joy. The soup didn't even taste all that bad anymore.

After the two left the restaurant, they strolled around for a while until they came upon a commotion on the street. A crowd surrounded a spot that had been set up with an array of little trinkets. One by one, people were tossing rings onto the ground.

"This one's good." Wei Wuxian pulled Lan Wangji over and took three rings from the vendor's hand. "Lan Zhan, have you ever played ring toss before?"

Lan Wangji shook his head.

"You never have?" Wei Wuxian said. "Let me explain it to you, it's very simple. You take these rings and back a short distance away, and then you try to toss them onto the things on the ground. If you snare anything, it's yours."

"Anything I snare is mine," Lan Wangji echoed.

"That's it," Wei Wuxian confirmed. "Which one do you want? I'll get whatever you choose."

"Anything," Lan Wangji said.

Wei Wuxian leaned his elbow on Lan Wangji's shoulder and tugged at the tail of his forehead ribbon. "Hanguang-jun, you're not giving me any face by being so easygoing."

"I want whatever you snare," Lan Wangji said in all seriousness.

Wei Wuxian was momentarily taken aback. "You... Why are you like this in public?"

Lan Wangji didn't get it. "What?"

"You're tantalizing me," Wei Wuxian said.

"I am not," Lan Wangji answered, his expression calm and unperturbed.

"You are!" Wei Wuxian insisted. "All right, then I'll snare...that one. Yup, that one!"

He pointed at a big white porcelain turtle displayed far, far away. He took a few steps back. When he was about three meters away, the vendor gestured and called out, "That'll do! That'll do!"

But Wei Wuxian said, "No, no."

"Gongzi, you're standing too far away. You won't be able to hit anything like that," the vendor yelled. "Don't say I scammed you when that happens!"

"If I don't stand farther away, you'll have to worry about losing everything!" Wei Wuxian quipped.

The crowd hooted with laughter. "This gongzi is so confident!"

It was a simple game and seemed easy on the surface. However, each object on the ground was set some distance apart, and it could be difficult for ordinary folk to exert the exact degree of strength required to target a specific prize. But such things were a breeze to a cultivator, so what fun would there be if he didn't aim from far away?

Wei Wuxian kept retreating, even turning around so his back faced the stall. The bystanders hooted louder with laughter.

Wei Wuxian weighed the ring in his hand and launched it with a backhanded toss. To everyone's surprise, the ring easily landed on the porcelain turtle, snaring its head.

The vendor and the crowd were both astonished and speechless.

Wei Wuxian looked back, and a smile spread across his face. He raised the remaining two rings and gestured to Lan Wangji.

"Wanna try?"

"Certainly." Lan Wangji walked over to Wei Wuxian. "Which do you want?"

Small streetside businesses didn't carry any high-quality goods. There were only trinkets which looked decent from afar and had passable workmanship. The large porcelain turtle Wei Wuxian had won was already the best-looking prize of the lot. He looked over the remaining prizes, and the more he looked, the more he found them all ugly. He didn't want any of them, which made it tough to choose.

All of a sudden, he spotted an extremely ugly stuffed donkey, so singularly ugly among all the other items that no one who saw it could ignore it.

Elated, he said, "That one's not bad. It looks like Little Apple. Come, come, come, let's get that one."

Lan Wangji nodded. He retreated three meters further than Wei Wuxian had walked and also turned around. The ring hit the donkey with accuracy and precision.

The crowd erupted into cheers and clapped with gusto. Lan Wangji looked back at Wei Wuxian, who laughed heartily as he jumped into the stall to snag the little donkey on the ground and tuck it under his arm. He was clapping the hardest.

"Again, again!"

Lan Wangji still had one ring in his hand, and weighed it gently and steadily. This time, he took some time before tossing it and instantly turned around to check.

Exclamations of dismay rang out from all around the moment he threw the ring. As it turned out, the ring's trajectory was so awry that it did not even touch the perimeter of the street vendor's stall. Instead, it landed right on Wei Wuxian, snaring him.

At first, Wei Wuxian was taken aback. And then a smile broke out on his face. The crowd, finding this a shame, provided words of consolation.

"Not a bad attempt!"

"Yeah, you got quite a few."

"It was already really impressive!"

Thankful for the miss, the vendor rolled his eyes and heaved a sigh of relief before he sprang to his feet and gave them a thumbs-up. "Yeah! So amazing! Gongzi was so right. If you'd managed to nab any more, I'd be operating at a loss!"

Wei Wuxian laughed. "All right, I know you're scared to let us keep playing. We've had our fun, anyway. Lan Zhan, let's go, let's go."

"Take care!" the vendor said happily.

It was only after the pair disappeared side by side into the bustling crowd that the vendor suddenly remembered, "The third ring! They didn't return it!"

Wei Wuxian walked with the turtle hugged under his left arm and the donkey tucked under his right. "Lan Zhan, why did I never realize that you're such a little schemer?"

Lan Wangji took the large, heavy porcelain turtle from him, while Wei Wuxian removed the ring from his neck and slotted it over Lan Wangji's head. "Don't pretend you don't understand what I'm talking about. I know you did that on purpose."

Lan Wangji held up the big turtle in his palm to inspect it. "Where shall we display this when we return?"

His question stumped Wei Wuxian.

The turtle was bulky and heavy, and its workmanship was nothing to write home about. It had an absolutely foolish-looking head and at best, could grudgingly be considered "cute." But on closer inspection, Wei Wuxian realized the craftsman had been shoddy in his work—its beady pupils had been painted cross-eyed. No matter how he looked at it, it was completely at odds with the Cloud Recesses' aesthetic. Deciding where to put it was a problem, indeed.

Wei Wuxian thought for a moment. "The Tranquility Room?"

He'd only just voiced the suggestion when he immediately shook his head and vetoed the idea. "That room's only suitable for playing the guqin and burning incense. It would be an utter eyesore to dump a giant turtle in a place like that, a serene spot swirling with sandalwood smoke."

When Lan Wangji heard him state that the Tranquility Room was a "serene" place suitable only for "playing the guqin and burning incense," he cast him a sideways glance. He made as if to speak but ultimately held back.

"But it'll definitely get thrown out right away if we put it anywhere in the Cloud Recesses that isn't the Tranquility Room."

Lan Wangji nodded silently.

In the end, Wei Wuxian exhibited restraint and was too abashed to say, *"Let's secretly put it in your shufu's room, don't let him find out that we did it."*

Suddenly, he slapped his thigh. "Got it. Let's put it in the Orchid Room."

Lan Wangji thought for a moment. "Why the Orchid Room?"

"Lemme explain it to ya," Wei Wuxian said. "Put it in the Orchid Room, and if you're asked about it while teaching Sizhui, Jingyi, and the others, you can tell them that the turtle was specially designed by an elusive and talented master craftsman to commemorate your defeat of the Xuanwu of Slaughter. As such, it carries a profound significance. Its aim is to inspire the juniors of your Lan Clan of

Gusu to look up to their seniors and strive to advance themselves. Although the Xuanwu of Slaughter is gone, there must be others lying in wait—a Zhuque of Murder, a Baihu of Massacre, a Qinglong of Carnage, and so on. The juniors must do great deeds that surpass their predecessors and shock the world."

Lan Wangji was struck speechless.

"Well, what do you think?"

After a while, Lan Wangji said, "Very good."

Many days later, every time Lan Sizhui, Lan Jingyi, and the others looked up during their lessons with Hanguang-jun, they would catch a glimpse of the large, crudely made porcelain turtle on the desk behind Lan Wangji, staring back at them with dull, lifeless eyes.

Deterred by some inexplicable force, no one actually dared to ask why it had appeared there. However, that was another story for another day...

After tucking their spoils into their qiankun sleeves, the two left in triumph.

Before their visit, Wei Wuxian had bragged to Lan Wangji for a long time about Yunmeng's gorgeous scenery—specifically the sight of the vast emerald-green lotus lakes meeting the blue line of sky. Naturally, he had to drag him out to tour the waters. He had wanted to get an extravagant pleasure barge, but after searching for a long time, could only find a tiny wooden boat tethered by the shore. It looked weak and rickety enough to sink as soon as someone lightly set foot on it. Loading two grown men into it seemed a little much, but there was no other option.

"You sit on this end. I'll sit on the other end," Wei Wuxian said. "Sit tight and don't move around. This thing will capsize if we're not careful."

"It is fine," Lan Wangji reassured. "I will save you if you fall into the water."

"Listen to you, saying that like I don't know how to swim," Wei Wuxian quipped.

The small boat brushed past large and luxuriant lotuses, each blooming with pink abundance. Wei Wuxian lounged on the boat with his head pillowed on his arms. The boat was truly too small—his legs were almost resting on Lan Wangji's lap. Lan Wangji did not say a word about this brazen, uncouth behavior.

A gentle breeze blew across the lake, stirring the tranquil water.

"This is the season when the lotuses are in bloom," Wei Wuxian said. "A pity the lotus seed pods aren't ripe yet, or I could've taken you to pick some."

"We can come again," Lan Wangji said.

"Right!" Wei Wuxian agreed. "We can still come again."

He absentmindedly paddled with the oars as he zoned out, gazing into the distance. "There used to be an old man who grew lotus seed pods around here. It looks like he's gone now."

"Mn," Lan Wangji said.

"He was already really old when I was little," Wei Wuxian said. "It's been over ten years since. If he's still alive, he's probably too old to walk or move a boat out."

He turned his head and said to Lan Wangji, "When I was at the Cloud Recesses way back then, I kept urging you to come visit Lotus Pier. I especially wanted you to come with me to steal lotus seed pods from him. Do you know why?"

When it came to Wei Wuxian, Lan Wangji always answered every one of his questions and acquiesced to all his requests. And so, he answered him seriously, "I do not know. Why?"

Wei Wuxian winked at him and snickered. "Because that old man sure was something whenever he hit people with his boat-pole. It hurt way more than your family's disciplinary ferule. I thought I just had to trick Lan Zhan into coming here and let him take a few beatings too."

Lan Wangji smiled slightly at this. The cold glow of the moon-light on the lake melted at the sight.

In that instant, Wei Wuxian felt dizzy. A smile also unconsciously rippled its way onto his face.

"All right, I admit—" he began.

The sky and earth spun. There was a massive splash; the wave of water rose several meters high.

The boat had capsized.

Wei Wuxian broke through the lake's surface and wiped his face. "I said to sit tight and don't move! That the boat would capsize if we weren't careful!"

Lan Wangji swam over. Seeing that he remained unperturbed even after falling into a lake, Wei Wuxian laughed so hard he almost gulped down several mouthfuls of water.

"So who tipped the boat? Look at this mess!"

"I do not know," Lan Wangji replied. "It could have been me."

"All right," Wei Wuxian responded. "It could've been me too."

Amid smiles and laughter, they grabbed hold of each other and embraced in the water before exchanging a kiss.

After their lips parted, Wei Wuxian raised his hand and continued their earlier topic of conversation. "I admit it, I was talking nonsense. I just wanted to hang out with you back then."

Lan Wangji lifted him from behind, and Wei Wuxian clambered

back onto the boat. He looked back and held out a hand to grab Lan Wangji.

"So tell me honestly, Lan Zhan."

Lan Wangji got on the boat and handed him a red cord. "Of what?"

Wei Wuxian held the red cord with his mouth as he pulled back his hair, which had come loose in the water. "Tell me if you felt the same way," he said solemnly. "You know, your callous rejection of me every single time I asked really made me lose face back then."

"You can try and see if I would deny you anything now," Lan Wangji said.

The unexpected statement hit him right in the heart. Wei Wuxian choked for a moment, but Lan Wangji was still as composed as ever, like he didn't fully grasp the weight of what he had just said.

Pressing his palm to his forehead, Wei Wuxian said, "You... Hanguang-jun, let's agree that you'll give me a heads-up before you say sweet nothings in the future. Otherwise, I won't be able to take it."

Lan Wangji nodded. "All right."

"Lan Zhan!" Wei Wuxian said, "Oh, you...!"

Of all the millions of possible words, there was nothing left to say. There was only laughter and hugs.

HAI TIME HAD LONG SINCE come and gone, but the person he waited for had yet to return.

Lan Wangji stared unblinkingly at the hazy glow of the paper lamp on the table. The flames had yet to die. After a while, he rose to his feet and walked to the entrance of the Tranquility Room to open the wooden door and stood there for a moment.

Just as he was about to step out, there came an odd *thud* from behind him.

Lan Wangji whirled around. The window had been opened without him realizing it. The shutters gently fluttered with the night breeze, opening and closing. There was a large, strange lump under the thin blanket on the bed. Something had broken in through the window, tumbled inside, and was currently curled up and wriggling beneath the covers.

First struck speechless, Lan Wangji then gently closed the door and returned inside. He blew out the lamp and closed the window before climbing into bed and settling down next to that giant hump. He silently pulled another blanket over himself, closing his eyes.

It didn't take long before a large frozen thing suddenly burrowed beneath his blanket.

That large frozen thing wriggled on top of him and pressed itself against his chest. "Lan Zhan! I'm back!" it happily cried. "Say 'Welcome back.'"

Lan Wangji hugged him. "Why are you so cold?"

"Been out in the blowing wind for half a day and night. Warm me up a bit," said Wei Wuxian.

No wonder he was covered in dirt and bits of grass—he must've taken the Cloud Recesses' juniors out into the wilderness to wreak havoc on the fowls and beasts and other nefarious creatures. Despite him being so filthy as he rolled about in bed and wrapped himself up in their blanket, the neat and tidy Lan Wangji didn't mind one bit. Silently, he held Wei Wuxian tighter.

He warmed him with his body heat for a while. "Remove your boots at the very least," he said at last.

"Sure thing," Wei Wuxian agreed easily enough. He kicked off his boots before shrinking back into the blanket to freeze Lan Wangji more.

"Stop moving," Lan Wangji said evenly.

"I'm in your bed, and you want me to stop?" asked Wei Wuxian.

"Shufu has returned," Lan Wangji explained.

Lan Qiren's residence wasn't far from Lan Wangji's Tranquility Room, and he already disliked Wei Wuxian—if there were any indecent disturbances, he just might beat his chest in anger, stomp his feet, and bawl Wei Wuxian out.

Wei Wuxian inserted both knees between Lan Wangji's legs, teasingly and maliciously nudging against him a couple times— his own frank way of expressing his opinions on the matter.

After a brief silence, Lan Wangji abruptly twisted, pinning Wei Wuxian under him. His movement was too large, too forceful, and when the two of them landed on the wooden bed, the impact produced a loud *thud*.

"Easy, easy, easy... Ea...sy!"

Lan Wangji pinned Wei Wuxian on the bed with deadly strength.

He speared him open and slammed inside, bottoming out in one single thrust. He only stopped when he was completely pressed against Wei Wuxian's naked hips, and then only because he could press no closer.

Wei Wuxian sucked in a few sharp breaths and shook his head, a little afraid to move. His eyes darted, and he twisted his waist in his discomfort, hoping to make that hard thing inside him withdraw just a little. But Lan Wangji sensed his intention and locked his waist, then immediately filled him up again.

"*Ah!*" Wei Wuxian yelped. "Hanguang-jun!"

Lan Wangji forced himself to hold back for a while, then said, "You asked for it."

After that momentary pause, he began to thrust in earnest.

Wei Wuxian was firmly pinned beneath him, his legs bent, his black hair spread loose around him, and face flushed. His body rocked along with Lan Wangji's every thrust. Every time Lan Wangji drove into him, Wei Wuxian would let out a moan in concert, two thrusts, two moans. Lan Wangji lowered his head and plowed away for a while, until he could finally no longer allow Wei Wuxian to continue his cries.

Forcing down the harsh breaths that caught in his chest, he rasped in a low voice, "Keep...keep it down."

Wei Wuxian raised a hand and cupped his face, and thought about how strangely thin-skinned Lan Zhan could be. His cheek was obviously overwhelmingly hot to the touch, but the blush didn't show at all. His complexion was like frost, finer than snow, so handsome it left Wei Wuxian breathless and unable to contain himself. Only his earlobes were tinted with a bit of pink.

"Er-gege, you don't want to hear my cries?" he asked through his gasps.

Lan Wangji fell silent, caught between an obvious truth and a reluctance to lie. His conflicted expression filled Wei Wuxian with indescribable pleasure. He wanted to swallow him whole.

"It's simple," Wei Wuxian said. "If you don't want anyone to hear me, cast the silence spell."

Lan Wangji's chest heaved, and his eyes appeared slightly bloodshot.

"Come on! Silence me," Wei Wuxian egged him on. "Then you can do whatever you want with me. You can fuck me into the ground and I won't be able to make a sound—"

His voice cut out abruptly as Lan Wangji had leaned down and sealed his lips using his own.

Once his mouth was stopped, Wei Wuxian wound his arms and legs around Lan Wangji, and the two rolled and turned on the bed, competing for dominance. The blanket had long since been pushed to the floor.

Lan Wangji didn't often change positions while making love. After being held down and fucked for an hour, Wei Wuxian was stiff from his back down to his hips and legs. He highly suspected he would be screwed in the same position for the entire night, and considering Lan Wangji showed no signs of stopping, that was likely the case. Thus, Wei Wuxian took the initiative to flip them over. He straddled Lan Wangji, hooked his arms around his neck, and started rocking himself up and down.

He bit Lan Wangji's earlobe and whispered into his ear, "Is that deep enough?"

The whispering in his ear; the wetness and the warmth... Lan Wangji seized Wei Wuxian's shoulders and pushed him down hard. This dreadful move ripped a startled cry from Wei Wuxian's throat, who then hugged Lan Wangji tight.

Lan Wangji rubbed the small of Wei Wuxian's back. "Is *that* deep enough?"

Still shaken, Wei Wuxian could only move his lips. Before he was able to answer the question, he scrunched up his face and yelped. "*Ah!* Hang on! Nine, nine, nine shallow thrusts to one deep one!"

One hand shielded his stomach in vain, and the other gripped Lan Wangji's strong shoulder, his fingers digging deep into the toned but lean muscles as he was all but fucked out of his wits. "Lan Zhan!" cried Wei Wuxian. "Don't you know that you're supposed to do nine shallow thrusts and then one deep thrust?! You...don't... have...to...go so...so...every time..."

His perfectly fine speech was broken by each thrust, voice hitching each time Lan Wangji pushed deep.

"I do not!" answered Lan Wangji.

Though Wei Wuxian's cries and pleas for mercy in the first half of the evening could be considered quite pitiful, half the night and two rounds later found him with his legs still firmly locked around Lan Wangji's waist. He refused to let him leave.

Lan Wangji's body was draped entirely over Wei Wuxian, though he was careful not to let his weight crush him. The space where their bodies joined was wet and slippery. He made to get up, but he had only moved a little before Wei Wuxian squeezed his legs, and the small distance created by this short parting was immediately and seamlessly closed.

"Don't bother. There's a breeze. Stay with me for a bit," Wei Wuxian said lazily.

Doing as he was told, Lan Wangji didn't move. "Are you not too full?" he asked, after a time.

"I am," Wei Wuxian whined, piteously. "I'm sooo full. Didn't you hear how awfully I was crying?"

"...I will come out," Lan Wangji said.

Wei Wuxian's expression immediately changed. "I like being filled up by you like this," he said bluntly. "It feels nice."

He clenched down hard. Lan Wangji's face changed, and even his breathing faltered briefly. He held it in for a bit before he rasped out, "...Shameless!"

Seeing that he'd nearly hit his limit, Wei Wuxian laughed heartily and kissed his lips. "Er-gege, what *haven't* we done? Why are you still so shy?"

Lan Wangji shook his head slightly, resigned. "Release me," he said in a low voice. "You need to bathe."

Wei Wuxian was a little sleepy by this point. "Nah," he said, groggily. "I'll do that tomorrow. I'm exhausted."

Lan Wangji dropped a kiss on his forehead. "Go bathe. You must be mindful of your body."

Wei Wuxian was so sleepy he couldn't keep Lan Wangji locked inside him anymore, so he relented and let his limbs fall away. The first thing Lan Wangji did as he climbed out of bed was to pick the discarded blanket off the floor. He firmly covered Wei Wuxian's naked body with it before hanging the clothes that had been strewn across the floor over the screen. After swiftly dressing himself and making himself decent, he went outside to draw water for a bath.

An incense time later, after Wei Wuxian had nearly drifted off, Lan Wangji picked him up and placed him in the bathtub, which had been set down next to Lan Wangji's work desk. As he soaked and played in the water, Wei Wuxian's energy returned to him. He patted the edge of the tub.

"Not joining me, Hanguang-jun?"

"In a moment," Lan Wangji said.

"Why wait? Come in now," Wei Wuxian said.

Lan Wangji gave him a look. He seemed to be contemplating something, then said after a moment, "In the four days we have been back, we have broken four bathtubs."

That pointed look made Wei Wuxian feel the need to defend himself. "Last one wasn't my fault."

Lan Wangji placed the soap box within Wei Wuxian's reach and answered evenly, "The fault was mine."

Wei Wuxian cupped a handful of water and splashed it down his neck. The field of red hickeys became more vivid and vibrant the more he washed. "Yeah, and the second to last time wasn't my fault either. If we're gonna be fair, you're the one who's wrecked the tub every single time. You've had a tendency to do so from the start—one that's never been addressed."

Lan Wangji rose to his feet. When he came back, he placed a jug of Emperor's Smile by Wei Wuxian's hand before he sat back down by the desk.

"Yes," he admitted.

Wei Wuxian only needed to reach a bit further to tickle under Lan Wangji's chin—and he did just that. Lan Wangji picked up a few sheets of paper that were dense with writing and began to look through them, leaving short annotations here and there as he did.

Soaking in the water, Wei Wuxian opened the jug of Emperor's Smile and tossed back a gulp. "What's that you're looking at?" he asked idly.

"Night Hunt reports," Lan Wangji replied.

"Written by the kiddos?" asked Wei Wuxian. "You're not grading them, are you? I remember it's your shufu's job."

"Shufu is occupied of late. On occasion, I assist," explained Lan Wangji.

It was probably because Lan Qiren was busy with more important matters that Lan Wangji had temporarily taken over the job. Wei Wuxian reached out and took two of the pages.

"Your shufu would leave hundreds of words' worth of comments every couple of paragraphs back in the day. He'd write nearly a thousand more in summary at the end. I don't even know where he got the time to write all that. You leave barely any," he remarked, leafing through the sheets.

"Is that not acceptable?" asked Lan Wangji.

"Oh, it's very acceptable!" Wei Wuxian said. "Concise and easy to understand."

Less commentary was most definitely not slacking on Lan Wangji's part—he would never leave a job half done for anything, even when it came to the simplest things. Succinct language without any unnecessary elaboration was simply his habit, in both speech and writing.

Wei Wuxian sank his head under water and only re-emerged after a while with a splash. He grabbed the soap and started rubbing it into his hair while his other hand grabbed a sheet from the desk. One quick scan of it and he snorted despite himself.

"Who wrote this? So many incorrect characters," he said. "Ha ha ha ha ha ha ha ha, I just knew it'd be Jingyi. You gave him a yi grade."

"Yes," Lan Wangji affirmed.

"There's so many reports here, but he's the only one with a yi. How sad," Wei Wuxian said.

"It has excessive writing errors, and its prose is cumbersome."

"What happens when you get a yi?"

"Nothing," Lan Wangji said. "A rewrite."

"He should be grateful. It's better than having to rewrite it while doing handstands," Wei Wuxian said.

Lan Wangji silently collected the sheets Wei Wuxian had scattered and reorganized them in his hand, placing the now-neat stack aside.

Wei Wuxian's lips curved upward naturally while watching him work.

"What grade did you give Sizhui?" he asked.

Lan Wangji picked out two sheets of a journal and handed it to him. "Jia."

Wei Wuxian took the proffered papers and looked through them. "*Great* handwriting."

"Well constructed, organized thoughts. Contains substance. Pertinent and accurate," noted Lan Wangji.

Wei Wuxian finished flipping through the report in his hands, then looked at the unmarked stack. "You have to go through all those? Let me help with a few."

"Certainly," said Lan Wangji.

"Just underline and comment on anything that's incorrect, right?" Wei Wuxian asked.

He reached out and took over half of the stack. Lan Wangji moved to take it back, and Wei Wuxian shrank away from his hand.

"What're you doing?"

"That is too much," said Lan Wangji. "Take your bath."

Wei Wuxian took another sip of the Emperor's Smile, then grabbed a brush.

"I am," he said. "It's not like I have anything else to do in the meantime. It's pretty fun to look at the kiddos' reports and their writings."

"You must also rest after your bath," Lan Wangji insisted.

"Do I look sleepy to you? I could go another two rounds, even," Wei Wuxian boasted.

Watching him lean on the edge of the tub to carefully review the reports, resting his arm on the desk to write every so often, there seemed to be warmth flickering in Lan Wangji's eyes that could not be attributed to the lamplight alone.

Although Wei Wuxian talked a big game, declaring among other boasts that he could still go for another two rounds, it was hard not to feel drowsy as he marked batch after batch of reports. He had been running around the entire day, after all, first leading a group of boys, followed by a bedside entanglement for half the night afterward. Wei Wuxian forced himself to carefully and seriously mark his portion of the assignments, tossing the stack onto the desk but nearly slipping into the water with the motion. Swiftly and gently, Lan Wangji caught him and hauled him up. He toweled him dry and carried him to bed.

Lan Wangji quickly took his own bath, then climbed into bed and pulled Wei Wuxian into his arms. Wei Wuxian roused for a little bit, mumbling groggily into the crook of his neck.

"Your clan's kiddos write pretty good essays. They're just lacking a little bit when out at Night Hunts."

"Mn," Lan Wangji answered.

"But that's okay... I'll help them cram while we're here in the Cloud Recesses," Wei Wuxian said. "Tomorrow...I'll take them to disturb the one-footed mountain spirit nests."

The one-footed mountain spirit was a creature covered in black hair. It possessed enormous strength and could crunch humans in its mouth like vegetables. But Wei Wuxian made it sound like he was just taking a bunch of snot-nosed children to go poke at bird nests on the rooftops.

The corners of Lan Wangji's lips twitched, almost curling upward.

"Did you go capture one-footed mountain spirits today as well?"

"Yeah," Wei Wuxian confirmed. "That's why I said they still need training. Those mountain spirits only have one leg, y'know, and the kids *still* only barely outran it. If they encounter a four-legged lizard, an eight-legged spider, or a hundred-footed centipede in the future, they might as well just lie down and wait for death... Oh yeah, Hanguang-jun, I'm out of money. Please grant me more allowance."

"Take the jade token to make a withdrawal," Lan Wangji said.

Wei Wuxian gave a muffled laugh. "That thing you gave me already lets me go in and out of the barrier...it can make money withdrawals too?"

"Yes," Lan Wangji said. "Did you destroy a bystander's stall or dwelling?"

"No...we didn't... The money's all spent 'cause...after the Night Hunt, I took them to that Hunan restaurant in Caiyi Town... It's that one I kept trying to drag you to and you kept refusing to go... God, I'm so sleepy... Don't talk to me anymore, Lan Zhan..."

"All right."

"...I said stop talking... If you say even one word, I can't resist responding... All right, Lan Zhan, go to sleep. I...can't hang on anymore... I'm really gonna fall asleep now... See you tomorrow, Lan Zhan..."

He pecked a quick kiss on Lan Wangji's throat, then indeed fell into a deep sleep.

Darkness and silence blanketed the Tranquility Room.

Some time later, Lan Wangji brushed a light kiss against the center of Wei Wuxian's forehead.

"See you tomorrow, Wei Ying," he whispered.

Grandmaster of Demonic Cultivation

- FIN -

英语读者们好！
　谢谢你们阅读《魔道祖师》
得知大家喜欢这本书后，
　我感到很高兴！

Hello, English readers!

Thank you for reading *Grandmaster of Demonic Cultivation.*

I'm so happy to know everyone likes this series!

-Mo Xiang Tong Xiu

Grandmaster of Demonic Cultivation

MO DAO ZU SHI

Character & Name Guide

Characters

The identity of certain characters may be a spoiler; use this guide with caution on your first read of the novel.

Note on the given name translations: Chinese characters may have many different readings. Each reading here is just one out of several possible readings presented for your reference and should not be considered a definitive translation.

MAIN CHARACTERS

Wei Wuxian

BIRTH NAME: Wei Ying (魏婴 / Surname Wei, "Infant")

COURTESY NAME: Wei Wuxian (魏无羡 / Surname Wei, "Having no envy")

SOBRIQUET: Yiling Patriarch

WEAPON:

Sword: Suibian (随便 / "Whatever")

Hufu/Tiger Tally: Yin Tiger Tally (阴虎符)

INSTRUMENT:

Dizi (side-blown flute): Chenqing (陈情 / "To explain one's situation in detail." This is a reference to a line in a collection of poems, *Chu Ci* [楚辞], by famous poet Qu Yuan)

Unnamed dizi (side-blown flute)

In his previous life, Wei Wuxian was the feared Yiling Patriarch. He commanded an army of the living dead with his wicked flute Chenqing and laid waste to the cultivation world in an orgy of blood that eventually resulted in his death. Thirteen years later, a troubled young man sacrifices his soul to resurrect Wei Wuxian in his own body, hoping the terrible Yiling Patriarch will enact revenge on his behalf. Awakening confused and disoriented in this new body, Wei Wuxian stumbles forth into his second chance at life. Now, he must piece together the mystery surrounding his return—and face the lingering consequences of his last life, which continue to dog him even beyond death.

Wei Wuxian is mischievous and highly intelligent. He seems physically incapable of keeping his mouth shut and also can't seem to stop himself from teasing people who catch his interest—with Lan Wangji being a perennial favorite target, even after thirteen years away from the land of the living. He has a soft spot for children and can often be found scolding junior disciples for endangering themselves during missions.

Lan Wangji

BIRTH NAME: Lan Zhan (蓝湛 / "Blue," "Clear" or "Deep")

COURTESY NAME: Lan Wangji (蓝忘机 / "Blue," "Free of worldly concerns")

SOBRIQUET: Hanguang-jun (含光君 / "Light-bringer," honorific "-jun")

WEAPON: Sword: Bichen (避尘 / "Shunning worldly affairs")

INSTRUMENT: Guqin (zither): Wangji (忘机 / "Free of worldly concerns")

Lan Wangji's perfection as a cultivator is matched by none. Shunning petty politics and social prejudices, he appears wherever there is chaos to quell it with his sword Bichen, and evildoers quake in fear at the sound of strumming guqin strings. His remarkable grace and beauty have won him renown far and wide, even though his perpetual frown makes him look like a widower.

Younger brother to the current Lan Sect leader, Lan Xichen, Lan Wangji is stern, reserved, highly principled, and an avid fan of rabbits. While he was easily affected by teasing in his youth, he seems harder to perturb these days.

SUPPORTING CHARACTERS

Baoshan-sanren

COURTESY NAME: Baoshan-sanren (抱山散人 / "To embrace," "Mountain," "Scattered One")

A mysterious immortal cultivator. She lives the life of a hermit on a secluded mountain, far removed from the chaos and pain of the outside world. She frequently takes in orphaned children to be brought up as cultivators under her tutelage and has but a single rule for her students to follow: If they ever choose to leave the mountain, they will never be allowed to return. She was the teacher of Xiao Xingchen and Cangse-sanren.

Cangse-sanren

COURTESY NAME: Cangse-sanren (藏色散人 / "Hidden," "Colors," "Scattered One")

A famous cultivator of remarkable skill and beauty who studied under Baoshan-sanren. Upon leaving her teacher's secluded mountain, she fell in love with Wei Changze (魏长泽 / Surname Wei, "Long-Lasting" or "Large," "Benevolence" or "Lake"), a servant boy from the Jiang Clan of Yunmeng, and they ran away together. They eventually perished during a Night Hunt gone wrong, leaving behind their young son, Wei Wuxian.

Jiang Cheng

BIRTH NAME: Jiang Cheng (江澄 / "River," "Clear")

COURTESY NAME: Jiang Wanyin (江晚吟 / "River," "Night," "Recitation")

SOBRIQUET: Sandu Shengshou (三毒圣手 / "Three Poisons," a reference to the Buddhist three roots of suffering: greed, anger, and ignorance, "Sage Hand")

WEAPON:

Whip: Zidian (紫电 / "Purple," "Lightning")

Sword: Sandu (三毒 / "Three Poisons")

Jiang Cheng is the leader of the Jiang Sect and Jin Ling's maternal uncle. Known to be stern and unrelenting, he possesses a long-standing grudge against Wei Wuxian even after the latter's death. This is a far cry from the way things once were—Jiang Cheng and Wei Wuxian grew up together at Lotus Pier when the homeless and orphaned Wei Wuxian was taken in by Jiang Cheng's father, and were the closest of friends as well as martial siblings. However, after Wei Wuxian's rise as the Yiling Patriarch, their friendship ended alongside the many people who died at his hands...or so it seems.

Jiang Fengmian

COURTESY NAME: Jiang Fengmian (江枫眠 / "River," "Maple," "To sleep")

The former head of the Jiang Clan of Yunmeng, husband of Yu Ziyuan, and father of Jiang Yanli and Jiang Cheng. Jiang Fengmian is a mild-mannered man who prefers keeping the peace. He is rumored to have been in unrequited love with Wei Wuxian's mother, Cangse-sanren. He took in the orphaned Wei Wuxian and maintains a warm and fatherly relationship toward him. He treated Wei

Wuxian with visibly more affection than his biological children, which further aggravated his already strained relationships with his wife and Jiang Cheng.

Jiang Yanli

BIRTH NAME: Jiang Yanli (江厌离 / "River," "To dislike separation")

WEAPON: Love, patience, soup

The eldest daughter of the Jiang Clan, older sister to Jiang Cheng, and older martial sister to Wei Wuxian. She is Jin Zixuan's wife and Jin Ling's mother, and is warmly remembered by Wei Wuxian as being unconditionally kind and caring—and also an amazing chef. Though she possessed weak cultivation and no talent for combat, Jiang Yanli's boundless compassion touched the lives of many and changed the course of the cultivation world more profoundly than any bloody war ever could.

Yu Ziyuan

BIRTH NAME: Yu Ziyuan (虞紫鸢 / "Apprehension" or "To worry," "Purple," "Kite [species of bird]")

SOBRIQUET: Zi Zhizhu (紫蜘蛛 / "Purple Spider")

WEAPON: Whip: Zidian (紫电 / "Purple," "Lightning")

The wife of Jiang Fengmian and mother of Jiang Yanli and Jiang Cheng. Originally from the Yu Clan of Meishan, she was a famous cultivator in her own right. She was a stern and unrelenting woman but loved her children deeply. That being said, she never warmed up to Wei Wuxian, the orphaned ward her husband brought home against her wishes. She was close with Madam Jin, and it was their lifelong friendship that prompted the arranged marriage of Jiang Yanli and Jin Zixuan.

Madam Yu has two personal maidservants who serve as her right and left hands when it comes to sect matters, named Jinzhu (金姝 / "Golden Bead") and Yinzhu (银姝 / "Silver Bead"). They are able to interpret their mistress's commands without a single word being spoken.

Jin Ling

BIRTH NAME: Jin Ling (金凌 / "Gold," "Tower aloft")

COURTESY NAME: Jin Rulan (金如兰 / "Gold," "Like" or "As if," "Orchid")

WEAPON:

Sword: Suihua (岁华 / "Passage of time"),
    previously owned by Jin Zixuan

Fairy (spirit dog)

Unnamed bow

The young heir to the Jin Clan and son of Jin Zixuan and Jiang Yanli. Jin Ling grew up a lonely child, bullied by his peers and overly doted on by his caretakers out of pity. Though Jin Ling remains quite spoiled and unmanageable in temperament, he strongly dislikes being looked down upon and seeks to prove himself as a cultivator. He is often seen squabbling with his maternal uncle and sometimes-caretaker Jiang Cheng or hurling himself headlong into mortal peril alongside his loyal spirit dog Fairy.

Jin Guangshan

COURTESY NAME: Jin Guangshan (金光善 / "Gold," "Light and glory," "Kindness")

The former Jin Sect head and father to Jin Zixuan, Jin Guangyao, Mo Xuanyu, and many, many more. He was a womanizer who would abandon his lovers just as quickly as he would any children born of his dalliances. Despite this ravenous appetite, he only sired one child (Jin Zixuan) with his lawful wife. Under his rule, the Jin Sect was loathed by the cultivation world for its shameless abuses, corruption, and excess. Thankfully, he eventually died of exhaustion during an orgy and was succeeded by Jin Guangyao.

Jin Guangyao

BIRTH NAME: Meng Yao (孟瑶 / "Eldest," "Jade")

COURTESY NAME: Jin Guangyao (金光瑶 / "Gold," "Light and glory," "Jade")

SOBRIQUET: Lianfang-zun (敛芳尊 / "Hidden fragrance," honorific "-zun")

WEAPON: Softsword: Hensheng (恨生 / "To hate life/birth")

INSTRUMENT: Unnamed guqin

The current Jin Sect leader. He is half siblings with Jin Zixuan, Mo Xuanyu, and countless other children born of Jin Guangshan's wandering libido. He is also sworn brothers with Lan Xichen and Nie Mingjue, and together, they are known as the Three Zun. He is particularly close to Lan Xichen and could easily be named the man's most trusted companion. However, Jin Guangyao had a considerably more troubled relationship with Nie Mingjue before the man's death, and they frequently had heated disagreements over their conflicting worldviews.

Jin Guangyao rose from humble circumstances and became not only the head of the Jin Sect but also the Cultivation Chief of the inter-sect alliance. His work as an undercover spy was instrumental in the success of the Sunshot Campaign. His skill at politicking and networking is matched by none, and through restructuring and reparations he was able to largely make up for the damage done to the Jin Sect's reputation by his father's rule.

Jin Zixuan

COURTESY NAME: Jin Zixuan (金子轩 / "Gold," common male prefix "Son," "Pavilion")

WEAPON: Sword: Suihua (岁华 / "Passage of time")

The Jin Clan heir and the only legitimate son of Jin Guangshan. He married Jiang Yanli and together they had a son, Jin Ling. He attended school at the Cloud Recesses in his youth and was classmates with Wei Wuxian, Jiang Cheng, and Nie Huaisang. Due to his status, his natural skill, and his good looks, Jin Zixuan was generally rather prideful and arrogant, and was disliked by his peers.

He was initially resentful of his betrothal to Jiang Yanli, as it was arranged by his mother without his input or consent. However, he eventually began to regret his rude behavior and developed real feelings for her. Jiang Yanli seemed charmed by his earnest and extremely inept attempts to woo her, and the result was a brief but happy marriage.

Jin Zixun

COURTESY NAME: Jin Zixun (金子勋 / "Gold," common male prefix "Son," "Meritorious deed")

Jin Zixuan's younger paternal cousin. Like his cousin, he is arrogant and prideful regarding his appearance and skills, but unlike his cousin, these feelings do not have much basis in reality. Jin Zixun's cultivation level is unremarkable, and this coupled with his inability to keep a cool head often makes him a liability in tense situations.

Madam Jin

The lawful wife of Jin Guangshan and mother of Jin Zixuan. While her proper name is never revealed, her forceful personality is not so easily forgotten. She was close with Madam Yu, and it was their lifelong friendship that prompted the arranged marriage of Jiang Yanli and Jin Zixuan. She despises her husband's constant philandering (as well as any reminders of it in the form of illegitimate children), and although he fears her wrath, it does not stop him from continuing apace. She is equally unamused by her son's attitude problems and not afraid to reprimand him in public should the need arise.

Lan Jingyi

COURTESY NAME: Lan Jingyi (蓝景仪 / "Blue," "Scenery," "Bearing" or "Appearance")

WEAPON: Unnamed sword

A junior disciple in the Lan Sect. He is close friends with Lan Sizhui and appears to have a special kind of admiration for Lan Wangji. Although he was raised in such a strict sect, Lan Jingyi is distinctly un-Lan-like in his mannerisms, being loud, bluntly honest, and easily worked up into a tizzy. That being said, like any Lan, he is still very quick to spot and accuse instances of rule-breaking on the Cloud Recesses' premises.

Lan Qiren

COURTESY NAME: Lan Qiren (蓝启仁 / "Blue," "Open" or "Awaken," "Benevolence")

WEAPON: Long lectures, closed-book exams

A Lan Clan elder and the paternal uncle of Lan Xichen and Lan Wangji. He is well known across the cultivation world as an exemplary (and extremely strict) teacher who consistently produces equally exemplary students. He loves his nephews deeply and is clearly extremely proud of their accomplishments and skill as cultivators and gentlemen both. However, he does not exclude them from the prescribed clan punishments on the rare occasion that such things are warranted. Lan Qiren saw how his older brother Qingheng-jun was ruined by love and is desperate to keep his nephews from making the same mistakes as their father.

Lan Sizhui

BIRTH NAME: Lan Yuan (蓝愿 / "Blue," "Wish")

COURTESY NAME: Lan Sizhui (蓝思追 / "Blue," "To remember and long for")

WEAPON: Unnamed sword

INSTRUMENT: Unnamed guqin

A junior disciple in the Lan Sect. He is close friends with Lan Jingyi and appears to have a special kind of admiration for Lan Wangji. Lan Sizhui is poised and quite mature for his age and is a natural leader of his peers when the juniors are sent out on investigations. Although raised in such a strict sect, Lan Sizhui retains an air of warmth about him. He is kind, intuitive, and willing to see beyond surface appearances.

Unbeknownst to most, he is the last surviving member of the Wen Clan as the child of Wen Qing and Wen Ning's cousin (paternal side). Lan Sizhui does not remember his childhood years. He was raised by Lan Wangji after the first Siege of the Burial Mounds, who changed the writing of "Yuan" from 苑 / "garden" to 愿 / "wish" and gave him the Lan clan name, as well as the courtesy name "Sizhui."

Lan Xichen

BIRTH NAME: Lan Huan (蓝涣 / "Blue," "Melt" or "Dissipate")

COURTESY NAME: Lan Xichen (蓝曦臣 / "Blue," "Sunlight," "Minister" or "Subject")

SOBRIQUET: Zewu-jun (泽芜 / "Moss-shaded pool," honorific "-jun")

WEAPON: Sword: Shuoyue (朔月 / "New moon")

INSTRUMENT: Xiao (end-blown flute): Liebing (裂冰 / "Cracked," "Ice")

Unnamed guqin

The current Lan Sect head and Lan Wangji's elder brother. He is also sworn brothers with Jin Guangyao and Nie Mingjue, and together they are known as the Three Zun.

Lan Xichen possesses a warm and gentle personality and can easily get along with anyone and everyone. He possesses the unique and curious ability to understand his reticent little brother at a glance. He is as calm and undisturbed as the shaded pool from which he takes his sobriquet and will lend an ear to anyone who approaches, whatever their social standing.

Luo Qingyang

NAME: Luo Qingyang (罗青羊 / Surname Luo, "Green," "Sheep")

FORMERLY KNOWN AS: Mianmian (绵绵 / "Continuous")

A female cultivator who travels across the land with her husband and young daughter (who has inherited the nickname "Mianmian"), seeking to right wrongs and defend those in need. She is not affiliated with a sect. Her husband was once a merchant, but he gave up his stable life in order to follow his wife on her journeys.

"Mianmian" was a nickname originally bestowed on Luo Qingyang by Wei Wuxian many years ago. It references the lady lead of a romantic folksong from the Han dynasty. The verse in question is Mianmian si yuandao, *Unendingly do I long for [my husband]."*

Mo Xuanyu

COURTESY NAME: Mo Xuanyu (莫玄羽 / "Nothing" or "There is none who," "Mysterious" or "Black," "Feathers")

The young man who offered up his own body to bring Wei Wuxian back into the land of the living at a most horrible price: the obliteration of his own soul. He is one of the many illegitimate sons of Jin Guangshan. After he was expelled from the Jin Sect, the humiliation took a dreadful toll on his mind. He endured years of relentless abuse by the Mo household and eventually turned to demonic cultivation to exact revenge on those who tormented him. With his soul destroyed, Mo Xuanyu himself is now but a memory, and Wei Wuxian inhabits his body.

Nie Huaisang

COURTESY NAME: Nie Huaisang (聂怀桑 / "Whisper," "Cherish," "Mulberry")

SOBRIQUET: Head-Shaker (一问三不知 / "One Question, Three Don't-Knows")

WEAPON:

Unnamed saber (ostensibly)

Crying (actually)

The current Nie Sect head and Nie Mingjue's younger half brother. When they were young, he attended school at the Cloud Recesses with Wei Wuxian and Jiang Cheng. Nie Huaisang is a dilettante dandy who possesses a passionate love of fashion and the arts, but unfortunately possesses no such innate genius for politics or management. He is frequently seen looking stricken and panicked, and largely relies on the compassion and assistance of his older brother's sworn brothers (Lan Xichen and Jin Guangyao) to keep the Nie Sect struggling along.

Nie Mingjue

COURTESY NAME: Nie Mingjue (聶明玦 / "Whisper," "Bright" or "Righteousness," "Jade ring")

SOBRIQUET: Chifeng-zun (赤锋尊 / "Crimson Blade," honorific "-zun")

WEAPON: Saber: Baxia (霸下 / "To be ruled by force," also the name of one of the mythical Dragon King's nine sons.)

The former Nie Sect head and Nie Huaisang's older half brother. He is also sworn brothers with Lan Xichen and Jin Guangyao, and together they are known as the Three Zun. Nie Mingjue was a fierce man who was quick to use violence as a solution. He was unable to tolerate injustice or underhanded behavior, and was fearless in calling out even those in the highest seats of power. Unfortunately, his temperament eventually got the better of him, and he died at a young age from a qi deviation.

Ouyang Zizhen

BIRTH NAME: Ouyang Zizhen (欧阳子真 / Surname Ouyang, common male prefix "Son," "Genuine," "Truth")

WEAPON: A sentimental heart

One of the junior disciples who was rescued by Wei Wuxian as they found themselves lost in Yi City's fog. He is described by Wei Wuxian as having a sentimental outlook on the world. Ouyang Zizhen does not forget the kind deeds others have done for him, and he will not hesitate to stand up to defend a friend even in the face of an army.

Sect Leader Ouyang

NAME: Sect Leader Ouyang (欧阳宗主 / Surname Ouyang, "sect leader")

The leader of the Ouyang Sect and head of the Ouyang Clan, based in Baling. He is Ouyang Zizhen's father.

Meng Shi

NAME: Meng Shi (孟诗 / First month [of a season] or "To strive," "Poetry")

Jin Guangyao's birth mother. Meng Shi was once known for her skill in the Four Forms and the Four Arts, a rarity for a prostitute. Her reputation attracted the attention of Jin Guangshan, and though he broke his promises and abandoned her, she dreamed of a better life for herself and her son. She spent all her meager income on Meng Yao's education, and until her dying breath she kept faith that Jin Guangshan would one day come back and rescue them from the brothel.

Qin Su

BIRTH NAME: Qin Su (秦愫 / Surname Qin, "Sincerity")

Jin Guangyao's wife. Despite her high social status, she pushed to be allowed to marry for love and got her way. She is devoted to her husband, Jin Guangyao, with whom she had one child, Jin Rusong (金如松 / "Gold," "Like/as if," "Pine tree"), who died tragically at a young age. Jin Rusong's name uses the same character for "pine" that is in the poem from which the Cloud Recesses takes its name, in honor of the close friendship between Jin Guangyao and Lan Xichen.

Young Master Qin

NAME: Young Master Qin (秦公子 / Surname Qin, honorific "-gongzi")

The scion of a wealthy non-cultivator household who has recently encountered issues with a strange fierce corpse. He seeks out the assistance of Lan Wangji and Wei Wuxian after hearing that there are cultivators visiting the area and is completely unaware of their renown. Young Master Qin is quick to anger and slow to take personal responsibility in matters, and has a poor opinion of those born into the lower classes who don't know their place in society.

Bicao

NAME: Bicao (碧草 / "Green grass") [no family name given]

The ex-handmaid of the late Madam Qin of the Qin Clan of Laoling. She was deeply trusted by her late madam and watched Qin Su grow up.

Sect Leader Yao

NAME: Sect Leader Yao (姚宗主 / Surname Yao, "sect leader")

The leader of the Yao Sect and head of the Yao Clan. He is very quick to speak in public and does so at great length and with considerable pretension.

Sisi

NAME: Sisi (思思 / "Pining" or "Longing") [no family name given]

An ex-prostitute with a heavily scarred face. The sole surviving witness to a shocking incident, she was secretly held under house arrest for over a decade. Thanks to the assistance of a mysterious benefactor, she recently escaped her imprisonment and is now determined to tell the world the truth of what she saw that fateful day.

Su She

BIRTH NAME: Su She (苏涉 / "Tassel" or "Revival," "Experience" or "Involve")

COURTESY NAME: Su Minshan (苏悯善 / "Tassel" or "Revival," "Compassion" or "Kindness")

WEAPON: Sword: Nanping (难平 / "Difficult to quell")

INSTRUMENT: Unnamed guqin

The leader of the Su Sect of Moling and head of the Su Clan. Originally a disciple of the Lan Sect, Su She eventually left to form his own sect. Insecure about his abilities as a cultivator, he has a tendency to copy Lan techniques, which has led to bad blood between the sects.

Wen Ning

BIRTH NAME: Wen Ning (温宁 / "Mild" or "Warm," "Peaceful")

COURTESY NAME: Wen Qionglin (温琼林 / "Mild" or "Warm," "Beautiful" or "Fine jade," "Forest")

SOBRIQUET: Ghost General (鬼将军)

WEAPON: Fists, feet, and metal chains

A fierce corpse known as the Ghost General. One of the Yiling Patriarch's finest creations, Wen Ning retains his mind and personality. Coupled with the strength to crush steel to dust with his bare fists, it is no wonder that he was once Wei Wuxian's right-hand man.

Wen Ning wasn't always so powerful, nor always so dead. In life, he served under the Wen Clan as the leader of a minor squadron. His compassion and meekness were always at odds with the orders passed down from on high, and he also suffered from a minor stutter. Despite the lack of respect from his peers, he maintained his position in the Wen Clan due to family ties. He is the beloved younger brother of the Wen Clan's most famous doctor, Wen Qing, and the son of Wen Ruohan's cousin.

Wen Qing

COURTESY NAME: Wen Qing (温情 / "Mild" or "Warm," "Sentiment"; 温情 taken as a single word means "Tenderness")

WEAPON: A steady hand and an endless supply of acupuncture needles

A famous and highly decorated doctor and a member of the Wen Clan. She has a no-nonsense personality and a decided lack of bedside manner. Although she can come across as arrogant, no one in the cultivation world could deny that her abilities are truly exceptional. Wen Qing is the daughter of Wen Ruohan's maternal cousin and is a personal favorite of the mad tyrant himself. While she does not share her relative's taste for cruelty, she doesn't consider it something she needs to personally concern herself with—after all, her prime directive is to ensure the survival of her beloved younger brother, Wen Ning, at all costs.

Wen Ruohan

COURTESY NAME: Wen Ruohan (温若寒 / "Mild" or "Warm," "As though," "Cold" or "Tremble")

The leader of the Wen Clan of Qishan and an immensely powerful cultivator. He is cruel and power-hungry, and will stop at nothing to ensure that the Wen Clan crushes all other clans beneath its heel. He has an extensive collection of torture devices and does not hesitate to use them to toy with his victims until death releases them.

Xiao Xingchen

COURTESY NAME: Xiao Xingchen (晓星尘 / "Dawn," "Stardust")

WEAPON: Sword: Shuanghua (霜华 / "Frost Flower," referring to the natural phenomenon when ice crystals form on long-stemmed plants)

A mysterious and once-highly regarded cultivator. He is close friends with Song Lan and dreamed of founding a sect with him. He lived on a remote mountaintop for most of his life under the tutelage of his shizun, the immortal Baoshan-sanren. He descended the mountain to do good deeds for the common people of the world, and was well known for his skill and sense of justice.

Song Lan

BIRTH NAME: Song Lan (宋岚 / Surname Song, "Mist")

COURTESY NAME: Song Zichen (宋子琛 / Surname Song, a common male name prefix "Son," "Gem" or "Jewel")

WEAPON: Sword: Fuxue (拂雪 / "To sweep away snow")

A Daoist cultivator and close friend of Xiao Xingchen. He was known to be quiet and stern, and dreamed of founding a sect by Xiao Xingchen's side.

Xue Yang

BIRTH NAME: Xue Yang (薛洋 / Surname Xue, "Ocean")

COURTESY NAME: Xue Chengmei (薛成美 / Surname Xue, "To become," "Beautiful")

WEAPON: Sword: Jiangzai (降灾 / "To call forth disasters [from the heavens]")

On the surface, Xue Yang is a petty thug with a penchant for violence. Below the surface, he is still a petty thug with a penchant for violence, but with a strange knack for understanding the dark arts—a truly terrible combination. Xue Yang's courtesy name is derived from a Confucian proverb describing the conduct of the ideal gentleman, 成人之美 / cheng ren zhi mei, or "help others accomplish good works."

Fairy

WEAPON: Claws, jaws, and the only brain in the room (usually)
INSTRUMENT: Woof!

Jin Ling's loyal spirit dog. As a spirit dog, Fairy possesses intelligence of a level above the average canine and can detect supernatural beings. Regarding the pup's name, "Fairy" could refer to the Chinese *xianzi* (仙子), a female celestial being, but it is also a common way to describe a woman with ethereal, otherworldly beauty. That being said, Fairy's gender is never specified in the text.

Little Apple

WEAPON: Hooves, teeth, and raw fury

A spotted donkey that Wei Wuxian stole from Mo Manor as he made his escape after the ghost arm incident. Little Apple is imperious, hard to please, and very temperamental; however, it possesses a strong sense of justice and a heart brave enough to put even the most renown cultivators to shame. It also really loves apples. Little Apple's gender is never specified in the text.

Locations

HUBEI

Burial Mounds (乱葬岗)

A foreboding mountainous ridge located near Yiling. It is said to be the spot where an ancient and most terrible battle was waged. It is heavily ravaged by resentful energy and packed to the brim with walking corpses and vengeful ghosts. It has proven to be extremely resistant to any attempts at purification from top cultivation sects, and as such it was sealed off with magical barriers and written off as a lost cause. That is, until the dreaded Yiling Patriarch claimed it as his base of operations.

Lotus Pier (莲花坞)

The residence of the Jiang Clan of Yunmeng, located on the shores of a vast lake rich with blooming lotuses. The picturesque scenery is a perfect setting for a myriad of outdoor activities, such as boating, kite-flying, and playfully roughhousing with one's martial siblings.

Lotus Pier is always bustling with cultivators and common folk alike, which is in stark contrast to other sects. Merchants line the piers to hawk food and wares, and local children scamper about to gawk in awe as the disciples of the Jiang Sect do their daily training.

Yiling (夷陵)

An area located near Yunmeng. While Yiling itself is bustling with life, it is most infamous for its proximity to the Burial Mounds.

Yunmeng (云梦)

A county in the Hubei area. Its many lakes and waterways make it a prime juncture point for trade.

Yunping(云萍)

A city in the Hubei area, near Yunmeng. Located on the shores of a river that cuts through the region, it sees a considerable amount of trade and tourism. It also boasts a most peculiar feature: a temple located in the heart of the city that is dedicated to the beloved goddess Guanyin.

JIANGNAN

Cloud Recesses (云深不知处)

The residence of the Lan Clan of Gusu, located on a remote mountaintop. The Cloud Recesses is a tranquil place constantly shrouded in mist. Beside the entrance there looms the Wall of Discipline, carved with the three thousand (later four thousand) rules of the Lan Clan.

The Cloud Recesses is home to the Library Pavilion where many rare and ancient texts are housed, the Tranquility Room where Lan Wangji resides, and the Orchid Room where Lan Qiren hosts lectures. There is also the Nether Room, a tower in which spirit-summoning rituals are performed, as well as a cold spring for bathing. On the back of the mountain is a secluded meadow where Lan Wangji keeps his pet rabbits.

The Cloud Recesses' name translates more literally to "Somewhere Hidden in Clouds" (云深不知处) and is a reference to a line in the poem "Failing to Find the Hermit," by Jia Dao:

I asked the young disciple beneath the pine;
"My master is gone to pick herbs," he answered.
"Though within this mountain he is,
The recesses of clouds hide his trail."

Gusu (姑苏)

A city in the Jiangnan region. Jiangnan is famous for its rich, fertile land and its abundant agricultural goods. Its hazy, drizzling weather and the soft sweet dialect make it a popular setting in Chinese romance literature.

HEBEI

Qinghe (清河)

A county in the Hebei region. Qinghe is the home territory of the Nie Clan and is where their residence is located.

Impure Realm (不净世)

The residence of the Nie Clan of Qinghe. Its name may be a reference to Patikulamanasikara (in Chinese, written as 不淨觀 / Impure View), a set of Buddhist sutras meant to help overcome mortal desires. It thus serves both as a goal for the Nie Clan to aspire to and a reminder of their background as butchers.

SHAANXI

Qishan (岐山)

A county in the Shaanxi region. Qishan is the home territory of the Wen Clan and is where their residence is located.

Nightless City (不夜天城)

The residence of the Wen Clan of Qishan. Its name is derived from the fact that the expansive complex is vast enough to be comparable to the size of a city, as well as the brazen declaration of the Wen Clan that the sun never sets upon their domain—since it is their clan crest. The Scorching Sun Palace is the seat of Wen Ruohan's power, and the Inferno Palace is where he stores and demonstrates his vast collection of torture devices on unlucky guests.

SHANDONG

Lanling (兰陵)

A county in the Shandong region.

Golden Carp Tower (金麟台)

The residence of the Jin Clan of Lanling, located at the heart of the city of Lanling. The main road to the tower is only opened when events are being hosted, and this grand avenue is lavishly decorated with murals and statuary. Upon reaching the tower base, travelers must scale the numerous levels of steep staircases that lead to the tower proper. These staircases are a reference to the legend from which Golden Carp Tower derives its name—it is said that if an ordinary carp is able to leap to the top of a waterfall, it can turn into a glorious dragon.

Once the arduous journey to the top is complete, one will find themselves overlooking the city of Lanling from on high and vast gardens of the Jin Clan of Lanling's signature flower: the cultivar peony, Sparks Amidst Snow. The Jin Sect's wealth and influence, as well as current leader Jin Guangyao's position as Cultivation Chief, sees Golden Carp Tower hosting frequent symposiums and banquets with VIP guests from the cultivation world's most powerful sects.

MISCELLANEOUS

Dongying (东瀛)

The name used for the country of Japan in ancient China.

Qiongqi Path (穷奇道)

An old road running through a mountain valley. It was previously a tourist attraction that boasted murals depicting the brave deeds of the Wen Clan's founder, Wen Mao. After the Sunshot Campaign's conclusion, the area was reassigned to the Jin Clan of Lanling, who wasted no time in removing the Wen murals to rebrand it as their own.

Name Guide

Courtesy Names

A courtesy name is given to an individual when they come of age. Traditionally, this was at the age of twenty during one's crowning ceremony, but it can also be presented when an elder or teacher deems the recipient worthy. Generally a male-only tradition, there is historical precedent for women adopting a courtesy name after marriage. Courtesy names were a tradition reserved for the upper class.

It was considered disrespectful for one's peers of the same generation to address someone by their birth name, especially in formal or written communication. Use of one's birth name was reserved for only elders, close friends, and spouses.

This practice is no longer used in modern China but is commonly seen in wuxia and xianxia media. As such, many characters have more than one name. Its implementation in novels is irregular and is often treated malleably for the sake of storytelling. For example, in *Grandmaster of Demonic Cultivation*, characters as young as fifteen years of age are referred to only by their courtesy names, while traditionally they would not have been permitted to use them until the age of twenty.

Sobriquet

The term used in this translation for *hao* (號). Hao can also be translated as "art name." These names are generally chosen by an individual for themselves, but they can also be bestowed upon them in light of their accomplishments or traits. They were often used as pen names or respectful titles for scholars, government officials, or martial heroes.

They could be derived from a number of possible subjects, including their place of birth, a poetic quote, a feat that the person in question was famous for, and more.

NAMES, HONORIFICS, & TITLES

Diminutives, Nicknames, and Name Tags

XIAO-: A diminutive meaning "little." Always a prefix.

LAO-: A diminutive meaning "old."

-ER: A word for "son" or "child." Added to a name, it expresses affection. Similar to calling someone "Little" or "Sonny."

A-: Friendly diminutive. Always a prefix. Usually for monosyllabic names, or one syllable out of a two-syllable name.

   EXAMPLE: A-Qing, A-Yuan, A-Xian (for Wei Wuxian).

Doubling a syllable of a person's name can be a nickname, and has childish or cutesy connotations.

   EXAMPLE: Xianxian (for Wei Wuxian, referring to himself).

FAMILY

BOMU: Aunt (non-biological, wife of father's elder brother).

DI: Younger brother or younger male friend. Can be used alone or as an honorific.

DIDI: Younger brother or a younger male friend. Casual.

XIAO-DI: Does not mean "little brother" and instead refers to one's lackey or subordinate, someone a leader took under their wings.

GE: Older brother or older male friend.

GEGE: Older brother or an older male friend. Casual and has a cutesier feel than "ge," so it can be used in a flirtatious manner.

JIE: Older sister or older female friend. Can be used alone or as an honorific.

JIEJIE: Older sister or an unrelated older female friend. Casual.

JIUJIU: Uncle (maternal, biological).

MEI: Younger sister or younger female friend. Can be used alone or as an honorific.

MEIMEI: Younger sister or an unrelated younger female friend. Casual.

SHUFU: Uncle (paternal, biological). Formal address for one's father's younger brother.

SHUSHU: An affectionate version of "Shufu."

XIAO-SHU OR XIAO-SHUSHU: Little (paternal) uncle; affectionate.

XIONG: Older brother. Generally used as an honorific. Formal, but also used informally between male friends of equal status.

XIONGZHANG: Eldest brother. Very formal, blood related-only.

XIANSHENG: Historically "teacher," but modern usage is "Mister." Also an affectionate way for a wife to refer to her husband.

If multiple relatives in the same category are present (multiple older brothers, for example), everyone is assigned a number in order of birthdate, starting with the eldest as number one, the second oldest as number two, etc. These numbers are then used to differentiate one person from another. This goes for all of the categories above, whether it's siblings, cousins, aunts, uncles, and so on.

EXAMPLES: If you have three older brothers, the oldest would be referred to as "da-ge," the second oldest "er-ge," and the third oldest "san-ge." If you have two younger brothers you (as the oldest) would be number one. Your second-youngest brother would be "er-di," and the youngest of your two younger brothers would be "san-di."

Cultivation and Martial Arts

GENERAL

GONGZI: Young master of an affluent household.

-JUN: A suffix meaning "lord."

-QIANBEI: A respectful suffix for someone older, more experienced, and/or more skilled in a particular discipline. Not to be used for blood relatives.

-ZUN: A suffix meaning "esteemed, venerable." More respectful than "-jun."

SECTS

SHIDI: Younger martial brother. For junior male members of one's own sect.

SHIFU: Teacher/master. For one's master in one's own sect. Gender neutral. Mostly interchangeable with Shizun, but has a slightly less formal feel.

SHIJIE: Older martial sister. For senior female members of one's own sect.

SHIMEI: Younger martial sister. For junior female members of one's own sect.

SHINIANG: The wife of a shifu/shizun.

SHISHU: The younger martial sibling of one's master. Can be male or female.

SHIXIONG: Older martial brother. For senior male members of one's own sect.

SHIZUN: Honorific address (as opposed to shifu) of one's teacher/master.

Cultivators and Immortals

DAOREN: "Cultivator."

DAOZHANG: A polite address for cultivators. Equivalent to "Mr. Cultivator." Can be used alone as a title or attached to someone's name.

EXAMPLE: Referring to Xiao Xingchen as "Daozhang" or "Xiao Xingchen-daozhang."

SANREN: "Scattered One." For cultivators/immortals who are not tied to a specific sect.

Pronunciation Guide

Mandarin Chinese is the official state language of China. It is a tonal language, so correct pronunciation is vital to being understood! As many readers may not be familiar with the use and sound of tonal marks, below is a very simplified guide on the pronunciation of select character names and terms from MXTX's series to help get you started.

More resources are available at **sevenseasdanmei.com**

Series Names

SCUM VILLAIN'S SELF-SAVING SYSTEM (RÉN ZHĀ FǍN PÀI ZÌ JIÙ XÌ TǑNG):
ren jaa faan pie zzh zioh she tone

GRANDMASTER OF DEMONIC CULTIVATION (MÓ DÀO ZǓ SHĪ):
mwuh dow zoo shrr

HEAVEN OFFICIAL'S BLESSING (TIĀN GUĀN CÌ FÚ):
tee-yan gwen tsz fuu

Character Names

SHĚN QĪNGQIŪ: Shhen Ching-cheeoh

LUÒ BĪNGHÉ: Loo-uh Bing-huhh

WÈI WÚXIÀN: Way Woo-shee-ahn

LÁN WÀNGJĪ: Lahn Wong-gee

XIÈ LIÁN: Shee-yay Lee-yan

HUĀ CHÉNG: Hoo-wah Cch-yung

XIĂO-: shee-ow
-ER: ahrr
A-: ah
GŌNGZĬ: gong-zzh
DÀOZHĂNG: dow-jon
-JŪN: june
DÌDÌ: dee-dee
GĒGĒ: guh-guh
JIĚJIĚ: gee-ay-gee-ay
MÈIMEI: may-may
-XIÓNG: shong

Terms

DĀNMĚI: dann-may
WǓXIÁ: woo-sheeah
XIĀNXIÁ: sheeyan-sheeah
QÌ: chee

General Consonants & Vowels

X: similar to English sh (**sh**eep)
Q: similar to English ch (**ch**arm)
C: similar to English ts (pan**ts**)
IU: yoh
UO: wuh
ZHI: jrr
CHI: chrr
SHI: shrr
RI: rrr

ZI: zzz
CI: tsz
SI: ssz
U: When u follows a y, j, q, or x, the sound is actually ü, pronounced like eee with your lips rounded like ooo. This applies for yu, yuan, jun, etc.

Grandmaster of Demonic Cultivation

MO DAO ZU SHI

Glossary

Glossary

While not required reading, this glossary is intended to offer further context to the many concepts and terms utilized throughout this novel and provide a starting point for learning more about the rich Chinese culture from which these stories were written.

China is home to dozens of cultures, and its history spans thousands of years. The provided definitions are not strictly universal across all these cultural groups, and this simplified overview is meant for new readers unfamiliar with the concepts. This glossary should not be considered a definitive source, especially for more complex ideas.

GENRES

Danmei

Danmei (耽美 / "indulgence in beauty") is a Chinese fiction genre focused on romanticized tales of love and attraction between men. It is analogous to the BL (boys' love) genre in Japanese media. The majority of well-known danmei writers are women writing for women, although all genders produce and enjoy the genre.

Wuxia

Wuxia (武侠 / "martial heroes") is one of the oldest Chinese literary genres and consists of tales of noble heroes fighting evil and injustice. It often follows martial artists, monks, or rogues, who live apart from the ruling government, which is often seen as useless or corrupt. These societal outcasts—both voluntary and not—settle disputes among themselves, adhering to their own moral codes.

Characters in wuxia focus primarily on human concerns, such as political strife between factions and advancing their own personal sense of justice. True wuxia is low on magical or supernatural elements. To Western moviegoers, a well-known example is *Crouching Tiger, Hidden Dragon*.

Xianxia

Xianxia (仙侠 / "immortal heroes") is a genre related to wuxia that places more emphasis on the supernatural. Its characters often strive to become stronger, with the end goal of extending their life span or achieving immortality.

Xianxia heavily features Daoist themes, while cultivation and the pursuit of immortality are both genre requirements. If these are not the story's central focus, it is not xianxia. *The Scum Villain's Self-Saving System*, *Grandmaster of Demonic Cultivation*, and *Heaven Official's Blessing* are all considered part of both the danmei and xianxia genres.

Webnovels

Webnovels are novels serialized by chapter online, and the websites that host them are considered spaces for indie and amateur writers. Many novels, dramas, comics, and animated shows produced in China are based on popular webnovels.

Grandmaster of Demonic Cultivation was first serialized on the website *JJWXC*.

TERMINOLOGY

ARRAY: Area-of-effect magic circles. Anyone within the array falls under the effect of the array's associated spell(s).

ASCENSION: A Daoist concept, ascension refers to the process of a person gaining enlightenment through cultivation, whereupon they shed their mortal form and are removed from the corporeal world. In most xianxia, gods are distinct from immortals in that gods are conceived naturally and born divine, while immortals cannot attain godhood but can achieve great longevity.

BOWING: As is seen in other Asian cultures, standing bows are a traditional greeting and are also used when giving an apology. A deeper bow shows greater respect.

BUDDHISM: The central belief of Buddhism is that life is a cycle of suffering and rebirth, only to be escaped by reaching enlightenment (nirvana). Buddhists believe in karma, that a person's actions will influence their fortune in this life and future lives. The teachings of the Buddha are known as The Middle Way and emphasize a practice that is neither extreme asceticism nor extreme indulgence.

CLANS: Cultivation clans are large blood-related families that share a surname. Clans are led by family elders, and while only family members can be leaders, disciples can join regardless of blood relation. They may eventually take on the family name, depending on whether the family chooses to offer it. This could be accomplished via adoption or marriage. Clans tend to have a signature cultivation or martial art that is passed down through generations along with ancestral magical artifacts and weapons.

Colors

WHITE: Death, mourning, purity. Used in funerals for both the deceased and mourners.

BLACK: Represents the Heavens and the Dao.

RED: Happiness, good luck. Used for weddings.

YELLOW/GOLD: Wealth and prosperity, and often reserved for the emperor.

BLUE/GREEN (CYAN): Health, prosperity, and harmony.

PURPLE: Divinity and immortality, often associated with nobility.

CONFUCIANISM: Confucianism is a philosophy based on the teachings of Confucius. Its influence on all aspects of Chinese culture is incalculable. Confucius placed heavy importance on respect for one's elders and family, a concept broadly known as *xiao* (孝 / "filial piety"). The family structure is used in other contexts to urge similar behaviors, such as respect of a student towards a teacher, or people of a country towards their ruler.

CORES/GOLDEN CORES: The formation of a jindan (金丹 / "golden core") is a key step in any cultivator's journey to immortality. The Golden Core forms within the lower *dantian*, becoming an internal source of power for the cultivator. Golden Core formation is only accomplished after a great deal of intense training and qi cultivation.

Cultivators can detonate their Golden Core as a last-ditch move to take out a dangerous opponent, but this almost always kills the cultivator. A core's destruction or removal is permanent. In almost all instances, it cannot be re-cultivated. Its destruction also prevents the individual from ever being able to process or cultivate qi normally again.

COURTESY NAMES: A courtesy name is given to an individual when they come of age. (See Name Guide for more information.)

CULTIVATORS/CULTIVATION: Cultivators are practitioners of spirituality and martial artists who seek to gain understanding of the will of the universe while also attaining personal strength and expanding their life span.

Cultivation is a long process marked by "stages." There are traditionally nine stages, but this is often simplified in fiction. Some common stages are noted below, though exact definitions of each stage may depend on the setting.

◇ Qi Condensation/Qi Refining (凝气/练气)
◇ Foundation Establishment (筑基)
◇ Core Formation/Golden Core (结丹/金丹)
◇ Nascent Soul (元婴)
◇ Deity Transformation (化神)
◇ Great Ascension (大乘)
◇ Heavenly Tribulation (渡劫)

CULTIVATION MANUAL: Cultivation manuals and sutras are common plot devices in xianxia/wuxia novels. They provide detailed instructions on a secret/advanced training technique, and are sought out by those who wish to advance their cultivation levels.

CURRENCY: The currency system during most dynasties was based on the exchange of silver and gold coinage. Weight was also used to measure denominations of money. An example is something being marked with a price of "one *liang* of silver."

CUT-SLEEVE: A term for a gay man. Comes from a tale about an emperor's love for, and relationship with, a male politician. The emperor was called to the morning assembly, but his lover was asleep on his sleeve. Rather than wake him, the emperor cut off his sleeve.

DANTIAN: *Dantian* (丹田 / "cinnabar field") refers to three regions in the body where qi is concentrated and refined. The Lower is located three finger widths below and two finger widths behind the navel. This is where a cultivator's golden core would be formed and is where the qi metabolism process begins and progresses upward. The Middle is located at the center of the chest, at level with the heart, while the Upper is located on the forehead, between the eyebrows.

DAOISM: Daoism is the philosophy of the *Dao* (道 / "the way"). Following the Dao involves coming into harmony with the natural order of the universe, which makes someone a "true human," safe from external harm and able to affect the world without intentional action. Cultivation is a concept based on Daoist beliefs.

DEMONS: A race of immensely powerful and innately supernatural beings. They are almost always aligned with evil. Evil-aligned cultivators who seek power are said to follow the demonic cultivation path.

DISCIPLES: Clan and sect juniors are known as disciples. Disciples live on sect grounds and have a strict hierarchy based on skill and seniority. They are divided into Core, Inner, and Outer rankings, with Core being the highest. Higher-ranked disciples get better lodging and other resources.

For non-clan members, when formally joining a sect as a disciple, the sect becomes like the disciple's new family: teachers are parents and peers are siblings. Because of this, a betrayal or abandonment of one's sect is considered a deep transgression of Confucian values of filial piety. This is also the origin of many of the honorifics and titles used for martial arts.

DIVINE BEASTS: Refers to the four holy beasts that are considered guardians of the cardinal directions, as well as their associated seasons / elements.

> **AZURE DRAGON:** (青龍 / *Qinglong*) Associated with the cardinal direction of east and the season of spring.
>
> **VERMILION BIRD:** (朱雀 / *Zhuque*): Associated with the cardinal direction of south and the season of summer.
>
> **WHITE TIGER:** (白虎 / *Baihu*): Associated with the cardinal direction of west and the season of autumn.
>
> **BLACK TORTOISE:** (玄武 / *Xuanwu*): Associated with the cardinal direction of north and the season of winter.

DIZI: A flute held horizontally. They are considered an instrument for commoners, as they are easy to craft from bamboo or wood.

FACE: *Mianzi* (面子), generally translated as "face," is an important concept in Chinese society. It is a metaphor for a person's reputation and can be extended to further descriptive metaphors. For example, "having face" refers to having a good reputation, and "losing face" refers to having one's reputation hurt. Meanwhile, "giving face" means deferring to someone else to help improve their reputation, while "not wanting face" implies that a person is acting so poorly/shamelessly that they clearly don't care about their reputation at all. "Thin face" refers to someone easily embarrassed or prone to offense at perceived slights. Conversely, "thick face" refers to someone not easily embarrassed and immune to insults.

FAIRY/XIANZI: A term commonly used in novels to describe a woman possessing ethereal, heavenly beauty. *Xianzi* is the female counterpart to *xianren* ("immortal"), and is also used to describe celestials that have descended from heaven.

FENG SHUI: *Feng shui* (風水 / "wind-water") is a Daoist practice centered around the philosophy of achieving spiritual accord between people, objects, and the universe at large. Practitioners usually focus on positioning and orientation, believing this can optimize the flow of qi in their environment. Having good feng shui means being in harmony with the natural order.

THE FIVE ELEMENTS: Also known as the *wuxing* (五行 / "Five Phases"). Rather than Western concepts of elemental magic, Chinese phases are more commonly used to describe the interactions and relationships between things. The phases can both beget and overcome each other.

Wood (木 / mu)
Fire (火 / huo)
Earth (土 / tu)
Metal (金 / jin)
Water (水 / shui)

Flower Symbolism

LOTUS: Associated with Buddhism. It rises untainted from the muddy waters it grows in, and thus symbolizes ultimate purity of the heart and mind.

PEONY: Symbolizes wealth and power. Was considered the "emperor" of flowers. Sparks Amidst Snow, the signature flower of the Jin Clan of Lanling in Grandmaster of Demonic Cultivation, is based on the real-life Paeonia suffruticosa cultivar (金星雪浪).

PINE (TREE): A symbol of evergreen sentiment / everlasting affection.

WILLOW (TREE): A symbol of lasting affection and friendship. Also a symbol of farewell and can mean "urging someone to stay."

THE FOUR FORMS AND THE FOUR ARTS: The Four Forms (诗词歌赋) refer to the four forms of Chinese poetry, which are defined by the poetic meter used: *shi, ci, ge,* and *fu.* The Four Arts (琴棋书画) refer to guqin, weiqi (a strategy game known also as "qi," or as "go" in Japan), calligraphy, and painting.

FUNERALS: Chinese funerals last anywhere from three to seven days, and the mourning period lasts for forty-nine days. A Buddhist or Daoist ceremony is held every seventh day during these seven weeks. A vigil is held during the first week and ends when the body is interred. During this period, a family member (usually the eldest son or a spouse) needs to remain with the deceased's body for companionship. This duty is usually shared in shifts.

During the funeral ceremony, mourners can present the deceased with offerings of food, incense, and joss paper. If deceased ancestors have no patrilineal descendants to give them offerings, they may starve in the afterlife and become hungry ghosts. Wiping out a whole family is punishment for more than just the living.

After the funeral, the coffin is nailed shut and sealed with paper talismans to protect the body from evil spirits. The deceased is transported in a procession to their final resting place, often accompanied by loud music to scare off evil spirits. Cemeteries are usually on hillsides; the higher a grave is located, the better the feng shui. The traditional mourning color is white.

Keeping the corpse intact is a demonstration of respect for the dead. Dismemberment and cremation with no proper burial is a sign of profound disrespect and hatred and is mostly reserved for criminals.

GHOST: Ghosts (鬼) are the restless spirits of deceased sentient creatures. Ghosts produce yin energy and crave yang energy. They come in a variety of types: they can be malevolent or helpful, can retain their former personalities or be fully mindless, and can actively try to interact with the living world to achieve a goal or be little more than a remnant shadow of their former lives.

GOLDEN CROW: A Golden Crow (金乌)—also known as Three-legged Crow (三足乌)—is a tripedal crow that is often used to represent the sun. A myth explains that there were once ten of these crows, which nested in the Valley of the Sun and came out one at a time to cross the sky. One day they all came out at once and began to cause chaos, causing the world to burn. The divine archer Houyi shot down nine of the ten crows to save humanity. This myth is directly referenced in *Grandmaster of Demonic Cultivation* as the meaning behind the name of the Sunshot Campaign.

GRADING SYSTEM: A "jia" grade corresponds to an "A" in the American school system. A "yi" grade corresponds to a "B."

GUQIN: A seven-stringed zither, played by plucking with the fingers. Sometimes called a qin. It is fairly large and is meant to be laid flat on a surface or on one's lap while playing.

HAND GESTURES: The *baoquan* (抱拳 / "hold fist") is a martial arts salute where one places their closed right fist against their open left palm. The *gongshou* (拱手 / "arch hand") is a more generic salute not specific to martial artists, where one drapes their open left palm over their closed right fist. The orientation of both of these salutes is reversed for women. During funerals, the closed hand in both salutes switches, where men will use their left fist and women their right.

HAND SEALS: Refers to various hand and finger gestures used by cultivators to cast spells, or used while meditating. A cultivator may be able to control their sword remotely with a hand seal.

IMMORTAL-BINDING ROPES OR CABLES: Ropes, nets, and other restraints enchanted to withstand the power of an immortal or god. They can only be cut by high-powered spiritual items or weapons and often limit the abilities of those trapped by them.

INCENSE TIME: A common way to tell time in ancient China, referring to how long it takes for a single incense stick to burn. Standardized incense sticks were manufactured and calibrated for specific time measurements: a half hour, an hour, a day, etc. These were available to people of all social classes. When referenced in *Grandmaster of Demonic Cultivation*, a single incense time is usually about thirty minutes.

INEDIA: A common ability that allows an immortal to survive without mortal food or sleep by sustaining themselves on purer forms of energy based on Daoist fasting. Depending on the setting, immortals who have achieved inedia may be unable to tolerate mortal food, or they may be able to choose to eat when desired.

JADE: Jade is a culturally and spiritually important mineral in China. Its durability, beauty, and the ease with which it can be utilized for crafting both decorative and functional pieces alike has made it widely beloved since ancient times. The word might cause Westerners to think of green jade (the mineral jadeite), but Chinese texts are often referring to white jade (the mineral nephrite). This is the color referenced when a person's skin is described as "the color of jade."

JOSS PAPER: Also referred to as ghost paper, joss paper is a form of paper crafting used to make offerings to the deceased. The paper can be folded into various shapes and is burned as an offering, allowing the deceased person to utilize the gift the paper represents in the realm of the dead. Common gifts include paper money, houses, clothing, toiletries, and dolls to act as the deceased's servants.

NEW BABY: New baby traditions: A mother is confined to the house to recuperate for the first thirty days after giving birth. This postpartum confinement period is known as zuoyuezi (坐月子 / "sitting the month"). During this month, new mothers are tended to by their mother-in-law (or their own mother). Visitors, sometimes even immediate family members, are barred from entry until the period is over.

The conclusion of the thirty days is known as manyue (满月 / "full month") or miyue (弥月 / "complete month"). The occasion of the baby's birth can be celebrated at this time, and it is known as zuomanyue (做满月/满月酒 / "doing the full month" or "full month banquet"), or miyuezhixi (弥月之喜 / "complete month bash"). This is when the baby is formally inducted into the family and presented to the ancestors. During the full month celebration, family and friends are invited to a banquet and to witness the zhuazhou (抓周) tradition, a ceremony in which various symbolic items are placed in front of the baby. Whichever item the baby selects first is said to predict their future fortunes. (For example, picking up a pen indicates they will be a scholar, picking up an abacus means they will be successful in business, etc.)

The Chinese calendar uses the Tian Gan Di Zhi (Heavenly Stems, Earthly Branches) system to mark the years. There are ten heavenly stems and twelve earthly branches, each represented by a written character. The set of characters associated with the year/month/date/time of a person's birth is known as 生辰八字, or "eight characters of birth date/time."

Numbers

TWO: Two (二 / "er") is considered a good number and is referenced in the common idiom "good things come in pairs." It is common practice to repeat characters in pairs for added effect.

THREE: Three (三 / "san") sounds like *sheng* (生 / "living") and also like san (散 / "separation").

FOUR: Four (四 / "si") sounds like *si* (死 / "death"). A very unlucky number.

SEVEN: Seven (七 / "qi") sounds like *qi* (齊 / "together"), making it a good number for love-related things. However, it also sounds like *qi* (欺 / "deception").

EIGHT: Eight (八 / "ba") sounds like *fa* (發 / "prosperity"), causing it to be considered a very lucky number.

NINE: Nine (九 / "jiu") is associated with matters surrounding the Emperor and Heaven, and is as such considered an auspicious number.

MXTX's work has subtle numerical theming around its love interests. In *Grandmaster of Demonic Cultivation*, her second book, Lan Wangji is frequently called Lan-er-gege ("second brother Lan") as a nickname by Wei Wuxian. In her third book, *Heaven Official's Blessing*, Hua Cheng is the third son of his family and gives the name San Lang ("third youth") when Xie Lian asks what to call him.

PAPER EFFIGIES: *Zhizha* (纸扎) is a form of Daoist paper craft. Zhizha effigies can be used in place of living sacrifices to one's ancestors in the afterlife, or to gods. Joss paper can be considered a form of zhizha specifically for the deceased, though unlike zhizha, it is not specifically Daoist in nature.

PILLS AND ELIXIRS: Magic medicines that can heal wounds, improve cultivation, extend life, etc. In Chinese culture, these things are usually delivered in pill form. These pills are created in special kilns.

PRIMORDIAL SPIRIT: The essence of one's existence beyond the physical. The body perishes, the soul enters the karmic wheel, but the spirit that makes one unique is eternal.

QI: *Qi* (气) is the energy in all living things. There is both righteous qi and evil or poisonous qi.

Cultivators strive to cultivate qi by absorbing it from the natural world and refining it within themselves to improve their cultivation base. A cultivation base refers to the amount of qi a cultivator possesses or is able to possess. In xianxia, natural locations such as caves, mountains, or other secluded places with beautiful scenery are often rich in qi, and practicing there can allow a cultivator to make rapid progress in their cultivation.

Cultivators and other qi manipulators can utilize their life force in a variety of ways, including imbuing objects with it to transform them into lethal weapons or sending out blasts of energy to do powerful damage. Cultivators also refine their senses beyond normal human levels. For instance, they may cast out their spiritual sense to gain total awareness of everything in a region around them or to feel for potential danger.

QI CIRCULATION: The metabolic cycle of qi in the body, where it flows from the dantian to the meridians and back. This cycle purifies and refines qi, and good circulation is essential to cultivation. In xianxia, qi can be transferred from one person to another through physical contact and can heal someone who is wounded if the donor is trained in the art.

QI DEVIATION: A qi deviation (走火入魔 / "to catch fire and enter demonhood") occurs when one's cultivation base becomes unstable. Common causes include an unstable emotional state, practicing cultivation methods incorrectly, reckless use of forbidden or high-level arts, or succumbing to the influence of demons and devils.

Symptoms of qi deviation in fiction include panic, paranoia, sensory hallucinations, and death, whether by the qi deviation itself causing irreparable damage to the body or as a result of its symptoms such as leaping to one's death to escape a hallucination. Common treatments of qi deviation in fiction include relaxation (voluntary or forced by an external party), massage, meditation, or qi transfer from another individual.

QIANKUN: (乾坤 / "universe") Common tools used in fantasy novels. The primary function of these magical items is to provide unlimited storage space. Examples include pouches, the sleeve of a robe, magical jewelry, a weapon, and more.

SECT: A cultivation sect is an organization of individuals united by their dedication to the practice of a particular method of cultivation or martial arts. A sect may have a signature style. Sects are led by a single leader, who is supported by senior sect members. They are not necessarily related by blood.

SEVEN APERTURES/QIQIAO: (七窍) The seven facial apertures: the two eyes, nose, mouth, tongue, and two ears. The essential qi of vital organs are said to connect to the seven apertures, and illness in the vital organs may cause symptoms there. People who are ill or seriously injured may be "bleeding from the seven apertures."

SHICHEN: Days were split into twelve intervals of two hours apiece called *shichen* (时辰 / "time"). Each of these shichen has an associated term. Pre-Han dynasty used semi-descriptive terms, but in Post-Han dynasty, the shichen were renamed to correspond to the twelve zodiac animals.

ZI, MIDNIGHT: 11pm - 1am

CHOU: 1am - 3am

YIN: 3am - 5am

MAO, SUNRISE: 5am - 7am

CHEN: 7am - 9am

SI: 9am - 11am

WU, NOON: 11am - 1pm

WEI: 1pm - 3pm

SHEN: 3pm - 5pm

YOU, SUNSET: 5pm - 7pm

XU, DUSK: 7pm - 9pm

HAI: 9pm - 11pm

SHIDI, SHIXIONG, SHIZUN, ETC.: Chinese titles and terms used to indicate a person's role or rank in relation to the speaker. Because of the robust nature of this naming system, and a lack of nuance in translating many to English, the original titles have been maintained. (See Name Guide for more information.)

THE SIX ARTS: Six disciplines that any well-bred gentleman in Ancient China was expected to be learned in. The Six Arts were: Rites, Music, Archery, Chariotry or Equestrianism, Calligraphy, and Mathematics.

SPIRIT-ATTRACTION FLAG: A banner or flag intended to guide spirits. Can be hung from a building or tree to mark a location or carried around on a staff.

SWORDS: A cultivator's sword is an important part of their cultivation practice. In many instances, swords are spiritually bound to their owner and may have been bestowed to them by their master, a family member, or obtained through a ritual. Cultivators in fiction are able to use their swords as transportation by standing atop the flat of the blade and riding it as it flies through the air. Skilled cultivators can summon their swords to fly into their hand, command the sword to fight on its own, or release energy attacks from the edge of the blade.

SWORD GLARE: *Jianguang* (剑光 / "sword light"), an energy attack released from a sword's edge.

SWORN BROTHERS/SISTERS/FAMILIES: In China, sworn brotherhood describes a binding social pact made by two or more unrelated individuals. Such a pact can be entered into for social, political, and/or personal reasons. It was most common among men but was not unheard of among women or between people of different genders.

The participants treat members of each other's families as their own and assist them in the ways an extended family would: providing mutual support and aid, support in political alliances, etc. Sworn siblings will refer to themselves as brother or sister, but this is not to be confused with familial relations like blood siblings or adoption. It is sometimes used in Chinese media, particularly danmei, to imply romantic relationships that could otherwise be prone to censorship.

TALISMANS: Strips of paper with incantations written on them, often done so with cinnabar ink or blood. They can serve as seals or be used as one-time spells.

TAPIR: A mythical chimeric beast. Although it shares its name with a real animal, the two are not to be confused. The *baku* of Japanese mythology is derived from this creature and created its association with dreams and nightmares.

TIGER TALLY: A *hufu* (虎符 / "tiger tally"), was used by Ancient Chinese emperors to signal their approval to dispatch troops in battle. A hufu was in two parts: one in the possession of the emperor, and the other in the possession of a general in the field. To signal approval, the emperor would send his half of the hufu to the general. If the two sides matched, troops would advance.

VINEGAR: To say someone is drinking vinegar or tasting vinegar means they are experiencing jealous or bitter feelings. Generally used for a love interest growing jealous while watching the main character receive the attention of a rival suitor.

WANGXIAN: Shortened name for the relationship between Lan Wangji and Wei Wuxian.

WEDDING TRADITIONS (BOWING): During a wedding ceremony, the couple must bow three times: one bow to worship the heavens and earth, one bow to respect their parents, and one bow to respect each other.

WHISK: A whisk held by a cultivator is not a baking tool, but a Daoist symbol and martial arts weapon. Usually made of horsehair bound to a wooden stick, the whisk is based off a tool used to brush away flies without killing them, and is symbolically meant for wandering Daoist monks to brush away thoughts that would lure them back to secular life. Wudang Daoist Monks created a fighting style based on wielding it as a weapon.

YAO: Animals, plants, or objects that have gained spiritual consciousness due to prolonged absorption of qi. Especially high-level or long-lived yao are able to take on a human form. This concept is comparable to Japanese yokai, which is a loanword from the Chinese yao. Yao are not evil by nature but often come into conflict with humans for various reasons, one being that the cores they develop can be harvested by human cultivators to increase their own abilities.

YIN ENERGY AND YANG ENERGY: Yin and yang is a concept in Chinese philosophy that describes the complementary interdependence of opposite/contrary forces. It can be applied to all forms of change and differences. Yang represents the sun, masculinity, and the living, while yin represents the shadows, femininity, and the dead, including spirits and ghosts. In fiction, imbalances between yin and yang energy can do serious harm to the body or act as the driving force for malevolent spirits seeking to replenish themselves of whichever they lack.

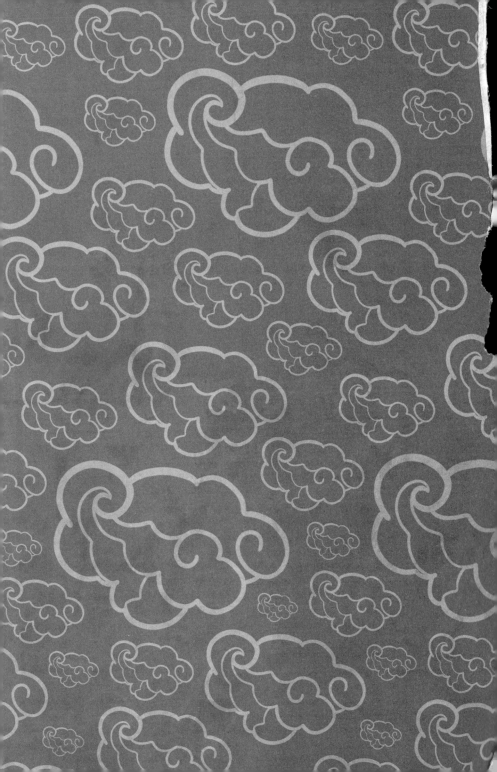